BLUE

a novel

MIGUEL A. FENRICH

Supernova Press

P.O. Box 1973 Battleford, SK S0M 0E0

www.supernovapress.com

Blue: A Novel

1st Print Edition 2022

ISBN: 978-1-7781844-5-1

Cover Design by Brianne Hager

This novel contains triggering or sensitive material that may be upsetting to some audiences. These include: Infrequent sexual violence, abuse, torture, drug and alcohol use and abuse, frequent use of harsh language, violence, suicidal themes, and warfare. This books contains rampant injustice & anti-blue-eye rhetoric. Reader discretion is advised.

Dedication

Though I would like to say that *Blue* was created solely by my own effort, that could not be further from the truth. I dedicate this novel to my grandmother who listened to my every rant and concern under the sun, my mother, who without her the book would be just a jumble of words on paper, and my grandfather who gave me hope. Without their support, spiritually, physically, and emotionally, there would be no book to read.

I also dedicate this novel to the hundreds of millions of long dead people who lived entire lives that weren't their own, who lived lives of hate instead of love, who lived under tyranny, and who never got a happy ending. May they rest now. You are remembered. I dedicate this novel to God, for without their spiritual energy there would be no book at all. Pen and paper are my closest friends for their tireless work.

I also thank an old friend who without our conversations I would never have written this book in the first place. It is to them, ironically, that I owe the life and story of Wolfe, and so many more.

Lastly, if you're reading this, I thank you, truly, honestly, and supremely, from the bottom of my heart for supporting *Blue* and myself. Enjoy.

A Letter from the Author

In 2020, while the COVID-19 pandemic was raging and civil unrest over the killing of George Floyd swathed North America and beyond, I was *angry*. During conversations with people during these protests against institutions of power, I realized something needed to change, intrinsically, in the conversation. *Blue* is my attempt at education and discussion, shifting the power of conversation back to a place of potential enlightenment.

I wrote *Blue* because I realized people rarely understand the scale of racism in the Americas, past and present. The scope at which dehumanization happens and how easily the apathy of the masses empowers the hatred of a few to perpetrate cruelty on a massive scale, the enormity of it, is nearly incomprehensible unless you're placed in that situation. I wrote *Blue* to condense the absolute horror of being seen as less than human into a single novel, despite being an uneasy, and sometimes horrific topic, the unavoidable horror of blind ignorance must be brought to light, examined, and understood.

Racial science is nothing new. We've used "science" to justify genocide against the Jewish people, Africans, and Indigenous communities. When we allow ourselves to be divided on trivial characteristics like skin color, sex, where we're born, the color and shape of our hair, what language we speak, etc... we allow ourselves to forget our shared humanity. We say *We Remember* and *Never Again,* but we never remember; at some point, we forget. One day, eye color might matter more than skin color ever did, and could you imagine how dark a world like that would be?

I'm sure I'll get angry messages asking how I could write something like this, of my sadism and evilness, to even create the scenarios you'll read about. I remind you, I drew from the real-world atrocities that have actually been lived by real people. The transatlantic slave trade, The Holocaust, indigenous residential schools, Irish indentured servitude, and so on. Every horrific, torturous experience is drawn from the lived experiences of people long gone. Honor them through remembrance.

At the end of the day, I didn't write *Blue* to anger, hurt, inflame, and certainly not to deride blue-eyed people, but to educate. I want people to imagine an "impossible world" lived by ethnic minorities for centuries and beyond, situations that have risen over, and over, and over again in "civilized" countries that would "never" do something like *that*. Never assume we've put the darkness behind us. Fight for people that don't look like you because tomorrow, you might be the one targeted.

Don't take your humanity for granted,

Miguel A. Fenrich

Chapter 0

Rogue Lightning

She was born in what had been Armenia before BESNA came. There had been joy before the ships, before the guns, before the stench of rot and death. Now her family was curled together in the hold of a moaning ship as it caressed the waves of the Atlantic ocean. They lived in a hovel along the eastern seaboard while the camps were built and Hurricane Pauline picked their lives apart.

"We believe some of you to be in legion with those who would wish to destroy this great country. Due to a…regrettable event surrounding blue-eyed communities, unfortunately several of you may have to be detained until our amazing officers can sort out this corruption and stamp it out at the roots. I'm sure you all agree?" Prime Minister Windthorst said to them with cherry red lips, his face plastered on every screen in their slums.

Men dressed in black came for them at night, shuffling them across the greatest country in the world and into the ghetto along the edge of Redemption City. The world grew darker, the light of her childhood was harder to find when she dreamed, and when selection came, and Daddy was shot, the rest of them were dragged into giant copper vans with golden eyes in the corner. The little girl cried for the first time since leaving her kitten behind in Europe.

—

Somewhere, at some point, lightning struck the desert. The black strip of road wedged between an ocean of gnarled black trees and sand, hissed against the tires of a thousand copper trucks. The air flashed white as another lightning bolt turned the shimmering grains to glass. The girl pushed her face away from the blistering heat into the curl of her mother's arm. It all came back as static when she thought of her childhood, her home, her cat, and her brother. The doors on the trailer swung open, and her heart dropped.

A swell of black arms grappled with her. The metal spears opened like mouths and devoured her, coiling her in black nets and metal handcuffs. She'd screamed, she must have, but not that she could remember. Her mouth opened, and no words came out. In her head, she strung together a single word:

Liberty. Liberty. Liberty.

She repeated her mantra in silence as she watched her mother's glassy eyes. Her mother was dead, but the girl was only eight. How could she read death on her lips?

Liberty. Liberty. Liberty.

She watched the black figures hop into the back of the truck with their guns pointed down. She waited for her mother to get up, for the skin around her soft blue eyes to crinkle like silk, but they didn't. The girl watched her mother cease to exist. When she cried herself to sleep that night, she slept beneath a starless sky.

Liberty. Liberty. Liberty.

She listened to cries echoing in the wind.

—

The little girl closed her eyes and tried to think of home, ignoring the clambering bidders with their flagging arms desperate to stare at her naked flesh. She was eleven, and she was being sold. She'd stopped repeating her sister's name, the trail of *Liberty. Liberty. Liberty.* fell off her tongue, and she knew she'd failed. The sisters were orphans, and each was alone.

A tall, greasy man reeking of smoke picked and prodded at her, staring into every dark crevice that eyes should never see before stealing her away into the plains. Once he'd taken and bred her and she'd grown heavy with his child, she tried to imagine all the ways she could kill him: a knife against him when he mounted her, a needle filled with bleach while he slept beside his infertile wife, rat poison in his food until he bled to death. Once she'd planned his death, she returned to her cabin and pretended life wasn't so bad.

—

She fell in love with a man whose name didn't matter, but love only goes so far. Master killed him with his fists when he planned to escape and claimed her like an animal in the yard reeking of his blood. She was pregnant again and birthed another worker. She bore four children for Master before one of the babies kept its blue eyes into adolescence:

"I don't understand. I'm only twenty-three. I can't be, your test must be wrong, he'll sell me if I can't give him more brown-eyed kids."

"Your guess is as good as mine. Women saddled with the mutation struggle with infertility more than normal women, you should know that. Blue-eyed women have higher rates of cancer too. It's just how God designed you. I have to inform your Master."

"Please, sir. I can't…he…he'll…" She could feel the slap before it even touched her face.

"Don't ever raise your voice to me again, it's my obligation to report this to Master. Now shut your whore mouth and get back to work." She'd been sold before she had a chance to beg.

—

As the world grew hotter, rumours of caravans fleeing northbound to escape the heat reached them. A man came to auction and bought a handful of slaves: the infertile woman, a young musician, and a mother. Master and their new owner smiled, shook hands, pointed, and inspected them before leaving with the best mother in Texas, the best musician in Texas, and the best sex in Texas.

He turned to them with his brown hair, white teeth, and green tie, and he spoke to them. But it didn't matter because she'd die with a handful of broken promises, a life spent running, and betrayal on her tongue. She was twenty-seven.

Texas had ceased to exist.

Chapter 1

The Bitter Sting of Chains

The world ended long before we knew it was ending, and by the time we noticed, we were too late to stop it. The man thought to himself as he crawled in the sunbaked earth, feeling the pebbles and twigs cast imprints across his hands. The sun split his forehead, and sweat trickled across his parched skin, stinging his eyes. A hot, shaky breath crawled from his lips as they parted, pushing past his swollen throat. His knees burnt against the boiling soil and his back threatened to shatter. He felt the dirt under his clothes, scratching at him like bugs beneath his peeling, blistered skin.

"Worker WLL29809NC, I have removed seven credits from your account citing section thirty-two of the Workers Protection Act..." The cool, iced voice of electronic chips and wires hissing together spoke from the soil beside him. The round, metallic orb heaved a cart of dead corn stalks beside him, informing him as he worked. It had tiny wheels spun from resin over steel rims, digging ruts in the earth as it rambled off its reasoning: quotas unfilled, unremarkable work, and floundering company time.

The man felt rage simmering beneath his skin. *That's a full day's work gone. Now I can't buy new work boots tomorrow.* He thought.

"Verbally respond," the voice said.

"Yes," Wolfe muttered absently, listening to the incessant humming of the ball.

The robot was no larger than a grapefruit, a resin ball wrapped in an aluminum shell. The metal ball went quiet, regaining its lethargic march across the hillside, dragging its cart behind it as Wolfe followed, picking the dead stalks from the field. The workers aptly named the robots Slow-Mos or just Mos for short.

He leaned back on the balls of his feet and rolled his neck around in circles. He blinked dirt loose from his eyebrows as he rubbed his face with a clean elbow, looking up from the fields and towards the horizon. A mirage spread before him, encapsulating the hills in a shimmering cloud of light. He squinted through the haze, gazing over the arid landscape alive with ants like himself, mulling in the thousands. The unseen, unskilled figures, shapeless in their multitudes, ambled through the same sandy soil as him.

The year was 2067, the May rains hadn't come as they should, and the crops withered, leaving nothing but an accumulation of death in place of corn. Now the workers would collect the remnants, and the sky would burn russet with smoke for months. Then, BESNA would spray the fields to simulate a faux spring, manipulate the skies to force the rain, and the workers would pick it endlessly until the winter came.

Wolfe rose at dawn, crawled through the fields during the day, and slept when the sun slept. Since his 'temporary relocation' three years ago, his two-week stay bled into months and the months into years. He felt himself dampen under the sun's oppression.

Two months after he'd arrived, they had stood in the darkness and the rain, watching the screen above them in the plaza. The grass sank into a grayish sludge during the long winter months, and the rain had fallen endlessly. Winter lightning shattered the black porcelain sky as the air shook, and claps of thunder tore the heavens in half, letting loose torrents of rain, stirring between antiquated cobblestones and washing them free of dirt. A man stood on a freshly erected podium, hands crossed, head arched. His gray tie was shining black, slick with rain.

"I had prayed we would live in peace," he had said. "That your savage, lazy instincts wouldn't take over as they have before."

A video played above his head. They watched it twice in its entirety and each time, a new host of horrors they missed the first time came to light: A brown-eyed woman was raped in front of them by blue-eyed assailants, feral white dogs with cobalt eyes feasted on school children, blue-eyed men wielding spears of glass screamed with blood on their tongues as they dragged men and women down alleys.

Officers dressed in black, each with a golden eye sewn on their left arm, right breast, chest, and plastered on the forehead of their black visors, trolled around the plaza in trucks. The letters BESNA, standing for The Brown Eyed Society of North America, were sewn across their chests. They carried large metal poles with spinning, twitching spikes in each of their hands. Wide golden eyes were shining on every wall, etched into every glass window, hung from every windowsill, and flown from every roof.

"I am afraid of what this country has become. We are not a country of violence or anger, but instead we are the most peaceful country on the planet. Why must you fight us? Why must you be so ignorant of facts, breeding riots and terror on the streets?" he cried, tears on the edges of his eyes, spit flying from the corners of his lips.

"They attacked my daughter in her bed three days ago," he said, his chest rising and falling.

Wolfe could feel the same chill he'd felt that night run down his back again, staring up at the brown-eyed man standing beneath the canopy of rain. He told them how thousands of high-ranking officials' personal information was leaked to the public, making them the targets of extreme violence. He had told them it ends today.

"To address the large breaches of privacy, BESNA has lobbied congress to pass the Peoples' Endangered Privacy Act or PEPA for short." And they all watched, waiting to see if they would live or die.

He said they would increase security by almost double. He told them that all rumours and fabricated information would be strictly controlled. He said that all information about parliament and publicly owned businesses would be made unavailable to the public for their safety. With an evil glint in his eyes, he told them that they would begin questioning certain individuals deemed to have sensitive information in the transgression of PEPA.

"Lies led to the death of my colleagues," he said finally before slipping off the stage.

They lost any idea of the outside world from that day: what countries remained or who the prime minister was, what laws passed or fell into oblivion. The weekly updates turned into monthly updates, then bi-yearly updates, and then not at all.

No news. No elections. No changes. Nothing but whispered rumours and thoughts.

"Your shift has finished for the day. Due to exemplary service in your field, you are eligible for the one thousand credit raffle this week," Mo said. The moment he finished speaking, the cart rumbled between the rows and sunk into the setting sun, kicking up dust behind it that glittered against the crimson light. Wolfe never knew where it went; no one did, but it would be empty and ready to be filled tomorrow morning.

Wolfe stretched his back, feeling his vertebrae cry. He watched through parted eyes as figures listed towards the hill in front of him, congregating in a dark, trembling mass a few kilometres ahead of him. Wolfe dug the heels of his ruined boots into the crackling earth beneath him, and he walked until his throat burnt.

The sun felt hotter, the air hung heavy, and the lack of moisture pulled water out of his eyes and skin, baking him from the inside out. A layer of dust shimmered in the air, basking in the burgundy heat as Wolfe came up to the group of workers. At the center of them, a tall, erratic woman flung her arms open, her lips and head shaking back and forth as she spoke.

"—and that's not even the worst of it. I lost half my credits today," she yelled. "I'll have to skip supper tonight!" she yelled louder. The workers gave a symphony of sighs, ticks, and tuts in her defence. "A pregnant woman on top of it all..." she added, cradling her swollen stomach.

"Fuck'n animals," a short, fat, beetle-shaped man grumbled, pacing around in circles, waddling more like a penguin than a man. "Then they wonder why we'd try to kill 'em out east," he said, sinking into a circle of people, whispering rumours to each other of an army pushing down into what was once California.

"No, it's true. I heard that they've been lynching any blue-eyed escapee from any of these sorta places," a woman whispered, her eyes pinched shut like a rat, her gangling legs stuck beneath her like a scarecrow. "Yes, yes, that's what I'd heard," a pumpkin-shaped man crowed. "The country has been broken up into over a hundred tiny provinces, all with their own horrible punishments if you're caught. It's a different world out there for sure."

"And the hospitals. They say if you get sent there you come out a different person. More beast than man."

The rumours came back from the ditches, the fields, the factories and the re-education camps. They ranged from Prime Minister Windthorst being a blue-eyed man in disguise, the BESNA officers actually being cyborgs behind their visors, there was a gigantic war pushing into the country from the Rockies to free them all, this was just a massive alien conspiracy to show them humanities true colours, and the list went on forever. Every rumour had a hundred alternatives, and every alternative had a thousand variations.

Wolfe didn't care for rumours, yet he still heard them: whispers of oppressive overseas regimes, assassinated prime ministers, festering decade-long wars, and wicked plantations in the east. The whispers came and went, but nothing ever happened. At best, they got him hopeful; at worst, they depressed him. He stood and listened while he waited, watching the other faces move and swirl, cast eyes over the shoulders, and sink closer against each other as they murmured.

Eventually, the earth creaked and cracked beneath them as the familiar sound of heavily armoured trucks rumbled up the dirt road, coming to collect them and take them back to the Redemption City Workers District. They clambered into the truck beds as silent, armed guards dressed in black watched them while clinging to the back of the trucks with guns in hand.

A plume of brown and gray dust oscillated in the air behind

them as they rode on raw, heat-shattered hills, desiccated and devoid of movement or life. They all sat in absolute silence, eyes always trained on the guards, disciplined from years of practice. They swept through the fields beneath the waves of heat and blinding sun like they had this evening and every evening before. The self-proclaimed 'jewel of the coast' towered over the horizon as they rode.

Sunburnt walls floated along the edges of the sea, pushing the swell of water back along the relic of an ancient coast. Twenty years of swollen oceans and melting ice caps rammed an extra thirteen feet of water against the off-white hydroelectric dams that allowed for kilometres of white, sandy beaches to run the course of the city, their surface spotted with beachgoers.

Monstrous skyscrapers disappeared thousands of metres into the sky, twisting glass and metal physiques tapering off above the clouds. The workers' eyes trained down the white towers to their bases where the suburbs and parks lay, buzzing with millions of tiny shadowed bodies, the distance shrinking them into non-existence.

Even in Wolfe's youth, the city was heralded as one of the world's environmentally friendly cities, second only to Mexico City. A city free from emissions, guilt, and smog. A city of the future, of glass and metal, of wooden roofs and solar panels. The south sides of the towers were sparkling green over their white frames, crawling with enough vegetables and hemp to feed and clothe the city for decades. The rooftop fans spun, walls of black solar panels reflected the sun

down on them, and the entire city hissed with life.

They gazed down towards their homes as they wound down the dusty hills. At the base of the city, the former towers and skyscrapers of the future looked like primordial huts with their dated veneers. Their lack of glass perforated space and time; their ashen hue a blight against the edge of Redemption City.

Wolfe and the other workers were packed into those archaic, crumbling buildings like rats on a ship. They were boxes to be stacked and unstacked, moved and shuffled wherever someone thought best. They ate on top of each other, pissed on top of each other, and slept on top of each other. *It's easier to treat us like animals if you make us sleep in filth. If they make us look and act like animals, it's easier to pretend we aren't prisoners. Not humans.* Wolfe thought, souring what bitter remnants were left of his mood.

They crawled down the hills into the only entrance to the Redemption City Workers District. Tall, tepid stone walls adorned with barbed wire circled their home while guards watched them in silence, marching in long lines with guns. The officers lived in the black and gray walls, watching the workers through the dark glass windows, waiting to destroy workers with their turrets if they stepped out of line.

The guards claimed to be unbiased.

"We only wish to uphold a good understanding between different people. There are only a few bad guards if any. We're not all bad!" Everyone knew it was a lie, as when the batons came out and the bullets flew their dark black wings into the workers' skin, there was only silence. The well-reasoned guards, if they existed, were silent. There were only violent oppressors and those who watched violent oppressors.

Wolfe stepped out of the truck, across the threshold of the ghetto, and over a carcass undulating with maggots.

"A teacher from Colorado."

"Taught calculus for fourty years."

"Broke bylaw fourty-seven." Wolfe heard murmurs as they passed. Wolfe didn't know the bylaws. No one knew the bylaws.

This was simply life in this new world. Work. Earn credits. Listen to orders. Sleep. That was it. Sure, maybe once in a while they'd splurge their hard-earned credits on a phone call, or a drink, or a fuck, but mostly Wolfe spent his credits on extras like toothpaste, clean socks, and new work boots.

Wolfe walked against the string of machines lined against the courtyard's edge and held out his arm. It spat out a block and apartment number onto his wrist, followed by a golden eye, and he started drudging himself through the streets under the dusty monoliths and waving gold and brown flags.

Every night the workers were sent to a new building, a new floor, or a new apartment. Wolfe had yet to see the same room twice. The gangs, viruses, families, and drugs swirled through the ghetto like a typhoon battering its long limbs against the walls.

Wolfe moved through the streets towards one of the several mess halls at the bottom of the office buildings. Throngs of people passed by, all covered in blood, dirt, or manure. The tallest concrete skyscrapers between them were filled with metal beds and factories pumping steam out into the air. Millions of them lived crammed together in what was once the northeastern corner of Los Angeles.

Wolfe tapped his wrist against the plastic square embedded in the counter, taking three credits from his account. He grabbed a plate of slurry off the counter and slurped at it: A mashed pile of unknown vegetables, a lump of plant-based meat shaped like a ball of rubber, and a handful of pills and vitamins, the only thing keeping them from slipping into skin and bones.

Wolfe scraped the last of his food into his mouth and ambled back into the street, head down, eyes turned towards the pavement.

Every thirty feet, there was a PNT dispenser in places where benches and planters used to be. Men and women were curled around it, pouring credit after credit into oblivion, huddled in masses along the gutters, weeping and gurgling, crying with joy and shaking with need. Wolfe watched their faces, warped in their own individual pleasure. Everyone knew they'd reach the point when you took the tiny yellow pill that let you glide through your day without caring. He would, eventually, inevitably. Wolfe walked past them.

Wolfe turned his head away from the wall of building-length billboards beside him that shone day and night: C list celebrities that had fallen into obscurity tried to remind the workers that drugs numbed all pain, sex kept your mind busy, and gangs gave you a sense of community. And they did, for a minute, and then you came back to reality, desperately searching for your moment of peace.

Wolfe continued towards the end of a line of apartment buildings, then turned down a street of sixty-year-old office buildings. The brilliantly black pavement sat unused and unbroken, blistering and shining in the heat. There was no garbage and no piles of decay. Everything was clean, immaculately polished, and primed.

Wolfe looked farther to the north, walking with apartments on his left and tall office buildings and condos to his right. Once, the city was divided by class and not eye colour, an ideology that had long fallen through the cracks.

"Blue-eyed people have always been public enemy number one." They were told through their screens and their ads. Every CEO and politician reminded everyone that anyone who dissented was a liar, a traitor, and a communist.

Two guards stalked the street across from him, and he slowed. *Is your head too low? Too high? Are you looking suspicious or uppity?* Alarms rang in Wolfe's head. He dusted his shirt, hoping he wasn't too clean but not too dirty. *Try not to look sick. Don't look too happy either.* It was a familiar waltz he danced endlessly. You stole, or you're acting above your station, you're sick, or you're too happy, you're suspicious-looking or guilty. There was no winning.

Behind him, five more guards came around the corner of the street and stopped to harass a young woman and her boy standing in the street. Children were a foreign sight in the city, and Wolfe let his eyes follow them as he walked. Most of the children of the past were skeletons by now, and city officials forbid children born under their constant surveillance from reading or writing. That requires thinking; thinking will turn them against them.

Don't think, they whisper, *believe.*

They were testing the boy impromptu in the streets. Two guards held the mother back while the others lulled the boy into a false sense of security. They spoke to him in soft voices and gentle, laughing whispers, just long enough for him to point out a few signs, correctly babbling out the few words he could read. What child doesn't want to flaunt his knowledge? Wide, starry eyes smiled into their black visors with pride. Then, they were gone in a blink, taken to be punished and separated.

Wolfe tried to pretend things like that didn't bother him, but he was lying.

Wolfe came to the far northwest corner of the ghetto; a tall cream-coloured condo towered above him, a mere fifty stories high. The numbers on his wrist matched the numbers on the side of the building. Above him, a quote hung in gold lettering.

"Intellectual honesty is at the heart of all we find pure."

As if, Wolfe thought to himself. The Order of Truth and Justice was an eighty-eight-page novel that dictated their place in the world. Written by Dr. N.B. Hanley, he believed that the 'dominant' brown-eyed majority were superior to those saddled with the blue-eyed mutation. Hate crimes rose, the news spewed rhetoric day and night, politicians yelled over their podiums promising to solve the blue-eyed 'problem,' and still, it wasn't enough to push blue-eyed people into action. By the time the first ghetto was built, it was years too late.

The hate had been bred in silence, in all the dark, recessed places where disillusions of truth grow. When the first people were shipped into clearings and shot by black-suited men, it was too late. When BESNA lobbied the government to create brown-eyed 'protection' acts, it was too late. When Wolfe saw the leaflets raining over his school, telling the world that blue-eyed violence was the single greatest threat to the country, it was too late. When people cared more about the innate colour of one's eyes instead of their intrinsic humanity, it was too late.

What could I have done? Wolfe asked himself, *I was just a kid.*

"People with blue eyes are more prone to alcoholism."

"Despite making up only eight percent of the population, they account for almost half of all serial killers."

"If you have blue eyes, you're more likely to develop stage one diabetes, more likely to go deaf, and more likely to have endometriosis. It's nature's cripple."

They did this. Who are they? Wolfe asked himself. A conglomeration of corporations that wanted cheap labour? A rogue government that wished to gain an iron hold over their citizens? Or was it a group of brown-eyed people that wanted to be on top so severely that they made this world a reality?

Yes.

Wolfe held his wrist out to the sleek metal scanner mounted to the right of the doors. The scanner beeped, the doors pushed open, and a burst of air rushed over him. They closed behind him as he stepped through the doors, locking him in until morning.

Wolfe passed through the packs of people talking on the floor, refusing to look down, ignoring their empty words and meaningless chatter as they tried to pass the time.

A couple was nestled in the corner near a laundry machine, rutting feverishly against each other. The intimacy that should be there was replaced with glazed eyes and still hands. Wolfe locked eyes with her. No anger, no joy, no fear, no love. Nothing. A lonely, dark chasm Wolfe could lose himself in and never be found again. She seemed to study Wolfe. Then she blinked and refused to open her eyes again as Wolfe passed.

Wolfe walked upstairs, listening to their stale moaning dissipate beneath him. *Who could she have been? A teacher? A writer? A farmer? A mechanic? What were her dreams, her aspirations, her passions?* Then it didn't matter, and Wolfe pushed her black, devoid eyes out of his mind and thought of nothing again.

The next day, week, month, year, and decade would be the same. Though Wolfe wanted to sleep, he feared the nightmares. The memories would come back when he was too incapacitated to hold them at bay, and he would be forced to relive his life from sixteen to twenty again. Then when he awoke he went back to his life without an end in sight.

Chapter 2

Selection Day

2067 slipped into 2068. Summer came and melted into fall. The driest autumn in memory gave way to the winter rains that turned the hills to mud. The workers toiled in the fields regardless, wrapped in plastic, spraying the fields, burning the refuse, and digging stones from the soil with bare fingers until their skin slipped from their bones.

Selection Day, as it was called, came on the first of every month. The city officials told them that a lottery would be the best way to ensure *true* impartiality, and the BESNA-owned ghetto, in partnership with the city, entered the workers' codes into an A.I. algorithm. Every month Wolfe had worked in the fields. Until the autumn. Two weeks before the rain started to fall, Wolfe was selected to spend the winter working in a canning factory on the south side.

Every morning he stuffed the cans with meat and vegetables, carving out the rot and dodging the gigantic presses that claimed a life a week. After a month in the cannery, it became two, then three more. Six in total. Then it was spring. The sky cleared, the earth dried, and dried, and dried. The whispers said it was the hottest May on record, that the plants would not grow in dust, and that the fields were a death sentence.

Wolfe saw the workers, walking with heads held high towards the covered vans, sputtering to start against the heat. By the end of the first week, they limped; by the end of the second, they crawled; by the end of the third, they were drug back in the wheeled carts by a swathe of Mos.

Yet, not everyone was selected to work. A sparse collection, maybe a thousand workers a month, were led backward from the fields, through the streets, and towards the black metal gates that led towards the urban sprawl behind them. The selection was tomorrow, and the fields were almost clear of workers.

Everyone theorized what would become of them. What happened when you were led beyond the shiny black gate? Would it be preferable to die underneath the sun? They were seen as products, not people, and the workers knew they would be used until broken. If there came a time when it was more expensive to fix them, they ended up in the scrap heap, disposed of in the cheapest way possible. There were no medics in the ghetto.

Friday night was spent spending credits: some workers spent their credits calling directories, searching for family members to no avail, others carried drugs in their pockets, slinking upstairs with their eyes blurred and hands trembling, while some scrimped and saved for the big-ticket items like work boots, gloves, desserts after supper, toothpaste, new clothes, and hair gel. Anything that made them feel more human. On the evenings before selections, the workers sat around the massive gathering rooms and talked to anyone who would listen. Wolfe caught the conversation of a group of women chatting on a long couch against the wall.

"I heard it was plus sixty-three today," one short, squat woman said to the others. Once lush fields became desert, rolling grape fields soured into brown, arid hills.

"Think about those poor souls out in the fields," another woman cried. She had a small mousy face and gray whiskers underneath her chin.

The shorter woman spoke up again. "As if we have it easy?" she cried. "We're forced to do hard labour every day too, look at my hands!" she said, holding out her stained and rippled fingers, wrecked from years of water and chemical.

The other women went to object, but no one could speak fast enough.

"I remember a time when our biggest concern was the climate," she mumbled. She was the youngest of them, maybe fourty, judging from the age of wrinkles across her forehead and the shadows sinking beneath her eyes. "We were fighting our grandparents to have a say in the world, in politics, in life, in—" Her words slid together as she spoke, and she was cut off.

"Look where that got us. Stop complaining and just let it go," one woman said, jumping in and interrupting the woman to try and get her point across.

"It was just so quick. While everyone cried, 'That can't happen! We live in the safest country in the world. What about the law? We're living in the twenty-first century.' they shuffled us into semi-trailers and sent us off into the void. But what could we do if none of the brown-eyed people spoke up? Even if we tried to fight back, they told everyone only *violent* blue-eyed radicals, criminals, and terrorists would be sent to prison or executed. Then, they told the world that every blue-eyed man or woman was almost always in league with violent radicals. What could we have done?"

"Oh, as if Madison," the woman grumbled. "You're acting like it was brown-eyed people, and you and I both know it was the fucking Jews. They let them come in and pull apart the fabric of our country. That's why everything is profit, profit, profit. Then the diaper heads were bringing in their sharia law, prancing hand in hand with all them dirty niggers. But in the end, it was every shit-eyed brownie who wouldn't do anything." The moment the word 'brownie' crossed her lips, she knew she had made a mistake. She looked up to the ceiling, the five cameras above trained unwaveringly on her face.

Wolfe felt his skin recoil; a trail of goosebumps trembled down his spine to his fingertips. The room drained until only the woman, and Wolfe remained. She begged the cameras above for salvation, looking through Wolfe, alone as much as he was.

Wolfe stepped out as she wept, heading upstairs to bathe. The shower stalls and baths were full, so Wolfe wandered an empty floor. He looked at the scratched, foggy windows, the light fixtures swimming with dead flies. Dust was stirring in the street, and the faint outline of where artwork and coat racks used to hang was plastered on the walls. A slew of BESNA officers swept towards the building, their golden-eyed visors shining in the darkness.

The walls were pearlescent, alabaster white. A thousand shades of white and gray seemed to dominate his life. *Where were the colours?* The rich, opalescent shimmer of plum-coloured silk curtains, the rising indecency of vermillion flower petals, the thick, twisting amber shades of melted butter. When life lost its colour, life lost its excitement. *Maybe I'm being dramatic*, he thought to himself. But life had lost its gleam. Life was all dust, no joy. All work, no play. What is the purpose of life if not to live it?

Wolfe looked up towards the towers shining from within as people went about their lives deep within the behemoths. *What do they do? How do they live?* Wolfe asked himself. He tried to imagine their lives and only thought of darkness. Their apexes pierced the clouds, letting the dying sunlight ripple down like the golden blood of demigods.

He thought about his first trip to the city, a liberating escape from the dusty prairies of his youth. A glittering world, a world in movement, a life spent running, a life he longed for. But after his Great Grandmother's funeral, whose face was lost to the memories of his youth, they went home again. They never saw the city again. Wolfe was seven. Eight years later, he'd been sitting in class when BESNA came and changed everything.

He let his eyes shut for a moment. His eyes didn't ache, his limbs didn't burn, but he was tired. Tired of moving, tired of doing, tired of thinking. He looked out towards the horizon. A shimmer of beaches lined the coast. He wouldn't make it much longer. He watched the sun sink, watched the sky go shades of scarlet, burgundy, then plum.

The last years had taken their toll. Wolfe's eyes were sunken in their frames, his black hair was buzzed short along his scalp, his clothes were almost rags, and a few lines of scars from beatings and machinery malfunctions over the years had bruised and damaged him. He was tall enough, but his back ached when he stood tall. Wolfe had long, delicate fingers but bulges spread between the knuckles from injuries long forgotten. He had more muscle than he had ever wanted, but his fingers were calloused, and the feeling had left the tips from overuse. His pale, almost white-looking blue eyes had stopped shining just like everyone else. Wolfe was one of millions, wholly fungible and regular among the masses. His family wouldn't even recognize this foreign man he'd grown into alone.

Maybe he would dream of Arcola tonight, his brown-eyed sister who'd worked at the library before BESNA overcame their little town. Or Ogema, his equally brown-eyed grandmother working as the Bruno town hall office manager until retirement. Or possibly even his uncle, who told the world he'd run away to Bermuda before having to kill innocent blue-eyed people. More likely, however, he'd dream of his parents, Elrose and Allan, his brother Blaine, his dog, cousins, and aunt who'd met their individual fates somewhere with or without each other.

Wolfe heard a shuttering beneath him as the solar generators slowly shut off power to the lower levels of the building. Wolfe stepped into a dull, dirty maze of dividers, metal beds, stairs, and shambling figures. The light was a practically non-existent throb, throwing the shadows of bugs and moths around the light bulbs.

He wandered between the hallways. Men with their faces pushed deep into bottles were slumped against walls, their voices slipping and tumbling over themselves in a drunken haze. A toothless old man sat slurping at a plastic cup filled with murky brown liquid that smelled like cow shit and acid. A gigantic green and purple bruise crept across his bony face as a vast, throbbing vein pulsed around his eye. Two people sat huddled together by the entrance to a cubicle. A man with dark hair and brilliant green eyes and a brown-haired older woman with eyes like murky water flashed weary smiles at Wolfe as he walked by.

He saw a young woman farther down the hall laying on her stomach, her back exposed, as a few teenage nurses worked quickly to stave off bleeding from a fierce beating. Deep gouges were carved into her, and as they tried to treat her wounds, they were met with muffled screams and cries. Wolfe pondered her crime. *Insubordination, or is it more straightforward? Walking on the wrong side of the road, breathing at the wrong time, eating at the wrong time, being at the wrong place at the wrong time like everyone else.*

Wolfe found his cubicle. The words 11748B were marked above it. The scanner waited before him as he raised his wrist, and the door jumped open. Two bunk beds sat in each corner of the eight-foot cubicle. Two men were already in one, and the other one was empty.

"Got any smokes?" one man asked, sitting up sharply, leaning over to make eye contact with Wolfe.

"Sorry, man, I don't. I already spent all of my credits this week," Wolfe lied. He sat down on the bed and pulled off his boots, the pads of his toes aching as he did. *God, I'd love a smoke; it just might feel normal.* Wolfe thought. It was the last 'normal' thing he'd ever done, heckled into smoking beneath the gray school he'd seen razed.

"Ah, no problem. Who thought *this* would be the answer to my nicotine addiction," the man snorted before rolling over in bed again.

Wolfe pulled the thin sheet up over himself, laying down on his pillow. His neck craned backwards, his body sinking into the abused springs. The man on the top bunk rolled over again and hissed down at Wolfe.

"Pssst…Psssssssst…Hey. Hey man."

"What do you want?" Wolfe snarled back, a little more bitter than he meant.

"Oh, I'm sorry your majesty. Jesus, a little conversation won't get you shit these days," he said, thumping his head down into what was left of the pillow.

"Sorry. I'm just tired. Selection Day is tomorrow and all that."

"Oh, Selection Day?" he said, propping himself up on his arms to get a better view of Wolfe. "Let me tell you, I've been working out in these fields since before the world was like this, and I'll say it, it never rains anymore." He was squinting in the dark, trying to see Wolfe's face.

Wolfe stayed quiet, hoping he would stop talking.

"Oh, it's horrible. Before all this, we had these um…whatcha call 'em…" He went silent for a moment, obviously deep in thought. "Grapes. Yeah, that's it. Grapes. You know what I mean?"

"Mmhm," Wolfe responded, trying his best to signal to the man that he didn't want to have this conversation.

"Oh, and I'm praying for an inside job, I'll tell you that. It's a death sentence out there now. I've been doing mostly mechanical work. Do you have any mechanical background? Electrical?" Before Wolfe could respond, he spoke again. "It was hard enough back in the forties, right before that drought, you know? Still hasn't changed, and it's been up on twenty five years since then."

Wolfe prayed he would shut up.

"Ey, it was good back then, I'll tell you that much. Good work, good ethics, good rain, and now it's all gone to shit," he continued, making a weird ticking noise with his tongue.

"You worked here back when there were still avocados?" Wolfe pried, willing to risk sleep tonight for some actual information.

"Oh yeah," he said. "The hills were lush like you wouldn't have known. We got rain out the wazoo back then, wouldn't you believe it?"

He went on to list regional rainfall averages back then versus today and the different vegetables and fruits they grew. The golden years he called them. He finally stopped talking, and Wolfe let his eyes fall shut.

"Have you heard any of the rumours that have been going around?" the man asked, lowering his voice.

"No, and I don't wanna hear them, either. I don't believe any of the shit we hear," Wolfe snapped.

"Oh," he said, momentarily stunned. Then he went on. "I plan to wait until they reissue marriage licenses for us, and I'll settle down with my girlfriend, have a couple of kids, you know, the simple life," he said, seeming to swell with pride at the idea of it. "I just wanna get some roots down, you know?" he asked, craning over Wolfe.

"Yeah, but wouldn't you want to be free *and* get married? Like all the brown-eyes do?" Wolfe pointed out, waiting for the idea to strike him.

The man was silent for a moment.

"Well, I guess. But I don't think there is anything you or I could do anyway, so I may get on with accepting it. Are you up for going to Selection Day together? It'd be nice to have someone to walk with."

"Mhmm," Wolfe responded. He was so done with stupid people. *Would he just shut up?* Wolfe pleaded, waiting for him to stop talking.

"Did you hear? Apparently, there is going to be a rebellion at the Tobin's plantation. The Valparaiso's. Possibly even the Bredenbury's too," he said, his voice dropping to a whisper.

"Where?" Wolfe asked, picking his ear off the pillow to listen.

"You haven't heard of the Tobins? They own breeding farms on every continent. The Valparaiso family owns the biggest weapons company globally, and the Bredenbury family has the biggest monopoly on produce and animal feed in North America. They all buy workers out of here every month. You haven't heard people talking about them?"

"I asked where, not who. I try not to listen," Wolfe said, but he still heard the whispers; the murmurs of whips and bullet holes, missing digits and rotting corpses. But the whispers of rebellion were new to Wolfe, and he was piecing things together in his mind.

"Is that where those workers go every month? Past that gate?" Wolfe asked. Wolfe and the man could see the gate now, pulling the light from the moon towards it's smooth, darkened surface.

"Not just the Valparaisos, the Bredenburys, or the Tobins. The Wilkies. The Dorintoshs. We're the cheapest labour they can find."

"But how do you know they're planning a revolt?" Wolfe asked, every sense lit alight, their voices nothing more than a hum.

"I don't. Just a rumour." His voice went back to normal.

"Isn't that a huge risk to take? Hoping to get selected to go to a plantation all because you heard some rumours about a rebellion?" Wolfe asked, feeling his entire body shake with nervous energy. "From what I heard, It'd be safer here. It's hell out on those plantations."

The man thought for a moment. "Who said anything about hoping to go to a plantation? I'd rather take my chances in the fields. It's just a rumour. I doubt it's true. We owe people like the Tobin family our lives."

The silence grew between them.

"What's your name then?" The man asked.

"Wolfe."

"Craik."

Craik was still talking, though he hadn't noticed Wolfe's silence. Wolfe only caught bits and snippets of what he was saying.

"—though of course I hadn't always loved metalworking, but it's better th—"

"—the credit system is a piece of work though, makes you wonder why someone would—"

"—ow long have you been here? I got shipped out from the east six months ago by the—"

"—they always make it sound like it's for our good, but I'm not sure that—"

As Craik dithered on, Wolfe found his voice. He wanted to tell him how stupid he was for falling for half-baked lies and propaganda, how easily Craik gave up his rights, how he could be so stupid for not being angry. As his voice found him, his will gave out.

"Well, goodnight," Wolfe found himself saying before rolling over in bed for a final time; the rusty metal shifting under his weight

"Oh," Craik said, the silence filling the room. "Well, goodnight," he said, far too happy to have grasped the implications of Wolfe's silence. Wolfe listened to Craik roll over, falling into a sleep fit for kings. Wolfe felt a flash of fear. *What if I get selected to go to one of the plantations?* Wolfe thought. Then he wondered if he should hope for it. *What if I get chosen to work in the fields?*

The black metal gate shimmering in the boiling night pulled at the back of Wolfe's mind, and he imagined the world beyond it. *I could go home.* He had never honestly imagined what freedom would look like; what would he do with his life; what would a future of possibilities look like? The idea of escape hummed away inside him as Craik snored.

The air feels different tonight. Wolfe thought.

Chapter 3

The Man in a Suit & Tie

Wolfe and Craik were tightened to the pavement, repeating their numbers in their heads. They had both been given the same number this morning, Z13. They were standing in the courtyard, the earliest rays of light beaming down over them, flickering through the windows.

"We'll be some of the last people to be named…" Craik said, a noticeable tremor in his voice. He was starting to shake and perspire, sweat beading down the nape of his neck and staining his shirt black. "The livestock and agriculture jobs are gone, the cooking, the tech, and the mechanic work too."

"Section Z1…" a speaker in front of them said, cutting off Craik's whispers and leaving him twitching, his lips pressed together, his eyes pinched shut.

"…will be sent and trained as house and yard staff for the Burstall family," she finished loudly and clearly, enunciating her words so that they could hear adequately through the microphone.

"Section Z2 has been selected for training in the Matterson City Housing District."

The air buzzed with heat. Wolfe felt his skin sliding from his face, and he was confident he would collapse into a puddle of skin, bones, and muscles. His clothes were soaked with sweat; the smell of people, bodies, and perspiration swam between them. Wolfe's eyes stung as droplets fell across his forehead. They had been standing in the sun since sunrise, and from where the sun rested in the sky, Wolfe guessed it was around noon.

"Z4 will be sent overseas for training to work at the Atom Energy Corporation."

Wolfe heard the woman speak but paid her little attention. The surrounding plaza was practically empty now, maybe nine hundred people spread out into their own tiny groups. Talking was strictly forbidden during the selection.

"Z7 will be sent to the southwestern transfer station and will await further instruction within the next two weeks."

Their group, the Z13s, totalled about two hundred people. The next group, the largest group of nearly five hundred men and women, were sent to a factory making yarn, string, and clothes for the Dundurn family company.

"The Z10 section has been purchased by the Tobin family for domestic service at their farms." Wolfe and Craik let out sighs of relief. Of everything he'd imagined could happen at the Tobin family, none of it would happen. He and Craik would continue living their lives as they were now. The PDT dispensers hummed in the street behind them.

"The Z12s will be trained to serve the Atoon family in their penthouse for the month."

The Atoon family owned a sizable chunk of all electricity generated in the country. They had bought out electric vehicle companies, oil and gas empires, and swathes of wind turbines and dams decades ago, forcefully overtaking the market. Now, you'd be lucky to find an energy company that wasn't connected to them in one way or another.

"Lastly, Z13!" The woman called out with an enthusiastic grin. On an average day, stragglers would mill around between shifts. The emptiness made it look freakishly destitute.

"You will be trained to serve the Bredenbury family. They look forward to having you with them as soon as possible." She stood up with her last words, the mic cutting off as the anthem blasted through the speakers.

Wolfe looked over at Craik, whose eyes now gazed ahead unseeing. He shut his eyes, and they started darting frantically behind his eyelids. His hands twitched, his lips muttered, flushed hot against the rest of his skin. The sound of boots stirred behind them, and they walked in silence, eyes straight ahead.

As they walked, the screens the length of condo buildings flickered through a collection of technicolour ads: offering lotteries and free condoms, vivid, glitter-dusted sex scenes painted in neon shades and the cheapest PDT on the market, overdose warnings and cheap alcohol. The ads flashed videos of naked, sex wild men and therapy for the genuinely lost among them at the meager fee of five credits per minute. When Wolfe closed his eyes, he could still see the flashing white, yellow, and purple neon lights through his eyelids.

Workers leaned against their factory windows to watch the doomed workers pass by. Wolfe could feel their eyes on them, hear their whispered prayers on the wind, blessing the doomed souls being led through the black gate at the back of the ghetto.

An army of BESNA officers led the freshly purchased workers past relics of scanners, hissing and shrieking as the outdated models fought to scan the horde of bodies brushing past waist-high quackgrass, thriving under the midday shade of the apartment buildings beside them. Wolfe dropped his hand and felt the seed heads tickle his palm as they attacked his waist.

They marched them out through the suburban sprawl that crawled along the city's edge in the blinding sunlight. The older, weathered apartment complexes shrunk into rows of identical houses, their colours dull and muted like unripe peaches, rotten strawberries, and boiled ashes. They were all the same, each a carbon copy of the next and the one before it. Slivers of manicured lawns with the same dull, unmarked grass ran beside wide, overbearing streets. People dressed in muted clothing to match their muted homes peered out of gardens and window sills to watch the funeral procession.

The streets were silent like before a storm. As Wolfe and the workers walked, windows closed, curtains drew shut, and parents shuffled their children inside, leaving nothing but an empty city and a vast, gaping silence. A long, deathly hush fell over the workers as they walked, two hundred of them with eyes upturned to the brilliant, azure sky.

As they came over the crest of a hill, Wolfe glanced down at the winding, boiling cement, and his eyes danced as he fought to take it all in. Sunlight hit the billions of dark green windows along the millions of buildings and shattered, twinkling and hitting the ground like a trillion diamonds. The air seemed to hum, vibrating like a lifetime of birds beating their wings in unison against the sky. Slices of clouds in the sky above the city were polluted coppery with flashing ads: cheap medical insurance and the freshest tablets on the market. Credit card companies, car finance corporations, sleazy buffets and cheap plane tickets, travel companies, and notary publics. Smiling faces and flashy cars shone in mirages over the city like giant beasts reaching down from the heavens.

Sprawling green parks and man-made rivers lay for kilometres before them. They pushed past farmers markets, ice cream parlours, gift shops and patio bars, outdoor swimming pools, and artisan bakeries. Speakers stood like trees at every corner, broadcasting news and playing songs while recanting ads and political campaign promises.

"We're in it for you!" a man cried, trying to weasel his way onto ballots and into wallets.

As they pushed down the hill, the heart of the glimmering city sank beneath the horizon. Train tracks hummed above them, and the scents of ethnic restaurants pooled their sounds and tastes into the street: tamarind, anise, cardamom, turmeric. A spice market was sitting across the street: men heaved giant bags of tiny, tumbling black seeds onto heaving tables while a woman haggled with a vendor for a handful of plump, tanned roots glistening in the sun. A boy carried a white bag of spices that plumed as he walked, bouncing and diving like the tail feathers of a cardinal diving into snow.

Humming electric cars coasted past them in the street. Bikes whizzed past them while clanging their bells. Buses languished under the sun as they slipped from building to building in an effortless purr. Wolfe looked up, and the condos sprouted so high that they lost themselves to technicolour clouds at dizzying heights. A woman beckoned tourists towards history tours and ghost walks, while men with heaving pockets tried to peddle their cheap electronic pieces to tourists. They turned to their right and walked towards a sleek silver building built maybe twenty feet in the air. Men and women crowded up the stairs in droves, chattering on phones, lost in their tablets with beady eyes.

Wolfe watched as they passed a group of children shrieking on a playground. A man was selling frozen treats from a silver cart to their right. They twinkled translucent in the light, melting and glistening in every shade and colour. Wolfe watched a father tap his wrist against the cart, and a group of kids swarmed around it, leaving with hands laden with sugar and ice.

Wolfe watched as the man saw the approaching horde and swivelled the children away, glaring at the workers and the suited BESNA officers. Wolfe barely noticed; he was staring at the ice cream cart that listed each treat for fifteen credits.

"Fucking bluies! Mutts!" the man yelled at them, pointing at their 'mutated' blue eyes.

"You should be fucking ashamed," one woman said, hacking up a glob of spit and shooting it at Wolfe's feet as he passed. "People like you shouldn't see the world that we've built!" she screamed, the veins in her neck straining. Wolfe looked forward again, eyes trained on the loose pebbles in front of them.

"These people are the reason your father isn't with us. They're TERRORISTS!" another woman screamed, spitting the last word at a worker's face. Her young son stood beside her with his mouth hanging open and his mini tablet dangling from the tips of his fingers. He was dressed in soft yellow and brown pieces of cotton, his hand-sewn trousers were strung from hemp, and his hat, printed with a company logo Wolfe had never seen, was askew.

Wolfe remembered the world before this. A world filled with overcrowded cities and disease-filled produce, smog that clogged the sky, and plastic that plugged the rivers. Motorways roared eleven lanes wide, chemicals leached from factories into rivers and oceans, and men and women squished in shoebox apartments died from various ailments and cancers. He remembered the world watching the richest and the strongest build dynasties that eclipsed the wealthiest monarchies of history, as the poorest toiled like rats on treadmills, all in a desperate attempt to keep their heads above the rising oceans. Illness swept the globe killing indiscriminately, while war wiped country after country off the face of the earth. The famines killed babies and the elderly without a batted lash. Humanity was sinking. The world needed a scapegoat. The world needed more money, more resources, cheap labour, or fewer people.

They walked towards the silver building as a train whizzed over them. It felt like Wolfe's organs were sucked out of his body. The carriage moved so fast it pulled a bubble of air behind it across the country. Wolfe watched its smooth underside, black and glossy, crackle with energy along the uncut edge of the track. He marvelled at them when he was a boy, wondering how they could get someone from Vancouver to Miami in two hours.

Wolfe could see the men and women above them, hopping aboard the hovering train carriage. The speakers promised a seven-minute ride to Boulevard. And then it was gone, leaving a vacuum where it had been that popped Wolfe's ears.

Wolfe marvelled upwards as they were led up the etched metal and polished stone steps. An arched wooden roof curled and weaved above them like a piece of silk fluttering to the ground had suddenly solidified. It was perched on the wooden frame of the building, protecting them from the harsh sun.

Wolfe was speechless. He looked around at the glossy station, shiny with copper and bamboo. Another train was resting above the station floor, and again it was gone. The ceiling was flushed with glass and glistering lights, speakers lined the oak and bamboo walls, and at least ten screens were set into the smoothed stone and black metal floors. The screens flashed never-ending videos of brown-eyed women dressed in vibrant red and orange hues, the hair around their faces shone like halos, stunning the world with their beauty at some Parisian fashion event in a world removed. The world slipped into a sophisticated, intellectual ardour while Wolfe was gone.

As the workers piled up the steps, a few disembarking passengers glared at them. But Wolfe noticed most people didn't even see them. Going on about their days running, playing, laughing, eating, and loving. He felt almost invisible, watching eyes glide through him as they walked, their eyes not even seeing him.

They had stripped the world around him of colour. Famous brands had gone monochrome or sunk into browns, grays, peaches, and whites. Celebrities held up their earth-tone makeup palettes and flashed their red carpet dresses dripping with glimmering golds, browns, and saturated velvets. The colour leapt through the screens, leaving him spinning with ecstasy.

Wolfe felt his ownership close around his neck like a choker. This was all theirs. *We dug their metals, chopped their wood, sewed their clothes, and grew their food. We built those towers, built that train, and don't even get to savour it. We made this. Why don't we get to stake our claim?* Wolfe felt a sinister feeling bubbling below the surface of this new world: brown equalled divinity, blue equalled calamity. It was hinted at, sewn into the fabric of this strange new world.

They pushed their rhetoric in children's books about the brown-eyed bunny and the blue-eyed fox. Popular songs lamented about the heartless, love stealing, blue-eyed demons of their youth, while the villains in every movie had crystal blue eyes and brewed sinister plans. While every girl dreamed of her brown-eyed adonis in history class, kids watched blue-eyed drug abusers beaten down by valiant brown-eyed officers. While the brown-eyed prime minister addressed the horrors of blue-eyed mercenaries and terrorists in third-world countries, BESNA killed blue-eyed kids in Wolfe's first-world country.

Another train exploded out of the station, shattering over the horizon in a wink. Wolfe followed the train with his eye until it was nothing but a glimmer of light on the horizon. When he looked back, another train had taken its place.

This one was different. The usually large, crystal windows were completely black. The doors did not open, nor did anyone step towards the train to enter. A circlet of braided stalks of golden wheat, wrapped around a thinly scribbled signature, was etched into every window. The doors jettisoned open, and a man stepped out with a broad smile on his face to match his shoulders.

He was tall, probably near six-three, dressed in a trimmed brown suit. His hair was cut short, brown hills styled into rolls of fluff along the rim of his head. The man's eyes lashed Wolfe, and they were the darkest brown Wolfe had ever seen, nearly black in their severity, like roasted coffee beans and dark chocolate. His pointed chin was dusted with stubble, and it hovered above them, assaulting them with accusations.

He was wearing a white shirt and a green tie, brilliant like forest floors and evergreen trees or a wall of thick ivy. He held himself tall, his hands in front of him, a slight smile poking across his face. The man was the most attractive person Wolfe had ever seen in his entire life.

Wolfe's gaze rolled down. His body squeezed against the suit, muscles rippling beneath the fabric. His shoes were a dark brown, made from either hemp or algae. Wolfe couldn't help but feel something, a familiar stirring in his stomach that made his toes curl and his eyes wander where they shouldn't have.

"You will call me Mr. Kelvington," he said, stepping out of the train car. His hopeful eyes surveyed the group. He spoke in a no-nonsense tone that commanded obedience and respect, yet Wolfe sensed an air of lightness, a kindness on his breath.

"I am the Administrative Overseer for the Bredenbury family, and I will be training you to care for the house, the grounds, and the crops of the Bredenbury family." He walked gently between the rows of men and women, pacing back and forth between them. Wolfe kept his eyes trained on Mr. Kelvington's shoes.

"I am not here to be friends, but to ensure the family gets the service they paid for," he said, walking back to his spot in front of them. "Some of you may live, and some may die, but I hope we can reach a mutual understanding of one another." Wolfe listened intently, clinging to every word that floated from Mr. Kelvington's lips to his ears. He spoke with a power that commanded everyone to stop and be silent in his presence, and Wolfe felt the trembling in his stomach again.

He stooped down in front of a man standing before Wolfe.

"Am I clear?" he asked in a cruel-sounding tone. He took the silence from the man to be a yes. "Very good. I see you have experience in subservience. That will guide you well in the coming months and years." He smiled, patting the man on the shoulder as he walked over to the door he had come from.

"Alright, group Z13," he said, pulling out his tablet and scrolling for a few moments before continuing. "It says here most of you worked in the textile industry. A few mechanics and a few farmers." He looked up at them and chose his words carefully.

"That is…not ideal…but we will make it work," he said, stepping aside to allow the workers to scan their wrists as they entered the train. Once they were all aboard, the train hummed. Then, when Mr. Kelvington spoke again, Wolfe noticed they were moving. He felt like he weighed less, like the train's movement seemed to push him up and off his seat, hovering.

"Now," Mr. Kelvington began. His voice seemed to carry through the cabin easier, his words and enunciation sharper and more precise. "If I find any of you don't put their blood, sweat, and tears into their work here, I will make sure you live to regret it." He scanned the room; his tone dropped; no one dared to meet his eyes.

Wolfe noticed the tablet never left the man's hand. He would glance down at it frequently before swiping or clicking on its glowing white surface. Its edges were seamless. It glowed so softly it seemed to hover in a crown of light.

"We divided the family's summer home into four main distinctions. The yards, the gardens, the fields, and the house. We have well over five hundred people on duty day in and day out. We are most in need of house workers, so I hope you all have experience in domestic work."

"I will say now, the family will take nothing less than perfection in every sense: in your cleanliness, in your work ethic, in your efficiency. It's a deep shame to be sold by the Bredenbury family, so for many of you, this will be your last home." He smiled again, his eyes briefly flickering against the ceiling.

The workers looked up to him, clinging to every word. Everyone except for Craik. He sat silent. His eyes stagnant, hands in his lap, face frozen, staring at the floor. Wolfe felt a twinge of guilt, he had considered praying for this, and now they had been whisked onto a train heading toward what might be hell.

Mr. Kelvington continued, "any questions?"

"Mr. Kelvington, how're da jabs gonna be pfiled wen we get der?" a tall, lanky woman asked through a barely understandable accent and few teeth.

"Well, it's based on the skills listed in your files, the positions that need to be filled, and your physical status. Next?"

"What if I get all confused?" another younger, well-rounded woman asked. Lines of tattoos ran up and down both arms, and her teeth stuck out of her mouth like a jack-o-lantern.

"We highly discourage it, so please pay attention. But, these things happen, and we have procedures in place. We'll cover that later once we've gotten settled in." He checked his watch as he stood up, brushed himself down, and readjusted his tie.

"Questions?" Mr. Kelvington asked again as Wolfe felt the weightlessness sink away, settling him further down into his chair.

"Is the family as mean as the rumours say?"A young man spoke up, his eyes trained on the floor to avoid the man's gaze.

"Whispers mean nothing to the family. Act respectfully, and they will treat you accordingly," Mr. Kelvington said sharply, turning himself to face the door. Wolfe felt himself sag like he'd gained twenty pounds. Mr. Kelvington touched the tip of his tablet against the wall, and the doors swung open.

Heat and pressure descended on them like the dark wings of bats, and with it, chords of pounding anxiety rushed in Wolfe's ears. Somewhere in the heavy, pounding heat, his new life awaited. Whether it be escape or death, it would be out there.

Chapter 4

A New Gilded Age

As they stepped off the train, their clothes sagged from the boiling moisture in the air. Thick tendrils of moss were hung between the trees, and bugs screeched and howled towards the microscopic sneeze of a town behind them. Grain elevators peaked their dark, soulless faces over the kilometres of wagging crops, while church steeples and spiked rooftops poked above the horizon as they disembarked.

The train station was older and heavier than the one they had just left; there were no screens, no ads, no scanners. The building was brown, held by heavy, mud-stained pillars, and built like a box. When the last of the workers stepped off the train, it shot away, kicking up plumes of dust in its wake. Wolfe turned, and he saw what the train had blocked.

A towering manor stood down a long stretch of winding gravel in the heart of a wooded enclave. Its two stories were held up with black granite pillars, and its aged roof was bristling with flapping black shingles while a sturdy oak and walnut porch hugged the sides of the manor. Giant black gargoyles carved from obsidian swung around the edges of the roof, watching her bustling frame. She was alive with shifting bodies; people glowed in the brightly lit windows and raced around her edges. The path led up the incline towards the house, winding between willows as a mist of gravel dust settled.

The house looked archaic, somehow ancient yet modern. The windows glittered, shining with crisp white light while paint flaked around the edges of the window sills. The heavy black doors looked venerable, gleaming with fresh paint. The lawn sagged and rippled, but it was cut in a perfect diamond shape pattern around the stone walkways and water fountains bristling with every shape and size of bird. The manor shrieked of elegance, silent solemnity, style, and grace from an age long gone.

Mr. Kelvington stood at the top of the steps, his eyes trained on the gathering of men and women below him. Wolfe fell to the front of the group, face to face with Mr. Kelvington, trying not to wither under the gaze of his dark brown eyes.

"Make your way down the steps slowly, single file, so I can tally you up. Dr. Wolseley, the Medical Overseer, will issue your standard immunizations and antibiotics. You'll go to him in the case of an accident," Mr. Kelvington said.

They stepped down onto the sun-warmed gravel below them, one after the other as Mr. Kelvington checked off numbers on his tablet. The highway behind them was cracked with age, split along its white lines, and chunks of pavement were heaved into the vibrantly green ditches. No cars ran its length, no bikes tittered along its edges, and no one walked its ditches. Along the line of trees, an old-fashioned train track was nestled into the dirt heading towards town.

Wolfe stepped up to the lanky metal desk where Dr. Wolseley sat. His eyes were the softest brown he'd seen, like the churned earth in the spring or lightly toasted sugar. They were light, warm, and flickering dangerously. The doctor looked up at him, gave him the slightest smile while meeting his eyes, then gestured towards the end of the table. He was a titan, bulging over his chair as he worked. A beard grew across his chin, and a halo of dark black hair hung in coils around his head.

Wolfe smelled something like sulphur. A coolness ran down his arm, and he felt a pinprick high on his shoulder. The doctor passed him a cup of pills and whisked him forward. The line behind them grew as Wolfe stepped off the path to swallow the pills.

Huh. Wolfe thought. *Where are the officers? The gates, the guns, the scanners?* The grounds were unblemished. Then fireworks exploded. *Maybe this was it.* He let his eyes wander into the rippling underbrush. Roots curled and wove in and along the ground, thick with dirty brown leaves, dipping behind the drooping branches. *Maybe if I just hide…*he thought, slinking closer to the whispering willow trees.

Wolfe stepped farther near the edge of the bushes as the gravel past Dr. Wolseley filled with more immunized workers. Mr. Kelvington sighed in relief, scratching off a final number on his tablet, tucking it into his pocket and hopping down the steps two at a time.

Wolfe inched closer to the shrubs.

He turned around slowly, touching up the branches of the nearest willow, its soft and scented blooms filling the air around him, wilting in his fingers.

Wolfe tossed the pills into his mouth, swirling them across his tongue. Then, when both men turned their faces, he spit them against the dirt and watched them drool off his tongue. Their bitter tang choked him as he let them shrivel against the tree's roots, swallowing the water.

Fuck 'em, he thought.

Wolfe slid back into the crowd, wiping his lips with his shirt and losing himself to the group while surveying the land above the bobbing heads.

The grounds were a cosmic space of lush green grass, punctuated sporadically by towering trees pressed against the sky. The yard had curving stone walkways that drifted alongside the road. Flower gardens, fountains, tiny stone labyrinths, and hedges speckled the yard. A mahogany gazebo flickered in the heat in the centre of the yard, aligned with the front door.

"Let's continue. The family will be here in three days, so we have lots of time to learn the ropes," he said. Wolfe watched the doctor walk past, smiling, eyes churning with thoughts Wolfe couldn't read.

They walked in silence. "Please don't be afraid to ask questions," Mr. Kelvington said as their feet crunched across the gravel. The air was littered with pieces of fluff drifting in the wind; twisting leaves and twirling branches chased them in the hot breeze. Yet the air carried the stench of rot. Wolfe felt phantom fingers crawl up his arms, and he shivered in the heat.

Wolfe drew his attention to the towering oaks. Metal rings were dug into the bark, and large lumps seemed to bulge from underneath their torn skin. Straps of leather, rope, and pieces of chain hung from the trees, draped between them like connective tissues between pockets of pus. Wolfe felt his stomach churn. The uneven trees cast diseased-looking shadows across their faces as they walked.

"What are those?" a man asked, pointing his finger to the knobbly trees. Wolfe watched the colour drain from Mr. Kelvington's face as he looked up. He turned his head away, eyes fogged over, staring ahead. He let his eyes close, thoughts streamed behind his eyelids, and he muttered.

"Right." He turned his face to them, stopping in the middle of the gravel road, flicking on his tablet. "During your immunization, we placed microchips beneath your skin," he crooned. His eyes danced, sure to never meet anyone's eyes. The air shifted. Some stood silent, some gasped, and others just felt along their shoulders where the needle had entered, tracing the itching bump underneath their fingers.

"This will show the family your work ethic, when you take your bathroom breaks, how much time you spend at dinner and so on. We will constantly be watching your movements and actions." Wolfe finally met Mr. Kelvington's eyes, and they stared at each other before he continued.

"The family feels the scanners are a cluttered, ugly addition to their summer home, as well as the scanner codes deface and devalue their property." He sighed as if it were the most boring thing he'd ever said, like this was normal.

The smell came again, this time stronger. It burnt Wolfe's nose, threatening to overcome him. He burped up a mouthful of puke and swallowed it again. It threatened to burn out his throat, and he rubbed the dribble along his chin into his skin. Wolfe let his eyes drift to the tiny black boxes that dotted the edge of the property.

"Those—" Mr. Kelvington said, following Wolfe's eyes to the

boxes. He pulled at his tablet and slid his finger along its edge. Immediately, a crushing weight worked its way through his shoulder and into the back of his neck. It threatened to tear every molecule in his body apart until he was dust on the wind.

"—are to keep you on the property. The feeling can be slightly uncomfortable, a gentle pressure at best, but you will get used to it." When he met Wolfe's eyes again, Wolfe saw nothing but a frigid stare, devoid of life and black in its intensity.

"The chips target a particular area of the cerebrum, keeping you from stepping over the boundaries by forcing electronic pulses through your neurological system and into your brain. As your muscles freeze and your nerve endings burn, you'll be left in such an excruciating agony you'll wish for death. The tablets serve as controls, allowing us to forgo scanners." He sounded bored, like he was talking about cattle or government deficits.

"We will dole out punishments to workers who don't meet their daily quotas, miss their shifts, refuse to provide exemplary service, or take part in prohibited actions without mine, other overseers, or the family's consent. And although all punishments fit the aforementioned crimes, some may feel harsher than necessary. Yet you must understand that the family tries hard to instill a sense of comradeship, togetherness, and equality among their workers." His eyes darted up, eyeing the tallest boughs of the towering trees.

Lost between branches, high in foliage, swinging between the spindles of towering boughs, bits and pieces of rotting, decomposing bodies hung. Toes and fingers, teeth and eyes. Entire bodies with charred ankles, dripping wrists, and fat swollen tongues. The source of the fetid, rotting stench wafted down towards them.

Wolfe's hands fell to his face, his stomach churned, the world spun, and he found himself on the ground with acidic bile trickling from the corners of his mouth in a steady white dribble. He heard a woman sobbing, an older man was cursing, and another man was hacking up puke like Wolfe as blood pounded in his ears. Wolfe looked up with stinging, watery eyes at Mr. Kelvington and saw impatience stirring across his face, eyes rolling, fingers moving towards the tablet.

Wolfe felt an electric roaring in his neck that burnt his organs. Knives dug across his skin in strips, beetles dug holes in his neck, and rodents tickled the inside of his lungs. The air lashed him, and the gravel bit him.

"This is what insubordination will get you. Stand up," he snapped, rolling Wolfe over with the point of his shoe. He watched him with a cursory glance, disinterest flung across his shoulders, humour building at the corner of his lips.

"Please," Wolfe begged.

"Get up," he barked, threatening to turn the pain up even higher on the tablet. Wolfe gasped through the pain. His extremities were freezing, boiling, burning, then gone.

By the time Wolfe struggled to his feet, the pain was almost unbearable. Through a burning haze, static swung from the corner of his vision; light filled his head, and his breathing slowed. Then the pain boiled down to a simmer, an irritation pulling at his scalp. Wolfe fell again.

"I will have to write you up for this, you know. Failure to obey orders is a serious crime." He laughed, staring down at him. Wolfe felt tears sticking to the corner of his eyes. He watched Mr. Kelvington's face shift into shadow. He could see it now, the tyranny in his eyes, the callous disregard for the power he held at his fingertips.

"You look no one in the eyes; that would be rule number one," he snarled, gleaming his onyx eyes against Wolfe's. He held the silver tablet in his fingers, letting it dangle lazily, aloofly from his wrist. *No*, Wolfe thought, *he is well aware of the power he holds*. Wolfe hated him. He was a monster, dangling his victory above Wolfe's head.

"You're going to spend the rest of your life here. You will die here," he whispered, leaning closer to watch the tears paint the gravel brown, a sad, sarcastic little pout playing across his lips. Wolfe kept his eyes down, feeling the stones pressing ridges into the bottoms of his feet. *How stupid can you be?* Wolfe thought. *This is what a monster looks like.*

"Now. I'll show you the grounds, the house, and the fields. Follow me please," he said, walking up the path towards the house.

The workers swelled around Wolfe as he fell back down to his knees. Wolfe looked up as his tears trickled over his cheeks, leaving trails across his gravel-dusted face. He saw Craik, hidden by the sun, as an aura eclipsed him. He held his hand out and grabbed Wolfe, pulling him to his feet.

"We're in hell, aren't we?" Craik asked.

"I think so."

Wolfe looked up the road and saw the man brandishing his hands out, his mouth moving in circles with a wide smile. The way the sun caught his hair and lit his skin made Mr. Kelvington look like an angel. But Wolfe was in hell, and he was looking at the devil.

Wolfe glanced around as they rejoined the congregation at the base of the steps. The grounds were teeming with soulless, pale-eyed workers teetering in circles. Two women watched the ground as they walked, pushing a cart of cleaning supplies. Men crawled down rows of plush, bloated dirt, picking weeds with their arms wrapped in scars. A man walked by carrying a bundle of wood in his arms, with one eye shining white like the first snow in January. Two men walked by, dragging a wheelbarrow of manure; their legs were a network of wires and metal up to the knee.

Men ran past them dressed in ornate brown and green suits, framed with golden trim. They worked in groups, unrolling gilded rugs painted with scenes from the Iliad and the Fall of Icarus. They trimmed topiaries into preening beasts, sculptures that could have leapt into life; teeming masses were born again from the clusters of leaves and branches.

A shot broke the air, and Wolfe jumped. The smoke still hung in the air, and a bird had stopped its flight. It hovered in the air, invisible against the sky until the bluebird fell, leaking into the grass before being swept away into a black bag.

A few handfuls of men patrolled the grounds in groups of five. They were dressed in plain brown jeans and boots. Their dress shirts, all shades of gray, were pulled up around their elbows, milling around each other while they spoke. They held no contempt or hatred in their eyes, but when they looked at the workers, their eyes cast through them, and the silver tablets never left their hands.

"—and I told you to let me know if anything fucking changed," Kelvington whispered furiously. The man next to him was dressed like the other men, though he had a shiny silver badge that said GUARD on it pinned above his heart. The guard seemed to shrink next to Mr. Kelvington's rage, yet he held his ground.

"I informed you of their change of plans as soon as they made it aware to me. You may, if you wish, take it up with our employer?" he replied as Mr. Kelvington steadied himself, taking deep breaths in an attempt to hide his irritation.

"Fine. I don't know how I'm supposed to do it on such short notice, but if everything goes wrong, it's in your hands."

"Scott, I found out five minutes ago…" an air of disbelief clung to his words like flies to flesh. Scott turned around; his face was redder, his eyes rolled, but his lips and cheeks were flat like he'd just had the wind knocked out of him.

"Due to an…unprecedented—" he shot a look over his shoulder at the man, "—change. I will have to teach you all the ground rules tonight."

He lifted his hand and pointed to a series of cabins refurbished out of shipping containers, pushed into the trees at the edge of the lot nearest to the entrance they'd just come from. "I live in the green one on the far right. If you forget anything, I will allow you to visit me there for the next few days."

"What is that?" a young woman asked with tiny strands of wispy black hair dusted across her fat, egg-shaped head. Her finger pointed to a hut, backed firmly against the trees near the back edge of the grounds.

"Oh, that's the guardhouse. There are maybe fifteen guards on patrol at any given time. There is rarely any use for them, so they watch from there," he said, leading them around the edge of the house.

The tour began with a full inspection of the grounds and the garden. They moved clockwise around the house, down the gravel path that surrounded the front of the manor, and onto the cobblestone pathway.

"This is the main garden," he said. "We grow almost every plant known to man here," he added, turning around to throw his arms out, beaming with pride.

The garden was immense. About the size of an entire city block filled with the ripest, plumpest vegetables and fruits churning in black soil Wolfe had ever seen. The corn was nine feet tall and ran the length of the garden. Tomato plants as round as the guardhouse bristled against each other, jostling with fruit. A wall of beans taller than Wolfe grew broad beans as thick as his wrist.

"Mrs. Bredenbury likes the weeds to be pulled diagonally so you would grab a weed like this, here, by the base—" He crouched down on the neat cobblestone paths that weaved in and among the rows of perfect vegetables, grabbed a weed by its base and pulled it straight up, making sure the roots came with the plant.

"See! That simple," he said, standing and dusting his hands against each other, never letting them touch his side again.

They followed Mr. Kelvington through the rows of plants, past glass fountains shaped like elephants and ostriches, trickling with crystal clear water. Then past little benches with lions and pegasuses worked into the framework, lining each side of the garden. They walked underneath ornamental berry and apple trees heavy with fruit as workers gently plucked the fallen fruit from the paths and washed the stones with a bubbly solution that stank of chemicals and acid.

"The family prefers to stick to an all-natural eating regime, so all food is fresh, made on site." He smiled, glancing over his shoulder.

They passed through the gardens and into the greenhouse. The heat hung over them like the looming brow of a dictator. In here, watermelons the size of barrels lumbered in the humidity, coconut and banana trees lusted over them, and avocados the size of grapefruits hovered in the air. He saw a teeming grassland moving like golden waves through the frosted glass, with green tractors sailing through the blonde sea.

"The family owns over a hundred and fifteen thousand square kilometres of farmland and contributes over twenty three percent of all global food production. This is what they do best," Mr. Kelvington said, beaming. *How many people do they own?* Wolfe thought to himself, horror falling over him as he understood the scale. He was a pawn of hundreds of thousands, maybe millions. He was nothing, as inconsequential as a flurry of snow, as dandruff, as wind.

On either side of the greenhouse sat huge Quonsets filled with metal, tractors, rusting machinery, and crates of parts. Sparks flew, machinery whirred, and the banging of metal on metal filled the air. Just as Kelvington led them to leave, he turned towards the building and smiled as a man walked towards them.

"This is Mr. Watson, the Mechanical Overseer."

Wolfe held back a scoff. He was a short, beetle-like man with eyes that hid behind rolls of fat. He smiled at the group of workers in front of him and spoke in a tiny squeaky voice that would fit more of a field mouse than a man. He had more body than leg, and he limped heavily, waddling back and forth as he moved.

"Only about…two hundred I see. Well done, Mr. Kelvington, you're well down from last month after May Day, and that was on less than four hours notice." He wiped his greasy, blackened hands with a dirtied cloth and glanced around.

"Thank you, Mr. Watson."

"Mmm. Well." He seemed very bored to be here and wobbled himself back into the metal buildings he came from. He slipped past the walls hanging with tools, plastic sheeting, spare furniture, and paint cans.

Mr. Kelvington guided the group back towards the towering house in the centre of the yard. "Remember to always enter the house through the back door, even if the family isn't home. Always." The workers nodded their acceptance. They stepped up the golden brown steps onto the porch, and he guided them through a heavy mahogany door into the most luxurious house Wolfe had ever seen.

"Don't touch anything!" Mr. Kelvington called in after them, and Wolfe snatched his hands closer to his sides.

The inside of the manor was nothing like its rustic exterior. Solar-powered electric fireplaces lit every room, light bars flicked on or off via voice commands along the walls as Mr. Kelvington spoke, and 3D printing stations and wireless charging ports hanging with tablets replaced the dumbwaiter system along the edge of the stairs.

The wooden hallways led to marble rooms heated from the bottom up. Vintage rugs spun from cotton adorned the oak floors shining like tempered chocolate. The red and brown sofas were like pillows of mousse to sink into. The walls were decorated with every size of screen and bookshelf. Books and busts sat on wide side tables, heaving under the weight of glass art pieces and expensive bottles of alcohol. *How stupid.* Wolfe thought. Who could justify wasting the space in a world where every book could lie at your fingertips through your tablet? They were bound in genuine leather that still reeked of a cow. Paintings Wolfe had seen before, even faintly in memory, stared at him from the walls; A peasant woman stood smiling in front of farm gates, a woman cloaked in brown with russet eyes sat and smirked at him, a girl dressed in brown frolicked in poppy fields with cold, dead eyes.

"Yes, that's a Clausen, a da Vinci, and a Monet. In that order. The da Vinci was rescued from the Parisians," Mr. Kelvington said.

Even before this new world came to fruition, it was never like this for him. Wolfe felt like he was standing in an ancient library, a mausoleum where demons hissed down his neck, pulling their eyes down his back in constant warning.

Workers rushed past them as the new workers gawked. Women carried white sheets like swan feathers up the stairs as soiled sheets descended. The worker's eyes followed them wherever they walked, either with fires of contempt, longing, or sadness. A hundred painted eyes, broken, twisted, and misshapen, watched them endlessly from the walls.

Mr. Kelvington stepped past them into the house.

"This is the main house where a fraction of you will do your work." He gestured to the hundred workers milling back and forth.

"Your job is simple but a precise one. You will be in charge of keeping the family living in their pristine surroundings. However, if workers were allowed to mill around the house, it would go against our strict moral policies. All work in the house is done on Sundays, between meals, or when the family is on an excursion. The family is not to see you in the house, not under any circumstances."

They moved to the base of the main staircase leading to the upper levels of the house.

"You're also never to touch anything in the house without gloves lest you dirty their belongings. Several of which are well over millions of credits," he bragged, seeming to get pleasure at flaunting his employer's wealth.

They ascended the charred, dusty brown staircase. Large enough that six of the workers could climb abreast. The glittering chandelier twinkled above them, older than Wolfe's great-great-grandfather by fifty years at least. It was powered by rooftop solar panels that charged the house, Mr. Kelvington had told them. The sun shone through a stained glass window that showed the resurrection of Jesus wrapped in brown cloth with chestnut eyes, a halo of white light, and tight ebony curls of hair running past his radiant face. It lined the entire back wall of the house behind the staircase.

They walked past an enormous grand piano with pristine black and white teeth, lavishly set dining rooms with expensive china and golden foot long candles, and past sealed wooden doors with brass doorknobs. They were led through guest bedrooms, past brown and red satin curtains hung with gold chains and delicately threaded scenes of biblical scenes.

"I'll show you examples of the rooms you will be cleaning."

They walked into a room at the end of the hallway with its large double doors flung open, exposing the rich, velvety heaven beyond it. A large king-sized bed was draped with thick, opulent plumes of crimson and burgundy blankets. The floor was covered in thick rugs that held Wolfe as he walked. The room smelled of citrus and delicate perfumes, plums and must, aged paper, and age kissed leather. An applewood desk with a shiny leather chair rested against the corner, and lounge chairs and sofas were placed against the opposite wall from the large screen farthest from them.

"You will dust, vacuum, sweep, wash the carpets, remake the beds, and do all the laundry, to name a few things. I will include the rest on the full weekly schedule posted in the workers' barracks."

Then he took them through the rest of the guest bedrooms that paled in comparison, then through the bathrooms and the supply closets.

"You will never enter a closed room, and you will never enter those rooms, regardless." He pointed towards the far end of the manor. "Both the study, the library, and the nursery are strictly off limits. We have our own people clean them, and it's not your concern."

They descended past the main floor again and down the stairs nestled behind the grand staircase. Rather than the smooth, wooden steps they had grown used to, a narrow, rickety metal staircase could only fit them in sequence as they descended into the basement, lowered into the bowels of the house.

Chopping boards and knives, vegetables and slabs of fresh meat larger than Wolfe's head, and dusty wines and cream-coloured sauces flew around the kitchen. Brown-eyed men shimmering with sweat carted crates of eggs, mutton racks, and spices bags into the back room. Spicy-smelling sauces and marinades twirled around the room, and fresh loaves of bread cooled on the counter while steaming soups and desserts went into the fridge to chill. They pulled the finest champagnes from the cellar in dozens, lining them in front of glasses on the counter.

"Drop them over there if that's alright," a snooty-faced man said, brandishing his eyes sharply over his glasses perched on his nose. He was far too young to be the chef, but here he was regardless. He stood with his hair stuffed into a black ball cap, his arms crossed over his starched coat, looking like a ruffled chicken.

"Our Kitchen Overseer is preparing the menu for the highlight of our year. The Midsummer Night's Festival," he said, beaming again. "The family will welcome the highest members of society inside these very walls for food, wine, and dancing. Still three weeks out, but lots to be done for the tasting."

"It would have helped to know they were coming tonight," the Kitchen Overseer muttered from across the kitchen in a surprisingly loud voice considering he barely moved his lips. He glanced a short, tart smile towards Kelvington and let it fall when he turned his back.

Further down the stairs, they came into the workers' common room. It was a vast circular room with a flat grungy ceiling caked black with cooking grease and dust. A snaking series of corridors branched off from the main room with MEDIC, LAUNDRY, BARRACKS, FUMIGATION, PANTRY, ADMINISTRATION, HOUSE, and GARDEN were written above each hallway. They spidered outwards, dizzying Wolfe in their complexity.

The concrete, painted walls dripped with gray moisture as acidic green pipes slithered above their heads. Red and yellow wires tracked along the sides of the hallways. Little black boxes were stuck above every door, constantly emitting the tiniest humming noises.

To their left was a small canteen, and to their left sat about twenty large planks and tables. To their right was a small gathering area of chairs, drinking water, and a clock on the wall above the stairs that said EXIT above them.

They mulled through the crowds around them, and Wolfe looked down at them eating their supper at the tables. He couldn't shake the idea he had seen some of these people, but their hunched backs and knobbled fingers betrayed their images in Wolfe's mind.

They followed closely behind Mr. Kelvington as they weaved around women carrying laundry and past dirt-caked men descending the stairs after a long day in the fields searching for food. The clock chimed to three p.m. exactly as he pushed into the hallway with the words BARRACKS wrapped across it in black letters.

"And these are the state of the art windows that simulate the sun, the moon, and the natural vitamins you would receive from such. The family thought it would boost morale despite the expense. Come along," he called after them. He pointed towards windows that shone sunlight, flickering beside them as they walked past door after open door.

They took a right, a left, then one more left, and Mr. Kelvington showed them an immensely long hallway that seemed to snake inward. Rooms lined the corridor in constant repetition. Each room was relatively small and housed six people in bunk beds, two on the right, two on the left, and two against the back in front of the windows.

"There is no need to look. There are no scanners," he said as a young man stealthily searched the edge of the door. "The chips automatically scan you when you pass through the doorway, either upstairs or in the barracks."

They walked through hallway after hallway, and Wolfe lost his way. The paint-chipped, bone-coloured walls shone blindingly against the fluorescent light. Wolfe felt a headache stirring behind his eyes from the overload of information and the glaring lights.

Mr. Kelvington paused in the circular common room, turning to face the workers, wiping his forehead with the back of his sleeve.

"Quite a workout, isn't it!" He smiled. The group was silent, and none of them had broken a sweat.

"Well. This concludes our tour of the barracks. Any questions?"

Wolfe felt his stomach-churning. What if there is no escape plan, and he had been hoping and praying for this fresh new hell? He hadn't seen, heard, tasted, or smelled any evidence that any form of escape was brewing.

"The rules are as follows." He led them on a tour of the laundry rooms and supply closets as he spoke. "Don't speak under any circumstance, never shake your head, never touch another worker under any circumstance, do not be seen by the family, wear gloves at all times, do not look anyone in the eyes." Wolfe tried to listen, but the other twenty-eight rules were lost in the melee of the common room.

"Right. Please follow me," he said, turning again and leading them through another series of corridors before they came to the start of a long hallway. At the end of the hallway sat a woman. She gently typed into her tablet, ankles crossed, at a tiny oak desk. She lifted a pair of petite brown glasses, unfolded them, and perched them delicately on her nose. She wore nude lipstick, and her nails were transparent and glossy; her brown eyes stirred like chocolate.

"All right," he murmured, coming up to stand beside the desk and flipping out his tablet. He scanned it for a few moments before letting it ghost down onto the table like dusting flour over a workbench.

"These are the new workers?" The woman beamed out at them.

"One hundred and ninety-two in total," he said nonchalantly, yet a tinge of pride came over him before he quelled himself into silence. The woman started clicking and tapping against her tablet, glancing over at the list as names flurried onto the glass screen beside them.

After about fifteen minutes, she looked up. "You can explain the work timetables to them while I finish up, Mr. Kelvington."

"So," he began, "there are seventeen different jobs here on the plantation. You have three shifts per day between four and five hours each." He directed them to look at the large screen to his right.

A black screen took up the entire wall to Wolfe's left, and Mr. Kelvington shot his hand in front of it. A giant project management board was clustered with people's names, tasks, asterisks, shift titles, and times bouncing and changing every few seconds.

"Every job here on the plantation has a corresponding buzz. A garden shift is three buzzes, whereas a laundry shift is nine," he said. "If you ever forget your next shift, you can look at this timetable here on the wall during your lunch or supper break." He beamed at them as if he had come up with the idea himself.

"Ready, Mrs. Briercrest?" he asked, looking over at her, typing away before she kissed the final key with her ring-wrapped finger.

"Yes, sir."

The buzzes started in their necks without warning. Like a moth was furrowing around inside their necks, crawling between the cracks of their vertebrae. It was such a strong vibration Wolfe's vision went blurry while Mr. Kelvington listed off the jobs and their according buzzes. Wolfe tried desperately to count the whizzing in his neck, and he knew he had counted six at least. Wolfe didn't know what he expected, but it wasn't laundry work.

Above Y.L. Bredenbury, Wolfe looked at the screen and saw his initials. W.L. Bredenbury. In horror, he realized that he didn't have his own last name. As more names rolled onto the board, the name Bredenbury spilled across the wall like a bloodstain.

"Ah, yes," Mr. Kelvington said, watching as the men and women stared agape as their names were wiped off the face of the earth. "As legal property of the Bredenbury family, you've adopted their last name until you're sold to another family, at which point you will take your new family's name." Wolfe was petrified. He was nothing more than a dog, a bitch that takes the name of whoever owns 'it.'

Wolfe saw that C.T. Bredenbury was listed under the mechanic shifts. At least Craik was safe. Empathy came over him in waves. He had seen the fear across his face; it was apparent he didn't want to be here. Wolfe searched the crowd for Craik, but he couldn't see anything through the swathes of bodies.

"And…that's everyone," he said, running his eyes over the list and looking at the woman at the desk to confirm. She nodded, and he smiled at her. "Thank you again, Mrs. Briercrest. If you have any questions about specific shifts, she can help you. Mrs. Briercrest is the House Overseer, and she will be keeping a close eye on the workers."

"Of course, sir, my pleasure as always."

"Now, if you look at the screen, you'll see that most workers' second shifts end in seventeen minutes. You can also see that the in-house cleaners and the laundry workers have just started their second shift ten minutes ago. But you'll also see that field workers start their first shift at four-thirty rather than nine like most," Mr. Kelvington said to the group.

"The algorithm is well written, and you'll never get both a field shift in the morning and a laundry shift at night. The algorithm ensures a full night's sleep and adequate food rations to ensure no one goes hungry."

He smiled at them and walked towards the workers as they merged like water around the bulk of a ship. They reached the main common room again. The clock on the wall read three-twenty-six as the sun continued its journey to the sky's apex.

"This is my wife and the other Administrative Overseer for the plantation. If you have questions, you ask one of us, yes?" The group ahead of Wolfe nodded. The wall of bodies ahead of him made it impossible to make out a face.

Wolfe gazed around the room as Mr. Kelvington and his wife led the group through the main dining area and stood idly as they walked past them to get their meal. The room was already packed. Workers lingered along the walls with trays, men and women spoke freely, and children snaked between their feet.

"After dinner, we will come and show everyone to their rooms. We believe you'll all have enough understanding of how life goes on here to get to your shifts in the morning, but your second or third shift still applies tonight," Mr. Kelvington said to the group as they spread themselves out through the maze of tables, chairs, and tired field and garden workers shovelling food.

"If you're confused, please check with us or consult the timetable," the woman said above the roar of scraping tables and cutlery.

"Maybe the rumours were wrong, and we're not going to die here," Craik said, materializing beside Wolfe and shooting him a grimace. He ran his fingers over his arm, massaging the bump beneath his skin.

"Maybe the rumours are true, and we're going to escape," Wolfe said.

Wolfe tried to catch a glimpse of the woman's face out of curiosity but only saw a flash of brown hair. She said something and pointed to a table across the room.

Then he heard her voice again, and this time it scratched an itch he didn't know he had. "Look where you're goi—" she said as Wolfe turned around and bumped into her. And in the silence between them, eyes greeting each other, Wolfe could only squeeze out a single word to greet his sister.

"Arcola?"

Chapter 5

Reunification

Arcola gasped, shutters running the length of her face as she trembled. She was frozen, shaking with either fear, surprise, or both at once. Her soft brown eyes, like tanned leather and freshly woven cloth, flickered. She smelled of sandalwood, freshly baked bread and sun-warmed rosehips. She smelled the same way she'd always smelled.

He let his eyes drift downwards, rooted firmly to the spot as the swarm of bodies parted around him. Her dress was knee-high, and the bottom half of her legs were wrapped in coffee-coloured leggings. She was wearing black leather heels strapped with gold up to her ankles. Not a hair was out of place. She was immaculate, a creature of perfection slowly tumbling out of grace.

"Don't forget..." Arcola muttered indistinctly and halfheartedly over her shoulder towards Kelvington. Her hands moved without thought, sliding over papers, stacking and reshuffling them in circles. Her eyes were unyielding. Wolfe studied her face. Every crease and line, every movement of age across her skin gliding over muscle and arched bone.

Then Wolfe turned to Mr. Kelvington, and the realization sunk in. *How could she?* He cried to himself. Mr. Kelvington studied the pressure between them, gauging it with an unwavering facial expression.

"Yes, I almost forgot. I need to take you for disciplinary action," he said, the same shadows as before eclipsing the light of his eyes.

"What?" Arcola said, dropping her gaze from Wolfe and peering up at her husband.

"Yes, well, he refused to follow orders this afternoon," he said.

"Scott…" Her voice dropped. "Scott, listen I—"

"Why are you acting so weird? Get back to work, and I'll take Mr. Wolfe." He spoke over her, reaching out to grab Wolfe by the wrist. Wolfe watched her drop her face to the floor, running her fingers over her hair in subservience. But when she looked up again, her face was rumbling, waves were breaking across her eyes, rippling beneath her skin.

"I'm always sorry to have to do this type of stuff, but—" Before he could continue dragging him down the hallway, Arcola had nudged past Kelvington and grabbed Wolfe's wrist in his place.

"Wolfe, could you please come with me? I have a few questions for you before you begin your shift this afternoon." She promptly turned on her heel, but Wolfe could see a glimmer in her eye. The same glow he had grown up with, the face of a warrior, ready to fight to the death.

She was the volcanoes, the mountains, the storms. She was everything Wolfe had dreamt of being when he was young. When she was a teenager, she would bottle herself up for days at a time, exploding in bouts of shrieking violence whenever she was crossed. But the older she got, the more she honed it into a passion, a cunning, a determination. She won the arguments, her battles, her wars. She was always the winner.

As Wolfe followed her, he felt a sharp strangle on his arm. Wolfe automatically froze. His heart stopped beating, and he felt his life flash before his eyes. *This is it.* Nevertheless, he was still walking. When he looked up behind him, he saw a man. Not Kelvington, not the devil, just a man. There was a blink of vulnerability, fear, concern, or all at once. Then it was gone, and he budged past him up to Arcola, rushing to her side and flicking nasty glares over her back at him.

"Who the fuck is that?" he asked. She ignored him. Down one hallway, then another, until the sounds of the clanging and calling of the common room were a distant hum. She pulled Wolfe into a storeroom, arms already wrapped around his back "What the fuck, Arcola!" He gaped. Again, she ignored him.

"I'm so happy you're okay. When everyone disappeared, and no one could find you…I'm just so happy you're okay." Her voice cracked.

"ARCOLA!"

Wolfe turned to him, smiling directly into his eyes. Wolfe devoured him with his eyes, gloating in his minor victory as Arcola clung around him. He reached up a hand to shake it, and Mr. Kelvington yanked it back instinctively.

"Hmm. I didn't want to shake your hand either, but that's no way to treat your brother-in-law," Wolfe said, mocking him. He watched Kelvington's face glaze over. For the second time, emotions swirled in his eyes undisturbed. "I. Eh. we…but…" He tried to say something, but Arcola cut him off.

"Why are you here? Where is Blaine? Dad?" she asked, pushing them apart and wiping her eyes.

What was there to say? Wolfe asked himself. He hadn't seen his sister in over five years, and this is how he has to break it to her? In a dingy old storeroom, creeping with dust and age, water dripping off leaky pipes. The afternoon light trickled in through the cracked window, leaking golden sunlight into swirling pools on the floor, stirring in the dust.

He tried not to meet her eyes and failed. The light had left her irises, and she tried to keep a strong face, trying not to let her smile crack, but Wolfe could see the tears brewing in her eyes.

"And mom?" she asked, staring out through the window; the light caught in the frames of her eyes and torched them.

"I don't know."

"We can talk again later. I just had to see if you're okay," Arcola said. She fixed her eyes on the foggy glass door, watching shadows weave past and dissipate. "Tonight, after your shift, come to our cabin on the south lawn."

Kelvington was absent. His eyes flicked back and forth between his wife and the strange man beside her. His brows were thick with distrust; his eyes were thin like a knife blade, cutting back and forth between them.

"But—" Wolfe had gone to say, but she was gone. She had stepped back towards the door, dusted herself, and tightened the buttons on her blouse. She straightened her jacket as she walked.

Wolfe watched Kelvington put his hand across her shoulder, and Wolfe watched his touch shift her. They whispered back and forth, eyes darting, angry growls and purrs looming across the room. He seemed to make himself taller, straightening his neck, lording his shadow over hers.

"Wolfe…" she called to him, grabbing him by the shoulders and thrusting him through the crack in the door, closing it behind him. He watched their shadows sink back into the room, leaving him alone in the hallway.

His heart was pounding, and his mind sank into a frenzied delirium. *Maybe this will be my way out. Maybe something can be done,* he cried to himself. The air was lighter; the walls were cleaner; the people moving past him looked happier as he walked. Life slowly fell into proportion.

The shadows came back; the grime showed at the corners of the walls; the darkness ran down his spine again. What about *Mr. Kelvington?* Wolfe still felt the rage in his soul, the hatred like electricity coursing through his veins like blood turned to ice. Workers stirred past him. The odd guard walked by, eyes lost in their tablets.

Well, it's better than nothing. Wolfe told himself as his neck buzzed.

———

Wolfe walked through damp green grass as the rain lifted, but it offered no relief from the day's sweltering heat, only adding to the wicked humidity that sagged across the lawn. Thick brown water beetles swam through the soggy air, fat mosquitoes hovered lazily, and tiny black flies swarmed around him like smoke as he walked.

The grounds were empty; the heavy lull of the simmering afternoon hung in the air. Somewhere, the soft cry of violin strings drifted across the lawn. The late sunlight was creeping over the trees, painting a rich apricot blur over the grass, leaving the last few raindrops to frantically hover between the honed blades.

The work was fine. Wolfe thought. He and another woman had spent a quiet afternoon cleaning the master bedrooms along the first floor. They made the beds up with fresh sheets, primping and priming them into perfection. They ironed and hung laundry, scrubbed every surface with cleaner, and polished every inch of wood until it shimmered.

Then they did the next one. And the next one. And the one after that. A mechanic followed them, checking lights and rewiring tablets and screens. The woman had stayed silent except to whisper to him as they walked from the basement to the first room.

"Watch your back for him," she had said, flicking her head towards Mr. Wolseley as he carried two briefcases back towards his cabin beside the Kelvington's.

Wolfe tried to whisper back, attempting to compel her into speech, but she had fallen mute. She pretended his words meant nothing, and they fell on deaf ears. He wanted to ask her why, but she refused to listen, trembling as she passed the guts of a piano, the neck of a gown hanging in the closet, the eye of a cherub hanging above their heads along the walls.

Wolfe sauntered between the tall grass along the yard's edge, looking at the cabins in the bushes. There were seven in total, lined halfway around the grounds, backed into the trees. They were nearly invisible from the manor, lost in the network of roots and moss.

He stood in front of the cabin, reading the small gray slate beside the door. *Mr. and Mrs. Kelvington.* A plume of dust caught in his throat. He stepped up towards the door and hesitated for a moment, daring himself to knock. Then he heard the unmistakable sound of tires crunching on gravel. Then he was tugging on the door, pounding against its crisp white wood until it was flung open.

Kelvington was standing in the door in a state of undress: His shirt was half unbuttoned, leaving his tanned chest exposed, revealing golden chest hair. His tie was half undone, hanging around his neck like a noose; his sleeves were rolled up, exposing the lines of veins across his arms. Then he was gone, scrambling across the kitchen for his tablet.

Trucks threw their headlights against the trees, flickering through the raw green leaves like dancing fireflies. Then, as they rounded the corner into the yard, a train arrived, sucking the oxygen out of the air. Wolfe looked forward again, and Kelvington had grabbed him by his shirt, yanking him onto their living room floor.

"What are you doing here?" he hissed, slamming the door shut behind him.

"She told me to come tonight!"

"Wolfe…" Arcola was wrapped in a bathrobe. Her hands were clasped to a wardrobe as tires rubbed on the dewy grass outside the trailer. The sound of voices and footsteps on dirt echoed through the open window, and she flung open the wardrobe and threw Wolfe in. She stared into his eyes for a second before the door snapped shut.

A second later, Wolfe heard a sharp rap on the door. When Kelvington answered it, a middle-aged man entered through the low-hanging entrance as Wolfe watched him through the slats on the front of the wardrobe.

It looked like a homeless man had stumbled into the cabin. His dirty, graying hair, coated with a thick layer of rancid grease, was tied up in a bun. His beard was patchy across his chin, and his clothes were almost rags. He smiled when he saw the couple and greeted them with a nod of approval, looking genuinely happy to see them.

Yet as he entered the home, the atmosphere died. Scott and Arcola dropped their voices, refusing to let any emotion slip that might betray them. The man looked around and spoke. His voice was nothing like his face. Cold, unloving, and calculated with each response.

"Are the cabins ready? Are the boilers fixed? The water systems are operational? The house is ready? The new acquisitions are briefed?" he asked rapidly.

"Yes."

"Yes, of course."

"Yes, sir."

Eventually, he nodded, walking around, picking things off shelves, reading papers, ruffling through their lives.

"We didn't think you'd be here until the morning," Arcola said. "Sir," she added.

"Yes, and I'm so sorry you found us in this state of undress," Kelvington said, pulling his shirt shut.

"Please don't worry. I'm not concerned." He laughed. His voice was thick like butter, soft and palpable, yet it cut like a cold knife.

Then the man spoke again, and the coolness was gone, replaced by a warm, silver glow hanging around his neck. Wolfe could see his eyes through the crack in the door; a genuine kindness turned in his pupils. "What did you think of the municipal elections? Did Alameda get in?" he asked them kindly, lifting a paper transcript off the kitchen table and silently reading it.

"Oh, I think so, sir. She's ready for the post, sir," Arcola spoke, holding her hands behind her and smiling. Beads of sweat hung on her forehead. Wolfe was acutely aware of his breathing. It sounded heavy in his ears, and the air around him grew hotter. Wolfe could count each individual vein in his neck.

He picked up a miniature figure of a cruise ship and read the name aloud, gently letting it rest on the shelf.

"SS Normadica…" Wolfe was sure every word and step he took or said had a motive.

"And how are you both doing? The newlyweds are enjoying their own home I'm sure?" He smiled, tilting his head ever so slightly.

"Yes, sir," they spoke in unison.

"And I assume your accommodations are treating you well?"

"Of course, sir. The personalized pillows were a special touch." Wolfe could practically hear Arcola swallow. He waited for him to jump to his feet, swivel around and rip open the cabinet, and the world would crumble around him. He could feel his heartbeat in his ankles.

"Is the food satisfactory?"

"Oh yes, sir," Arcola said again.

The man sat in a lounge chair near the door, his back leaning against the wardrobe behind him. Wolfe could smell him; the air became an ocean of wildflowers and salt. Wolfe held his hands against his face to silence himself, to stop the trembling in his hands.

"You're quiet, Kelvington, is something wrong?" His voice was filled with passion, like Scott's well-being was his utmost concern.

"Just a little tired sir, we both planned to turn in early tonight."

"Of course, I'll be on my way," he said, smiling again.

He popped up, and the chair bounced against the wardrobe, gliding open a few inches and bathing Wolfe in light. Arcola smiled, stepping over towards Wolfe and sliding the chair against the wall, shutting the door again.

"But I must ask before I leave. How *are* you?" He smiled, putting a heavy emphasis on his words. "I'm well aware that you were in a camp for insurrectionists when I hired you, Arcola, but are you thrilled with this new world? New countries, new alliances, new governments, new businesses…How are you *really* doing?" He spoke fast and pointedly towards Arcola. She barely had a moment to cobble together a response before he pulled a soft manila folder from his back pocket, flicking it open and reading from it.

"Of course, sir—"

"Scott. You were born in Toronto. You had two siblings, you being the oldest. Your sister killed herself, and your youngest sister rebelled against her owner and was killed. Makes you wonder if the apple didn't fall too far from the tree."

Scott stood there with his mouth askew. His arms were pinched close to his chest, and he trembled. His eyes darted around the room, looking for an escape.

"Well?"

"This is the right option going forward, and I know my family's actions are poor indications of my character. I am very sorry, sir. I should have mentioned it." He looked tearful, but his voice sounded monotone like he'd said this a hundred times.

"I require loyalty, Scott. You should have informed me about your family issues. I always find out. You insult my intelligence. I will remember this."

"Yes, sir. I'm sorry, sir."

"Very good. I'll leave you to your evening. Goodnight."

"Goodnight, Mr. Bredenbury."

After the sound of his feet on the gravel had shrunk into the evening, Scott pulled Wolfe out of the wardrobe and threw him on the floor.

"Get him out of my house, Arcola. I don't ever want to see him step foot in here again," he murmured, refusing to look down at either of them.

"Scott! He's my brother, I can—"

"You will. We're not going to risk our lives for him," Scott hissed.

"Please!" she cried. She was on the floor, her arms wrapped around Scott's legs while his chest swelled, his eyes turned into black holes.

"Don't come back. If you say a word about this to anyone, I'll have you killed," he said, glowering his dark eyes down at him. Tears licked the corners of his eyes, threatening to spill over his bare chest.

"Please, Scott, Please, I'm sorry. I couldn't bear it," she cried, sobbing puddles across the floor. When Wolfe looked into his eyes, he wondered how anyone could love them. *How could anyone stay with this man.* Then he left, Kelvington's eyes burning holes in his back. A worker shovelled a wheelbarrow full of manure against immature trees, the sunset heaved colour through the trees, and the curtain in Dr. Wolseley's house trembled as Arcola's cries broke the heavens.

Chapter 6

A Midsummer Day's Festival

I guess the rumours weren't true. Wolfe thought to himself as he stretched under the heat of the afternoon sun like a cat. Day after day, week after week, he'd been working in the laundry rooms. Every day, he watched the sun rise and fall through the tiny spotted window where he worked. Every Sunday, an army of workers attacked the house while the family was away at church, fixing, cleaning, and mending until the house glimmered again.

Twice a day, just before noon and around eight, Wolfe usually had his meals. On Mondays, they were free to roam the grounds, and Wolfe had taken to lounging in the skirt of the yard and listening: the chirping of birds lost among branches, the wind in willow leaves, and the humming of distant tractors.

Just three days ago, Mr. Kelvington had cut Wolfe's meals in half, and now there was nothing but bitterness and hunger swirling in his gut.

Wolfe laid in silence, letting the sun warm his eyelids, feeling the grass tickle him. He loved the sunlight, anything better than the fake sun that woke him every morning, stretching its artificial tendrils across his eyelids, devoid of warmth. Wolfe found himself clawing at his skin every morning when the nightmares subsided, and he remembered that eight feet of earth bore down on them from above, pushing in on the cement walls and cracking the stark white paint with pressure.

He cracked open an eye, squinting away from the sun trembling in the branches. He sat up, staring out over the yard. Every day for weeks, more and more pavilions rose in the yard like snow-capped mountains. Tables littered the grounds, posts hung with fairy lights, and tents and blankets swirled like snowdrifts in the sun.

Every year, the family hosted the socialite gathering of the season, coinciding with the summer equinox. A night of drinking, feasting, dancing, and gossip for every actor, politician, and basketball player in the country. The Midsummer Night's Festival went from sunset to sunrise, and if the rumours were true, it comprised some of the most debauched acts known to man.

Wolfe pulled himself to his feet and out of the bushes and thought of the costumes. He had spent the last three days cleaning some of the most stunning clothes he'd ever seen. The brightest pinks, the softest yellows, the most beguiling greens. They twinkled like faerie wings, shone like sunsets, and dissolved through the air like cotton candy and silk.

The work wasn't hard, no harder than anything else. The food was delicious, nights weren't as hot here, and they got breaks. Wolfe had fallen into a paradise, and his mind drifted to Craik. *It wasn't like it was my fault. We would have both ended up here, regardless.* He walked himself back along the edges of the yard, waiting to find the staircase sunk into the ground across from the gazebo that led to the barracks, thinking about the gossip this morning.

"They couldn't pay me a hundred credits. I wouldn't do it," the tall, thin woman who stood like a scarecrow hissed across the room as she washed another batch of delicate white bedsheets.

"You've heard the same?"

"Mhmm. Every year."

"Mmhm…"

The women shook and hissed at the thought. Wolfe didn't ask, and he didn't want to know. Then they fell into silence again, wondering if the chips in their arms could read their minds, tell the Bredenburys their most personal ambitions. That was the consensus, but Wolfe would have been dead if that were the case.

"Hello, Wolfe," a woman said as they passed under the eaves of the house. Wolfe looked back at her, then again as he walked past. He'd never met that woman in her life. *How does she know my name?* Wolfe looked back again and saw her glance over her shoulder. They met eyes for a moment, and she bore into him with such intensity he knew he'd have to find her again. *What could she possibly want from me?*

As he turned the corner into the common room, his mind swimming about the strange woman in the hallway, he walked into Craik, wandering around the room. Craik's face was gaunt and hardened, unlike the Craik he had known three weeks before. His eyes were distant, sunken into his skull, and dark shadows beneath his eyes bore holes into Wolfe's soul.

"Craik?" Wolfe cried, grabbing him by the shoulders and backing him towards a bench along the wall.

"We're never going to escape," Craik whispered. His hands bounced along Wolfe, twittering off him, arms trembling.

"What?"

"We can never be free."

"Craik…" Wolfe backed up, watching the thoughts shift over his face. His eyes moved back and forth across his face in circles. He flung his head over his shoulders once each time. His eyes swivelled in his skull, spinning around him in erratic orbits. "They listen to everything, they see through your own eyes, change what you believe you've felt…" His hands played with each other, wringing in circles.

"Craik I…what are you…come here." Wolfe pulled Craik up by a shaking arm and led him towards the doorway that said MEDIC. Across the cafeteria and towards the stairs leading into the Bredenbury's kitchen, two women dressed in neat pantsuits decked in gold, red, and fancy lace trim were standing with impatience painted across their faces.

Somewhere upstairs, fingers kissed piano keys. The sun was setting, and tires rumbled on the gravel outside. Wolfe watched her eyes glide around the room, and Wolfe found a deep interest in the scratches on the cement floor as he walked a shaking Craik towards Dr. Wolseley's office.

He pinched his eyes shut as Wolfe reached the door, listening to their heels snap against the tiles.

"W.L. Bredenbury?" one of them said.

"Yes, ma'am?" Wolfe asked, staring at his reflection and their faces behind him on the shining wall in front of him.

"It seems our normal servers are unavailable, and there wasn't enough forethought to schedule them." She glared at the woman beside her who stood defiantly, rolling her eyes in deep arching circles. They were both extremely short, and they tied their hair back behind their heads in tight, slick buns.

Wolfe didn't respond.

"So you and a few others will do it in their place."

"Ma'am I…I'm blue-eyed. I can't serve the family…"

"Are you questioning me?" she snapped.

"No, ma'am, but I'm taking Craik to the medic, he is—" Wolfe was interrupted.

"Should I write you and C.T. Bredenbury up then? He looks fine to me."

Craik looked on the edge of tears, his hands were shaking, and his eyes darted from Wolfe to the women, each glance more desperate than the last.

"Please ma'am, I—I—I…can't. I."

"We will ma'am. Of course," Wolfe said. His words bolted out of him, knowing he didn't dare question a brown-eyed woman. She flicked something into her tablet and stood resistantly above him.

"Good. Follow me," she said.

On their way to the base of the stairs, they collected a small army of men from every nook and cranny until four dozen workers crowded around the bottom of the stairs: a mechanic on his third shift struggling to stay awake with hands larger than Wolfe's face, two men who had just started their day as night cleaners were plucked off the floor reeking of cleaning detergent, and an almost bawling Craik that looked like death. But in the end, all of them watched each other with trembling hands. Wolfe felt a rush of heat wash over him as he listened to the murmur of guests above him in the manor.

"Right. You take numbers six and eleven, you take tables fifteen and fourty two…" She thrust a small container into their hands and distributed them around the rest of the men. Wolfe looked up to meet Craik's eyes, but he was staring at his hands.

Wolfe felt the contact lenses against his palms and smoothed the tip of a small bottle of contact solution with his finger. It was heavy in his hands like he was holding dynamite. The room behind them had emptied as the dinner bell hummed its metallic cry, and the halls stayed barren.

"You all have to act like this is *normal.* Any of you step out of line, and it's death for you, and the re-education camps for us," the woman said as she stared down at her tablet. The other rolled out a line of suits from the supply closet nearest the stairs and passed them out. Wolfe felt the fabric of a soft pink suit with feathers sewn into the neckline.

"Now I remind you," the woman said, stepping between the rows of dressing men, "the act of serving high society is an arduous task but one that will reward you in mind and soul."

"Always hold your tongue."

"Never meet their eyes."

"Always be polite."

"Say yes, sir and no, sir. Yes, ma'am and no, ma'am."

As they rattled off rule after rule, proper poise after proper poise, Wolfe looked at himself in the reflection of the metal countertops. He was wearing a soft pink dress shirt, rolled up to the elbows. A pair of grassy brown suspenders and a bow tie touched by God itself in its shimmer. The complete outfit sparkled, twinkling like moonlight had kissed the fabric herself and hot pink feathers sprouted along its hemline.

They slid on masks and grew into horned beasts, mythological wonders of millenniums passed, into fairies and sea creatures, mossy statues and golden figurines. They had transformed into different people, their brown eyes glowing dark behind their masks. Music and voices hummed down through the floorboards, drifting into Wolfe's ears.

"Got it?" They all nodded. Wolfe had heard none of it.

He felt his gut clenching in on itself. He knew this was wrong and knew he would get caught. *It will be worth the punishment,* he told himself. *It has to be. You don't have a say.*

The women in charge of the party pulled the doors open, and the metal staircase fell open. As they began to ascend in silence, they walked past the kitchen doors to their right. Platter after platter of glittering plates and trays, adorned with every drink and delicacy the world offered, shimmered into their hands. The Kitchen Overseer twirled around the kitchen gleaming with sweat as he yelled orders to the blurring staff.

Despite every reason and path of logic in the world, Wolfe felt a twinge of curiosity merge into excitement. He saw figures moving upstairs, and he'd already forgotten about the women who knew his name. They rose into the glittering, shining world of the people who were, in all regards, better than him in every way as imaginary butterflies filled his lungs with every breath.

Chapter 7

A Midsummer Night's Festival

The stairs were silent beneath them, sparing the dull thump of polished black shoes as they ascended. Wolfe had a tray of hors d'oeuvres piled high with thinly sliced meats and slanted, stewed, roasted, and broiled fruits laying over soft cheeses, draped in extravagant sauces that smelled of unfamiliar spices. Piles of fruits he had never seen before, crimson and jagged, rich with white flesh, lay in heaps over platters in the manor. The scents wafted around the house as guests murmured in the study.

The men rounded the corner and stretched into various corners of the house. Wolfe looked over his shoulder for Craik, but he was lost in the crowd.

The library, rich with dusted novels and tablets, was packed with people lounging in each other's presence. The stairs were dusted with ghostly, colour-clad figures. A blonde-haired boy played the piano in the far corner of the living room, his fingers glittering over the keys. His eyes were tired yet listless, constantly moving to fight off sleep.

The living room swam with colours. Wolfe saw prime ministers and presidents, CEOs and A-list actors, porn stars and dictators. All unfamiliar but held together by two unifying causes; money and eye colour. Green-eyed prostitutes, male and female, wandered in circles. Their naked bodies were dusted with green glitter, wide eyes dazzling and dripping with seduction as the brown-eyed people devoured them with theirs. They shivered, yet their cheeks were flushed red. Their eyes were dreamy, hazed with pleasure, high on PDT.

A collection of brown-eyed women sat in the living room, flanked to either side of a regal-looking woman draped in gold.

They turned their noses up at the walking sex around them, their silently judging expressions and upturned noses flitting down over them, eyeing them with contempt as their husbands slobbered over their naked breasts and muscles.

The woman in the centre leaned her head and spoke to a woman on her left, a polite smile falling across the edges of her lips. She was royalty, grace, a Goddess. Their heads turned in unison to a woman with soft hazel eyes and then back to each other, continuous in their judgment with slight smiles and waving lips. The woman with hazel eyes watched her feet, and they went back to eyeing each other when she snuck out of the room and into the silence of the dining room.

The darker the eyes, the purer the soul, Wolfe thought to himself. It wouldn't be long until even the brown-eyed people shrank into tiny cliques searching for money and subjugation: hazel over amber, chocolate over ebony, amber over oak, acacia over chocolate, until finally, their greed would devour each other whole.

A clatter of whispering women moved past Wolfe, complaining about the paintings on the wall.

"It's obscene…"

"Well over a hundred and seventy thousand credits…"

"…and she doesn't even like it. I'd gladly keep it…" They eyed the walls with gluttony on their minds, dreaming of everything they'd never have.

Wolfe stepped out into the summer twilight. Tables of food running the yard's length teemed with guests draped in cloud white dresses and togas. Green-eyed women wrapped in green and gold dresses spun in hanging cages to music, fairy wings swirling over their backs as they sang. Flashes of lilac purple wine spun through the air as cries of laughter rang through the night. Men and women were dusted with gold dust, and their hair was filled with flower crowns weaved from yarrow and dandelions. Their masks shifted as they danced, eyes flashing in every direction.

The air seemed to swim with the smell of honeysuckle and

freshly baked blueberry tarts; the air tasted of daisies and goldenrod, and the grass hummed around his ankles as he walked. A young woman with an enormous smile giggled up to him and spun away with a handful of hors d'oeuvres, flashing her long eyelashes at him. He dipped beneath a pavilion and was handed a crystal decanter of honey-coloured liquid that smelled like sugar and flower petals.

He poured rivers of sunlight into glasses thinner than paper as a group of men chuckled around each other, faces exposed to the world, glowing under the glistening fairy lights that drifted lazily back and forth across the white cloth.

"He will lose. Aber just doesn't know when to shut up. If he keeps pushing that stupid blue-eyed bullshit, he'll definitely get cut down," a brown-haired man said to a group of nodding faces as he set his glass down on the side table.

"But here's the thing no one wants to talk about. Blue-eyed nationalists always say, oh well, Einstein had blue eyes, or Tesla, without ever looking at the big picture. It's their culture, their lack of drive, and motivation that got them in this place. Bluies made up over half of all domestic violence reports, half of all prison inmates in Canada, and a quarter of all violent crime. They were only eight percent of the population, so why is there such a huge disparity? We built this fucking country three hundred years ago. We created the biggest civilizations in the world: the Egyptians, the Mayans, the Mesopotamians, the Romans. That was us. The language we speak, the numbers we use, the Gods we worship? That was us." His drink sloshed up and over his hand into the grass as he ranted, spit hung off his lips like spiderwebs.

"It's true. There have been successful blue-eyed people, but they all come from a long line of brown-eyed ancestors. Look it up, it's true! They learned to be like us and act like us. We brought culture and civilization to the drooling, snivelling, inbred masses, and they're mad? Then they steal from us, wear our clothes, use our inventions, and blue-eyed people get the idea they are worth more than us?"

"Some of the world's most horrific tragedies can be attributed to the blue-eyed race. Famine, genocide, ethnic cleansing. It's sick. And people still want to defend them?"

The men spoke two separate conversations, and the closer Wolfe got, the more they looked familiar. Wolfe knew he had seen them both before. Prime Minister Windthorst and Mr. Kelvington were standing with their backs towards him. Wolfe walked around them and saw the prime minister up close, his hair was graying, his lips were bright red, and his eyes were tired but dignified.

Wolfe offered them a drink, and they dismissed him, pushing him aside with a flick of their wrists. *They are why I'm here. They did this to me. They are criminals. Yet they are so blase about it.* They flicked Wolfe aside, spoke down about 'bluies,' and they didn't even care about the millions of blue-eyed children who never got a chance to grow up. There was so much Wolfe wanted to say, so much he could do, and he did none of it.

Wolfe sunk into the fray again, losing himself among the edges of the tablecloths and dancing bodies. Gossip swirled around him, pulling him back and forth, but Wolfe knew who he was looking for. If one Kelvington was here, the other would be too.

"It's true! He bought thousands of those little green girls from overseas. He said he sells them before he gets them on the lot. Or, that's what he said…" the women around her gasped in a fake scandal, the stench of falsity and indifference thick in the air.

"Who?!"

"I shouldn't say…" the woman murmured in fake disgust.

"Oh you're bad!"

The woman looked ready to explode before splashing her wine onto the side table, heaving itself deeper and deeper into the mushy earth.

"Well. If you won't say anything…" she said, knowing they would talk as soon as they got home if they made it that long. "One of the Tobins. He has this whole setup from five to seventeen, girls and boys, all green, all shipped to anyone who can afford one."

"You're joking."

"Not at all. He ships most of the boys up north to those pervy faggots, and apparently, Leslie Valparaiso is running a breeding farm out west, built to breed more and more green-eyed sex slaves."

"Christ above…"

"I know, right…" she said, her eyes glimmering with excitement. They gasped and shrieked together, holding each other's hands and delving deeper into their madness. "He makes millions pimping out these greenies. I heard even the little ones have an intrinsic understanding of sex. Sex fiends. The younger they are, the prettier they are, and the better they…are…" she flung her arms up, sending tributaries of wine trickling down her bare arms.

"I visited Ireland on a mission trip ten years ago, and greenies are just so… exotic. Their culture is so… rich," another woman whispered, her eyes dreaming of the emerald eyes and freckled bodies.

Men and women teetered around in circles. One woman, naked as the day she was born, tore across the grass, much to the delight of the howling, clapping men in the garden. The dishes piled, and the food kept coming. The music played louder, and the voices talked faster until a pounding delirium grew around him. Guests snorted lines of powdered sunshine up their noses, rubbing the PDT along the rims of their mouths. Still, Arcola was nowhere to be seen. Towards the edge of the trees, their cabin was glowing. A figure moved behind the blinds.

"Have you gone shooting lately?" a man asked Mr. Bredenbury, leaning on his shoulder.

"Why would I? I'm the best shot here!" he said as a group of men laughed around him.

"And the war?"

"What are a bunch of blue-eyed Latinos gonna do? The war will be over by the end of the summer. The Old Cobalt Society will fall."

Wolfe carried out a platter of desserts as a train flashed by the trees, signalling to him that it was morning. The train went by every night at three, shaking the roof over them as it shipped supplies down to the coastal cities.

A pile of chocolate delicacies heaped with toasted meringue came first for dessert, then a platter of twisted cinnamon pastries filled with cream and sprinkled with spices. Wolfe wanted to slip one past his lips, but he held himself back. A selection of stewed plum cocktails came next as another round of champagne was carried out, and with it came straight-faced guards hauling giant wooden structures across the grass. Fifteen giant 3D X's with thin black straps around the edges were rolled from the guardhouse, coming to rest in the centre of the yard, encircling the gazebo.

The crowd watched in silence; descending looks of shame, excitement, and distaste washed their faces. Most of the women trickled their way back towards the house, boasting loudly of their newest hobby, their charities, art competitions, and their children's successes overseas in academies and military training outposts.

Wolfe took a wide berth back around the gardens, watching Mr. Bredenbury step onto a table from behind a row of people. Wolfe peered through the topiaries, and just as Mr. Bredenbury spoke, a stream of bodies rounded the corner of the house.

Thirty men and women were led towards the X's in screaming rows. Some kicked, and some cried. Electricity coursed through their angriest until they were limp and the rest settled. The green-eyed sex dolls, with their plump lips and smoothed bodies, were already in the throng. A touch here, a rub there. They strapped two per X in place, crotch out, hands touching, legs spread like dolls.

"My dear guests, friends, and acquaintances. I'll waste no time introducing you to everyone," he joked, and the crowd laughed. "I hope you enjoy the staple of our Midsummer Night's Festival. The entertainment!" he cried.

Wolfe hurled into the topiary, spewing years of bile onto the thorny branches. His supper of stew clung among leaves. The guards stripped the worker's clothes to strips with knives as the guests removed their own clothes.

"—and remember," Bredenbury said to the crowd, hastily undoing their belts, slipping dresses off their shoulders, masks falling towards the ground. "They need to work tomorrow!" he finished, and the crowd erupted into a facetious cheer. Wolfe vomited more of his dinner, tasting the stew a third time.

The crowd cheered again as Mr. Bredenbury pulled his shirt over his head, exposing his chest, sprinkled heavily with salt and pepper chest hair. A few women stayed around to watch, fingers slipping between their thighs. Some of the guests were already nude, sauntering toward the helpless victims. Wolfe watched two girls no older than sixteen wrap their fingers together.

Wolfe dropped the tray, letting the desserts spill across the grass. The earth was moving around him as he jogged towards the front of the house, and Kelvington pushed past him, pants undone, cock in hand. Wolfe felt the bile rising again as light poured over him from the front door.

Puke flung from Wolfe's chin as he jogged, dribbling along his lips, stinging them like spider venom. He went back past the gardens, around the topiaries, and towards the cabins. Once he was out of the light, he ran as fast as he could. He collapsed against the door, begging to be let in.

Arcola opened the door, and to Wolfe's surprise, her eyes were bloodshot. She had been crying.

"Wolfe?!" she cried, dropping to the ground in front of him, wrapping her arms around his neck as he sniffed the tears away.

"I'm sorry, I know I shouldn't be here. I just…" Moans filled the air. The sound of pounding meat and violent slaps drew Arcola's attention behind him as men and women beat flesh against flesh. Sweat beaded across their face, digging at them with their clammy fingers. Wolfe could taste the puke again and felt another sob steal the air out of his lungs. *I don't want to be here. I don't want to be here. I don't want to be here.* Wolfe wished he could shut off his brain, stop watching the movie, close the novel, prevent the horror from following him into his dreams tonight, but he had no choice.

"Come on, you can't stay out here," she said, dragging him inside. In the light, Wolfe could see himself better. Dirt and the hints of grass stains were torn across his legs, puke ran down his chest underneath his shirt, and tears beaded against his collar. Arcola walked along the length of the cabin, flicking the windows shut and drawing the shutters as Wolfe sat, trying to stop the tears.

Their cabin was filthy. The wallpaper was a soft yellowish, floral shade that made the walls feel taller, but they were still brown along the edges. A bouquet of wildflowers arched their tall necks across a sticky table. The house smelled of a dinner freshly cooked of onions and carrots, garlic and balsamic vinegar, brown sugar and celery, all with the notes of mould.

"Would you like some roast?" she asked, sniffling as she walked towards the stove, wiping her eyes.

"Arcola, what's wrong?"

"I just made gravy a little while ago. It should still be warm."

"Arcola."

"I also have some beets…"

"Arcola, please…" Wolfe begged, more tears falling against his hands on the floor. "I don't want to eat. I want you to talk to me."

"Oh Wolfe…" she cried, dropping to her knees beside him and leaning against the wall.

They just looked at each other and sat there for a moment, breathing in each other's existence. They both let the tears fall, their hands laying on each other. Then Wolfe let himself slide down so his head was resting in her lap, and she smiled down at him.

"What are you wearing?" she asked, staring down at his clothes and tilting his head back to look at his eyes.

"We're serving the family tonight…and I can't take it, Arcola. I can't. I'm gonna go insane. I'm not going to make it much longer," he said, tears welling again.

"You're wearing contacts. Who's idea was this? Are they

trying to get you killed? They must have disabled your chips," she said, wiping her eyes and pulling the hair out of her face, leaning back against the wall. "Oh, I'm sorry, Wolfe. I'm so sorry."

"Don't they notice that four dozen workers are just…gone?" Wolfe asked.

"The guards never pay that close attention, and the overseers…are busy." Arcola gulped.

"And why are *you* apologizing to me? How is this your fault?"

"I guess it isn't, but—"

"I know." They were silent again for a minute. "Why were you crying?" Wolfe asked.

"Because I hate my husband," she said, smiling.

Wolfe could see Mr. Kelvington's face twisted with pleasure, rutting against the girl in the yard, ass bare, knees shaking. He was angry again, saw vermilion visions of his death at his own hands, saw his guts squished between his fingers. Wolfe saw his pain and languished in it.

"Then why are you married to him? He's a monster."

"Wolfe, I do love him, and he has his issues, but… I love him."

"Why? You're crying because of him. He hurts me at every chance he can get, he's out there fucking some sixteen year old girl, and you love him!?" Wolfe felt his heart shatter, crystalline pieces falling against his rib cage and growing into the soft, delicate skin.

"Wolfe stop. Just stop. I…"

"Why him?" Wolfe could see it plain as day. That man was a shifting devil, changing when the mood required him too. He cared about one person, himself, and Mr. Kelvington would do anything to protect that. *He's evil. How can she not see that?*

"I don't know. It's a lot to explain."

"Try."

Arcola mulled for a moment. Then she closed her eyes.

"We met in one of the eastern re-education camps after I got a little aggressive at home. Our fucking bitch of a grandmother was the one who turned me in. I can still see her smug face when she phoned the hotline for snitches." Arcola sneered at an imaginary vision of their grandmother floating in the reflection on the stove.

"Anyway, Scott was a BESNA officer, and he spent his days enforcing the thousand fucking rules they had in that place. I on the other hand spent my days fighting with all of my teachers and getting punished for it. You just write all day, re-learning everything about BESNA and the country until they deem you brainwashed enough to send you out into the world. I would have been there for years. Fuck, I'd still be there. He needed to get married and settle down. I needed to prove to the parole officers that I wouldn't relapse."

"He just…married you?"

"He isn't what you think he is," She said. "He just wanted out, and he would do whatever it took. He stopped me from getting beaten to a pulp, and in turn…I let him root around for a little bit."

"Arcola, that's terrible."

"I enjoyed it. I felt powerful, like I was in control for once in my life. We got married, I got out, how else was I going to help people?"

"Who have you helped, Arcola?"

"I…I will help people. Just wait and see…" she said, a glimmer in her eyes. She was about to say something but closed her mouth again, looking through the kitchen window. "He got hired here. I came with him. And I do my part, I give people food, I don't hurt people, I'm a good guy here, Wolfe."

"He basically raped you, and you love him?" Wolfe asked, ignoring her question.

"It's difficult, Wolfe."

"I could never."

"That's up to you, but even though he can piss me off, he isn't that bad. I'm sorry if he's mistreating you, but… It's a game, Wolfe. It's all a game here, of appearances and acting, and… I don't know, but I am glad you're okay." She smiled at him and rubbed his knuckles.

"I'm glad you're okay Arcola…" he said, smiling, wrapping his arms around her, breathing in her scent. They didn't let go; they couldn't let go. Wolfe could breathe again knowing she was okay.

"Give Scott some time. He'll get over it. You're the only actual family I have left."

They waited for a moment, knowing Wolfe had to leave, neither of them wanting to be the first to say it.

"I'll come for you. Just be calm Wolfe, it'll be okay in the end. I promise."

"So I'll see you later then?"

"Of course, you'll always have me, even if it doesn't feel like it. I mean, you found me after five years of me thinking you were dead." She smiled.

"Forever."

"Forever." She smiled again, giving him one more hug and flicking off the lights so Wolfe could slip out into the darkness.

——

When Wolfe entered the living room, the walls were still adorned with tapestries, and the paintings still started judging from their hallowed homes clinging to the walls. He straightened himself in the mirror. He raked through his hair, wiped his face, and tied his mask on again. The boy was playing something by an obscure Austrian composer who had died centuries ago, and his eyes were drifting aimlessly.

A man came past, smiled at him, then leaned against the wall. He was pulling up his pants as he came by, feral noises drifting in the door as he clutched the staircase. Wolfe watched him drag his sweaty fingers up the stairs, painting the wall darker where he touched it.

The women whispered in the living room, and when he came around the corner, the women were still spread across the living room, immaculately placed, sparing a stray hair or a missing ring. Finally, it dawned on him. A family portrait hung above her, and she was a porcelain replication beneath it. Mrs. Bredenbury glared up at him.

"Yes?" she drawled, looking into his soul.

She drank deeply for a moment, and with all eyes on him, she rose gently. Wolfe saw her form, delicate and shadowy. She wore a dark brown dress like burnt sugar, a golden shawl wrapped around her elbows. She clutched it over her breasts and ruffled her green blouse as her bare feet drifted across the floor towards him. As she moved, her dress parted around her legs, and a pair of black leather pants shone beneath them. She was transcendent, a ghost, a spectre. She slid across the room like the dying whispers of a cigarette or a lioness stalking her prey.

"Where are you from then…Mr…"

"Bracken." Wolfe whispered the first name that had come to mind. In his memories, Bracken was still dead on the street where he'd been shot by that BESNA officer. He wished he could remember him as something else. He wished he could forget the past hanging like a silver dagger above his head.

"How…archaic…" she whispered. Mrs. Bredenbury glided around Wolfe as he held his breath and watched her head bob around him. A golden circlet of leaves was worked into her inky hair. She smelled of rose petals when she walked, her sweat leaving sweet notes lingering in his nose.

"I'm not going to do anything to you. Unless…" she stepped around in front of him and stared at him directly. She stared until an eon almost passed, but Wolfe never looked away. Instead, he studied her in return, watching the movement in her pupils, watching galaxies explode in her irises. And then she sank backwards and rested herself back in her chair, folding her legs across one another, black leather stretching against her legs.

The women reeked of alcohol as he served them, all except for her. She was poised. Not a word would pass her tongue that she didn't want to. As the men waddled in, the surrounding women peppered him with questions.

"Where are you from?"

"What do you do for a living?"

"What is your name again?"

Wolfe tried his best to respond. "Town. A field hand. Braden"

Mrs. Bredenbury looked up at him again when he said his name, then smiled back down at her drink, showing off a row of the whitest teeth he'd ever seen.

"Champagne," Mrs. Bredenbury barked. Wolfe walked quickly and without hesitation. His heart pounded with every step as he moved across the room. The semicircle of women sat with their backs to the growing light. Wolfe felt as if he had been brought before a council. The women were married to some of the wealthiest, most influential people in the world, and with those marriages came power, alot of it.

"Well. As far as I'm concerned, I'm voting for the IPNAP, only because they can get the country out of the emotional rut we're in," Mrs. Bredenbury said.

"Agreed. The National Party espouses ideals that will get this country into the best place it could be, but they don't have a moral leader in place," Mrs. Meota said. Through the night, Wolfe had learned more than he should have. She and her husband owned over half of all privately owned nature reserves on the continent.

"Though the country is new, the world knows we're an economic powerhouse. No one would question us regardless of who we elected." The woman next to the bookcase chuckled, her mouth stuffed with cranberry and goat cheese panini. She owned most of the lithium mines, spread across a hundred subsidiaries.

"True." Mrs. Bredenbury laughed. "At the end of the day, it's all the same shit. It doesn't matter if it's the Nationals or the IPNAP; they let us do what we want. I don't care who can marry who or what countries they bomb. Who gives a shit?" She laughed.

When she finished talking, her eyes fell on Wolfe again. It felt like she could see through the contacts and straight into his soul. Like she was picking through his thoughts, fears, and opinions. It felt like she was taking them as her own.

"Well, they expect the EU to issue tariffs against us."

"What? So seven minuscule countries with less GDP than my left toe?" a woman laughed. A woman Wolfe understood was the daughter of a water tycoon and owned half of the old Canadian boreal forest.

"Will that affect my black cards for my next trip to Warsaw?" Madame Kincaid gasped, fear trickling in her voice. She and her husband, both eighty-seven years old, owned seventeen of the big car companies.

Was that all they were scared of? How could they sleep at night knowing what they do during the day? Was that the worst thing that could happen to them? Wolfe asked himself, disgust flaring again. He was among monsters.

Another round of food came out, and Mrs. Bredenbury began her spiel.

"These truffles had to be brought in specially from Asia. And it's been a bitch to grow them, pardon my french, because of all the droughts over there, and the water we had to spend to grow them. They almost didn't let them leave the continent!" she cried, and Wolfe watched her guests flicker their eyes at each other. They wanted those truffles. Her money. Her water. Her power. They craved it like the lungs crave air.

When Mr. Bredenbury came in behind them, he came with a reek of sweat. Wolfe and the other servers backed against the walls. Mr. Bredenbury was half undressed, whispering to his wife and rubbing her shoulders as he scanned the room between the guests.

The party had wound down; the birds had started to chirp and whistle, scaring the stars back into their hiding until tonight, when the moon would rise again and they would return. Pale grey light slid its ambling fingers over the yard. Trains had begun to arrive at the dirty station down the sweat-stained approach. The guests started dispersing into the night, flashing away into trains that would take them halfway across the world in minutes.

"Servers. Go let the workers out and take them back to the barracks," he said, zipping up his pants and laughing at the other men in various states of undress.

Wolfe was one of the first men out the door. When he was down off the porch, he peeked over his shoulder. There were no prying faces in the windows, so he sprinted across the lawn to the nearest wooden cross.

A boy no older than fifteen was stretched across an X, still and unmoving. They had streaked his naked body with shiny fluid and bruises. His soft skin was marked with aching bursts of colour pulled across his flesh. His eyes saw nothing, and his tear-stained voice spoke a thousand words as he muttered something incomprehensible. Another boy, maybe nineteen, watched Wolfe with a tear-pocked face on the other side. The two of them had clasped their fingers together, sweat dripping where their hands met.

Wolfe fought with the constraints, and the boy fell to the ground. Wolfe wrapped him in one of the unused towels, feeling his goosebump-covered skin chilled from the cool morning air. The sun peeked its fiery lashes out from over the horizon, bathing them in warmer light, and they still shivered. The shortest night of the year was over, and Wolfe dragged the boys across the lawn.

Wolfe and the others walked them directly to the bushes nestled deep within the trees and down the steps into the barracks. Some wandered off aimlessly like ghosts, and others pretended nothing had happened as they spoke to other workers. Wolfe hurried back up the steps as the cooks started breakfast. He sighed a breath of relief; it was almost over. Cars petered out of the driveway and down the gravel approach. People milled back down the steps and over the porch, watching them come back from the bushes.

Wolfe came back to the front porch with the other servers behind him. The two women were probably just downstairs, waiting to congratulate them on their excellent job. Nothing felt so bad under the light of day. Wolfe came in the front door, turned into the living room, and stopped. A handful of people remained. He could sense a feeling in the air. It wasn't unfamiliar, but he couldn't place a definite note on it.

Mr. Bredenbury's back was turned, but a few men wandered around him, tapping away furiously on tablets. But one thing was for sure. The silence throbbed; it painted their faces with a look

Wolfe had seen many times before. His heart sank. Disgust weaved across the faces of the men and women standing with judgment in their hands.

"It is very peculiar, I have found…" he paused for a moment, never turning to look at them, "…for the men whom I have never employed, just happen to know the precise location of the workers' barracks." Mr. Bredenbury held a glass in hand while he spoke, something red and toasty clinked around with frozen stones.

How could I have been so stupid? He thought to himself. Mr. Bredenbury held the tablet, and with a tap, Wolfe felt his world around him fracture, falling through the static recess of his mind and into darkness.

"I can only imagine that you weren't the ones who found brown contact lenses, so you won't be disposed of," he said, a vast, wicked grin spreading across his lips. "Though we have already found the perpetrators, and we will deal with them accordingly. Bracken, was it? Or Braden?"

The men and women crowded around Wolfe, staring down at him in their simple suits, fancy dresses, and full stomachs as he lay waiting for death. Mr. Bredenbury reached down and flicked his mask aside, studying his face.

"Though you may not die, some of you might wish for it."

Chapter 8

The Rapture

Wolfe felt the clothes fall off his back in strips. He heard the sound of feet, knowing a thousand eyes watched over his naked skin. They had stirred a congregation behind him, and the workers watched with flitting eyes, never looking directly at Wolfe.

The first lance pierced his skin against the backdrop of the muggy morning. The empty pavilions watched, standing like ghosts across the lawn. He looked up as the front door opened, thinking of anything other than the searing pain across his back. The two women from earlier, with bruised faces and torn clothes, were drug down the steps to either side of him. They were crying, reaching out toward invisible forces. They fell down the steps towards the trucks, a rope tied to each corner.

Even the whip had stopped falling when their torsos were liberated from their limbs. Wolfe looked back to see her rise into the sky, followed by the other woman. A man a few years older than his father was claimed by a guard. Another man was led to the next tree for the same punishment. He didn't scream, didn't cry, didn't beg. He simply prayed as he walked. He yearned for divine intervention, prayed that God would spare him, that he would be the one God listened to, unlike the millions before him and after him, who begged and would beg towards the same saviour. God didn't hear.

A ring of dogs prowled forward, their necks bristling with spikes honed into spears. Their collars shone like the sky, like iced ponds, like baby blue porcelain, dripping with red paint.

A girl rushed forward, maybe seventeen, bloated with pregnancy. She ran towards the guards, screaming, trying to rip the tablet from their fingers. Another woman followed in an attempt to save her husband. They threw the girl to the ground, and as she clutched her stomach, a pool of water spilled around her. She gave birth in the dirt. Then, Wolfe listened to the bloodsucking, bone-rattling howls of a woman watching her newborn baby get taken away to be sold.

Wolfe couldn't comprehend the sound and he thrashed in an effort to squeeze his ears shut. He imagined other sounds to fill the void. *A churning flour mill, ice clinking in a glass, the flutter of water on sand.* Mr. Wolseley had arrived, surveying the scene and pointing an unwavering finger to the weakest among them. They were dragged, crying away from the children towards the trucks, taken to be sold. Wolfe bawled for them, knowing they would never see each other again.

The air seemed to shimmer, the air burnt metallic and hot, and the stench of ammonia burnt at Wolfe's nostrils. The smell of roasting meat made him wash the steps with vomit. The workers screaming shattered the crystal bowl of the heavens. Wolfe saw a child trying to run to her mother within his peripheral vision, bawling with snot dripping down her face. The guards removed her. Wolfe could hear the sizzling of brands warming in the fire, the sound of chains behind trucks, the sounds of nails behind hammered into barrels. *The crinkle of paper, the crunch of dried dirt beneath boots, the smell of lavender.* Wolfe thought.

Wolfe looked left and right at the men flanking either side of him, each dripping with tomato sauce, their backs open gifts to the air. He heard the cries of men beside him like he'd never heard and saw a red liquid with a yellow shimmer spread across their spines. Wolfe felt a hand on his back and jumped away, only receiving a sharp blow on the back of his head that made his ears ring.

Wolfe guessed what the substance was from the pain and smell alone. It felt like someone had poured acid on his back. They rubbed the paste over him as it slid and fell over his elevated skin. They'd ran a zipper down his spine, and he dropped out of his skin. *The burning reek of peppers, the fresh assault of vinegar, the sting of salt.*

The pain had no meaning anymore. He wasn't even in his body. Blood, not even his own, rushed down the surrounding steps. His back was fire, electricity, both. The pain had no name, nothing to compare it to. The pain made him scream and thrash, the only way he could try to deal with the agony.

Wolfe looked up for the last time at the family as his vision gave out: Two young girls to his right, a ten and a seventeen-year-old boy to his left, with their parents in the middle. They didn't even blink; the parents had a slight smirk, but the children did nothing. Their faces were empty and emotionless. They were bored, tapping their feet, swinging their arms behind their backs.

As his neck slumped forward and the morning reverted into the night, the last sight he saw was their towering figures over him, and then, vividly, he saw six pairs of shoes that were etched into his memory. A couple of brown, genuine leather dress shoes, two pairs of light brown girl's shoes laced with pink and golden trim, a pair of delicate black dress shoes with a slight heel laced tight above the ankle, and two smaller versions of Mr. Bredenbury's.

The distant sound of a coming storm, the smell of dew on grass, the taste of freshly baked cookies.

—

Wolfe was in darkness for eons at first before the dreams came to him again. Like a dam, memories he didn't know he had come rushing back. Faces torn and disfigured, things with missing limbs and the smell of cooking meat.

Wolfe pushed himself up on one arm and felt something heavy and damp rise over his back with him. He rubbed the sleep out of his eyes and peeled them open. He was lying in a large room filled with other bodies; some slept along the walls like him, and others lined the floor in rows. Blue-eyed women rewrapped bandages and fed medicine to their bodies. Most of the room was silent, sparing the odd grumble and soft whimper.

Wolfe held back coughs with every breath as his lungs filled with the stench of freshly made plastic and disinfectant. He sat up on the cot and held his hand to his back, feeling what they had wrapped him with. His mind was foggy; he didn't know where he was or what he was doing, but Wolfe knew he was hungry, and he was going in for supper.

"Please lie back down," a nurse begged. Her eyebrows were deep furrows above her gaunt face, and her eyes shook. Her entire body was stiff, and what her voice tried to convey, her eyes did better.

Through his plastic casing, he heard the odd thunk from outside the door. Every few seconds, thunk after thunk after thunk. The air coming under the door seemed to whisper at Wolfe, a low gentle murmuring smelling of barbecue. He felt his stomach grumble again, and he stood up abruptly.

"Please…" the woman said, looking over her shoulder again as she and an older nurse fought with a man's leg. Wolfe tilted his head like a confused dog. Whatever they gave him, his mind was heavy like oatmeal boiled into sludge. *Don't most people have two legs?* He thought to himself, looking at him over and over.

He scanned the room slowly, counting legs. *Yup, they have legs; I have legs, everyone has legs…wait…*one man had a stump where an arm should be. His right. Now Wolfe was confused. He had an arm too. *One and two.* Wolfe struggled to think.

"Just lie back down, and we'll get you some more pain medication…" she said, resting her arms on either side of his shoulders. *I'm not in any pain. I'm perfectly healthy.* He took a few steps backwards and tripped over some loose plastic wrapping, barely catching himself before he stumbled into the door.

The smell was stronger near the door, and it clawed at his stomach. The woman stood there staring at him, begging with her eyes. "Please, sir, if you'd just…" Wolfe felt tears brimming at the cusp of his eyes. He knew he was in the wrong room, and he knew he was going to go get supper, he'd miss it if he was late, and he didn't want to wait until lunch tomorrow.

The nurses struggled with a man who was now crying and

trying to get out of bed, and at the moment they both went to help him, and Wolfe was left alone, he fumbled to open the door.

The smell hit him first. The smell of a freshly butchered animal, the reek of ammonia from stale piss, of bleach and sanitation. Then, the smell of barbecued steaks and roast chicken. The scent pulled at his stomach, but his feet touched a body, and he couldn't move forward. He looked down and saw a face. *Or something?* The face looked vaguely human. They had realigned his features like a Picasso painting. An eye wasn't where it should have been and he was sleeping with his eyes open. His nose was pressed backwards, his forehead was dented, and Wolfe looked into his sleeping eyes. Wolfe blinked. The man did not.

"Are..youokay..?" Wolfe grumbled. He wanted to crouch beside him, but the room got hotter, and he steadied himself on the door handle behind him. He looked out over the common room. He knew where he was now. He was in the room with word MEDIC etched above it.

The main common room was empty. The chairs and tables were thrown up against the walls, and the floor had changed too. Instead of pale white tiles, all Wolfe saw were bodies and clothes. The air burnt his eyes, and he struggled to place what he was hearing.

The floor was alive with squirming. A swelling, rippling sea of fluttering bodies shifted over the ground like waves. Makeshift cots hung on the walls, swinging with more bodies. Men dressed in overalls stepped through the throng, picked up people, and heaved the bodies up the stairs and into the darkness.

The cold air came down the stairs, chilling him, and Wolfe squinted his eyes. *Why were the stairs painted?* The stairs to the outside had been painted a bright, shiny red. How much time had passed? It was night, at least. Shadows threw themselves across the walls. Moths, in their barbarity, beat their bodies against the dull yellowed lights.

Wolfe leaned back and looked at the wall across from him. Dr. Wolseley was working with enormous, red metal tools. They covered him in red juice and a sheen of sweat while he sawed, and as he would take a something and sear it off, the floating smell of cooking meat wafted from the wrong area, not the kitchen, but from the doctor with his flaming metal and heavy tools.

Somehow, the doctor knew Wolfe was there, and they looked at each other. His eyes were like a softened caramel, but his face was a shine of red paint. Maybe Wolfe imagined it, or perhaps his memories betrayed him, but he shook his head. He was telling him no. *How does he even know me?* Wolfe had asked himself before he lost track of his face.

Wolfe saw a train of people coming down the stairs: *They must be new.* Some looked sunburnt, others looked like their clothes had been eaten by fiery moths, others had glued pieces of gravel to their face, and some had been born without ears or fingers. A few of them had wide, red birthmarks covering their faces and arms.

Wolfe watched men, women, and children brought down the red stairs as another load of sleeping workers were removed by hand. The cycle would begin over and over again as the scent of roasted meat wafted through the room like a thick, poisonous smog.

Through this, his back itched. Annoying at first but quickly turning unbearable. The scratching started out as relief before turning from bliss into an aching and stomach rumbling pain. It grew worse and worse while Wolfe scratched furiously, then he let his arms fall to his side.

As he looked down, he saw his fingers covered in something red and sticky, like sweet and sour sauce or ketchup. He was standing in a pool of red blood. *Why was there blood?* He watched the liquid seep its way across the floor and matte itself into the hair of the sleeping, wide-eyed man at his feet. A fly crawled across his open eye.

Then, as a bout of dizziness and exhaustion, hunger, and confusion overwhelmed him, he reverted into darkness again.

—

The abyss was darker than darkness. Darkness is simply the absence of light; the darkness Wolfe was engulfed in now was the opposite of light. Black was white compared to the gaping void before Wolfe. Over the next few weeks, he came in and out of consciousness, lost to time.

The nightmares were worse.

Wolfe peeled his eyes open, and it was night. Then he would blink, and it was afternoon. Time moved backwards, forwards, within and without itself. Circular then linear. It was something. Somewhere in dreams, he heard the weeping.

The smell was worse. As time passed, it began to reek of rot and decay. The bodies had stopped coming in, and they only took bodies out.

"Nine thousand per head, I hear," a voice whispered, a nurse, a helper, someone. A shuffling sound pulled him from sleep.

"Why do you think they make every girl who comes through here have their children? Saves them from buying workers." The voice clicked its tongue in shame as the shuffling subsided, and Wolfe was back in his mind.

Time slowly regained its regular advancement. Wolfe sat up in a near-empty room. Five men other than him were wrapped in blankets and gauze. He sat up. The electronic window on the wall told him it was morning, but that could be a lie. Wolfe felt his cheeks; the slight burn of stubble scratched his fingers. Certainly not two weeks worth.

The itching, then the searing pain, had subsided. The night tremors, the sweats and fevers, the sickness and shakiness were over. They left him feeling weak and exhausted; he'd have laid down and died if someone had asked him.

"Morning, Wolfe," a woman whispered as she stepped in. She carried a few pairs of cloth bandages and crept in silence.

"Morning," Wolfe said back. He questioned whether he should ask what day it was and decided against it.

"How're your dressings feeling?"

"Fine." Wolfe tried to talk as little as possible. He just wanted to sleep.

"Mm," she murmured while she turned him around to check. "You got off easy, you know," she said as she pulled off his bandages. "Have you been scratching?" She told him he was lucky, like it was nothing, like she was just trying to make simple conversation.

"No. I don't think I did."

"Have you been scratching? Be honest."

"No."

"Mmhm." It seemed to be her favourite saying. "Mr. Bredenbury is furious. He is planning on setting changing the laws in the province. He's gone straight to the Premier's office this morning for all this disobedience. Lost a lot of money." Wolfe tried to figure out what side she was on as she wrapped him again with fresh bandages.

"Well, he wouldn't lose money if he didn't kill us. I don't see how he gets to be mad."

"He gets to be whatever he wants."

"And who pays for this?"

"For what?"

"The bandages, the creams, all of that?"

"Well, the Bredenburys need at least a skeleton crew to run the plantation, so they pay for that much. The rest...we have to make do. We'd prefer it if people didn't start things in the first place," she said, flicking her eyes over Wolfe.

"Have you spoken to Mr. Bredenbury personally?" Wolfe snapped, and her eyes screwed into him.

"Be careful, Wolfe. I don't blame you completely. But others aren't so lenient. The new ones always have to learn. The rest of us are smart enough to stay out of dodge and follow the rules," she said, standing to leave.

Fuck. You. Wolfe thought to himself. His back was still burning. He laid his head against the edge of his cot. *Was this all my fault? I had no choice.* Voices in his head argued with each other. *Scarier still. Would the other workers blame me?*

When Wolfe closed his eyes, he saw demons. Mr. Kelvington

was standing beside him, trying not to stare. The helper, the lover, and the saint standing idly as he was beaten. He saw now, for the first time, how little help he had.

How can you treat people like this, beat them, and still import more every month to do the same? How can you feel okay about that? Unless you look at the men, women, and children before you and see not people but ants to kill and keep subjugated. Something to play with, have fun with, make money off, and then discard.

Then his mind moved to Craik. *What did he mean? Is he alive? What if he's dead?* If Wolfe was alive when he woke up, he would go find him. *I must,* he told himself. Wolfe felt his head throb with each new thought as he fought against sleep. Slowly, he was losing the battle. Then there was that woman. *How did she know my name?*

It's not your fault. You're okay. One more day. Wolfe repeated this mantra in his head until a restful sleep took him for the first time in weeks.

Chapter 9

Reconfiguration

It had been a month.

After the Festival, life had gone downhill on the plantation.

The work had gotten harder, and the days grew longer. Wolfe picked stones and weeds until the tips of his fingers bled, dipped his hands into cleaning solution until the lines on his hands split, heaved hundred-pound boxes until he'd rather die than move again. Yet still, they watched him. A break warranted a beating; a breath deserved a punishment.

The nightmares were worse. Short, dark figures uttered broken words, chased Wolfe through bushes in the dark, and threatened his family's life. He dreamt of his brother, his father, and his friends that had been lost. They were all faces, watching him sleep. He dreamt of the woman last night. It was her and him alone, standing in darkness as she called out to him.

"Wolfe. Wolfe. Wolfe," she called his name repeatedly until it had consumed his mind, and there was nothing to picture but himself. *What did she want?* The question plagued him.

Wolfe had sought her and found her body outside. Nine days ago, Kendal had refused to work, overcome with the loss of her closest friend. As punishment, the guards took her and her children outside and sold her kids off to some slimy-looking buyer from Argentina. She still refused to work, then refused to eat. They had tied her beside the steps and released her from her teeth. They saved her from death with bowl after bowl of nourishing stew. Still she refused.

Wolfe saw her every day on his way to the gardens, swinging from the bows of the lumbering oak where they had executed her. *Where is the devil?* Where is the fire and brimstone, the cavernous hell where men boiled in pee and had pitchforks raked over them forever?

Wolfe sat in the sunlight during his break, resting his side against the bark of a tree. A few weeks ago, the new workers had arrived to replace the murdered workers from the Midsummer Night's Festival, and Mr. Kelvington had led them in their circles around the yard with the same cheery expression he had worn for them. He dreamed of them, Scott and Arcola, staring at him from their dark cabin.

He hadn't heard a word from anyone. Not from Craik. Not from Arcola. Deep purple, bulging scabs ran lengths down his back, pulling against the scratchy fabric of his shirt, aggravating his sores. He fought the urge to scratch.

As the weeks rolled together into their familiar blur, he grew indignant. *All of this for money?* There will always be more. More land. More money. More power. More, more, more. It would be endless. He wished people would call them what they were. *Slaves.*

Wolfe looked up at the sky. The air was softer this morning; the wind was warmer; the sky was bluer. Sunlight caressed the sores across his face, rubbing them into nothingness. When Mrs. Bredenbury returned from town, he heard her guests talk about the sky.

"It used to be brown, you know. It was God's punishment because we let Lucifer's mutation overwhelm us. Now, until we've had two thousand years of brown-eyed dominance, we have to stare at the blue sky as a reminder of our hubris," one of their constantly revolving guests told her as they climbed the incline towards their house.

"Oh?" Mrs. Bredenbury responded, arching an eyebrow and smiling with a morbid fascination.

"It's true, my pastor told me. After Krydor fell to the Archians, during the Monoplatian Reconstruction, God turned the sky blue after fourteen days of suffering and raining hell." *How could they be so dumb?* He wondered. *Mutations.* That's all blue-eyed people were to them.

"But of course, the house cost only a few hundred million credits to fix up, but what's a few hundred million?" Mrs. Brednebury laughed as she led her guests up towards the house, and they laughed with her. Wolfe watched them flick their eyes back at each other with a rise of envy, staking out everything they could try and take into their own little lives.

"It's exquisite…"

"How do you get the wood grain so shiny."

"Who do you use as your contractor?" They devoured the manor with gluttonous eyes.

Guards rumbled across the grounds in trucks, and two women Wolfe had never seen before stepped out, following Mr. Bredenbury around the side of the house. Craik must have died. *How did he die?* A wave of guilt overcame him.

"All workers, please come to the front porch for a very important announcement. Thank you," a voice spoke through the speakers around the edge of the house, all of which Wolfe was unaware existed. He pushed himself to his feet and set off through the yard. They stood in rows a few minutes later, their feet slowly aching into the overwatered green grass. The two women from the Midsummer Night's Festival hung on either side of the step, bare torsos growing plump and heavy in the summer heat.

On the porch stood Mrs. and Mr. Bredenbury.

Mrs. Bredenbury stood tall beside her husband. She was wearing a long pair of black velvet pants that grew larger around the ankles and swung over her strapped heels, and a brown matte shirt with golden trim that matched her lipstick. She glittered with golden and onyx jewellery, black and gold bracelets, earrings, rings, and a dark wooden cross, flecked with pieces of stone and gold, hung shallow between her breasts. She wore a half-smile, and her eyes flickered over them all, watching.

Mr. Bredenbury was wearing a pair of black loafers and soft brown khakis the colour of iced coffee or sun-tanned wood. He wore a polo shirt, three buttons undone and rolled up past his elbows. He had a pair of sunglasses pressed into his graying, greasy hair, and he was holding his wife's hand. Her diamond ring was biting into his palm's soft, sweaty flesh, and a line of sweat hung off his wrinkled forehead. He too was smiling.

On either side of them stood the house overseers. To his immediate right was Mr. Kelvington wearing nothing out of the ordinary. His head was turned down towards a tablet, but he flicked his eyes up and over, behind his shoulder, and into the crowd every few seconds. He was sure never to look even close to where Wolfe stood. Further to his right stood Dr. Wolseley, dressed in a pair of jeans and a t-shirt, standing out like a sore thumb with groggy, pinched eyes.

Looking over his face brought back the memories of his shaking head. No, he had tried to tell Wolfe while he dripped burgundy, splattered with muscle. Even though he spent most of his time in his cabin, he made his presence known. He was notoriously picky and doled out the nastiest punishments. He did the medical examinations, and on his suggestion, the Bredenbury family sold or kept workers. He had gotten Kendal's children sold to the smoked, greasy man from Argentina.

Past the doctor, the Mechanical Overseer was standing as dumpy as usual, with his dirty hands and greasy, bald head. The House Overseer, Mrs. Briercrest, was the same short, plump woman who sat behind her little desk every day. The Grounds Overseer, Miss. Eve was a severe-looking woman with a short neck and slow, mournful eyes that watched everything with an iron scowl. The Field Overseer was a shorter, rounder woman, built like an acorn. She shifted her weight back and forth gently, watching over them with an inattentive stare. Her eyes turned upwards, watching the clouds cover them in shadows every few minutes.

Mr. Bredenbury cleared his throat, pulling everyone's eyes towards him. Wolfe noticed the group had swollen, edging down the road and onto the grass in the front yard. They had called the fieldworkers in for the announcement.

"What the fuck is going on…" Wolfe heard a voice whisper. It felt like they were standing on the edge of a giant cliff with a horde of wild animals behind them, ready to push them forward before anyone even had a chance to beg. Wolfe was digging his heels into the dirt, bracing for impact.

"My dear workers!" he began, throwing his arms open with the sickly sweet smile Wolfe had become all too familiar with. "I have exciting news!"

Mrs. Bredenbury shifted beside her husband. Wolfe noticed she was several inches taller than him.

"I know that a lot of you here feel that you've been treated too harshly. Trust me, we are listening and understanding of your pleas." He paused for emphasis before continuing.

"I know few of you like me. As far as I know, all of you feel that I, and my family are too harsh to gentile workers such as yourselves. I would like to tell you, sincerely, I appreciate your input and want to move forward from here. Together," he said, stepping forward.

"We understand—" blurted Mrs. Bredenbury, stepping up beside her husband."—that there have been issues on both sides of the aisle, and we would like to step across. This is our gift to you, from us. To show our fair workers that isn't one-sided, we stomp out rebellion and injustice from all sides, whether it's your fellow workers or ours."

They both smiled again, sharing a few hot, sticky breaths between them. *Where is Arcola?* Wolfe asked himself as his breathing sped up. She should be up there, standing beside her husband and Mr. Bredenbury.

"My entire family strives for perfection. And while I know that we can be strict, we have a plan to help you all in this regard, along with a few words of wisdom, if we may. The harder you work, the better the reward. You can all live in the laps of luxury if you work hard and maintain loyalty to our cause," he said, smiling a wider smile if possible, showing lines of pink gums above and below boiled white teeth.

Out of a side pocket, he pulled a tiny metal blip and held it in his hand. It was no larger than a grain of salt but it dazzled. A breath fell over the crowd and a sombre gasp pushed through the crowd like a cool wind, rattling over reeds. Then, as quickly as it came, the breeze of whispers stopped, and silence sunk over them.

"These are your upgrades. We're about to get a shipment in for the first of August when the newest round of workers arrive. Truly a feat of engineering. Thanks to the testing of our Mechanical Overseer, Mr. Watson, with this tiny implant, we can now maximize productivity and time management," Mrs. Bredenbury said.

"Coupled with a new guard system and food rations, life here is going to get a lot more stable." Mr. Bredenbury walked across the porch, letting the tiny piece of metal glitter and prance in his hand, glimmering in the summer sun.

Mrs. Bredenbury smiled, stepping front and centre again. Wolfe watched her wide red lips spell out and speak over glimmering white teeth with her hands clasped together. Every time she moved her heavy black hair, rich with perfumes and oils, over her shoulders, she shook her arms, her golden jewellery clattering up and down her arms.

"—a new level of peace of mind for every worker here. You will no longer have to fear for your safety, nor will you have to worry about missing your quotas, as the chips will ensure you fulfill and surpass them every day. You won't have to worry about insubordination because the chips won't allow you to make decisions that break any rules!" she said, smiling out before the crowd.

Wolfe noticed guards closing in with tablets in hand.

"We expect everyone to get chipped by August first at the latest. Please talk to Mrs. Briercrest downstairs to consider inoculation possibilities. Thank you." Mrs. Bredenbury stepped back and let Mr. Bredenbury take front and centre again

The world shifted on its foundation. Just a smidgen, just an iota. But it was there, the balance of power was changing, and soon there would be no balance. There would be overlords and fleas.

"Now, for what we promised. Accountability from our side.

And how far we will go to sponsor equality. We will also welcome two new positions into our ranks here. Please help me welcome Mrs. Ester and Mrs. Hazy, the new Guard Overseer and Kitchen Overseer, respectively."

The two women Wolfe had seen earlier moved around the side of the house. They held polite smiles and a gentle exterior. The first woman was massive, taller, more muscled, and heavier than Wolfe, without a doubt. She trod carefully but walked with high shoulders and a bulging chest with the silver badge pinned to her chest. She climbed two steps at once and, with a swift movement, shook Bredenbury's hands and stepped into position beside a taller, larger Dr. Wolseley. Then the Kitchen Overseer did the same.

Wolfe felt a pit empty in his stomach. Wolfe scanned each face on the porch. No one faltered. Smiles where there should have been smiles, applause when there should have been applause.

"Now onto the main event. Mrs. Ester, the honours?" Mr. Bredenbury stepped away from the door and materialized a thin black pistol, quaint and delicate like lace. He rested it in her hands, and she smiled, a mouth full of crooked teeth.

"After you ma'am…" he said.

The doors behind them fell open, and a trail of men walked through the door. The crowd fell into a discomposed silence. They could hear their blood pounding through each other's ears, feel their heartbeats through the ground, and feel their lungs swell and collapse. Grasshoppers paused on their blades of grass to watch. The wind held its breath. The sky leaned its face down over them.

The guards led eleven bodies out of the house and into a line at the base of the porch. They pulled off their white hoods stained with blood. The first was the former Guard Overseer who had spoken to Mr. Kelvington on the steps when they arrived, the other being the Kitchen Overseer with a broken nose and a collection of faces from around the grounds and plantation. Brown-eyed cooks, cleaning boys, and valets, all trembling with terror.

"You may begin," Mr. Bredenbury said. A delicate glass table slathered with food materialized as they sat down to lunch on the porch. Wolfe smelled it from here, and it turned his stomach. *How can they eat?* A server brought out a platter of pears stewed in spiced honey, then a platter of cold soups and sandwiches, then a coffee and a tea for both of them. They poked and prodded their food with grace as Mrs. Ester read the crimes slowly and with pleasure.

"—insubordination—"

"—conspiracy to destroy private property—"

"— conspiracy to commit insurrection."

"—domestic terrorism—"

Mrs. Ester let the words slip down her tongue, savouring their pain.

"Please don't do this…" the Guard Overseer begged, his eyes glassy, his voice barley a whisper.

"Govan? Govan, what's happening?" a voice yelled across the grounds.

All at once, the crowd turned towards the source of the yell. A woman had burst from her cabin in slippers and an off-grey sweatshirt filled with holes, her hair flailing behind her as she crossed the yard.

"Stay with the kids!" Govan yelled back. Wolfe had never heard his first name before, nor had he seen his wife. As she ran, a handful of kids streamed backwards from their cabin and onto the grass. They were bawling while they watched her mother run.

—BANG—

The sound of a gunshot cracked the sky, shaking birds from the trees. The sound echoed across the walls and into the willows. It sank into the earth, muffled against the ground, holding the noise for the rest of time.

Somewhere a woman was bawling and clutching her chest.

"No. Please." She was numb, trying to fight back, but her eyes had been varnished. Her feet were kicking aimlessly as she was drug next to her husband, thrown away without hesitation.

—BANG—

Wolfe heard kids crying somewhere. Their cries were angelic, high, and wispy. Dazzling in their clarity. Wolfe looked up from the scene, over the house and at the sky. The sun was out again, bathing the back of his neck in warmth. *What a day to die.*

—BANG— —BANG— —BANG—

The crying stopped.

"They have been propagandized. They would have continued doing their parents' work. They are as guilty as the next, and there is nothing to be done. We all feared for our lives and we acted in self defence," Mr. Bredenbury said to them, not even bothering to look away from his soup.

It followed the same rhythm every time. Crimes. Begging. Silence.

—BANG—

Whispers. —BANG—

Questions. —BANG—

Begging. —BANG—

Wolfe looked away from the clouds and straight ahead. He studied the face of a boy in front of him, ringing with familiarity. His nose was twisted, his cheekbones bruised, and his eyes were closed. Every time a bullet shattered the silence, his lips trembled, but he stayed silent. He was covered with pimples, shaking in the heat.

His eyes flickered shut when the barrel was at his forehead. As they closed, tears breached the edges of his eyes and ran down his face. They gathered in the slightly trembling cracks beside his lips, hung like yarn along his cheeks, and slid between the bruised dents along his jawline. Wolfe refused to look away. When the boy opened his eyes one last time, he wasn't alone. He and Wolfe were together, and Wolfe tried to force a faltering smile.

—BANG—

—BANG— —BANG— —BANG— —BANG —BANG—

It was music. A twisted subversion of a song. A muttering of words in the choir. The crack was a reverberation. That's all music was after all. The noise was music; music was noise. So this was a waltz, a tango, an opera. The symphony fell on deaf ears.

"I hope you enjoy the rest of your day!" Mr. Bredenbury cried as he shattered an egg with the back of a spoon. A dozen of them were laying on the ground like lumber, all perfectly straight, sticking out like teeth below the porch. Somehow Wolfe didn't feel as bad as he should have. *At least it wasn't me.* He thought. *Why shouldn't they suffer every once in a while?*

Wolfe wandered back towards the edge of the yard, and finally, something fell into place. He'd spent almost two months here in a storm. A storm of feelings, fear, and wonderment at the horror encircling him, and he was no safer every day than the day before. *That boy, he'd thought he was safe. He had undoubtedly followed every rule, and still, he was dead.* There was no innocence, and there was no guilt. There were only impediments to the family's constant march for money and power. That's all it was. There was unimpeded progress, or there were obstructions to be smashed. Blue. Brown. Green. It didn't matter.

There will never be freedom.

Once he was out of sight, Wolfe slid into the edges of the property. He crawled over the vines, over the arched limbs of trees, and around the edge of the property until he was staring at Mr. Kelvington's cabin. Death was coming. If he stayed in the barracks and followed every rule, the end would still come. So instead, he put one foot up towards the door and knocked. He had to see Arcola again.

Mr. Kelvington alone opened the door, and as he went to close the door, Wolfe held it open with his shoulder. Wolfe watched Mr. Kelvinton's neck strain, his eyes boiling with rage. As he turned for his tablet, Wolfe followed him into the house.

He towered above him, tablet in hand. Wolfe closed his eyes

and took a deep breath.

"Do it then," Wolfe said, as he felt a lump in his throat catch his voice. The searing never started, and when he opened his eyes, he was staring into Mr. Kelvington's. Wolfe was ready to die, but he was done pretending. He was done with bowing.

"Get out," he hissed as tears formed at the corner of his eyes. His entire face was bloodshot; his eyes were boiled red around the corners. He'd been crying. His lip was shaking, and his head fell towards the floor when Wolfe spoke.

"No."

The door behind them swung shut, and Wolfe turned past him, walking through the house.

"Arcola!" he cried, pulling open kitchen cupboards.

"Wolfe," he said. It was the first time he'd heard him use his name like that, and shivers ran down his back. The way he hissed the F, the way he tried to command him with his own name. Wolfe turned to him sitting on the couch, rubbing his hands over a trembling face.

"Scott," Wolfe hissed back, watching him decay. His facade was crumbling around him, leaving him naked in front of Wolfe. Wolfe felt his pulse freeze in his wrist, and blood roared up through his neck. His eyes fluttered, and he already knew she was gone. There was no need to look for her. Arcola wasn't here.

"It's your fault! You did this!" When he yelled, it shook the ceiling and cracked the ground beneath them. Wolfe hoped the earth would open up and suck them down. *Why do I never get to say goodbye?* Sadness turned to rage.

"How is this my fault? How is any of this my fault? I didn't ask to be here. I don't have a choice. I go where I'm sent!" Wolfe yelled. He didn't care if anyone heard; he didn't care if anyone listened to them. *Let them.*

Scott spit against the floor and beat the wall with his fists. "You came here, you got seen, and *she* got sent away? If she dies, you killed her!" he screamed.

"Maybe if you'd helped her, maybe if you'd let us see each

other, I wouldn't have needed to come. Maybe you could have stopped us if you weren't fucking a child out on the lawn!" Wolfe cried, his heart breaking with each new word. He slumped his head against the wall, sliding down beside the couch and letting his tears water the fabric. It had been his fault; he had come to her, and they had seen him. *Why not me?* He asked.

Scott was silent now, but Wolfe could feel his fury. The tablet slipped out of his hand and onto the floor beside him. He could hear his breathing, heard him slump down beside him, and felt the change of pressure in the room. They were snorting and gasping, trying to hold back the tears that were coming. Together, they were alone.

Wolfe turned and looked at him: his eyes were fluttering, catching and flinging tears into a mist. They streaked his face, and his chest rose and fell sporadically. His bare skin shone with sweat beneath beams of sunlight.

Seeing Scott shudder, sniffing back the trail of tears, possessed Wolfe. *It wasn't fair.* Not to Wolfe, not to Scott. W*hy does it all have to be so hard?* He turned towards him and rested his arm on his leg. Wolfe just wanted to feel skin, feel warmth, feel something.

Scott went rigid for a moment, then he sunk into his touch. He pushed himself closer, just enough so that their sides touched. Wolfe tilted his head back and rolled it onto Scott. They sat forever. Eons passed. Souls were born and died, lives were loved and lost, the world kept spinning, and they were left together. Neither of them spoke. They sat there quiet and alone, dealing with their losses in their alien world together.

"You know I loved her…" he said, finding the strength to toss out a few shaky words, sniffing again.

"She knows," Wolfe choked. "She did say she thought you were an asshole, though…" Wolfe said, sniffing back tears and rubbing at his eyes.

Scott snorted, rubbing a stained cheek. "That too." His other hand found Wolfe's, and they laid there together, breathing in each other's scent. His sweat smelled like salted cedarwood, cloaked under a strong cologne. He felt Scott's fingerprints on the palm of his hand.

"I—I was so willing to change my life I'd've…I'd've married anyone, but she…God, she was amazing. She always told me off, which I thought was the funniest thing ever." He laughed, his chest still shaking with loss.

"I was scared and was alone. Arcola was there, and I…We got married within two weeks, got a house, got a dog, got jobs… We were happy. I worked for BESNA. She worked at a bookstore turned into a coffee shop, but we were trying." Wolfe could smell the aged paper, the roasted coffee beans cascading out of silver machines, and the murmur of lives beyond their own. "You're an uncle," Scott said, finally looking down at him. "He's staying at a boarding school. I don't know if they'll send him away like Arcola."

He stared down at Wolfe. His eyes were red, his cheeks still flushed. Wolfe saw a soul for the first time. He looked like a broken man, a mirror of himself. He pulled himself up by his neck and touched his lips to Scott's. Wolfe craved touch, craved love. Scott didn't stop him. Their lips quivered together for a moment, static dancing between their lips.

They sat there for a moment together, knowing that affairs between eye colours were illegal, refusing to care, knowing it would result in a castration for Scott and death for Wolfe. Somehow his touch numbed the pain a little. Wolfe buried himself into his chest, smelling of sweat and perfume, tangerines and earth. He kissed Wolfe again, then again, burying his hands in his filthy hair before pushing him off.

"I'm not going to do this to Arcola. She was my wife. She deserves better than this. I mean…you're my brother-in-law for Christ's sake. I can't risk my life; I'm not going to die like this," he said suddenly, sliding out from under Wolfe. His voice grew louder with each word, rising until Wolfe winced with each statement.

"Scott…please," Wolfe tried to ask him, begging him. Wolfe hated himself. He loved how it had felt, loved how the monster made him feel. He just wanted to hear him say his name once more, tell him he wasn't alone. Scott was right. After all, Scott was his brother-in-law. *Why am I like this?* Wolfe cried to himself.

"Get out!" Scott tore at his own face, trying to pull out his eyes. He stretched his face, trying to grapple with his feelings. His demons fought inside him, moving and stretching him like a ball of putty.

Wolfe felt his own emotions sag him down. The air almost hardened in his lungs, making each breather harder to inhale or exhale. He felt a hurricane growing inside him, shame, loathing, sadness, hatred, anger, fear, disgust…*Why did I kiss him? Why didn't he stop me?* But even before he could be shoved out, he turned to him with teary eyes.

"Why didn't she throw me under the bus?"

"I don't know Wolfe, but I wish she had." He hissed his name again, sending ripples through Wolfe's stomach.

"So do I."

Scott shoved him out the door and down onto the grass. *Where did they take her?* Wolfe asked himself. He wandered for the rest of the day, and sadness transitioned to anger one last time. *I will not die here. I will take them all with me*, he told himself. Wolfe didn't know how, but the first of August loomed, and he would kill them all before then. They were all going to die.

Chapter 10

The Plan

Rumours had spun since the Midsummer Night's Festival nights a month earlier. Voices suggested someone, a lone man, a worker, had manufactured the assault against the family. The contact lenses. The Festival. Getting caught. It was all the work of 'the rat.' The man walked among them, watched them, and reported them to Mr. Bredenbury for every minor mistake. This figment of imagination grew more and more real by the day. The mole was among them somewhere.

Eyes turned towards Wolfe, slowly at first, then they asked him questions he couldn't answer.

"How did you survive?"

"Why were you the first to be punished?"

"Why did the party organizers pick you first?"

Now Wolfe was having blue-eyed people sold, separating families, and working in tandem with the Overseers. It was easier to blame Wolfe than to grapple with the godhood of the family above them. *People with no control in their lives found the strangest ways to gain a feeling of it*, Wolfe thought, even if it came with his own villainization.

The family had decided there was too much work to waste the Monday on resting, and Wolfe was on his third shift of the day. Despite the complaints of other workers, he didn't hate the garden. He enjoyed doing something, feeling the churning black soil beneath his fingers. He felt at home, away from the reeking chemical stench of cleaning products.

He had filled a large basket with carrots and weeded a long spindly row of plump peas, bursting in their soft green sleeping bags, when he heard the soft rustle of grass in front of him.

Someone was coming from his right. He kept his eyes low and waited until he could see the shoes in his peripheral vision. Worker's shoes. He took the rare risk, and he glanced up.

A woman, probably in her mid-thirties, walked past him. She was taller than Wolfe, with a long, lanky torso. Her clothes looked saggy on her, probably a size too big. When Wolfe moved his head up, her eyes flickered down on him, and her electric blue eyes met Wolfe's. He watched a boy, comfortably into his pre-teen years, walk in front of her. He wore dark black circles beneath his eyes, his lids dipping with each step, his hands buried in his pockets. A third pair of boots followed them, and Wolfe flicked his eyes back down into the dirt as the guard passed.

His face was familiar. Wolfe had seen that boy before. He closed his eyes to imagine them. *Did she glare at me?* At the Midsummer Night's Festival, the kid was playing on the grand piano. Wolfe remembered Mrs. Bredenbury trembling with glee when she'd spoken about him.

"As gifted as blue-eyed children can be," she had said, "from a long line of brown eyes I've found." Wolfe felt his neck buzz, and all the workers in the garden moved towards the barracks. Wolfe stood on his toes to search a group of workers leaving the Quonset at the back of the yard. He couldn't spot Craik among them.

Wolfe sank into a dark corner to nurse his food as people around him pawed at it like starving beasts or pushed it around like hospice patients. He couldn't bring himself to eat it, so he slid the tray onto the nearest garbage can and walked past the whispering voices into the hallways towards the barracks. He slid a steak knife up his arm beneath his sleeve and felt a rush of heat. *Am I going to do this?*

"Have you seen C.T Bredenbury? Craik?" Wolfe asked a group of mechanics coming down the steps looking as full of dread as Craik had the day of the Festival.

"Craik? He went to the barracks," one of them said, looking sadly at Wolfe.

Wolfe turned and moved deeper into the heart of the

barracks.

"Have you seen Craik Bredenbury?" he asked a group of young women standing near the exit towards the guardhouse. They shook their heads but stared at him with distrust. Wolfe turned, walked back to Mrs. Briercrest's desk and asked her.

"Is there a reason you needed to speak with him?" she asked, smiling up from her desk, her mouth hanging slightly askew.

"No," Wolfe lied. In truth, he had a plan. And he was going to take Craik with him. Wolfe was past the common room when his neck buzzed, signalling another shift. The laundry room.

"Another shift? I've worked three shifts already. Come on!" he yelled at nothing. *Fuck it.* Wolfe sat down in the hallway, waiting for the end. He was done. In a few days, they'd chip him, and his mind wouldn't be his own. He'd be a puppet, a machine. At the very least, he didn't plan on giving himself up that easily for free labour.

What can they do? He asked himself. Torture me? Kill my friends? My family? He had no family. Craik was probably dead. Scott had thrown him out of his house. *There is no escape. I'd have rather died in the fields.* He sat there in the hallway for fifteen minutes, waiting for the end, but it never came. He was just sitting in a hallway under flickering fluorescent lights talking to himself.

Fine. If they weren't going to kill him, he wasn't going out without a fight. Every time he blinked, Mr. Bredenbury's dark eyes blinked back at him. If he was going to go, he would take him with him. *What will his face look like at the end?* Wolfe smiled to himself as he imagined. *Heaven.*

"Wolfe?"

"Craik?"

Craik was standing in the hallway in front of Wolfe. He had lost probably fourty pounds, and every bone on his face was pulled over a thin layer of skin. A scar was torn across his face, and one of his eyes was replaced with a white, glassy ball. Wolfe looked down his body and saw that Craik had five metal fingers sticking off a prosthetic arm beneath his sleeve.

"What happened? What did they do to you?" Wolfe cried.

Craik wrapped his arms around Wolfe and buried his face in his neck. Wolfe froze before wrapping his own arms around Craik's back. Wolfe knew Craik could feel the scars through the back of Wolfe's shirt.

"The Festival," was all he said, and Wolfe didn't ask anything else. "They're gonna get those chips in us and…we're gonna be as good as dead. What's the point Wolfe? I just wanted to propose to my girlfriend." A tear fell from his working eye, and Wolfe scanned the hallway for listening voices.

"Listen to me. A guard comes through the barracks every fourty-five minutes or so. Tonight, after supper I stole a steak knife…" Wolfe smiled at Craik, pulling the blade down from his sleeve, glinting in the fluorescent light. "…and I'm taking it to bed with me. When the guard passes, I'm going to jump him, kill him, and take his tablet. After that, I can disable our chips, and we can sneak upstairs and slit Mr. Bredenbury's throat. His bitch wife too. Then we can run away, we'd be free Craik!" The idea of having to kill a guard made him pause, but he pushed the thought aside.

I have to do this.

"That's fucking insane Wolfe. Guards are patrolling the grounds like locusts. There has to be three guards for every one worker, all walking in groups of three at least, seven at most. For the first time since we've gotten here, there are BESNA officers out there. What happens when they find us missing and re-enable our chips and we've passed the boxes?"

"We can dig the chips out with the knife."

"What?"

He's right. Mr. Bredenbury must be anticipating fallout over the new chips in two days and called in reinforcements. Shit. Fuck.

"Now what though? We have to try, don't we? We'll be as good as dead if they get those chips in us."

"But I'm alive still. Maybe I'll get back to my girlfriend. But I can't just kill myself."

Wolfe's neck buzzed again in warning.

"I'll come find you tonight after my shift."

"You have a shift tonight?"

"Yeah, right now," Wolfe said, tilting his head towards the laundry room behind Craik. "I'll find you tonight."

"Wolfe. Leave me out of it."

"Craik, please." But Craik was turning to walk away.

Wolfe pulled the door into the laundry room open and let it shut as quietly as possible, his conversation with Craik playing in his head. The walls hummed with washers and dryers, colossal fabric carts were filled with soiled white sheets, stained clothes lay around the floor in heaps, and dirtied upholstery was hung along the wall. An entire side of the room was lined with cleaning products that reeked enough to give Wolfe a headache.

"About fucking time…" a woman said, her back turned to him. "We've already packed the cart," another said. When they turned, Wolfe smiled at the woman he'd seen this afternoon and at another woman he had never met before.

"Fuck you," the shorter woman said, stepping into Wolfe's space. She was shorter than Wolfe, and she had wide, furious eyes and a curled lip. Her fingers were knobbly, and her cheeks were splayed with rows of tiny sunken spots.

"Unity, you're gonna get blown up. Let's just get going," the woman said, wrapping her hands in yellow gloves.

"Really, Sandy?" Unity cried out. She was livid, contorting into a gargoyle. She pulled her hair around her face beside her, pointing a long finger at him.

"You walked the entire serving group right into the lion's den. You got them all whipped."

"That wasn't my fault."

"Like hell it wasn't!"

"What makes that my—"

"Shhhh," Sandy said to them. "Let's get to work."

"No! He got your son beaten," she said.

"Unity. Let it go," she said, glaring at him.

"No, don't let it go. Tell me how it's all my fault again, lay it all out, make it make sense," Wolfe snarled as they pushed their cart back down the hallway and towards the schedule list, only to find they were cleaning the Overseer's cabins.

They heaved the cart, maybe sixty pounds of metal and plastic, back down the hallway, as Unity ranted. As they walked, a surge of BESNA officers dressed in black came around the corner. Their golden visors were up, and their faces were alive with laughter.

Wolfe turned his gaze to his shoes as their grating, high-pitched voices echoed against the walls.

"Hey, look!" one of them said.

"Cleaners! I've always found those are the ones who never spill a drop. Isn't that right, beautiful?" he said to Sandy.

"Look at that ass, what a fucking MILF!" another one yelled, grabbing his crotch and making barking noises that dissolved them into jarring laughter again. Wolfe prayed they didn't see him, pressed against the wall behind Unity.

"Wait, is that a guy? I didn't know they even bought fags. Imagine being a mutt and a faggot. Life really kicked you in the fucking teeth huh buddy?" Wolfe kept his eyes on the floor, watching the tiles move with each step.

"Hey, sweetie," one of them said to Unity. "Might have to rent you off Mr. Bredenbury for a night. What do you say? Are you still a virgin with tits like that, or are you a common whore?" he said, smacking her ass as they walked by. They listened to their voices follow them down the end of the hall.

"Disgusting," Unity said, spitting a glob of spit onto the floor behind them as they walked. "Bet those were one of your pals, huh? They just pretend not to know you while you're on the job," Unity snarled at him.

"Would you ever shut up?" Wolfe snapped.

"Not if I'm right. Besides—" Unity said before Wolfe cut her off.

"Do you hear yourself? What would be the point of getting myself whipped within an inch of my life? Wouldn't that make you think I was just a victim like everyone else?" When Wolfe thought of Craik, his eyes got misty.

"I—" she began as they entered the yard.

They weaved their way through the gardens. The air was still muggy and hot, but there was a coolness and the smell of rain. They walked through the long stretches of grass. Wolfe let his eyes glide shut. The sun was bulging in the western sky, sinking and dragging the dark veil of the night behind it. Arching shadows spread out across the lawn as they walked towards the far edge of the property. Along the south side, backed into the wooded edge strung around the yard, were the homes for the Overseers in order of rank; the Kitchen Overseer, the House Overseer, the Field Overseer, the Medical Overseer, the Guard Overseer, Mechanical Overseer, and the Administrative Overseer.

———

They cleaned until the sun had set. The first houses were simple, nothing out of the ordinary. Then they stepped into the Doctor's cabin. They were left spinning by how clean it was. There was not a dish to be washed; every blown glass trinket on the shelf shone and sparkled, and every framed photo and university degree was dusted into sharp edges. The entire house smelled of cinnamon and lemongrass. A black pistol peeked out from underneath a stack of papers with a pile of eight bullets, and Wolfe's stomach lurched.

They were so engrossed they barely heard the front door open behind them. When Wolfe, Unity, and Sandy came back together in the living room, they stared at Dr. Wolseley standing in the kitchen. His back was turned to them as he set down a pile of handwritten notes and a briefcase. He checked his watch, turning around and staring at them.

"Already?" he said to himself, more than them. As he walked past, they stepped out of his way, and he locked himself in the bathroom as the showerhead started hissing.

They left, moving on to the next house, and a group of men grumbled outside. It reeked of smoke, and thick black tar clung to the ceiling. The room was shattered; life had been torn apart.

Children's books were strewn across the floor, tablets were still humming, and stuffed animals were sitting on the floor where they'd been abandoned. The entire building reeked of smoke. The wallpaper was off-colour, and the pillows had turned gray.

They came out hacking and coughing, and a woman was standing in the group.

"What were you doing in there?" Mrs. Ester, the new Guard Overseer, barked. "There were no lights on."

"We—sorry ma'am," Sandy said.

"Name?"

"Sandy. Bredenbury, ma'am."

"Well, I know your last name, Jesus. The building will have to be demolished, don't bother, continue on." She had the foulest face Wolfe had ever seen, twisted into a supremely disdainful mess.

The Mechanical Overseer's cabin was filthy. Layers of grime clung to the mountains of dishes balanced like a curiosity act in the sink; Little dots of fly shit dotted the window, and the smell of garbage and unwashed clothes hung like smoke. Over the next two hours, the three of them cleaned it back to its luminous shine, exhaustion dripping from their pores.

After they'd finished, they stepped up to the door of the Administrative Overseer's cabin. Shadows moved in front of the walls inside; they heard the sound of breath through the thin door. Wolfe tried not to act strange. It was just Mr. Kelvington, even if he had kissed him on the floor, smelled his skin, and dreamt of him; obviously, it meant nothing. His lips were still etched in Wolfe's memories, and the fire Scott had set burnt his insides.

Wolfe knocked.

The constant pressure in their necks faded away. The door was flung open. Wolfe saw the outline of a man before the lights disappeared, and groping hands pulled them into the darkness.

The lights were off, the curtains drawn shut, and the door was locked and bolted with a flick of a wrist on glass tablets. Sandy, Unity, and Wolfe stared from one side of the room. On the other, the Administrative Overseer, the Medical Overseer, and the

Mechanical Overseer stared back. Eyes blinked in the pitch-black room.

"Listen," Scott said, standing in the room's corner, chewing strips off around his fingernails. A tumble of words, some without form, most without meaning, fell from Sandy's, Unity's, and Wolfe's mouths. A cluster of "Buts" and "Ums."

"No, I said listen…" Scott said. "We're going to escape."

From the outside, there was just a strip of empty houses. A shiny silver cleaning cart stood alone under a nearly non-existent moon, glimmering like diamonds and spider eyes in the darkness.

Chapter 11

The Plan Part II

Their eyes shone in the dark. The Mechanical Overseer's eyes rolled like dewy marbles back and forth in large swipes from window to window, curtain to curtain, person to person. The doctor's eyes were slicked with veneer as he sucked on his knuckle, his hand folded over his face. His hair was still wet and shiny. His eyes drooped with exasperation, but his tapping leg and nervous, darting movements told a different story.

"Here's how it is," Scott said, pulling up a chair for himself beside a glass of brown liquid, downing it in three gulps, and leaving it perspiring on the counter. "This is our plan, and you have to listen carefully."

"Why us?" Unity asked, interrupting him. There was hatred on her tongue as she stared at the three men in front of her.

"You happened to be with Wolfe when we gave him an extra shift tonight. We needed it to look normal."

"I knew you had something to do with this," Unity snapped.

"Maybe that would be the case if I didn't find out right now like you did."

This is a trap, Wolfe thought.

"My name is Scott Kelvington. These are my colleagues; Dr. Brieux Wolseley, the Medical Overseer, and Mr. Chester Watson, the Mechanical Overseer. We know you don't trust us, and I understand but…but we're trying to get everyone out of here."

"So?" Sandy said, speaking up with a tremble in her voice. "We all have names. I think it'd be safer for us if we reported you for conspiracy and escaped on our own." She moved towards the door, and the room tensed.

"You won't," Chester spoke from the table, his eyes still fixed on the manor on the hill. He smelled of stale motor oil, grease, and something metallic and cool.

"You underestimate us," Sandy said, with her hand on the doorknob.

"You overestimate yourselves," he said faintly. He turned and looked at them. "If you saw the executions as well as I did, you will recall the chips. My workers and I expected to spend weeks preparing them and fixing their flaws. There are none. You will be under the complete control of the Bredenburys within a day."

"Well, I guess we'll—" Unity began before being cut off.

"No. You won't. The chips you have in your shoulders are the biggest impediment towards your freedom, and these new ones will be a thousand times worse."

"An impediment I am almost certain I can remove," Dr. Wolseley piped up, standing up, hands out, begging. He had an accent, a guttural, throaty inflection that pulled apart his words in one language and put them back together in another. "Please, just let us explain. We want to get out of here too."

"Why?" Sandy asked. "You guys have it good. Money. Power. Control. Why would you want to run away? Why risk your necks for absolutely no reason?" She held herself against the wall, her eyes flickering between Wolfe and the others.

"Listen, and we'll tell you," Scott said.

All six of them shared a glance, plastered into the tiny room with nothing but opinions, a half-baked plan, and a deadline of twenty-four hours.

Dr. Wolseley spoke first.

"Over the last four months, I have been smuggling tiny amounts of topical anesthetic. Thanks to Chester—" Dr. Wolseley gave him a half-smile and a nod. "—I have been able to study the positioning of the chips, and I am certain I can remove them without causing permanent damage."

"So…you can get these out of us?" Unity asked.

"Yes. I think so."

"We have about eleven workers who know this is going to

happen. We had the Guard Overseer, but that's obviously no longer the case," Scott said.

"How'd they find out?" Unity asked, a flare of suspicion flashing across her eyes with every question.

"That I don't know. I can only guess that grayson kept his mouth shut, or we'd be dead by now. The Kitchen Overseer knew nothing, and all the brown-eyed employees weren't in on it. As far as I know, it was just him," Scott said. A moment of silence came over them. Darting eyes slid around the room together.

"We have an advantage then, don't we?" Unity said, pushing herself away from the wall. "If Mr. Bredenbury figured there was going to be a revolt, he thinks he's stamped it out, yes?" Unity smirked.

"Yes, she's right," Dr. Wolseley said, mulling it over.

"But what is the plan?" Sandy asked again.

"Right." Scott pulled out the thin, glass tablet from his inner pocket, and it flashed. He turned it towards them. "These tablets tell every officer, guard, and overseer on the plantation where every worker is at any given time: what they are doing, where they are going, etcetera. Any Overseer or guard with clearance here on the plantation can access it and override the system." He zoomed in over the workers' barracks with a flick of his wrist and showed white dots by the names of Sandy, Unity, and Wolfe milling around the laundry room.

"That's…" Sandy started to say

"Horrific," Wolfe finished.

"That's the only reason you're here. The day after tomorrow, when the new chips come, they're changing the operating system. A system Chester isn't certain we can work around," Scott said, looking toward him.

"No, I'm certain I can't work around it. This is Space Program, Intelligence Agency shit. We won't be able to do anything."

"So it's tomorrow or never?" Wolfe asked.

"Exactly," Dr. Wolseley said.

Wolfe's heart was pounding out of his chest. He felt anxious energy building from his ankles up to his collarbone. He wanted to scream, jump, vibrate, break something, do *something*.

"Tomorrow night, after dinner, I will remove chips in the common room. If the cooks and the Kitchen Overseer aren't with us, we will have to deal with them. I can get through the workers, with a few helpers, by eleven. Three hours."

"Wait. There's so much more than that. How do we stop the guards from stumbling across us and frying everyone?" Wolfe asked.

"How are we going to fight back against pistols and large pointy zappers?" Unity asked.

"And what about the people?" Sandy asked. "No one is going to go for this. People are going to get brutalized. My son is in that house with them. What about him?"

"Sandy is right. No one is going to show up. And what happens when someone snitches on us?" Wolfe asked, pacing back and forth between the couch and the counter.

"Whoa. One at a time, guys. We'll get there," Scott said. "Chester?"

Chester leaned away from the wall, and with the hints of a devilish smile flashing across his lips, he spoke. "Unity raised a good point. They're not expecting this. They think they've caught the rebellion, and they did in part, but not enough of us. grayson knew the guard layouts to a tee, and every fourty minutes, on the dot, a new rotation of guards will come into the barracks. So after that, we have to distract them with something else."

"Like what?"

"A fire," he responded.

"Where?"

"In one place it would hurt most. The guardhouse. It would cut down on the guards and cause enough confusion and panic that Dr. Wolseley could remove the last of the chips. People would forget about us for a few hours, and when they come back from fighting fires, they have an armed rebellion on their hands and half the guards to fight it." The guardhouse had grown to have an almost superstitious quality about it. No one dared go near its black plastic windows or its slanted tin roof.

"Armed? With what? Sticks and kitchen utensils?" Unity asked.

Scott leaned forward. "While I set fire to the guardhouse, Chester is going to rob the storehouse. It's rarely guarded, even normally. It'll be taken easily, especially by Chester. And with the guardhouse burnt, there won't be any electricity, which means they can't send out distress signals."

"Now, this is where you come in. Tomorrow your job is to spread the word to as many people as possible. Tell anyone who will listen." As Scott spoke, he ran his eyes up and down Wolfe's face.

"You never told us why, though," Sandy began, holding her arms wrapped around her chest. "You could retire in thirty years as the richest sons of bitches I've ever had the misfortune of running across. Why even stage this entire escape. You could have us shot and never think of this again."

The air was sucked from the room, and they were silent

Dr. Wolseley was the first to speak. "I can't speak for anyone else in this room, but I've had no other intentions. I need to do this, and I am going to try. I didn't think I would have to decide who lived or died, who got sold or not."

"I second that. If you guys want to stay here for Mr. Bredenbury to take his wrath out on you, be our guests. But everyone else here, the children digging mouldy bread and half eaten chicken out of the troughs with the dogs, the people who lost their family, everyone who's been hurt, they deserve a chance to make a run for it," Chester said, not moving. Not inching away or towards. A statue. A cold figure of stone in the corner of the room.

"For my wife. This is what she had wanted to do herself. I owe her that much," Scott said. Wolfe saw the memories of her in his eyes. "So. This is the plan. Get as many people down to the barracks by eight fifteen. The last of the guards should have gone through there by then. Within half an hour, emergency lights should come on; that's telling you to hurry up because the guardhouse is a fucking crater. With the electricity down, and the storehouse stormed, we should be ready to take the house, steal as much food and clothing as we can, before running for our lives."

"Okay. We have to try, right?" Sandy asked, her voice trembling. She was holding back tears. She was playing the scene of her son's death over in her mind, a constant reminder of what was at stake. "We have to get Lett out of that house."

"We will," Scott said, sucking on his fingernails.

"Craik. We have to get him too," Wolfe said suddenly.

"Who?"

"Uh. Craik, a friend from the city. He was so scared to get sent here, I can't leave him." He didn't mean friend, but it just fell out. He couldn't do it. He couldn't leave him here. *He didn't want to come, and I must have wished it into existence.* Wolfe imagined his missing arm and glassy eye and felt a wave of sickness wash him. His fear rested like steel chains in his stomach.

"We'll look Wolfe, don't worry."

"I'm still worried about getting the workers on our side," Unity said

"Still? They will come. You'll persuade them," Scott said dismissively. He was already standing up and peering at his watch.

"No, not for sure. The doct—"

"Call me Brieux. I'm not your master." He smiled.

"Brieux…God bless him—" she said, smiling at him, "—thinks he can do it. No one, no matter how beaten or broken, will sign up to be the first of a long line of experimental test dummies. Trust me, the easiest path will get followed every time."

"No, they—"

"No. They won't. Think about it for a second," she snapped.

"Overnight, we have to convince them to have a medical procedure, storm the house with weapons, and flee into the night to be brutally murdered if they're caught. That's a lot of ifs, ands, and buts."

Scott went to speak, indignation flaring across his lips.

"She's right Scott. I think I can do it, but what if I'm wrong? The entire operation is hinging on that. If those don't come out, we're dead in the water before we even get going."

Wolfe didn't even have to think about it. "I'll do it then. Test it on me, and if it fails, it fails, but if it works, I push everyone into action. Win win," he said, smiling them all into silence.

"Alright. Sandy and Unity. I need you guys to spread rumours. Only start with people you trust, then spread it out a little. Don't give names, just a location and a time. Wolfe, I'll go grab some tools."

Everyone nodded and gulped. Sandy and Unity slipped back towards the barracks, Chester and Scott went to a freshly cleaned cabin and planned their explosion of the guardhouse, Brieux went to find his briefcase, and Wolfe was left alone in a dark cabin.

—

Wolfe didn't know what to think, or to feel, or to pretend he felt. This wasn't his life. Certainly, he was in some sort of hell where the devil tempts you with what can never happen, only to rip it away at the last minute. Fifteen minutes ago, he was planning to attack a guard and slit Mr. Bredenbury's throat, and here he was, waiting to escape. Tomorrow night, they'd be free.

He walked through the thin hallway down towards the end of the house and into the bedroom. It looked untouched since Arcola had been here, like a mausoleum, a tomb just for her. Her slippers were still next to the bed, and her clothes were hanging on the mirror for the next day. Wolfe saw himself between brown lace and corduroy.

He stretched his arms, feeling the scars on his back fold and sway with him. He'd lost weight. His cheekbones were pointed, more wicked than they had ever looked before. His clothes were baggy on him, and his hair was filthy, matted to itself and dewy with sweat. He pulled open one of the closest windows, and felt the the breeze chill him. The air smelled of metal and stone. Rain was coming. A storm. Wolfe would welcome the relief from the heat. He laid down on the crisp bed, not slept in for weeks, and looked up at the ceiling fan, stiff and frozen.

When he was younger, he wanted to see the world. To pack food and a camera and run precisely southwest. Away from town, across the freeway, and down into whatever adventures lay before him. The lakes and rivers, the rippling hills of golden wheat in fall, and the silvery gray stubble in winter and spring. The buttery yellow hills would grin at him and flush gold as he passed.

He pulled himself up and moved down the hallway again, back into the living room. He flipped through some impoverished cabinets. The cutlery drawers held a single spoon, cup, knife, and fork. One bowl, one plate, one mug, and one glass. It was hard to think of Scott as married. It was hard to think of Scott as married to his sister, or…was…married to his sister.

Wolfe tried not to think about it. He would make his sister proud; he would not let her be forgotten like that. *It must be so hard to die,* he thought to himself. To look down the barrel of a gun and know, just know, that you're not going to make it. Who expects themselves to be the background characters, a name on a list somewhere with the J's or the B's or the M's or the F's

He pulled through the cupboards a little bit more. He found a heavy, dirty, well-used book behind a crumpled pile of dress shirts. He flipped it over, and the words 'the Order of Truth and Justice' beamed from the front. Scoffing, he tossed it back in the cupboard. He didn't know how Scott did this. The pretending. *It would kill me. There would be nothing worse.* He thought. Maybe that's why he is staging an escape, to go live somewhere away from *this*.

When Wolfe closed his eyes, he saw a house on the Mexican peninsula, staring over the Pacific every morning and night. He'd be an uncle to an army of little Scott's and Arcola's. He'd have fallen for a ranch hand; they'd kiss the nights away, and everyone would eat breakfast together in the morning. They'd be a family. He smiled to himself. Wolfe laid his head down on the couch and waited.

"I'm bored. I feel bored," he said aloud before smiling to himself again.

"What a luxury to be bored." He chuckled out loud.

Ten minutes later, the door opened again, and in came Brieux carrying a large brown suitcase and a weary smile.

"Well. Scared yet?"

"Not yet." Wolfe smiled, sitting up, rolling up his sleeve to the shoulder.

They sat in silence for several moments as he laid open his suitcase. Long, metal instruments smelling of ammonia and sanitization watched him. A brown case filled with needles, little brown bottles, scalpels, and a large pair of sharp pincers lay beside Wolfe on the couch.

"Now?"

"Less so," Wolfe said, swallowing hard as he watched Brieux gently uncap a thin white bottle and squeeze two or three heavy, weeping drops into a cup.

"Alright. Here goes nothing."

He rested his hand on the centre of Wolfe's back, and Wolfe felt an arctic wind on his side. Wolfe flinched when it touched him.

"Sorry, I know that's cold. Just relax, stay still, and keep talking to me."

"Okay. I can talk," he said.

Wolfe's shoulder itched. A little at first, then a lot. Then, just as it became almost too much to bear, it turned into heat, then disappeared altogether.

"Were you at the party?" Wolfe asked.

"The Midsummer Night's Festival? No. I tend to stay as far away from that sort of thing as possible. Grosses me out."

"And they don't suspect you then?"

"Not yet."

Wolfe wanted to mention Scott being there and grappled with it for a moment until he heard the metal instruments behind him, and he spoke up without thinking.

"I saw Scott there."

"I'm sure you did."

"Does…do you think…he um?"

"Enjoys it? I doubt it. But he has to go. We all have parts to play."

"So whose idea was this in the start?"

"It was Govan's initially. He had to carry out most of the punishments. He was apparently a fireman in York before, and wasn't made for this sort of violence. Even I wasn't expecting it to be so…bloody here. I wanted to be a doctor, not use my energy healing people that didn't need to be beaten in the first place. And let me say, I'm sorry I didn't get to you sooner, Wolfe. We left you in the dark longer than we needed to be safe," he muttered, barely more than a whisper.

"You were watching me? For how long?"

"I saw you coming out of Arcola's and Scott's trailer the night you got here. Govan and I planned to get you the night of the festival. We even sent Kendal after you, but…we were too late."

"Was Arcola in on this?"

Wolfe still saw Kendal walking past him. "Hello, Wolfe."

"No, but it wouldn't have been long. She was getting more and more desperate to save you. That's the biggest reason Scott is with us now. He knows how much you meant to Arcola."

Wolfe was lost for words. All for him. Brieux's smile made sense. The woman in the hallway made sense. Even then, there were forces he didn't know about yet working to save him. He felt a flare of indignation. Maybe these past months wouldn't have been so hellish if someone had told him right from the start.

"How does this feel? Nothing yet? Good."

Out of nowhere, he felt the pressure again, like an eight

hundred pound gorilla was swinging around his neck. He let out a grunt and a gasp for air. "Fuck," Wolfe gasped, grabbing the side of the couch. It didn't hurt, but it knocked the wind out of him.

"Just relax."

"MhhmHM," Wolfe grunted.

Then, a second later, the pressure stopped, and with it, the slight headache he had developed during the procedure disappeared. After a few seconds of silence, Brieux stood up, pulling him by the arm.

"You're done."

"Really?"

"Yes. It's an easy procedure. You can't even see a mark."

"Well, that was easy."

Wolfe turned to him and smiled. He was holding a chip almost twice the size of an apple seed in his right hand, shimmering green with tiny legs on each corner of the square. When he rubbed its surface, it doubled in on itself, collapsing into a dot no larger than a grain of sand.

"As long as you don't touch the surface, it's as easy as cutting a blemish out of an apple. So, how does it feel to be a free man?" he asked Wolfe, rubbing the side of the chip as it grew back to standard size.

"Pretty much the same." Wolfe laughed.

"Touche." They laughed together.

"And don't forget. Now, you have the biggest advantage and disadvantage for the next day. You can't be killed, or by the same thread. If someone, say…an overseer, decided to punish you tomorrow, it wouldn't happen."

"They'd know…" Wolfe said, staring at the tiny chip in his hand.

"Stay out of trouble, or the whole thing goes down. Take this." He handed Wolfe the tiny, slim, multicoloured chip. Wolfe held wiring and griding, shimmery little pieces of glass and plastic in his hand. All of it was nothing more than precious metals and resin to Wolfe.

"Keep this on you at all times tomorrow; that way, the tracker will stay consistent."

"Got it."

"But you should get some sleep. If all goes well, who knows where you'll be sleeping next. Just touch your pocket, and you'll be able to feel the buzzing. I'll see you tomorrow," he said, standing up. Brieux varied between shades of green and gray.

"Thank you, Brieux."

"Don't thank me yet."

—

Wolfe licked his lips out of nervousness. The fireflies had gone to bed, and a cacophony of shrieking frogs filled the night. The grass was slightly damp, and the sky was overcast. The stars disappeared behind clouds, and the wind carried the smell of rain.

Wolfe's mind wandered to the next shipment. They were fucked. He felt his heart break for them and swore to himself that he'd be back. He was going to put an end to this. *The next slaves that leave this place will walk down the road rather than have to run.*

As Wolfe came to the front of the house, the door to the guardhouse opened, and a dozen guards dragged a bleeding man, tied at the wrists, with a rice bag over his head towards the stairs to the barracks near the guardhouse. Wolfe watched another dozen BESNA officers spill out towards the grounds.

Wolfe leapt out of sight and ran towards the bushes on his right. Wolfe watched a light come on in Brieux's cabin, but Wolfe focused on the line of trees. A stream of light fell out over the lawn, and Wolfe could feel light on his back. He pushed himself faster than he'd ever gone before. The trees refused to come closer, and he could hear voices behind him. Wolfe could feel the grass digging into his heels. Someone yelled out behind him. Wolfe waited for the lights to bathe him.

Then he was in the bushes, and a second later, the shrubs were washed in cool white light. Wolfe could feel the chip buzzing in his pocket, and he pinched it in his fingers. He laid on the sun-warmed dirt beneath him, panting and watching the lights cast shadows over every branch and piece of moss. Then the lights turned away, and Wolfe looked into the yard and saw nothing. Wolfe pushed himself back and sat in the berm of the yard, watching and waiting, refusing to move. He'd wait to be sure.

Ten minutes later, Wolfe watched Scott dart across the grass. He was half nude, struggling with the buttons on his gray dress shirt, only wearing spotted socks on his feet. He ran so fast that Wolfe watched a spray of water behind him. Scott left big wet footprints up the porch steps, leaping them three at a time. Wolfe felt his stomach drop and his balls lurch up into his chest. His heart pounded with every step. *He must have gotten news about Arcola.* Wolfe thought. He contemplated going back to Brieux, but the light in his cabin had gone out. Wolfe forced himself to breathe. Most of the guards had gone back to the guardhouse, and the lights had been turned on in the common room for breakfast.

As he squeezed between the house and the ring of bushes around the plantation, he caught glimpses of the empty eastern fields. He could step over the tiny little black boxes around the yard and run. Run and run until his feet were sore and his throat was blistering, but god, he would be free. He pushed the thought away and watched a group of magpies fly above the house, almost invisible against the black night sky, as light filtered out of the common room and into the night. The yard was utterly silent, sparing the hum of a woodchipper, and Wolfe felt his heart rate return to an average pace.

Wolfe didn't question why the lights were on in the common room hours before breakfast. Wolfe didn't question why the sound of a wood chipper was humming in the yard. Wolfe didn't question why silence that only comes before a storm had laid itself across the plantation. A sea of clouds usurped the stars.

Wolfe put two feet into the common room, and his heart stopped. Every thought he had ever had, every plan, every instinct flashed through his mind in a millisecond. At the bottom of the stairs and maybe fifteen feet ahead of him, Mrs. Ester and Mr. Bredenbury were watching over the workers trembling on their knees.

At their feet was a pile of muscles, bone, blood, and organ that had once been Chester, who was only distinguishable by his face laying on top of the pile with open eyelids. His face was the island; the blood was the sea. It looked like they had fed him through a...*woodchipper*. Long strips of pink muscle were exposed to the air, and what looked like bones were broken and snapped into pieces no larger than Wolfe's fingers.

Wolfe heard Mr. Bredenbury roar, but he wasn't listening. Mr. Bredenbury was in the middle of a speech now, paused for emphasis with a shiny black pistol in his hand. He yelled again, promising to kill each of them until the men and women involved with the escape attempt stepped forward.

Chapter 12

The Execution

Wolfe watched Mr. Bredenbury's neck bulge purple as he spoke. "—plan to inspire an insurgency among the other workers." Even in anger, his voice was calm, but his tone told them their lives might soon end.

Wolfe noticed first the lack of blood. Mr. Bredenbury couldn't have been here long. The gun was still cold in his hand. Of all the things that could and would happen, no one was dead yet.

"I know some of you were working with him…" Mr. Bredenbury cried, pointing a hairy finger down at the pile of Chester on the floor. "And I will kill every mutation in this place until you talk," he said, clicking the edge of his gun with his fingernail.

He walked between the figures. They were kneeling on the floor, heads downturned, never looking where he stepped. Mrs. Ester stepped behind him, and on command, she grabbed a woman by her hair. She held back her screams and fought to stop her tears as her hair tangled between Mrs. Ester's calloused fingers. The woman held onto the hands above her, trying to shift her weight off her scalp.

Wolfe told himself to run. *On the count of three, you'll go find help. One. Two. Three.* He never moved. He knew he wasn't going to leave.

The woman tried to pull herself free between wails as the hand tightened into her hair.

"No?" He raised his gun to her head; she squeezed her eyes shut and tried to rip herself away.

Time moved in slow motion. He watched it slide back and out, pulling him further away. As Wolfe scanned the crowd, he saw

Unity and Sandy kneeling against the tiles.

As the trigger was being pulled, the woman started begging for her life. Wolfe looked at Sandy and saw her smile, and her eyes were trickling like streams. They told him something he didn't want to hear.

"N—" Wolfe had begun to yell. Without thought, without reason, he would call out to her, tell her no, tell her that her son needed her. She was asking Wolfe to do what she no longer could.

"It was me," she said, standing up suddenly.

—BANG—

He turned the gun and shot at the voice without even looking her in the eyes. The gun fired, and a second later, she was still standing. Then, she began to tremble, rocking back and forth to her knees. Finally, she was face down on the floor. Wolfe watched her blood snake between the tiles, painting the grout crimson and velvety as it ran towards the silver drain in the centre of the room.

No one moved. No one spoke. No one ran to her aid. Wolfe could hear her slow, raspy rattles, gurgling and creaky like winter air whistling in through cracks.

He was still standing there.

Move! He yelled at himself.

His mind was screaming; his voice was outside his body, roaring in his ears until that was the only thing he could hear.

—BANG—

The second gunshot. Point blank. The other woman fell. Mrs. Ester pulled a handful of hair from the dead woman and shook it over their bodies.

"Now, I was under the impression at least six workers were working with him. This is going to be an eventful evening."

Wolfe finally found the courage. His feet were moving, but his mind was still standing outside the doors waiting for the next to die. As he ran, he listened to death.

—BANG—

He heard another gunshot.

—BANG—

Then two more.

—BANG— —BANG—

God, this isn't happening. He ran around the yard's perimeter through the underbrush, praying he couldn't be seen. He jumped over wiry branches and ducked under leaning trunks, rotten from the base down.

The field opened to his left, and he was in it. He was tearing through the corn, gunshots echoing behind him. The ground was loose underneath him. His feet pounded the dirt repeatedly until he couldn't run anymore. He crouched on the ground, knees digging into the soil, staring at the sky.

"Why? Why us?" he cried, peering up at the cloud cloaked night sky. *Why us?* He asked again and again. What was worth this torment? He could see a glade in front of him, and beyond it, the smell of water pulled at him. If there was a creek or a river, he could follow it north and try to fight his way home. Maybe he could make it to the Rockies. He'd have a head start if he went now.

His pocket buzzed. He rooted through his pants and flung the chip onto the ground. It shook and spasmed, digging itself into a rut, thrusting dirt up over its shiny metal parts as it sank beneath the earth.

He stared at it like alien hardware. It was something; it was nothing, but it meant everything. The world was caving in; the earth was quicksand, pulling him closer and closer to the planet's molten core. When he closed his eyes, he could feel the world crushing him, his bones turning into diamonds, his body into oil.

Wolfe watched it shake out of existence, lost beneath the dirt, burrowing deeper and deeper. Another gunshot. Maybe this one took Unity. He dusted the earth off its back, plucking it an inch from the surface. It was quiet now, playing dead.

Enough. Wolfe pulled two rocks from the edge of the corn and thrust the chip between them, crushing it with all his force. It cracked like an eggshell. He hit it until the chip sputtered and shrieked as he ground its tiny metal instruments into powder.

It was dead. Wolfe held its body between his fingers, cradling its hissing frame. Then he picked its pieces out of the dirt and threw it as far as it would go towards the yard, sailing above the lines of corn. *Fuck it.* He looked up at the house, an island shifting above the sea of green.

The air moved quickly between the rows, and dirt swirled around his feet. The breeze had a twinge of coolness to it. He tilted his head back, drawing in all the air he could, yearning for the river. The air carried the smell of rain and lightning. Green, tumultuous clouds rose and fell with his breath along the distant cusp of the horizon. Somewhere, lightning and thunder broke. The corn around him hissed their praise.

He couldn't do it. Unity needed him. Sandy's son needed him. Scott needed him. He could be free and alone, but he refused to live with guilt looming over his shoulders. Wolfe forced himself to run back towards the ring of trees.

He pushed back through the bushes into the yard. Behind the wall of trees to the west, a black wall of rain was moving at a glacial pace towards them. Wolfe lay among the feathery green branches, watching three guards step out of the workers' barracks to his right, not fifteen feet away, muttering as light bathed them from behind.

Do I risk going back down? The gunshots had stopped; the guards seemed to have gone back to their regular rotations. Somewhere behind him, the sound of feet pushed across the grass. He waited and held his breath until they passed.

Brieux walked by with three briefcases. His hands shook along his cases as he chewed along his lip, watching the foliage. Brieux waited at the top of the stairs before he smiled a weary, trembling smile and descended. Wolfe watched the windows of the quiet house.

Wolfe waited until he heard the crash of metal against metal and a surge of voices and gasps. Wolfe crawled over the last trunk and around the entrance, slipping over the edge and down the staircase.

Wolfe had never seen so many people in the common room before. They had pulled the tables and chairs to the corners of the room, and the blood had stained the white floor pink. Unity was standing across the room, brandishing Brieux's black pistol towards the cowering kitchen staff while he tried to reason with the workers.

"Please, listen to me. It can be done," Brieux begged.

"And why should we trust you?"

"We're dropping by the dozens!"

"I wouldn't let you come near me with a ten foot pole."

"Please…" Brieux pleaded, "…we have to start now. You just watched your friends and family die!"

The room quieted as Wolfe came down the stairs.

"Oh look, it's the brownie."

"Oh, shut up!" Wolfe yelled, pushing through the hoard and next to Unity, who grimaced at him, barely taking her eyes off the captive kitchen staff. The Kitchen Overseer's tablet was a pile of broken glass on the floor.

"Did Brieux talk to Scott?" Wolfe asked

"I think so," Unity said

"We don't have time to fuck around. We have to get out of here tonight. Brieux is going to remove the chips from your shoulders, and we're going to storm the house," Wolfe said

"But…" a woman began.

"How many more have to die? How many children have to get sold? How many times will we get beaten? We aren't workers. We're slaves. We're things to them. Objects. Machines. They will kill, rape, torture, and sell us until the end of time." When he blinked, he saw a thousand eyes blinking back.

"I'm not letting him operate on me," another woman wailed from the back.

"He already did it to me, look," Wolfe said. "I have no chip." He lifted his sleeve and showed off his left arm. "It's easy and it's quick. You don't even have to stay and fight. You can go home. But only if you get those chips out. I am begging you, don't let more people die in vain."

Fifteen people pushed through the crowds. The younger ones, the angrier ones, the sadder ones. The mothers without children, the siblings without brothers or sisters, and the children without parents. Everyone who had nothing left to lose.

—

Ten of them were already chip-free, and the line was growing around the room. Wolfe guarded the kitchen staff stuffed in the back of the kitchen with Brieux's gun. By the time half an hour had passed, Wolfe's hands were shaking, both from a mixture of cold rippling out from his chest and from the palms of his hands. A cold sweat rested against the centre of his chest, and beads of sweat rimmed his scalp like a crown.

The room bulged, and it crushed people against the walls, pressing them up onto the chairs and tables. For being so packed, the room was deathly still, each breathing in and out in tandem. The surgeries in the middle of the room swelled with the help of two nurses working on the bodies beside Brieux.

"Don't. Come on…" Wolfe said, focusing back on the kitchen staff.

"We won't say anything. We—we'll just get our families and leave through the fields," Mrs. Hazy said.

"Really?" Wolfe said, brandishing the gun at arm's length again, and Mrs. Hazy and the two cooks jumped back against the wall. He saw the terror flashing across their faces, flaring with love and fear, memories and images of people they'd leave behind. Wolfe watched one of them dance their eyes to their left towards the hallway.

Wolfe heard it too: the dull, monotonous sound of another horde of guards coming around for their next rotation. Wolfe watched one of them round the corner, his lips moving as he chattered away with his coworkers.

He pointed the gun towards the staff again while the room collectively held their breaths, waiting in a joint agony. *Could we jump them?* Wolfe asked himself. He could see trembling shadows bobbing from the end of the hallway ahead of him.

Fourty-five seconds at best. He shifted his eyes back to the staff pressed up against the wall, and they jumped back, closing their eyes against each other again.

Wolfe was the villain now. He was holding a few men and women captive against their will. If he had to, would he pull the trigger? Wolfe didn't know, but his finger trembled beside the trigger, the same black gun he'd seen on Brieux's desk last night. He was waiting, heaving his lungs in fear.

"Come on, Scott…" he whispered. He glanced over the counter, and Unity was pushing as many people away from the view of the hallway as she could, just to give them a few more seconds. The air around Wolfe trembled. He could feel his heartbeat pounding on his tongue, pulling his spit back in his mouth, choking him, drowning him.

He could feel pots and pans rattle down behind him as he slid to the floor, his hand quivering as he stared at the faces ahead of him. The women were clenched together, dark brown eyes glowing in the twilight. Visions of lovers and children they may never see again played in their eyes.

"Come on, Scott, come on, Scott…" he whispered to himself, his name blurring into a flurry on his tongue. *Where is he?* He wanted to squeeze his eyes shut and wait. He didn't want to be here when it ended. Wolfe watched one of the captives slide his hand around a broom handle, the shadows down the hallway growing longer and harsher.

He met the man's eyes, not much older than him. Unquestionably married by now, maybe with kids. Wolfe aimed the gun, and he didn't drop the handle; it was all about to explode in their hands. Spit lept to the edges of Wolfe's mouth, his stomach erupted, and imaginary spiders walked up and down his arms.

"Scott plea—" The ground trembled, and it was nothing like Wolfe had felt before. The walls shattered in his mind, dirt vibrated down from the ceiling, and pipes cracked and squealed. Then another one, again and again, four in total. The captive stopped moving towards Wolfe. The guards stopped and listened.

Brieux stopped working. The world was quieter if it was possible.

Wolfe heard the guards whispering at the end of the hall, and in the moment it took for Wolfe to stop and listen, clench his eyes for a second and let the gun fall to his side, the lights had disappeared, plunging them into darkness.

Wolfe heard a shuffle, scrambling for the pale light coming down the steps behind him. Wolfe saw a figure above him. A female captive flew over the counter like a panther, pushing something to the floor. Wolfe could hear it, feel its presence beside him. It would alert the guards, and chaos would explode around them.

Or it would have had the sirens not gone off. The emergency lights had come on, flashing harsh, violent bursts of ruby light above them. Red, electric arrows painted themselves across the ceiling, pointing them toward the escape exits. Wolfe couldn't hear his thoughts or the sound of a metal salad bowl clattering to the floor over the howls of the alarm. It rang against his skull, his mouth formed words, but no one heard him.

The shadows were gone from the wall, but the man held a pan over his head, ready to swing it down on Wolfe. He felt the gun go off.

—BANG—

The man fell over Wolfe, and warmth trickled across his face. Wolfe pushed him off, and his body slumped backwards. Wolfe watched the lights in his eyes shrink, then blink out of existence. He tried to think over the roar of the sirens. Above them, the house was creaking. Outside, someone was yelling, voices were shouting, and short strips of red and orange light flickered across the yard in heavy-handed streaks.

He looked down over the counter as Unity swung her feet towards him. He watched her drag the two women who had tried to flee back over the counter. They cried and begged voicelessly, pulling the dead body back towards them into the corner, parting his hair with their fingertips.

"I'm going to go look for Scott!" Wolfe yelled, but his voice was lost over the sound of alarms. Unity opened her mouth to speak and stuttered something equally silent. Brieux and Wolfe looked at each other as Wolfe rubbed a strand of sweaty, bloody hair out of his face, slipping his jacket off his shoulders.

"Scott," Wolfe mouthed, and he nodded.

A group of fifteen workers had gathered around the edge of the wall, and Wolfe could feel their energy riveting. As he moved past them, they stepped behind him.

"Stay here," Wolfe mouthed, though none of them understood. "No," Wolfe yelled, turning around to face them and brandish a gun with which he had just claimed a life. It felt dirty in his hand like he was holding something evil, and it had leached its power into him.

The handful of men and women stopped; their sweat-shined figures flashed red and white. He mouthed it again, holding up his hand three times. "Fifteen minutes," he said, and it seemed to sate them. He turned and darted with a final glance, leaving them idling in the hallway.

The hallways had never been so quiet. No one moved, no one pushed, no one shoved. No one carried laundry, BESNA officers and guards didn't jeer, and voices didn't whisper. He ran through the corridor and stopped around every corner. His heart was pounding in his throat, and his pistol shook in his hand. He kept waiting around every doorway, hovered in front of desks and behind cleaning carts, waiting to run into the next group of people he had to shoot.

The eyes of the young man replayed in Wolfe's mind. The fear, the defiance, and the anger. He could see himself reflected in him, mirrored and opposite, both sides of the same coin. Each of them was caught in their own storm. *No,* Wolfe thought. *That man was the villain.* He would have killed Wolfe if he'd gotten the chance. But his mind fought him. They could say the same for Wolfe. *Did he deserve to die? Maybe,* he thought as he ran.

His mind was wrapped in itself, and he ripped around the corner without looking. He felt the gun get torn from his hand, the air move around him, the rush of water. Even over the sound of shrieking sirens, he could hear the crash of metal. He spiralled across the floor, and across the hallway, he saw Mrs. Ester staring back at him.

Her clothes were charred, dusted with smoke and dirt. She was dressed in a simple t-shirt and a pair of ripped gray jeans. She was drenched, her hair flat against the sides of her face. They stared at each other longer than he had ever stared at anyone in his life; then, she was scrambling in her pocket for a tablet. She fished the silver tablet from her pocket, and it fell from her wet hands onto the floor. She went to snatch it, and Wolfe kicked it away. She lurched again and caught it. Wolfe scrambled away from her towards the gleaming black gun shimmering against the floor like a beetle. Then he was above her, a weeping tablet in hand while she grovelled.

"But how…I…We…" She stuttered, her fingers drifting over her tablet uselessly. "Please, my parents need me, they're old."

As he pointed the gun, her screams stalled him. He thought momentarily of sparing her. "You didn't have to help them. You could have said no. You could have done something," he said, and the gun fired before she could cry out again.

—BANG—

He watched her crumple like the man earlier. Her body slumped strangely like a robot figure with no strength, and her skin, blood, and flesh stretched tenderly over her metal frame. She melted like wax, twisting and falling in on herself until she was slumped onto the floor. She leaked her red, synthetic oil into the puddle of water around her, curling against the wall.

Wolfe ran again, turning a final corner, and saw a gaping void into the outside world. The world was smoky and thick with ash. Snaking vines of fire roared above the guardhouse. When a hose touched one, it split like a fiery hydra, lashing its tongues against the trees. Blurred figures rushed around the base of the flames.

Wolfe sank back down the steps with a pounding heart. The wind stirred dirt into his eyes and down the stairs as he ran back through the hallways. Past the doorways, over the capsized cleaning carts, around corners and past desks. A headache clawed against the inside of his skull, running faster than he'd ever run; his lungs were fire, and his feet were floating.

The closer he got to the common room, the tide of workers swelled. The electronic windows flashed red and yellow in warning. People were flipping through their barracks, pulling clothes and trinkets out of cracks and crevices, stuffing their lives into pockets and backpacks. Chips were scattered across the floor as they hurried, spiralling out towards the rest of the barracks. Some were armed with brooms, kitchen knives, or glass shards wrapped in plastic and cloth.

Back in the common room, the hall was emptying. The masses shifted around him as he dropped beside Unity, sweat trailing down her arms as her shaking fingers dug chips out of her shoulders and into stinking piles on the floor.

"Unity, we need to get that boy!" Wolfe said, pulling his face right next to her ear so she could hear him. She looked back at him with terror in her voice. "We need guns first. Where is Mr. Kel…Scott. Where is Scott?"

There were ten people having chips removed at the same time. A hodgepodge group of older women and young men were shakily doing surgeries along the floor. Unity touched his shoulder and pointed a finger towards the steps.

"Wolfe…" she gasped. Covered in twigs and soot, Scott jumped down the stairs two at a time in a pair of clean, brown leather boots.

"SCOTT!" Wolfe yelled. He raced around the bodies on the floor and below the shrieking alarms and the flashing lights. "Are you okay?" he yelled, checking and pulling at his clothes, everything just as Wolfe had seen this afternoon. Flames still licked the air behind him as he looked down at him with twinkling eyes. Wolfe wanted to kiss him again, to thank him for everything, and Scott looked away, turning his face towards Brieux.

"How many are left?"

"I don't know."

"I think about fifty or so," Unity said, wiping her hand on her shirt.

"And you?"

"Good." She pulled her hair around the back of her neck with one hand and pulled up her sleeve with a smile.

"Alright. We need to go," Scott said. His eyes were wild and darting, refusing to look at them. He pulled Wolfe towards the stairs. "They're going to come eventually. We just have to go." Across the edge of the stairs, Wolfe could see the trees above the guardhouse had caught fire. They were painted red with flame, black and bony fingers burning alive. They had become dark, twisted figures; emancipated skeletons writhing and dancing in flame.

"Scott, the kid."

"We don't have time…"

"Scott, we have to…"

"Wolfe, don't be silly." Wolfe felt his hand tightening around his wrist with each word he spoke, dragging him onto the grass.

"Scott, stop—" He pulled his hand back, and Scott twirled around.

"WE DON'T HAVE…time…" He yelled, then whispered, looking over at the men dousing the trees encircling them with water. His eyes wanted to scream something at him, and his mouth faltered over the words he wanted to say.

"What?" Wolfe asked, staring up into his eyes. Scott looked back towards the house, and for the first time, Wolfe watched absolute fear fall across his face. When he looked back towards Wolfe, he couldn't bring himself to look into his eyes. His hands were as clean and as soft as they had been when he'd touched him last. He still smelled like heaven, unlike the smoke on the air.

"We don't have time, the overseers are trying to fight the fire," he hissed again. "Please, let's just go."

"We're getting that kid," Unity said.

"Scott. Sandy is dead. So is Chester."

Scott mulled it for a minute. His eyes moved between them, between the small army they'd amassed: dirty and black, shining in the pale light of night. They heaved together, breathed together, waiting for directions behind Scott and Wolfe while Brieux worked in the flashing lights below them.

"It's too dangerous."

"Arcola wouldn't do this," Wolfe said. There were only inches between them on the lawn but they were kilometres apart. Scott slowly let his fingers off his wrist, turning to look at the supply shed at the back of the yard.

"Go then. Meet me back here, I'll go take the storehouse," he said as he stared towards the back of the yard. Before letting Wolfe go, he touched his shoulder one more time.

"Don't hurt anyone, please," he said, rubbing his finger over his shoulder. Wolfe felt his stomach come alive and felt the churning start again. "Promise me," he begged.

"No," Wolfe said and watched an expression fall across his face. *Disappointment? Fear? Disgust? Shame?* Wolfe didn't know. A band of sweaty, black-faced workers followed Scott towards the back of the yard.

"Do you still think I'm a rat?" he asked Unity as they watched the fire burn.

"I don't think so. Maybe." She smirked at him, and they looked up at the face of the black manor. Scott's face stuck with him as they ran towards the edge of the house.

—

They lay against the damp latticework along the front of the porch, watching in darkness as spirals of smoke pulled up into the sky. The odd star peaked out from behind the clouds. Distantly, thunder rumbled. The flames carved shimmering lines of heat against the night, etching themselves forever among the constellations.

"Gun?"

Wolfe nodded.

"Okay. Let's go," Unity said.

They slunk up the stairs, past the smell of rot and to the front door. Wolfe's heart was pounding in his throat as they touched the cold metal knob and into the manor's foyer. The house was uncomfortably silent: like a tomb, a church, or a city street past midnight. The chandelier still twinkled with lights reflected against the stained glass windows, the vast arching staircase was empty, and the living room was dark.

Their steps were muffled, and their breaths were slow as they crept up the gold and brown carpets that slid up and down the stairs. A few figures moved on the balcony, and Unity and Wolfe pressed themselves against the wall. The lights hung black above them. The only light was coming from the flickering flames through the glass.

"It must have taken out one of the backup generators. Do they have it under control?" Mrs. Bredenbury whispered above. Wolfe could hear her fingers trembling on the banister, a rhythmic tap of nails on the hardwood.

Wolfe pinched his eyes and held the gun as it dipped against the carpet. He heard Scott's voice in his head. "Don't hurt them. Don't hurt them."

"Should we wake the guests, ma'am?"

"Go check on the girls," she snapped suddenly. As the other shadows slipped down the hallway above them, they heard mumbling. "Useless..." Mrs. Bredenbury's heels clicked on the wooden floor. She walked back and forth, creaking above them as the house groaned and settled.

Wolfe felt a rush of heat. *Why not hurt them?* Every time he blinked, he saw their cold, dark eyes staring back. He saw them eating lunch, sipping coffee and eating chocolates while people died. If they knew what was happening, they would act like their livestock were ransacking the house. Humanity had left them long ago. They were monsters. *Monsters. Monsters. Monsters.* The mantra repeated in his mind as he moved up the stairs, listening to the sound of her retreating heels towards the west side of the house.

Wolfe was at the top of the landing, with Unity to his right. He was crouched under a painting of a half-naked woman stretched over a birch log in a forest. They basked in the glowing fire, and with a glance, they shrunk around the corner, down the hallway opposite a nursery where the woman was whispering to a pair of young girls.

They practically crawled down the hallway. The lights above them flickered, flickered again, blinked on, and then off. The light from the fire lit the hallway as lightbulbs shattered in the hallway. The flames roared above the guardhouse, and for a moment, the house was lit again as the power surged. Wolfe could see the strands in the wallpaper, the ribbing on the back of books, the burnish of the walls of screens, and the edges of the diamonds on the chandelier. Then the lights went out for the final time.

"Mrs. Bredenbury?" a woman called from down the hallway. Ahead of them, they heard footsteps in the darkness; behind them, steps grew closer. He sat paralyzed with indecision, and without thinking, his legs were unbending, and the gun was raised. A moment later, he felt a hand around his waist, and Unity pulled him sideways, resting a door shut as voices spoke outside.

"Go fetch Mr. Bredenbury."

"Well, ma'am he…"

"NOW," she barked, and the woman shuffled away. They listened to her feet sink down the stairs, then the sound of a door heaving open, then shut.

Wolfe was sure he was in a bathroom. The cold tiles were a relief against his hands. His eyes adjusted to the darkness, and he could see the faint outline of lumps around the room. Toilet-sized lumps, bathtub-sized lumps, and sink-sized lumps. He could smell wood smoke heavy in the air.

"Grab those," Unity whispered, pointing to something moving in the corner of the room. He caught it in his hands, dancing in the breeze. He ripped the curtain off the wall and felt the silk on his face. The frayed, torn edge was dissolving into string around him, and he configured it into a shrinking knot of rope with sticky hands.

Unity pulled the door open, and they moved down the hallway again.

The hallway was alive with light, a shifting, unstable lustre cast from the glow of the fire. Wolfe could still see the paintings on the walls; the curtains twirled with light as the smoke coughed and hacked in through the closed corners of the windows. Sunbursts of light painted soft orange and pink shadows over their faces, casting them in colour.

They were outside her bedroom door when the music began to play. Keys sunk against the piano, bellowing. Then the piano danced, fingers shimmering from key to key. It was like listening to droplets of rain playing and splashing together, all to a rhythm that escaped the ears of angels.

"Ready?" Wolfe asked. He was up against the door, and Unity was across from him. They leaned against the door and listened to footsteps moving back and forth across the floor.

"No, not like that. Who taught you how to play?" she barked from under the door. "Do you need to learn again?" she asked.

"No ma'am…" a voice whispered back. It was a child's voice, rippled with fear and pain. Tears hung off the end of his sentence. *A child should never sound like that*, and before Unity could say anything, he pushed through the door.

He was on top of her before she could scream. Her tablet fell from her hand, throwing a blueish-gray light across the ceiling. He forced a loop of curtain into her mouth as she beat her fists against his head. He had never seen her this close before. Tiny wrinkles moved around her eyes as she tried to fight him off. Her hair was soft and smelled like nutmeg and lavender. Her eyes had a depth to them, a deep nutty black colour, like watching pools of churning earth alive and teeming with worms.

Wolfe flipped her over and tied her arms behind her back again and again. By the fourth knot, she let out a cry of pain. Wolfe felt his heart lurch. He could see her nose pressed into the carpet; a smear of makeup was rubbed across the rug.

"Here," Unity said, marching over to the walk-in closet and pulling open the doors. Wolfe heaved her by the waist and pushed her back into the closet behind a pair of suitcases and boxes full of running shoes. They shoved racks of clothes over her until a small jiggling pile of dress clothes, purses, and a soft whimpering emanated from the depths of the closet.

Then they turned to the piano pressed against the window. The boy he had seen first at the party, then later only yesterday, crouched behind the stool. He held his hands against him, turned in, and kept his head tilted low to the floor as if in prayer.

"What's your name?"

"Lett, sir."

"No, no, I'm not—" Wolfe didn't know what to say. He wasn't a what? What could he tell him?

"We're going to get you out of here," Unity said.

When the boy finally looked up, he refused to meet their eyes. He looked beside them, over them, around them, through them, but never at them. He was younger than Wolfe thought, maybe seven.

"How old are you?"

"Eight, sir."

But when he moved his hand to his sides, Wolfe could see red. He glanced up at the piano and saw smears of burgundy across the keys. "What happened?" Wolfe reached out to his hands without thought, and he jumped back, bumping into the stool and falling backwards.

"I'm sorry, sir, I didn't mean to. I'm sorry," he cried, holding his hands up above his head. Wolfe looked over his weeping palms. Lines of blisters were spread along the length of his hands, and blood dripped along the waving patterns of scabs cracking and falling off his knuckles. Against the corner of the room, a heavy stick was shaved down into a thin instrument, stained with spots of black from years of abuse.

"I'll take him down to Brieux." Unity grabbed the tablet off of the bed and held it against her chest. She beckoned towards Lett, who moved towards her arms slowly. Wolfe moved away from the bathroom toward the rest of the room. "Wolfe, what are you doing? Bredenbury will be—" As she spoke, a door crashed open downstairs.

"RICHLEA," Mr. Bredenbury yelled from downstairs. He still sounded calm, like he still had everything under control. Then, through the darkness of night, two gunshots rang out, then two more. Wolfe listened to the sound of something heavy scraping its way across the floor below them, followed by the grinding of metal and the crash of breaking glass.

"GO!" Wolfe yelled, pointing them towards the bathroom window. Wolfe leapt across the bed to the large makeup table in the corner of the room and ripped at it. He watched Unity push Lett towards the window, helping him onto the roof. She wrapped a purple scarf around her neck and up around her face, ringlets of hair falling back away from her forehead as Wolfe reached the makeup table.

Boxes of jewellery poured around his feet, sparkling in the darkness: golden bangles filled with diamonds, silver anklets shiny with green and golden stones, necklaces, rings, earrings, pendants, and brooches in every shade and size. He stuffed his pockets with handful after handful until he jangled as he ran back towards the bathroom. Footsteps climbed the stairs in bounds of two and three.

"Honey? Honey, we have to go," Mr. Bredenbury cried.

Wolfe helped slide Unity out onto the roof with Lett while the voices drifted through the bathroom door.

"—where are—"

"—have to—"

"—bathroom."

Wolfe heard the voices through the door, and as Unity slipped out of sight down the side of the roof, he pushed the cabinet laden with towels and glass jars against the door, jamming it shut as bath beads and pumice stones cascaded to the floor. Jars of oils shattered, coating the wood in purples and shimmering silvers, case after case of bathrobes tumbled like woollen sheep, dried herbs and medicinal salves crumbled to the ground, sticking to the floor.

"Who the fuck are you?" a man yelled through the door. "If you hurt Mrs. Bredenbury, we'll..." A monstrous crash overwhelmed Wolfe's thoughts as something hit the door.

Wolfe reached for the windowsill with outstretched hands while he kept his feet pushed against the door. With every smash, the door bulged more and more towards him. He squeezed one arm out, then the other, and pulled his torso past the frame. The cabinet was forced away from the door, and he could see arms and eyes moving their way into the bathroom like a horde of demons, waving tablets and batons as they screamed. Wolfe fumbled with the gun, turning it around to face the eyes behind him.

Hands grappled up and down his legs, pulling at his clothes and tearing at his shirt. Then Wolfe slipped backwards an inch, then two. A hand tightened around his torso as his legs flailed, and he lurched back again. Wolfe let go of the windowsill, the gun fell, he curled his legs against himself and pushed away from the hands, the bathroom, and the Bredenburys.

He was tumbling against sandpaper, scraping over his neck and arms, tearing up his body. He rolled to the edge of the roof and caught himself on the drainpipe, swinging down onto his back on the porch, and the air shot out of him. Jewellery ran down the roof, falling like golden rain around him as he listened to bullets tearing the wood into pieces.

The trees around him were spectres, bursting into dancing shadows around the garden. The windbreak around the yard seemed to waltz, ghastly figures writhing back and forth against the pitch-black sky. Their dance cast droplets of fire over them. The grounds were alive with light; the garden was trampled into nothingness; the winds screamed their applause around them.

The yard was dislodging into anarchy. Wolfe watched a group of young men armed with tree branches and hammers beating two guards on the stone path behind the house. Their hands repeatedly swung down as the guard begged for his life. He screamed a scream Wolfe had only ever heard from the workers.

He watched bodies slink into the night, shadows disappearing through the unburnt trees towards the east as the west burnt to embers. He saw men and women tearing through the cabins for food and clothing at the edge of the property as flames caught the brush behind the overseer's cabins. The guardhouse was a smoking hole now, and the storehouse had been torn to shreds.

Three women ran in tandem, sprinting across the gravel and into the corn towards the glittering lights of town, laughing and hooting.

Wolfe scooped up the gun and flew to the barrack entrance. It was chaos. People were running back and forth with guns and chips scattered across the floor. Tablets were lying across the counter, casting a barely noticeable white glint around the room as Brieux squinted at Lett's shoulder. Some of the workers were yelling with joy while others wept, dragging shot and injured men and women up and downstairs, begging them to keep walking.

"GUYS!" Wolfe cried, running down the stairs three at a time and landing at the bottom, sprinting over to them, working near the counter.

"Wolfe!" Scott yelled. His eyes were wild, leaping with each step Wolfe took towards them. They connected, wrapping arms around each other. Wolfe pulled himself away and dug into his pockets, pulling out handfuls of jewellery and gleaming at Scott.

"Wolfe, what did you do?" Scott yelled, pushing him back.

"What? We're going to need the money."

"That's good thinking," Brieux said, wiping his hands and moving on to the next woman with her side to him.

"No, it's not good thinking! You can't just steal from them like that, you're going to get in so much shit!" he yelled, raking his fingers through his hair and breathing like a wounded hog. His eyes flickered with anxiety.

"How are we going to get into more shit than we already are?" Wolfe asked, pulling Scott's hands to his chest.

"I—I don't...I...I..." he stuttered, and Wolfe watched the tears well along the edges of his eyes. His fingers moved absently over his face.

"I know, let's just—" As Wolfe was talking, the lights above them flickered to life. A quiet grinding filtered through the barracks as the sirens tried to cough back to life, warbling through the din. The house outside flickered into life, and Wolfe saw figures darting back and forth in front of the hallways, gunshots lighting windows.

"Hey, the light—" A second later, the handful of people gathered around them waiting to have their chips removed crumbled to the ground. They didn't move, and they didn't shake. They fell like piles of sand to the tiles, and their chests didn't rise or fall.

"They hit the fucking kill switch!" Brieux cried, dropping to his knees and flipping a woman over, starting chest compressions on the floor. He was filthy, soiled with dirt and blood, crusted with layers of sweat. The alarm warbled around them, struggling to sound, hacking and wheezing to life.

"We have to go!" Unity yelled, dragging Lett and Brieux away from the common room. The lights flickered on and off again as they climbed the stairs.

The house was flashing between white and red as gunshots ripped through the dissonance of the yard lit aflame. Wedges of boiling ash fell from the trees above them as the maples to the east roared with flame. The fire had surrounded them as the workers turned their attention toward the house.

The house was falling. Piss stained the walls, and almost every window was broken down into pointed teeth as workers clambered against them. Guards and officers alike fired shots aimlessly into the crowd, striking people at random; guests of the Bredenburys, a child and her mother trying to climb the stairs, other guards, and workers as they were devoured by bullets.

Wolfe stopped on the grass in awe of it all. Workers scaled the sides of the house with ladders and ropes, dragging themselves up with guns, knives, and rocks in hand. Scott caught his hand and started dragging him back towards the edge of the yard.

"Where is Craik?" Wolfe yelled as they looked towards the train station at the edge of the lawn.

"Just come on…" Scott yelled, yanking him by the wrist.

"LET GO OF ME!" Wolfe yelled, snatching his arm back as Scott turned towards him. Wolfe slipped out of his grasp, turned without hesitation, and sprinted back towards the house as they trailed behind him across the grass.

Wolfe dipped through the gazebo, across the yard and onto the porch. An army of men with guns were pushing into the foyer, and the guards were retreating up the stairs. The hanging branches had fallen across the roof, and flames slid across the shingles.

Mr. Bredenbury was standing at the top of the stairs waving a gun. His tablet was slumped by his side, and people moved around him, running upstairs, workers and guests alike. Officers were shooting, and bullets ricocheted against the wood, splintering it into sawdust as men and women fell.

A group of guards drug a boy up the stairs kicking and screaming. Dishes shattered in the dining room, and the chandelier flickered and jumped before falling into darkness for a final time. The lights shivered over Mr. Bredenbury, and through the clearing, they shared a mutual gaze, watching each other for the first time as equals. Then he saw Craik below him, wrestling an officer with his bare hands. His face was twisted with rage, and fury pulled Craik's eye back.

Wolfe leapt into the war zone, lost in a thrash of bodies. He tumbled over Craik and shot, striking the guard in the side.

—BANG—

"Craik! Come on, we have to go." And before he could grab his hand, Craik exploded in front of him. Chunks of brain matter and blood ran down Wolfe's face. He could feel blistering heat churning in his stomach as Craik ran out of his mouth, seeping into the rug as Wolfe tasted him, salty and almost sweet, creamy against his tongue.

Another bullet splintered the wood beside him, and something grazed his cheek. Looking up, he saw Bredenbury smile. After all this, after two months of abuse, after a lifetime of horror, he smiled. Then he disappeared up the stairs. Wolfe fired again, and two shots found their home in the large glass window.

—BANG— —BANG— It broke the fractured window behind them, sucking in smoke and embers down from the attic as it opened into the night air.

His entire body bristled with rage, and Mr. Bredenbury was gone. Wolfe could feel prickles of anger tracing fingers up his spine, stabbing pins along every nerve and joint in his body. Scott was gone. Unity was gone. Lett, Brieux, they all dissolved behind him. Wolfe was alone, and he didn't care. Mr. Bredenbury killed Craik on purpose, and now Wolfe would kill him. Wolfe was going to make it hurt, and he would savour it.

"Wolfe!" Scott called for him, but he was already in the hallway, lost beneath the fray of battle. The chaos overcame him as he leapt the stairs. Workers dragged workers along the floor, and Wolfe pushed them off, shoving them away from crying men and injured women.

The house was filled with smoke and ash, and people ran back down the stairs again. Guards were ripped and torn apart like animals at their feet, begging for their lives the same way workers had appealed to them time and time again. Wolfe burst into the study at the end of the hall, and two girls were crying in the corner with tear-stained faces.

Wolfe knew they were his daughters. He wanted to take his rage out on them; he wanted to get his revenge; he wanted to hurt their father. Flames licked out of the roof and down into the open windows. Workers pressed into the study behind him and tore the room to shreds. They ripped the backs off books, backed guests against the wall, and tore paintings off the walls. A swathe of workers had piled onto someone on the floor, and Wolfe knew it must have been Mr. Bredenbury. *He's dead. The monster is dead.*

Then Scott was behind him, grabbing him by the arm. The smoke was thick around them, turning the air misty. An officer fired at them, missing Scott by a millimetre. Wolfe turned, firing in his general direction and shot him between the ribs.

—BANG—

He crumbled, sliding down the stairs, trying to drag himself to his feet with organs that refused to work.

Wolfe and Scott hopped down the stairs over an officer ripping the pants off a woman beneath the staircase. Wolfe aimed, the bullet hit his neck, and he toppled off her instantly.

—BANG—

A man stood in the study, ripping the pages out of books and letting them flurry against the air like dragonfly wings. A woman poured bottles of alcohol across the piano, smashing crystal decanters against the wall and plucking a camera out from the chest of the piano. Across the hall, someone took a shovel to the pictures on the walls, breaking screens with his bloody fists. An older man ran naked, pouring wine down his chest, screaming into the void. Smoke ran down the stairs like a sweeping silver gown over Craik's body, flowing like water and reaching out like spectral fingers. The bust of a cherub on the wall was missing its face, and a camera dangled like an eye loose in its socket. They were free.

Outside, people chewed on muddy vegetables; they smashed and broke into the most significant fruits, shoving their faces against their sweet flesh. Heat shattered the greenhouse and cooked the vegetables; the Quonsets were writhing with flame as tractors and combines were incinerated. The entire house was glowing. Wolfe picked chunks of Craik out of his hair as they ran.

They carried a string of people to the trees alive. In the upper rooms of the manor, a woman was trapped. She banged her fists bloody on the unbroken windows, but they wouldn't shatter. The flames licked at her delicate skin as she and other guests flailed along the length of the house, bashing themselves fruitlessly as they burnt in the manor, locked in with all the stuff they desperately envied. Their hubris sealed them in their flaming tomb as the wood turned black, and they stopped moving.

The trees swung with guards like bobbles while the masses cheered them on.

Wolfe knew they had to get out; they had to run and leave before BESNA came. Wolfe beckoned Unity over, who helped Wolfe up onto the gazebo. He stood up, balanced himself on the rough curved roof and started yelling. As he did, he watched a noose get thrown over the branches of a towering in the yard.

Wolfe watched a woman with high heels and delicate gold bracelets get carried out by her hair and thrown into a noose. She only begged for a few seconds before they pulled the rope higher and higher, and Mrs. Bredenbury climbed into the night. Then her son was lifted beside her. Eventually, a string of them were dangling from the tree. Mr. Bredenbury's family was dead, and he was somewhere in his house, burning among his things. Corruption would die with them, and nothing would impede their escape.

"STOP!" he yelled, but no one listened.

Their liberation swirled around them. Months of suffering, years of death, separation, beatings, rape, and violence were over. They were free, and Wolfe would do it all over again if he could feel this feeling. They had done it. The main house was a bonfire: the flames licked out of the windows like tongues and arms, and screams rose above the sky as the wind carried the fire into the field. The world around them blazed, and Wolfe felt the power in his chest, soul, and heart. They had won.

"This is a revolution!" the crowd cried out. Wolfe looked down to see one of the boys he had taken back to the barracks after the Midsummer Night's Festival kiss a girl beneath the light of the burning manor.

"This is a rectification of justice!" a man said, swinging a flaming tree branch over his head.

"We will not be kept down! We were fighting for justice, and since they refused to give it to us, we took it!" They would have chased them to the edges of the earth; they would have beaten and abused them into the afterlife. *What else could we have done? At least we have done something.* Wolfe thought, watching their bodies swing from the trees. The crowd roared and leapt with jubilation. He had their attention now.

"But now you have to leave. Run, go north, south, it doesn't matter. But you have to go. We are not safe here. If they catch you, you will die a death unlike anything you've ever imagined." They milled around him, looking for an answer, overwhelmed by the idea. They were free; nothing held them back.

"GO!" Wolfe cried. Sirens wailed somewhere in the distance as night enveloped them.

They ran faster than light itself across the ashy earth. He

could just keep going. He did it. *I did it. We did it. They did it. We are free*, Wolfe told himself as they came towards the end of the yard.

The sound of sirens grew louder as people shrunk into the bushes through the smoking embers and into the fields. Wolfe and his friends darted straight across the road and into the corn. Just after, a trail of wailing black vans with large golden eyes painted on their grills, loaded with officers wrapped in black, eclipsed the hill. Wolfe listened to gunshots killing the stragglers who didn't believe Wolfe. Two older women were gunned down behind them on the road. They tried, but they didn't make it. Freedom was over for them.

Wolfe heard the snarling of dogs and the whispers of people that had died behind him. Sandy, Chester, Craik, and so many more. His throat tightened as he ran. He promised he'd stay alive for them. They deserved to be remembered.

"Thank you…" he whispered to himself as he looked over his shoulder, watching the columns around the plantation house crunch with pressure, collapsing the manor into a plume of fiery red glitter.

They sunk into the corn and ran faster, digging their feet into soft dirt. Among the stalks, the world became quieter until the orange blaze in the sky was the only reminder of the world they left behind. Lett ran like he hadn't lost a mother. Wolfe ran as if he hadn't lost a friend. Scott and Brieux, a coworker. Unity, a confidant and friend. Their losses plagued them in silence as they ran towards town.

Chapter 13

The Town at the Edge of the World

The plantation had slipped into history. The smouldering orange embers had gone out behind them, and the town ahead of them glowed at the edge of the field. The small, aging buildings were washed clean. They stood like tombstones, empty and blasé, though plastered with giant billboards and glimmering lights. Smiling faces shimmered, advertising vintage hotels and fast-food restaurants, all splashed with the same slogan.

"Landia, the town at the edge of the world!"

The town was lit with the flashy, dazzling signs of a tourist trap city with an emptiness that clung to the streets. No cars or bikes lined the roads, and no street lights shone down on the glazed, cracking highway. There were only the dim glowing lights in a few houses with their curtains drawn shut and the whirring sirens and dancing lights that painted the gray cement red and yellow.

The five of them crept into town: Wolfe, Scott, Brieux, Unity, and Lett. They crawled across the gravel approaches before they hit the pavement and dragged themselves through an empty train yard. The track crossed into a giant X, one going east and west, the other north and south. Wolfe prowled ahead with Scott by his side, Brieux behind them, and Lett and Unity between the three of them.

They sank into the edge of town and threw themselves behind a flickering gas station with pale winged moths clustering around the grimy plastic windows. As a cruiser prowled by, it sent thick swathes of pale light across the ground, stirring flurries of moths to life. Wolfe felt his heart in his throat.

As the car pulled by, flicking its long yearning lights back and forth, they dashed across the main street. As Wolfe moved, he froze in the street, staring down towards the west side of town, taking in the street in front of him.

He had only imagined ads like this in places like Old Nevada and York, not in a small, filthy, dingy little town like this one. The sky wasn't dark; not a star could penetrate the sea of lights if it wanted. True darkness would never come here. Flashing billboards showcased the newest robotic invention or clothing trends from the hottest fashion house out of York. At some point, the same words trolled across every sign. "The town at the edge of the world!"

The signs sold and advertised everything imaginable: tablet subscription services, brown-eyed families smiling back from tropical destinations, and sparkling new cars that could drive themselves, make your appointments, and do your schoolwork. Bank accounts with seven million credits limits for middle-class families, BESNA community centres, and an ad for the 2068 summer Olympics:

"One hundred years after the summer Olympics in Mexico City, BESNA attempts to liberate her brown-eyed civilians. This year's Olympics takes a sombre tone, as we reflect on the losses and the suffering of BESNA and her allies."

Wolfe saw a sorry excuse for a town beneath the signs. Restaurants begged people to take coupons for their Indian restaurants down the block while ads for cheap fast food restaurants flashed overhead. A rundown grocery store sat dark, while an ad for a free Bredenbury Grocery Delivery service above it sparkled in gold and brown. "Right to your door!"

Further down the road, a cracked clock on the top of a red brick building slid to one, sending rumbling chimes through the town like church bells but wiry and electronic, screeching out like a metallic bird call. Wolfe was pulled off the road, through a bramble of wiry bushes and branches, and behind a large green dumpster.

"Do we have an actual plan after this?" Unity snarled, rubbing a bleeding scratch on the back of her hand.

"Well, I don't know where he lives, but there is a man here in town that sells contact lenses. He has to be here somewhere," Scott said.

"Oh great, so we're dead. I may as well go flash the officers my tits for a shorter sentence."

"God, do you always have to be so hysterical?"

"Do you want me to be hysterical?" she bit back. Wolfe watched them all in the pale light of the signs as red lights flickered.

"*Shh,*" Scott hissed. "It's the same guy that sold those lenses. For the party?" He peeked his head out as a car turned off the road.

"The ones I got beaten for wearing?" Wolfe asked mockingly, nudging Scott with the back of his knuckles.

"Well, exactly I—" He curled his lip up. "Sarcasm isn't helpful or funny."

"*I* thought so. Lightens the mood."

"Whose mood!?" Scott asked, flinging his arms up and grumbling, causing the branches to rattle.

Everyone had concerns to voice, concerns that often sounded useless to another and worrying to someone else. Where to go, what to do, how to do it, and how to stay hidden.

"Well, we could go through the sewer systems?" Scott whispered, the anger in his voice rising decibel by decibel.

"Stupid," Unity said.

"Ewh," Brieux added.

"Come on…" Wolfe said.

"Fine!" he yelled, pointing a finger at Wolfe and refusing to meet anyone's eyes. "*You* do something."

"Fine," Wolfe snapped at Scott. Then, without a moment of hesitation, they moved again, led by Wolfe. He felt a hand on his heel, but he flicked it off, his knees stirring up dirt.

They ran past old gas stations and abandoned grain elevators. Past garbage bins and water barrels. A stiff wind carried the smell of rain and bitter, watery skunk. The wind stirred old fast food containers, rotten cardboard, and dead grass down the street. The crusty brown earth was unnaturally dry beneath their feet as they moved, hiding behind fences and in alleyways every time a BESNA car trolled by.

Soon they were near the centre of town, hiding in the alley behind a derelict, crumbling fire station. Every yard away from the main street was dead, filled with weeds and rotten ornamental berries. Trash lined the sidewalks; entire street blocks were filled with fluttering gray tarps and half dug holes for construction.

Only a few houses per block had their lights on, and the ones that did were barely lit; slightly flickering lights inside a skeleton of a home, the final wheezing breaths of a dying, oxygen-less flame.

"If we can't find that man, we're just going to have to clean out a house," Wolfe said, pointing Brieux's dirty, bloodstained pistol at the cold, dead windows of a house. In the distance, what looked like lightning painted the dark backs of clouds coming closer to town.

"It's in the northwest for sure," Brieux said, wheezing, out of breath and groaning, as he sat down on the weeds cracking through the cement.

"So we have to get across the main street again?" Wolfe asked. Wolfe pulled himself to his aching feet, pushed himself against the wall and peered around the corner. He saw a car rounding the corner into town and watched its headlights coat the streets.

"Just after this one," he said, looking back at them. He saw Lett's face flicker with terror, and he clenched his hand tight around Unity's. Wolfe tried to crack a smile, but his face barely twitched before turning around.

The lights were beside them now. Wolfe took a step back as the lights snapped over the firehouse, the officers watching for human shadows. As Wolfe looked behind himself, he felt his heart explode. Dizziness and stars fell over his head, and he felt his heartbeat pounding in his toes.

Two faces were staring at him from behind a garden wall.

Wolfe blinked.

They blinked.

Then he watched them slide over the next wall, dirty and hands caked with mud before they dissipated again. He felt his heart settle. They must have been escapees like them. He told himself he saw a flash of blue eyes.

"Now!" Wolfe whispered. They darted across the street under the harsh white lights moments before the next car rounded the corner. Just as Wolfe put his foot across the middle of the road, the billboards started screaming.

The ads dissipated: the cruise ships, the electronics, the meal planners, and the roadside attractions vanished. Replaced, horrifyingly, by Wolfe's, Lett's, Unity's, and Brieux's faces. Red caution signs flashed violently in strips across the top and bottom, flashing images of burning plantation houses, murdered guards, and a final frame of charred bodies dangling out of shattered windows.

A reporter moved silently across the screen as an obsidian gargoyle fell into the burning manor, pushing plumes of fiery embers into the jet black night. The hanging bodies of guards shifted. His lips moved with a microphone chip at his mouth, but no sound came through the signs.

The billboards flickered back to Wolfe's face, standing on top of the gazebo, holding a bloody gun in his hand.

"Danger! Danger! Danger!" The words said beneath him, rolling by endlessly, a stream of cautions and warnings about the violent escapees.

The car behind him turned onto the highway, and Wolfe felt a hand around his wrist again. Its sirens clicked on and flew, wailing, down the street towards them. They slid down the grassy ditch, tripping over a piece of tire wrapped under dead grass and twisted chicken wire. They pulled themselves over a starched white fence and into a garden.

The car trolled by shining lights all around them, searching into withering azalea bushes and pale green tree leaves. Wolfe closed his eyes, laying on his back, staring into the orange, milky sky.

Then the car was gone.

Light filtered over them, trickling out of an open kitchen window above them. A thin metal grate was over the window and baby moths clustered over the grate, trying to pull themselves closer to the dim, off-white kitchen lights. They listened to the door open and close, the rustling of jackets and boots. Movement across the floor. Moving dishes. A kiss.

"There's a plate in the heater."

"Have you checked on the kids?"

"Just now. They're sleeping in our room tonight."

"Ah shit. It's all so stupid," he hissed while the heater hummed away. They walked back across the floor, and they listened to the sound of cutlery scraping porcelain.

"Shush. The window is open."

"Then close it."

"I'm not suffocating myself in this sweltering prison of a house," Wolfe heard her hiss as she kept washing dishes. Silence fell over them again.

"I hope they're okay," She said from the sink.

"So you do know what's happening. Just on my way back from work I saw a group of men get arrested."

"Good."

Silence again. Wolfe looked to his right, and he saw Brieux shuffling his way around the side of the house. Wolfe pulled himself away from the edge of the house and to Brieux, who was fiddling with something in the shadows.

"Shaun said a few officers have died," she said as she pulled the plug from the sink.

"What are you doing?" Wolfe whispered. Then, as he rounded the corner on hands and knees, he saw water pouring from a garden hose. He pushed rows of pale, bug-bitten swiss chard back into the earth as he moved. They had crushed wilted brown roses and a whimpering rack of beans thinner than a strand of hair with their weight. Wolfe watched a few scratchy plants straining to birth cucumbers.

"Drink." He beckoned to Lett first. Lett suckled from the hose gulping down fresh water by the cups, and Wolfe, Scott, and Unity followed suit.

Wolfe rubbed the grime from his hands and face, letting it run over his shirt. He cupped it in his hands and rubbed it down his neck, under his armpits, and along his hair. He let it run down his throat, healing his sores, tasting Craik again as he gurgled him out of his mouth. The water was lukewarm, but it was electrifying. As the mud grew around his legs, Wolfe felt like he was pouring liquid gold over himself.

"Stop running water, you're running the well dry for a few dishes," the man in the house said. The water pump was hissing beneath the house. They sat in the mud under the window again. The darker clouds snuck over the edge of the town as heavier gusts of brisk wind quickly followed.

They were whispering now, and Wolfe strained to hear them.

"How can you say that?" the man asked.

"Easily. They were nice, they brought home baked muffins to church and gave our kids treats for Easter Sunday!"

"That's to their neighbours. How do they treat their workers?"

"Who cares!" she said a bit too loudly.

"You really don't care? Isn't it wrong? They do terrible things I've heard, why should I be happy about it?"

"Sure. Everyone gets angry sometimes, but why trust rumours? You have no reason to dislike them. What is one unpleasant experience you've had? One bad apple doesn't mean all of the Bredenburys are bad, don't be so close-minded."

The man was silent. Then he walked over to the sink and started rinsing his hands.

"Don't do this," she said.

"Do what?" the man asked, shaking his hands over the sink and rubbing them dry with a towel.

"Do what…I'm not stupid."

"There is no point. You'd be happy to have kids beaten and killed as long as you're happy, so don't worry about it."

"You wouldn't? It's strangers over our kids, our house, your job. Why would I put them above us?" she said, stopping him from walking out of the kitchen.

"But…"

"But nothing. You owe your job to the Bredenbury family. We owe it to ourselves to bask in the little bit of money we get, even if it means a few things happen. It's bad, maybe. But it's how the world works, that's just how it is and how it's always been."

"But I mean, isn't it…wrong?'

"You think it's okay for them to act like this? They're raping, killing, and robbing actual workers like you and they're looking for pity? You immediately lose my support when resort to any amount of violence, there are a lot better ways to get their grievances out."

"I…" the man said.

"Sometimes people get carried away, on both sides. But, would you or I ever kill people if we didn't get our way? They are violent. Those people you saw on the street might have killed a guard or raped someone. Raped me, raped your daughter." The woman had tears in her voice.

The man was silent, and Wolfe stopped listening. He leaned against the white plastic siding and stared into the sky, watching the clouds swirl and heave kilometres above them. He looked to his left, down the main street and saw flashing lights. Somewhere above the clouds, he heard a gunshot, then a cry. Someone gunned down; a woman, a sister, a daughter, an aunt, a granddaughter.

Sirens erupted somewhere deep in the town. In succession, the wailing rippled towards them. Alarm systems flashed and whirred at the edges of cracked windows, empty planter boxes, and fence posts. An emergency broadcast played out of each little black box. Red and white lights flashed out across every garden, behind curtains, open windows, and in every living room. The inhabitants of every house in Landia were stained red.

"Residents of Landia. This is an urgent emergency alert for the areas including…Buffalo Hills, Landia County, and the

Bredenbury family acre fields," the voice began, metallic and nearly unintelligible.

"The Bredenbury family is, currently, experiencing a violent insurgence amongst their workers at their summer home…north of Landia. The perpetrators are still at large."

The woman above them let out an almost silent gasp. The living room above them was awash with news broadcasts. Wolfe saw white screens crinkle into life along the street. Kitchen and bedroom lights flickered on as the broadcast voice rattled.

"Please turn off all lights, lock all doors and windows, and stay inside until further notice. If you have any sightings or information to report, call the report line at…17B30." The voice snapped off.

"We have to go…" Unity mouthed to the others, but Wolfe didn't move. The rest of them moved to the right, past the garage, to the road, and Wolfe watched them go. Before leaving, he turned himself around and flicked an eye over the windowsill as he backed away.

Wolfe glanced around the room lit by the screen covering the far wall. The kitchen was immaculate. Something straight out of an early two-thousand Martha Stewart magazine. White wooden floorboards shone polished and waxed. Wolfe stared at eggshell glass cupboards with decorative porcelain chickens housing salt and pepper. The walls hung with metal pots and pans. Small freezer-ready dishes of unknown food sat on the counter in front of an antique black and white microwave perched on a marble countertop.

The man and woman stood silently in front of the screen. He was dressed in a suit, half undone with a tie loose around his neck, and the woman was dressed in a loose-fitting nightgown. Wolfe watched with them. The man kept rubbing his head and letting out enormous sighs.

Wolfe sat, mouth hanging open at the scene painted before them. Pictures of officers charred to pieces, trapped behind fallen bricks and wooden beams in the guardhouse. The ambulances poured in as a helicopter broadcast the video live. Burnt, sharpened pillars jettisoned out from the smouldering mound in the yard's heart like rotten teeth. The wispy ashes caught the wind and clung to the sweeping branches of the hanging trees. The camera panned over the tree in front of the house, its long slender arms decorated with the hanging bobbles of the Bredenbury family.

"Those fucking bastards. You were right. You were right..." her husband snarled into the air.

"Let's go to bed," she said, and when they turned, he and Wolfe saw each other. Wolfe was painted in mud and sweat, and the man was painted with loathing.

"Call the line!" he yelled to his wife as he flung himself to the window. He was across the living room and into the kitchen in five steps, reaching through the window to grab a thick handful of Wolfe's hair.

"Getthefuckoffme," Wolfe gargled, bracing his feet against the wall and pushing. Leaving the man dangling out of the window with a handful of his hair.

Wolfe had never seen such a contorted image of rage. Every time he tried to pull a string of words out of his mouth, only a ferocious babble of curses and cries would come. The man flung himself off the kitchen counter, and a second later, the door to their house was wide open, his shadow crawling across the white fence that separated the alley and the yard.

The group scattered over bushes and around fences into the deeper parts of the town. Wolfe pulled himself running to his feet and lunged through the bushes at the back of their yard and into the alley. The shrubs pulled at his clothes and face, drawing blood as the branches thrashed him.

Wolfe heard a voice scream out behind him.

"YOU'RE SCUM! INBREDS! BASTARDS! MUTTS!" Then, the sound of cannons echoed through the sleepy hamlet turned wasp nest. Then again. And again after that. Wolfe's feet bit into gravel; he tasted metal in his throat. He heard nothing over the sound of the pounding feet and blood rushing through his body, drowning out the world around him.

He stopped at the end of the alley. His sweat-caked forehead was dry again, dredged with gravel dust that left trails of sweat bleeding down his forehead. He looked to his right, and Scott looked wheezy and sick to his stomach, even in the dull yellow light. Blood drenched his arm, and he looked like he was going to pass out. Wolfe caught Scott a moment before he keeled over. Every time he'd look at his arm, his face would go green again.

"Shit, I…I…" Wolfe tossed out words, but he fell short. The sirens lit up the alley behind them, and they had maybe a few spare seconds. Wolfe looked over his shoulder, expecting another bullet to hit Scott and kill him, but all he saw was an empty street where the man was standing with his gun.

"I—I…II…don't—"

"Just keep moving, Wolfe," a voice whispered from behind them. Brieux touched Scott from behind, and together they walked Scott away from the screaming lights; the windows cast whispers out into the alley as they held each other under the darkness.

Seconds later, a scream ricocheted off the buildings. A weeping cry that shook the air and begged for death. The wailing persisted longer as they sunk further into the dusty night.

—

"No, we have to stop. He's going to bleed out," Wolfe said a few minutes later.

"He's going to die if we wait, so let's just keep going."

"But he—"

"We need something to tie around his shoulder."

Finally, they stopped across from a park and behind an empty mechanic shop. They could hear voices yelling behind them as they lay on the sidewalk panting.

"Here," Unity said, untying Mrs. Bredenbury's glimmering scarf out of her hair and passing it to Brieux. Her hair was filled with branches and twigs, her knees skinned and bloody. Her clothes were ripped as she held Lett against her. The purple scarf went brown with blood the moment it touched his shoulder.

They turned down another alley rather than running down the

paved roads. They pushed past a rusting unused garbage can on wheels into a parking lot. They crawled along the edges of parked cars and trucks as men crowed and hollered somewhere to the north.

They slid through a group of spaced-out chain-link fences to the music of barking dogs and air ripping through helicopter blades. Lights shone down from the sky as they hid under the eaves of a pizza parlour closed for the night. They wove through the light and darkness, through the streets, through backyards, past pools and playsets, past sleeping dogs and parks until they came under the shadow of a towering church. A concrete platform was overgrown with weeds where a statue of the Virgin Mary once stood. Large rusting letters above the door said St. Mary of the Anglican Church.

"Okay, wait a second," Wolfe gulped, resting himself on the scratched-out sign of The Virgin Mary. A stitch in his side throbbed, his throat burnt, and his hands were torn and bleeding.

Brieux gestured to the vicinity with wide eyes. They were exposed. Anyone would spot them within a hundred yards if they turned down either street. Wolfe looked up, glancing at the weeping cross hanging above the brown doors, the rusted orange handles dripping.

The church was hideous: the roof was slumped and domed, the walls bowed out, a few windows were unbroken, and its once-white walls were stained with graffiti and ancient piss stains. Broken bottles and a shopping cart convulsed at the back door in the wind.

"What do we do? We're sitting ducks," Wolfe asked.

"In here." Unity pointed.

One window into the basement was broken, the edges of the glass jettisoned out like shark teeth. Wolfe and Brieux helped Scott through without question, sliding in after him and pulling in Unity and Lett.

The basement of the church was gutted. Grungy, slimy cement walls were sprouting outwards and cracked from a lack of upkeep. Empty cardboard boxes were taped up and tossed in each corner, dented, bruised and covered in stains. As they walked, the ground crinkled like thin ice, and pools of murky liquid swirled across the floor as they disturbed them. To the far right of the room, cement stairs led up to a doorway, blocked off with pieces of wood and more boxes. One of the large crates, each crudely nailed shut, had been torn off at the bottom of the stairs and its insides were half empty.

Wolfe stepped over and peered inside. Boxes of granola bars, water bottles, and canned goods lined the walls.

"Hey."

Brieux walked over to Wolfe as he was gesturing. He peered over the edge and saw the goods stacked in the crates.

"Are these all filled with food?" Wolfe asked the room, gesturing at the roughly fifteen crates plastered around the walls. Wolfe stopped, a glint of metal caught his eye, and his gaze fell upon a stained photo of The Virgin Mary. Her canvas was nearly ripped from her frame; her eyes were averted to the floor above them, listening to the aching of carefully placed steps in the church.

"Possibly," Briuxe responded.

Her hands clung to each other, her fingers clawing at her palms as her eyes followed him. She was glaring at him with evil thoughts as her halo glistened and shone above her, painting her in sombre light. Her eyes shone radiantly back at him as he watched her, a glimmer of red along the edge of her frame.

Wolfe dipped and pulled a pocket knife off the floor. He flipped it in his hand, stuffing it in his back pocket without looking at the painting.

"We should go," Wolfe said. The creaking above them grew into a rustling like wind through barren fields.

"We need supplies. Eat something," Brieux whispered, tossing a handful of granola bars to each of them. He looked through cardboard boxes until he had found some gauze and a gray tube of paste from a miniature first aid kit. Armed with a bottle of water, he cleaned out Scott's wound.

Wolfe imagined bountiful feasts of fresh vegetables and meats, glasses of wine and champagne, delectably braised salmon in some deeply stewed plum sauce served over legumes long thought to have gone extinct.

He sat opposite Mary, and she seemed to speak to him. There was rage where there should be peace, anger where there should be joy. She was hidden down here, cloaked in her blue cloth away from prying eyes. Wolfe thought about the night behind them, felt the coarseness of the stone, felt the soggy boxes. It wasn't much, but he was here. He was alive.

He paced back and forth from the windows, past Lett sitting in front of the painting and boxes, walking around Scott as he grimaced and shook. Sweat covered his body like a sheen.

"Wolfe, come help me."

Wolfe knelt in the dry spots of the basement where Scott was lying. His gray dress shirt had been ripped down his right arm, and at the top near the shoulder, blood trickled onto the floor. Wolfe lifted him, ran his hand against his side, and felt goosebumps run the length of his body while Brieux busied himself with the tube of paste.

They smeared Scott's shoulder with the gray paste and wrapped it with shredded pieces of linen towels that had packed the granola bars and water bottles.

"The bullet went right through his shoulder, so we're lucky. But we need antibiotics or it's going to get infected. If we don't find it soon the infection will set in and it'll be significantly harder to stop."

"Where do we find some?"

"A pharmacy?"

"That's not gonna happen."

"I know."

"Then what do we do?"

"I don't know."

They looked up when lightning shattered in the distance. The electricity hung in the air.

"I might know what this house looks like, but only if I see it.

They sent me once for medicine but…that was months ago."

"Okay well, we—"

Wolfe stopped. His eyes had drifted up to the top of the stairs, where the light was now falling towards them. Shadows moved under the door at the top of the stairs as voices rustled on the other side.

"Move," Wolfe whispered, pulling them both to the side as light burst down the stairs and nothing but the sound of rusty pipes dripping onto cement filled the room. Wolfe hadn't noticed how dark the basement was as the light burnt his eyes.

A lone man's shadow was cast in the lapping pools of water, still moving from their footsteps.

"Shhh," a voice hissed from the stairs.

The room went silent. The sound of feet. Wolfe tried not to move but shifted ever so slightly. The steps crept closer.

One.

Aching.

Step.

After.

The.

Other.

Wolfe listened to his heartbeat thunking away in his chest, growing louder and louder by the second. Wolfe's finger slid onto the trigger. His heart pounded, his eyes pressed together, trying to ignore the flitting shadows behind his eyelids.

The sound of scraping shoes on cement moved towards them. Wolfe held a hand, uncertain who he was holding, his other on the gun aimed towards the stairs.

A man arrived at the bottom of the stairs, glanced around and cast his shadow behind and over boxes. They tried to hide, but most of the packages were against the other side of the wall. They were trapped. It was hopeless.

The man turned and bathed them in yellow light. He held out his hands monetarily to show them he meant no harm. He dropped the light, and Wolfe squinted in the darkness.

"I ain't gonna hurtcha," he said. Wolfe slowly slid the pistol into the hem of his pants as the man beckoned them closer. He watched Wolfe's gun for a moment until he looked up the stairs again and nodded, flicking the five of them towards the stairs with his hands.

Brieux pushed Scott between him and Wolfe.

"We need some medicine."

"Let's see what we have upstairs."

—

With each step they took, the light grew around them. The walls were damp and mossy. Rotten drywall was puddling onto the ground, and mould snaked into the ceiling above them. They came out into a hallway off the nave of the church. To their right was a small confessional booth; to their left was the main altar. The lights flickered on and off like they were close to losing power.

"When they use all this electricity, it hits the lower income areas first. Always does. A lotta people are going to be without power or hot water in the morning, and it's a school night," he said as he pushed boxes and boards up against the empty door frame, sealing off the cooler draft pushing up from the basement below.

"Paynton," he said to a woman wrapped in black cloth, carrying a box of water down off the altar. "Could you see if you can find our first aid kit, please?" She nodded, then smiled as she retreated. Wolfe kept his head downturned, trying not to show his eyes.

"Religion ain't what it used to be, it just ain't. It's an empty gesture now, a place where people can one up each other, show off, prattle and gossip. No one worships anymore," he said, thrusting his hands up towards the Virgin Mary.

She was draped in crimson fabrics, and her nutty brown eyes shone like copper. Her hair swung down around her face, wrapped in ribbons draped in bangles and jewellery. A halo crowned her head like a sunburst, and a gentle warmth overcame him as she smiled with flushed, ochre cheeks.

"Where are y'all from?"

"We're heading north. Trying to get away from the war," Brieux lied.

"The cities?"

"Mexican panhandle."

The answer seemed to satisfy him.

"And the wound?" he asked, nodding at Paynton carrying a heavy bag under her arm.

"Shot. There are a lot of police around, something strange is going on tonight," Unity said. He didn't dignify her with a response.

"Everyone is welcome in my church. What little is left of it."

They had filled the main abbey of the church with cots and tents. People slept on and under the pews. People held onto their belongings under one arm, their food under the other. Thin blankets and bottles of water hung from every hand. The lights outside trolled back and forth, twinkling through the grimy, stained glass windows, sending images of Christian scenes over them. Colour burst from the windows; sparkling shadows painted the colours of roses and spring water, lilacs and melting snow.

A velvety purple rug led from the front to back as he walked them down the pews, thick with mud and dirt, soiled from years of never being cleaned. Light from outside shone up into the caste of the abbey, throwing beams of light off the tarnished bell, sending birds twittering out into the night.

"I think many people just need to let go of their anger. We're all people, we all have to work *somehow,*" he said, rustling his bag under his shoulder. "People make too big of a deal about all this eye colour stuff. Under God's eye, we will all repent in our last hours and be free from eternal suffering regardless."

Wolfe watched the bag crumple under his arms. His gut turned. Lights flickered over the edge of the broken window, and steps crunched on the gravel outside the doors.

"Then these people, they think they can burn, loot, and murder and think they are free from God's eye? From worldly retribution? You aren't one of those types? Are you?" he said, spinning around to face them.

"I think we should—" Brieux started, crossing his arm in front of Wolfe. Unity moved to turn around when three heavy knocks struck the front door.

"BESNA! Open the door!" a man yelled as lights shone through the windows and light hit their faces. Eyes in shades of green, gray, brown, and blue twinkled around them. Men and women, groggy with sleep, started to rush backwards through the church.

Wolfe pulled his gun out and aimed it at the officer. Lett pulled at Wolfe, and he aimed up, shooting a bullet, shattering the lone light bulb.

—BANG—

They spiralled into the darkness with hot glass falling like acid rain. Wolfe searched the darkness for someone. A moment in the hallway…darkness. On the altar…darkness. In the hallway… darkness. He threw the boards away from the door and searched again. Nothing. As he pulled the last board away, he felt a touch behind him. When he turned to look, he only saw the void and felt his own extinction.

Chapter 14

The Contact

Wolfe struggled to stand; arms grabbed at him as he connected with something hard and cool, and he fell back. His sense of smell returned first. The scent of heat-wrenched plastic, stagnant water, and dog shit flooded his nose, and a wave of nausea overcame him until he gurgled up stomach acid onto the slippery plastic beneath him.

Voices spoke to him, and mysterious figures glimmered at the edges of his mind. They looked like demons, spirits, and shadowy creatures from nightmares long forgotten. He tried to push himself away, but the hands grabbed him and pulled on his clothes, arms, and face until he stopped fighting. He pinched his eyes shut and listened to the crowing and whispering around him while he begged for sleep.

His mouth tasted like vomit, and something volatile burnt on his lips. The faces grew familiar around him. A smudge of clothing here, a crinkled nose, a bloodstained hand. Around him, blue and brown eyes looked back at him, eight to be exact, glimmering like owls after twilight.

Wolfe tried to stand, and a voice called him down again.

"Wolfe, stop…" It sang to him as gentle but rough hands guided him down onto his back, sliding against the rounded edge of this plastic tube they were hiding in.

"Where…" Wolfe began but couldn't continue. His head pounded furiously, and it stabbed him each time he tried to speak.

"No, don't worry about it right now," Scott said again.

Wolfe stopped, letting the relief rush over him as his surroundings came into focus. The red rounded plastic walls, the dangling rope ladders, a maze made with wooden farm animals.

Bouncy animals shimmered with dilapidated paint. Horses, giraffes, and elephants rocked back and forth, stirring in the gentle breeze. They were hiding in a playground. He opened his eyes again, and the boiling in his head calmed to a simmer.

"Did we find the guy?" He breathed gently between bouts of nausea and stabs in his head.

"No, not yet," Brieux said

"And we won't find him here," Unity said, sliding down the tube and onto the sand. Wolfe followed her, and the world hit him. He steadied himself on the cool metal of the playground, pacing his breath while his eyes streamed.

Wolfe felt thunder tremble through the ground as he stood there. He reached for his belt and felt the gun in the back of his pants.

Brieux came next. Then Scott slid down, with Unity helping him, grumbling about how heavy he was. He was still gray, and covered in a sheen of sweat.

"How much longer until he gets an infection?" Wolfe asked, pulling back the cloth and seeing a gory red hole in his shoulder.

"Could have already happened," Brieux said, ushering them against a line of bushes along the side of the park.

A reverberation ripped through the ground as the clock's chimes rang out its hourly toll. Wolfe followed the sound with his ears, trying to gather the direction. His eyes landed on the large brick post office with an enormous clock on it, the same he had seen from the road into town. The bell chimed thoughts into his mind.

"Do you think we could catch a train out of here?" Wolfe asked, looking back towards the tracks into town. "A train comes through every morning. The longer we stay, the less chance we have."

"We have to get Scott medicine first," said Brieux.

The wind was back again, stronger than before. It whipped the trees, and loose pine needles blew through the air. They moved across the street.

"Northwest," Wolfe whispered.

—

They crawled through vegetable gardens, avoiding barking dogs and the conspicuous prying eyes that leaned through the screen windows above their bedrooms and living room windows. They ducked through scrubby caragana bushes, over low garden fences, past windows where sleeping families lay, and the lights in the houses blinked out one by one. A cat had walked by; her trail of striped gray kittens had meowed at them before they split ways.

The street they had turned down was empty and lifeless, just like all the others. Then, on the right side of the road, third from the end, Brieux had spoken up.

"Wolfe, that's it."

He lifted a shaking finger and pointed to a ramshackle yellow house with chipping paint flaking off into the dead, crisp grass filled with sprouting weeds. Its red door was sunburnt and peeling, and a tree stump was standing in the centre of the yard. The roof seemed to heave under an invisible weight. The shingle-less roof wept with years of water stains.

Like most of the other houses, it was dark. The only light that grimaced across it was the flashing billboards that shone red like a portal to hell, bathing the streets in crimson, bloody light.

"Right. Scott and Lett can stay here. Me, Wolfe, and Unity will go in," Brieux said.

Scott and Lett stretched themselves across the dingy alley and under the garish, hazy lights that had flicked on as the darker clouds swooped over them. Brieux, Wolfe, and Unity crawled across the street beneath a net of moths. Most of the yards were devoid of grass; the cracked earth seemed to suck the cooler evening air into the earth's bowels.

As Wolfe heaved himself over the fence, he looked back. Across the road from them, crab apple trees clung to each other in an empty lot. Their twisted, cracking branches held each other limply as they dreamt of fruit. The earth was weeping outside of the constantly watered, lush fields of the Bredenbury family.

They scrambled themselves over the fence and landed in the front yard. The windows were dark and grungy, sticky with dead bugs and water stains. They crept around the side of the house, looking past the stained windows and into the darkness. They moved on their hands and knees until Wolfe ached. He stood up, arching his back.

"There's no way in. They're all locked."

"Well."

Wolfe listened to the sound of breaking glass as it trickled in through the floating dust and onto the floor. Brieux tossed his coat over the broken glass and helped Wolfe to his stomach before he backed his way in. Unity was next, throwing herself down through the window, trying to make as little noise as possible, and Brieux followed her.

They crept up the stairs and found an immaculate home. Paintings of naked women spiralling off gleaming animals hung on the walls, perfectly stained wooden floors ran the length of the house, and stone gray cabinets and appliances hung and sat on freshly painted white walls. They came up the stairs, into a kitchen, then a living room and a long hallway with closed doors along its length. When they got to the end, they pushed against the last door, and it creaked open.

A man was in bed, snoring like a chainsaw, and when the light hit him, he cracked open an eye. Wolfe raised his gun.

"Get out," Brieux said, and the man flipped off his covers. He was wearing a pair of striped black and gray briefs with holes along the band. He held his hands up and padded past them to the kitchen without a word.

Wolfe and the man sat at the kitchen table, listening to the clock tick and judging each other.

"It was my grandmother's. Family heirloom," He said, flicking a tooth underneath his nail and spitting out a lump of dirt. "I'm a very sentimental person."

"I'm sure."

"And he speaks…" the man said, smiling. When Wolfe didn't respond, he sighed and sunk into his chair, resting his hands in his lap.

Wolfe jumped.

"Hey. Hands on the table."

"Isn't it rude to have my elbows on the table? Jeez. My great-great-aunt is rolling in her grave." He smirked a lumpy, off-kilter smile that showed off the tips of his teeth.

He had to be in his forties. He was almost bald, and he was getting a beer gut from too much greasy food and alcohol. He folded his hands across from Wolfe and stared at him.

"You're not going to escape. You know that, right? You shouldn't even try. This is gonna be on the news day in and day out. You made yourselves look like idiots. This just proves that bluies are violent."

"Shut up, if you make any more noise I'm going to shoot you."

He smiled his crooked smile, and he ran a fake zipper across his lips with his fingers and flicked it behind his head.

Canvas bags and mouldy plastic grocery bags were strewn across the counter as Brieux and Unity packed the house into them.

The man laughed as Wolfe watched him up and down.

"Like what you see?"

"Shut up? Remember?" And Wolfe pointed the gun in on him. Sirens zipped down the street, and the guy smiled.

"Where are they?" Wolfe asked, cocking the gun in his hand.

"They?"

"Contact lenses."

"Oh. I think I sold them all a few days ago. I might remember if you give me something I want though," he said, dipping his head towards Unity crouched over by the sink.

"You're disgusting," Wolfe said as the man chuckled.

"I've never had a blue-eyed woman before. I've heard bluies are feisty," he said, pinching his lips together and squeaking at her.

"You dirty bastard. Keep to your fucking self or I'll…" Unity started, but he cut her off.

"A murderer too? How sexy…"

"Unity…come on," Brieux said, pointing back to the cupboards above the stove.

"Where are they? You aren't going to have sold them all."

"Oh?"

The man dropped his hands into his lap again, and this time Wolfe didn't notice. Wolfe leaned closer to ask him again, and the man fought the latch that held the silver gun strapped beneath the table.

"Hey. Hands up. If you aren't helpful we'll kill you."

"Fine by me."

He stood up and forced the table up by the edge, shoving the table's rim into Wolfe's chest. Wolfe's gun shot into the air and clattered to the floor. The man aimed his silver gun in and went to fire. Wolfe pushed the table back, pushing the man's arm inward and forcing his gun to the floor.

The man spun towards the fridge, reaching for the guns, and Wolfe jumped after him. They wrestled over the silver gun, and it slipped out of their hands again and over by Unity's foot.

"Unity!" Wolfe cried, and as she'd gone to grab the gun, the man was pointing Wolfe's gun at the two of them.

"Up against the counter," he said as Brieux came up from the basement. "I'm gonna call the line, and they'll have three bodies to dispose of. "Woman. Ox," he said, flicking his gun towards the edge of the kitchen. "You can watch this one die first," he said, pulling Wolfe towards him by the scruff of the neck. Wolfe tried to push himself away, but he clicked his tongue against his teeth.

"Tsk tsk tsk. Come here."

Wolfe hadn't come this far just to die. He rested his clammy, naked thighs on either side of Wolfe and pressed his crotch into Wolfe's back.

"Should I count to three or should I make it a surprise?" the man said. "No one breaks into my fucking house. I warned you didn't I? You weren't going to win."

"One."

Wolfe pinched his eyes shut. *What would it be like?* Would he hear the gunshot, or would his world just go black? *Would it hurt? Would Unity and Brieux escape? Would Scott take care of Lett?*

"Two."

"Wait—" Wolfe started to push his head away from the gaping black hole of the gun.

The man pulled the trigger.

Click.

Wolfe's gun was empty. Wolfe ran through every bullet. *The cooking staff, Mrs. Ester, in the plantation house.* Wolfe remembered the eight bullets on the shelf beside the gun when he'd seen it first, resting on Brieux's shelf. *The church.* The gun had been empty since the church.

"I—" the man began, but Wolfe flung his head back with enough force to break his skin. Wolfe pushed himself across the kitchen and snatched the gun off the counter. But by the time he'd turned back, Unity had already shattered his skull with a cast-iron skillet off the stove.

"Did you kill him?" Wolfe asked.

"I doubt it." Unity spit on his bleeding face, and Brieux started dragging him towards the main bedroom again, wrapping him in the sheets at the base of the bed.

"Are you okay Wolfe?" Unity asked, staring at him.

"Yeah. I think so."

The fridge was bare, the cupboards were empty, and they reeked of fake blueberries and cinnamon. They pulled together a handful of groceries from the basement but none of the elusive contact lenses. They drew closer to morning.

"Alright," Brieux said. In front of them was a pile of foraged loot. A few half-full bottles of water, snack bars, sugar, a bottle of cooking oil, some chips, a pot of salt, some cloth, some oversized shirts, a pair of jackets, canned tuna, a few lighters, an almost empty bag of flour, some matches, and their saving grace, a first aid kit.

They split the supplies between them. Wolfe pulled a canvas bag out from under the sink and stuffed it with some food and water, a kitchen knife wrapped in a kitchen towel, and a grocery bag of sugar. Then, some paper, a few pens, his gun, and the man's gun. He flicked on the tap and trickled water into his hand, pushing over his face and pulling it back through his hair. Then he rooted through the depths of his pockets, tossing a handful of jewellery onto the counter.

"Take these," Wolfe said, pushing two golden bracelets into Unity's hands. She slid them over both arms and wrapped a silver necklace around her neck, stuffing two rings into her backpack.

"Brieux," Wolfe called out, tossing a necklace, two more rings, and a diamond-encrusted brooch across the room, and he slid it into his backpack loaded with supplies. Wolfe stuffed the other pieces into random crevices and holes in their luggage.

The three of them heaved their bags out the front door as lightning snaked across the sky above them. The first fat raindrops fell across them, touching their foreheads, pecking them with tremendous relief. The fence creaked as the wind gathered strength.

"And the medicine?" Scott groaned from the ground. He was sitting propped up against a red and yellow fire hydrant.

"We'll do it on the train."

"Right. Is everyone ready?" Wolfe asked, passing out more jewellery between them. Earrings to Unity, a bracelet for Lett, and a ring to himself.

"Okay," they whispered to each other and set out across the town again, racing against time. They moved past a silent care home and an abandoned print shop. An old museum creaked in the wind as the storm gathered around them. The wind was loud enough to deafen them, ripping rotten shingles off the roofs of old buildings, swirling dust around them and blinding them.

The ground trembled with thunder, and lightning lit the sky above them. The smell of damp stone forced itself into Wolfe's lungs as they reached the old grain elevator again. The sound of metal wheels on a metal track rumbled into town. Across a large ball diamond, then an empty field, the train was hissing. Its brakes released, and the train ached to a slow gait.

They moved between trees and under the heaving behemoth of the grain elevator. By the time they had passed the grain elevator, the train was moving at the speed of a slow walk, slowly picking up speed again. When they came around the corner, they stopped.

The train was long enough that the engine was out of sight, and the caboose was still buried in the dark. Officers prowled against the sides of the train, crawling over cargo, glinting lights into train cars as the train moved forward again with rust and graffiti tags hanging off its edges.

"What do we do?'

"Hell if I know."

It couldn't be more than a thirty-second run.

The same trio of women Wolfe had seen earlier, had been caught trying to sneak aboard the train and screams filled the air. Wolfe heard the yelling of men and the sounds of guns, the cries and screams of injured women, then barking dogs and the sound of tires on dirt streaking away from the train.

Wolfe made a run for it. He dashed across the dirt as the first pounding of rain started to beat him. He felt the wind behind him, pushing and howling against his clothes, throwing him forward as lights shone on him. Bullets buried themselves in the dirt around him, and he heard them break the air like a whip.

He hit the train running and pulled himself up. He felt a hand behind him, and Unity yelled, catching Wolfe's hand as the train jolted. Lett was dangling off her shoulder as she swung, and a bullet buried itself in the wood beside her neck. Another shot and Unity was still holding on. She slid her hand onto the side of the train, and Wolfe fell back against the car, holding Lett in his arms.

Wolfe pulled her forward, and the three of them scrambled behind a mountain of boxes as screams and gunshots echoed against the side of the train. They lost Scott and Brieux to the roar of wind as the train picked up speed. They moved faster until the blistering wind stole the air from their lungs, pushing them out into the desert.

"Wolfe?!" a voice called above the wind. Two lumbering shapes were crawling towards them over the top of a train car. Wolfe heaved Scott over his other arm, and together he and Brieux pulled him into the open boxcar with Unity and Lett, breathing in the victory as the train moved south.

Wolfe held Lett as they rested over piles of sheet metal and wooden beams. He looked over the edge of the train car, rolling over a trellis that spanned a rocky ravine as spits of rain continued to pepper them with wet, frozen kisses.

Wolfe understood the town's motto now as the train pushed against the wind heading towards its destination. He gaped, looking out towards the edge of the town, nothing more than a glow on the horizon. Every flash of lightning illuminated a barren wasteland known as the Desolation that was once called the 'south.' The Desolation went on forever, hundreds of thousands of kilometres of sand and dry earth stretching around a blistering equator that was incapable of sustaining human life.

Chapter 15

Abyss

The storm kept overhead through the night, not unlike a giant crawling over them; its gentle swirling fingers extended, sending sheets of rain flurrying down in circles. The wind snapped violently around them. They watched the lightning baste the landscape in shades of red, white, and purple light, casting eerie silhouettes and shadows off and through branches and shrivelled towns laying cold against the barren landscape. The train barrelled forward.

Wolfe felt the wind give off a rattling gasp, sucking at his clothes. He shivered. The chilled sweat on his body clung to him as his breath turned to fog in the air. When the flashes would come, he'd search the sky for shapes in the churning, jumbled clouds. The ground seemed to hiss, the day's heat leaching out into the iced night like fog.

The five of them huddled together. Scott held the loaded silver pistol in his hand, never letting his finger off the barrel. Unity and Brieux clung to each other to stave off the cold, Lett was plastered between Wolfe and Unity, and together they watched the sky.

Wolfe felt an elbow into his ribs. Unity held out the dirty water bottle they'd been drinking from. He smiled, looking at the scarce inch or two of water that danced around the bottom of the bottle. He gently shook his head. Then he felt a hand on his arm. He turned and looked at Unity, and she flashed her teeth at him.

"What?" he asked, not able to hold his smile back.

"We're free."

That was all she said, looking back at the lines of gray painting down behind them. The moon fought to bounce its hovering, pellucid beams through apertures of clouds as the storm swirled around them again and again. Wolfe could see the rain like a silver curtain moving down from the clouds somewhere in the distance.

"Well…we still…" Wolfe began, thinking of the world ahead of them, the battles they'd have to fight, and the hurdles still to come.

"No. No matter what comes, no matter what happens, right now, at this moment…we're free." She smiled again, holding out a hand to catch droplets of rain in her hands. He watched the water hit her, dance down her hands and run up her arm. He watched little snakes of water run down the creases of her fingers, watched the bones in her wrist twist and dance under her skin as the water pooled in the divots of her hand.

"Just…stop. Listen for a second," she said, pulling Wolfe's hands out into the rain.

Wolfe stopped. He let his hands swing in the breeze. The air swirled around them; the drops were cold on his skin; he had skin that could feel. He listened to the cruel cracks of thunder and the soft rumbling in the distance; he had ears that could hear. The smell of churning earth disturbed by rain, the taste of the air on his tongue, the churning of the wheels beneath them. He was here.

The rain picked up again, flurrying around Wolfe, dousing him, peppering him with tiny kisses from God himself. Every touch imbued him with electricity and filled him with power. He felt like he could conquer the world.

"FUCK, THIS FEELS GOOD! WOOOOOOOOOH!" Wolfe cried out, hopping to his feet. The wind screamed with him; the rain washed his tear-streaked face. He knew he was crying. The sky cried with him.

Wolfe had lost his parents, brother, and friends in the camp before the ghetto when he was far too young. Craik's story had ended at the end of Mr. Bredenbury's bullet. At least Mr. Bredenbury died. He got what he deserved. *I'm sorry I couldn't save you.* Wolfe thought to himself.

Almost five years had been stolen from him, and he'd never get them back. Things were going to change; something had changed. He saw Craik's face, and he smiled. Somewhere, wherever he was, he would know. He'd know.

"Wolfe!" Scott yelled as Wolfe slipped over a sheet of wet plastic. He crawled over the lumber, tied down with slick, hydro resistant covering, and kissed him on the lips, using wet sticky hands to pull him closer with his shirt. He tasted Scott, smelled him, felt the stubble over his cheeks; plastic and sweat, anxiety and terror.

"Wolfe, are you okay?" he asked. When Wolfe stepped back, he could see a smile on his lips for the first time. Through flashes of lightning, he could see a sadness in his eyes lift, an end of misery, the first turnings of acceptance.

Unity screamed at the top of her lungs, the wind carrying the voices somewhere, hiding them where the wind hides her secrets. She yelled again, louder until she was out of breath, and her voice cracked in tune with the lightning.

"YELL," Wolfe said. His face was glued with hair as water ran down his face, under his shirt, through his pants, and into his shoes.

Lightning crashed into each other above them; the battle of gods since time immemorial rocked the sky loose. Wolfe saw his life dancing in those clouds.

Scott cracked a smile.

Brieux snorted behind him, letting out a howl and a bark above the broken and crooked trees as the train blurred them. He and Wolfe barked and howled together in the air with the distant yipping of coyotes.

"Really?" Scott smiled, then he laughed, really laughed. His voice was soft and light, airy like the silence before water crashed against a beach. He'd never heard him laugh before.

"FUCK YOU!" Scott yelled into the storm, his voice lost in the pounding rain and wind, the chiming of triumphant angels and symphonies lost to time. His voice carried high above them, resting above the storm with a backdrop of starry skies.

"Fuck who?" Wolfe laughed into his chest, the breath of rain and winds trickling down his wet skin, his shirt clinging to him, translucent and pale. He wanted to be closer to him. He wanted nothing but water between them.

"Everyone. Anyone. Someone?" he said, looking into his eyes. The two men saw each other renewed and born again. He wasn't the man he had met on the train or the man covered in dirt and ash from the night before. He was someone else. His eyes apologized; guilt from the past two months washed over his face.

They kissed again, a kiss that spoke a thousand words. Wolfe felt the curve of his neck with his palm. Scott pulled him in by the curl of his back and hissed when Wolfe touched his wound. Wolfe felt the fringe of his lips, rough and calloused, chewed into flaps of skin with anxiety. Wolfe realized he was relieved. He was terrified Scott was going to die. All the emotions he'd put on hold since Landia flooded him.

"You don't have to be nervous, you can stop chewing your lips to pieces," Wolfe said, pulling his face away and running his thumb along the edge of his lip, feeling the minuscule bumps and holes Scott had torn with his teeth.

"I want you to take this," Scott said. They were the only two people alive on earth. There was nothing but each other. Wolfe moved his eyes back up into Scott's, electrified by the flashes of light.

"What is it?" Wolfe asked. Off his neck, Scott slid a necklace he had never seen before. It was a thin, dark wooden cross. He had seen it before. Inlaid with a crust of diamonds along its breast, beads crawled up and down the string.

"Is this Mrs. Bredenbury's?"

"It was, yes. I want you to keep it on forever. Sort of like…" He didn't continue, guilt crawled across his face. He looked away, back over the rain, rubbing his palm over his lips to wet them. Wolfe reached up and tilted his face back towards his own.

"A protection charm?" Wolfe asked.

"No. More of…a peace offering. From me."

Wolfe turned it over in his hand, feeling the chiselled wood grain slip over and under his fingers. Wolfe had marvelled at it back at the plantation, but it looked even more stunning under the lightning. It had four tiny crystals laid into the wood at each corner of the cross. It seemed to sing to Wolfe, practically humming.

"I'm sorry." Scott dipped his face away, staring into the murky sky. Wolfe watched his silhouette, his outline iced with worry. He was thinking about the past or worrying about the future. Wolfe held his hand, dipped his head into his shoulder, and felt the water dribble underneath his nose.

"I forgive you," Wolfe said.

"For what?"

"For everything."

Wolfe wasn't sure he meant it yet, but the only thing he wanted at that moment was to see him smile. He just wanted to take away his pain.

They kissed again, but this was a different kiss. It wasn't a kiss of love but a kiss of reconciliation. It was an "I'm sorry" kiss, a "don't hate me" kiss, a "don't be stupid kiss," and an "I could never hate you" kiss. Wolfe never wanted to let go of his lips. If he died now, there was nothing heaven could offer him.

Wolfe pulled the necklace out of his fingers and pulled it over his wet hair. He pulled it down under his shirt and leaned up against Scott again.

"I think I'm falling in love," Wolfe whispered, surprised to hear his own voice say it aloud.

"If you're falling, I'm already in love." Scott smiled, rubbing hair out of his eyes, and kissing him one more time for good measure, then he turned to watch the clouds swirl.

"I think we should move," Scott yelled over the whipping wind. The first few chunks of hail had fallen, beaming them with masses of ice. It was small at first, like being pelted with frozen peas, but they grew larger and larger by the second.

"Sonofabitch." Scott spit, trying to pull himself to his feet as slowly as possible as he held his arm against him. Unity shielded herself from the hail as a large piece smacked Wolfe on the elbow, sending electric tingles up and down his arm. He held Lett under his body, moving across the tarp with Scott guarding them.

The train had straightened out, heading south again through the storm. Brieux heaved Scott over the tarp and under the eaves of the boxcar behind them. They all leaned against the door in silence. Nothing but a heaving, breathing pile of soaking wet bodies.

"Those bastards are enormous," Brieux said, watching chunks of hail the size of coins, then nectarines bounce down off the train car, sliding around in piles on the tarp, gathering in the mountains in the corners of the flat. They rubbed their bruises and bumps as they laughed. Wolfe looked at Lett, and he smiled back.

"Ummh…" He spoke up to Wolfe.

"Yeah?"

"When is Mommy coming?" Lett asked, looking between the faces sitting with him on the train. Wolfe congealed, and his heart sank. No one else said anything, so it left Wolfe with nothing but a lie.

"We're gonna meet her later, it's fine, don't worry about that." He smiled at him, and Lett beamed back. Lett curled into Wolfe's legs, wrapping his arms around them.

"What do we do?" he mouthed. He looked between Unity and Brieux, but they had already looked away, asking themselves the same question.

Wolfe came to rest his head on Scott's shoulder, trying not to think about it but unable to do anything else. *What am I going to tell the kid?* He asked divinity, feeling the cross swing against his neck.

He had never been religious, not before this anyway. But he hoped something out there was listening and told him what to do before he woke up. Wolfe closed his eyes and let the howling wind and the voices it carried on it lull him into the deepest sleep he'd had in ages, bundling himself up to Scott's body heat to stave off the oncoming chill.

—

Wolfe woke with a start, the unfathomable, sooty sky unending above him. Sprinkled with bits of fluff and twinkling stars. The storm had passed behind them, nothing but faint crackling energy in the distance. Brieux had stuffed the bottles with chunks of hail and rainwater, leaving them a single water bottle for whatever lay ahead.

Wolfe curled his face into Scott's arm, his right arm wrapped around Wolfe's side. Scott was lying gingerly beside Brieux, both covered in jackets. Lett was on Wolfe's right, and Unity even farther past that. Wolfe didn't know how to explain it or conceptualize the thoughts in his head, but his body told him he was home. The cold had fallen over them, and the wind blowing past them felt tinged with frost. Lett curled into Wolfe's back, and Unity curled into Lett.

"Scott, are you awake?" Wolfe chattered up to him. His lips felt frozen, and his wet clothes were sucked against him. The early glints of sunlight were just barely creeping over the horizon, painting a deep gray into the air and across their faces.

"Hmmm."

"We have to get off soon."

The sun was rising, and the train had turned southeast, rushing along the cliffs at the southern coast. The bottom half of Louisiana had been swallowed by the sea, and only rough, choppy cliffs remained, towering above a hot, gray gulf.

"Yeah but how?" he said.

"I don't know."

"And after that, and that, and that, and that?" Wolfe asked. "What is our plan after this?"

They all sat in silence.

"I have an idea, but it's going to be a lot of work," Brieux spoke up at last. Everyone but Lett was awake. They stared into the sky. No one moved. No one looked at each other. They spoke without faces.

"Well…we have to decide soon."

"This train will probably stop somewhere along the coast to either refuel or distribute their shipment. We can either sneak into whatever city they stop in for supplies, or we can say screw the supplies for now and start heading west through the lower Desolation."

"Why in good Christ would we go through the Desolation?" Unity asked, her facial features twisted in the growing light as the stars above them gently blinked their heavy eyes shut for the day.

"There is talk. Was talk…" he began.

"Rumors?" she whispered. Lett was stirring from his sleep, and Wolfe stretched his back against the boxcar behind him. "Rumors aren't going to save us." She said,

"Well then, what's the rumour?" Wolfe asked. Unity was standing up and stretching her back, her neck, rolling her fingers together.

"There are few places left where blue-eyed people can still live in freedom: Japan, Mexico, areas around Quebec, a few Pacific islands. There are some countries in Europe but we can't get across the ocean. But the vast majority of people support this now, it's just a fact. Mexico City is at war, it's our best shot. Maybe we could help with the war effort? Maybe we could do something?" he said.

Wolfe stood up, bathing himself in the rays of warm light that crawled unimpeded by the clouds over him. "And the fastest way is through the Desolation," he said, taking a light sip from the bottle, letting the still frozen water coat his parched tongue and calm his angry throat.

"We won't survive a trip through the Desolation," Unity said.

"She's right," Scott said. "We only have so much water, maybe if we could find more food and—"

The train lurched violently, and the wheels screeched as their motion slowed. The blur of the trees gained more texture, and the expansive blue wall turned back into an ocean. Tiny waves, without the blur of motion, crinkled.

Then, as the train snaked its way over hills and down a cliff, Wolfe laid eyes on the scene below them. Black, unmarked vans and hovering motorcycles, giant white tracking dogs with blue collars, and BESNA officers with large guns and weapons streamed in the streets below them. An organized army designed to keep blue-eyed people scared and beaten down had flooded what was left of the city by the sea.

Wolfe looked past a network of coastal shanty towns and hovels. Out to sea, Wolfe watched the relic of a city sinking beneath the lapping steel waves. Towers of metal and glass, covered in moss, were hanging with bird nests and sea creatures. Hordes of white flecks spun around the spires, casting shadows over the gray towers holding themselves up against the waves.

"New Orleans," Unity whispered to herself.

"I'm with Brieux. The Desolation is the only place they won't follow us," Wolfe said, pointing down at the valley. The train was slowing, still high on the cliffs as it drifted right, preparing for its descent down into the valley, the coast, and the city below them.

"The second the train slows before the dip, point yourself away from the train in case you fall. Then you have to run as fast as you can up towards the plateau." He pointed a waving finger up towards a towering point of orange stone.

"I'll jump with you," Scott said, holding Lett's hand.

At the edge of the wasteland, the rocky cliff gave way to a valley before meeting the sea where the ocean historically used to sit. The long valley ran a strip along the edge of the Gulf Coast. It housed a temperate rainforest, picking up moisture off the warm ocean edge before drying out in the flat midwestern Desolation.

"You'll have maybe a ten minute head start on the dogs."

"What?"

The train had crested now, and their car's movement had frozen as it heaved itself over the last hills down towards the remnants of New Orleans. The train was mere seconds from gathering its speed again.

"GO!" Brieux yelled, and in the second it took for Brieux to slip and cripple Wolfe backwards into the train, the others were gone. They were hurtling downhill. The wind whipped Wolfe's ears, and the tarp flapped and billowed like a giant silver bird. They screamed at each other over the roar of the wind and the screaming of metal on metal.

"What do we do—" By the time Wolfe had gone to speak, he was dragged over to the tarp. Brieux was fighting with the metal restraints, cool against his skin as he fought to undo the latch. It was free with a click, and it billowed up like a circus tent. Then it flew up flat against the boxcar, metal ringlets bouncing and clanging freely against the side of the train. It wagged over them, hiding them from the cameras and officers.

They had reached the bottom of the southern bay coast. Wolfe had never seen a city like that before. Towering out across the ocean before them was a city forgotten. The ancient monoliths of stone and glass were heaving under the sea, still towering along the ridge of rock and trees. Wolfe had seen the news broadcasts every other day as a child, the hurricanes battering the coast and sending millions fleeing. It had meant nothing to him then, and now it felt like a dream, a different world altogether.

Brieux pulled himself to his feet and leaned over the edge of the train car, looking at the jagged rocks beneath them. The train veered sharply to the left as it barrelled towards the town along the coast, swarming with officers and news cameras.

"We have to jump."

They looked out over the edge of the train and saw a dingy gray swamp floating with algae and animal life. Birds burst free from the water, shedding droplets of water that shone in the air, casting refractions through the sky.

It couldn't be over fifty feet, maybe less, but Wolfe was already moving backwards. "Brieux I don—" and he was tumbling through the air.

The world spun around him in an endless roll. A second later, Wolfe met water. He was trapped under inches of thick slime that stuck around his face, drowning him. He felt his ears pop, and his feet touched wide arms of mud trying to pull him towards the ground. He barely managed to kick the floor, feeling panic flare as he struggled for air.

Wolfe pulled his head up through green algae that swung from his face and neck. He choked as the grunge tried to pull him back beneath the surface. He watched Brieux heaving himself over the algae and into the water until he pulled himself up on the weeds and grasses that stretched from the rocky hillside out.

Wolfe tried the same, pulling himself up with his body weight and crashing down onto the bed of the murky swamp, but it was harder than it looked. By the time he'd pulled himself to the edge of the swamp, his lungs were burning, and his limbs ached. Brieux pulled Wolfe out by the elbow, throwing glances over his shoulder towards the town as the sound of air getting slashed by metal wings broke through the skies.

He felt his legs shaking from adrenaline, but he and Brieux ran towards the jungle and the hills ahead. His bag was still on him, soaking wet and leaking down his back. The grasses were dense and prickly, the ground cover of clover and mud pulled at them. He felt something stab through his shoe, but he focused on the dense forest that lay fifty yards ahead.

They tore through vines and tripped over bulging tree roots. Wolfe saw a blur of earth tones before landing hard on his side. He saw the armoured trucks roaring along the northern plateau before Brieux suddenly joined him. They lay there in silence for a moment, watching the sky swirl with clouds. What felt like an hour passed once the droning sounds of vehicles, hovering aircraft, and men shrunk into the distance.

"Think they saw us?"

"I don't know."

The tracks above them had stopped rattling, and the pounding in their ears had subsided. They crawled into the forest and pushed a path through the dense underbrush, weaving between towering trunks.

The forest was magnificent. Trees that should have taken centuries to grow sprung up seemingly overnight. They hung with moss and trembled with insects and wild animals. The entire Gulf of Mexico had become this foggy, humid marsh. Wolfe saw a group of blue mushrooms that seemed to push away when he eyed them and followed their trail after they'd passed. Above them, the dense foliage nearly blocked out the sun, only lightning bolts scratched between the trees in perfectly cut lines. Let light reach the forest floor.

The mud squelched against their shoes, stained with sweat and dirt. Wolfe panted. He was very much aware of the stench he was giving off, trying to rub the sweat back into his armpits while Brieux walked ahead of him.

The Bredenbury family no longer exists, Wolfe remembered suddenly. They're dead. And he had a considerable part to play in their death. BESNA wouldn't just kill him; they'd torture him until he wished for death. He shivered at the thought.

"Well. You must have something to say about your life. If you're a human, that is," Wolfe joked, catching up to his surprisingly enormous strides.

"I'm not that interesting." He smiled.

"Nothing?"

"I was born in Gatineau, back in the old days," he said.

Wolfe looked over at Brieux. His smile lines had vanished, and his eyes were wider than usual. Wolfe waited for him to speak again, but he said nothing. Wolfe accepted it, and they kept moving.

They climbed another steep hill covered with snaking vines before they came out on the dry ground. The arid plateau that signalled the start of the Desolation, seven hundred kilometres north, and probably five thousand kilometres west and east, yawned in front of them. The train tracks were nowhere to be seen, nor were there any noises to indicate BESNA officers were waiting to strike. They paused before clambering over a ridge of fallen trees and slippery moss-coated rocks before going west.

"Shit. We're really out in the open here," Brieux said as they ran towards the gigantic towering stone monolith they agreed to meet on. Wolfe's legs were pounding. The sun was already heavy in the sky, frying the air around them.

They ran like animals. Wolfe let himself go and lost all sense of time. He ignored the aching in the soles of his feet, his thirst, and his hunger. The monolith grew in Wolfe's vision until they could make out the specks of people sitting around its fat base. As they moved closer, they could make out faces, and as they climbed the rock's face, they could make out smiles. Scott, Lett, and Unity. Tired but alive.

"I'm glad you're not dead," Wolfe called, clamouring up the final rocky hill.

"Is Mommy coming yet?" he asked.

"Not yet." Wolfe smiled, feeling his guilt tear him apart. "It's going to be okay, we'll take care of you until she comes, okay?" Wolfe told the kid, trying to convince himself too. He was kneeling as the rest of them stared out over the horizon.

Wolfe pulled the small pocket knife from his back pocket.

"I have an important job for you though if you're up for it. You're our scout. You have to watch the hills for wild animals and people, warn us if there is trouble so we don't get ambushed by BESNA. You have to take this job very seriously," Wolfe said, knowing he wouldn't see anything before they saw it. Wolfe watched the spiel hit its mark.

"Maybe…" Lett said in a moment of uncertainty.

"Are you sure? Your mom sent this knife. She thought you could."

"I think I can do that Wolfe."

"We trust you," Wolfe said, knowing it would keep him busy. Lett was squirming with excitement, squinting ahead through the sun, scanning the horizon with fierce determination. As they readied themselves to climb down, Unity grabbed his arm.

"I didn't know you were such a kid person."

"Neither did I."

He hugged Scott, careful to avoid the bandaged shoulder and breathed him in.

"I thought BESNA was going to catch us," Wolfe said.

"Thank god they didn't," Scott said, kissing his forehead, and Wolfe closed his eyes to bask in it.

The Desolation was a sizzling abyss before them. A million dangers lurked out there, and a million threats prowled behind them. Brieux tied his hair out of his face and wrapped his wet jacket around his waist. His shoes were caked with mud, and his t-shirt was stained with dirt, sweat, and Scott's blood. Unity put her hair in a ponytail and held Lett's hand. Scott's dress shirt was torn, and his entire left arm was exposed. His torso was wrapped with gauze, and his pants were ripped on both knees. Wolfe tossed his bag over his chest so it hung on his side. He pulled a scarf around his forehead and tied it off, his neck dangling with gold and wooden necklaces as they stepped into the unknown together.

Chapter 16

The Southern Raiders

The sun broiled down on them through their endless trek. They had drug themselves through the Desolation by night and tried to find rest among the cracked and fallen trees along the rocky cliffs to the north during the day. The heat ate away at their lungs. Venomous animals hidden among the dry, terracotta earth watched them as they walked.

The officers in their shiny black trucks, with their wheezing drones and barking dogs, hadn't followed them. The officers must have assumed they would die to the elements or the animals and saved their energy for bigger and better things. *They may have been right,* Wolfe thought.

Wolfe had tried to count, but the limitless sun pulling its way through the sky and the dark, moonless nights stole his memories away. *Had it been three weeks, four? Has it been a month? A year? A day? A minute?* The days blurred together through a gauze of obscurity. The nights he lost jangled just outside of reach, just beyond what he could see while awake. Then the days were stolen away to a world of dreams and thoughts beyond his control.

Signs of humanity were few and far between. A burnt gas station: its coffers empty of money, its tanks empty of gas, its rotted sandwiches turned back to dirt. A filmy layer of dust had settled into rust, heavier than stone. Then they found a small town, broken glass blown into sand, wood reborn into trees, concrete into dried orange clay.

They trudged past a highway frozen in time: Burnt vehicles were lying in the ditch like burnt and plucked chicken carcasses, dwindled to ivory bone. Skeletons were fighting their way over dunes, black and crispy like obsidian shards, digging their way free from a phantom firestorm that had once torn across the counties, claiming their lives like a beast out for flesh.

The sky was pink, the sun dull and heavy in the sky like a red bowling ball. The acrid air sparked and ripped at the lungs like the vicious pack of wolves that wandered through the arid landscape, hungry for the few meals that sauntered unsuspectingly.

"Do you see that?" Scott pointed out, dragging the group to a halt as the melted asphalt and gravel path stirred beneath their feet. A small gray lump was sitting on a hill through a dusty haze, slumped under the fog of smoke. A rock? An animal? A falsification of the mind?

"It looks like a big rock…" Unity croaked. She looked at the rest of the party, and their undetermined journey through the Desolation had taken its toll. She limped heavily, carrying herself over the uneven terrain.

Scott's wound was sneaking into an infection. Brieux's right hand was gnarled and torn from a wolf attack three days earlier. Wolfe's own ankle burnt with each step, twisted while ambling over a fallen tree. Lett's forehead was burnt. They shuffled him between them. A fever had set in fourty-eight hours earlier, and he slept uneasily.

Wolfe knew they were in a dire state, and any amount of food or water, medicine or new clothes would save their lives. After killing the wolves, their new gun was empty, and they needed ammunition. He doubted they would actually find anything that wasn't robbed or razed, regardless. It was straight north of there, shimmering in silence, the opposite direction from where they believed Mexico was.

"What is it?" Scott asked.

"Probably a rock," Wolfe agreed, staring ahead of them towards the aimless mass of dirt and rocks, dried grass and blistering heat.

"Should we check it out?" Scott asked.

"We can't. We have to keep moving," Brieux said. He held his weeping arm against himself. It reeked of blood, peppered with flies and gnats. His entire arm trembled, and he glared up with grayness dotting his face. "We don't have the time."

"It might be a house, with people in it."

"Or it's not, and we waste a morning when we could be resting."

"Or it is, and we won't die. We have to try," Scott said.

The rest of them hung in silence, and Wolfe spoke up. "I'm with Scott, it can't hurt."

Unity spoke. "Well, I'm with Brieux," she said.

"Of course you are, you hate me."

"I don't care about you enough to hate you," she said, looking at Scott

"Well I'm going, and if you want to come, follow me, and if you want to leave me to die, then do it."

"I finally get a chance!?" she cried sarcastically.

Scott and Unity fought bitterly on and off their entire journey. They clashed harshly enough to put the plights of war victims, the spats of Roman gods, and the constant war between the elements to pale in shame. The earth stopped its fight against the sea, and the planets stopped their movement, all to watch their vicious fights over the correct way to boil water, the best way to walk through sand and over burnt sea glass, the proper way to start fires.

They jumbled forth in silence. They were blissfully aimless until the lump through the gauze became a figure, a proportion, a sum. The world around Wolfe had become nothing more than that. The same dusty landscape played tricks on the mind until suddenly, the world was nothing more than numbers and ideas. Skeletal tree branches to be counted, rocks gathered in his mind, cracks in asphalt neatly numbered away. Something exact. Normal. Familiar.

It gave substance to the dull days and the wordless afternoons; it pulled his mind away from aching ankles and the listless pounding in his legs. It distracted him from the migraines when the heat was most potent, and the air turned into acidic pneumonia in his lungs.

They finally came over the seventeenth hill, past the fourty-third tree, over the ninety-seventh rock, and the lump had gained a profile. Knobbly, arthritic fingers of wood danced around its side. *What is it called?* Wolfe asked himself. The brain's usual process of formulating opinions and ideas had died. Icy silence rang back. Wolfe looked again. Glass windows like frozen eyes sat haunted and sightless. Some eyes were broken, gouged open like animal carcasses mauled against perpetual rolling hills by nameless creatures.

The roof was sunken, hunched and ancient like it had seen a thousand years before and after the start of time. Knobbly banisters on the porch...*THAT's what it was called*, he thought to himself with relief. The rotting boards accented the knobbly railings on the porch. They stopped on the hill, and they let their voices shrink to whispers.

"Think there is anything in there?" Scott asked.

"Well, it couldn't hurt to try." Because Wolfe had agreed with Scott, Unity quickly turned her attention to Wolfe.

"It'd make more sense if we didn't waste the next two days wandering around this rotting dump like idiots and tried to find civilization."

"Well, she is right," Wolfe added. "There has to be people around here somewhere. I mean, who is doing all this looting?"

"Told you!"

"Shut. Up." Scott yelled. "The men are talking. Leave the thinking to us before you injure yourself."

Wolfe cringed. He watched him shake his head, and he smiled at Unity, trying to bridge peace with Scott's vulgar statement. Wolfe gripped his pistol and slipped down the dune, half on foot, half on his back. He pulled himself off the burning sand, holding his hand up to shield his eyes from the orb in the sky. He eyed the windows and the peeling roof, and Wolfe walked around to the front.

The house was nearly invisible from the road, and it would have been easier to miss from a distance since it was nestled in between two hills. What looked like the dried bed of a creek snaked out behind the house, once running water and rolling hills. Once upon a time, it would have been paradise.

The door was covered in built-up sand. The door was white, peeling like sunburnt skin. Wolfe ascended the steps as they cried beneath him. The sand crumbled like burning paper as he touched it, and cooler air crawled from the opening door, rustling his clothes and crawling over him like bugs.

The house was frozen in time. Sand washed rugs laid over heavy beech floors. The floral patterning along the walls cracked and peeled as if it had been burnt; invisible hands pulled it back with thin, skeletal fingers. The windows still had thin, sun-parched curtains, blowing in a non-existent breeze past the mayonnaise yellow cupboards. Tarnished metal faucets ran dry.

Wolfe had stepped back into a different world. He was the ghost in a time that was no longer his. He was a foreign entity that shouldn't even be leaving footprints on the red tasselled rug that ran down the slender hallway ahead of him. To his left, the kitchen beckoned him, so he turned right into the living room, ignoring the gentle tugs beckoning him to the rooms above him up the stairs.

White leather sofas had been chewed open by bugs and mice, and metal frames peeked out from their flared bases. Shelves along the wall were laden with books, wax melters, and vintage plates, all caked with dust. The carpet beneath his feet was soft, and a small, seventy-five-inch television screen was sitting on a glass cabinet.

Wolfe knelt, feeling tears at the back of his eyes. Someone had neatly stacked a backlog of magazine subscriptions in the cabinet. Television remotes, an old gaming system that children would have played on, rested in the corner. He stood again, looking into the living room as he imagined the joyful screams of children that would never step foot in here again.

A sizable oriental vase was stuffed with dead flowers against the side window. They drooped, wilting outwards like a head of hair, and half of them were strewn across the floor. The windows were open, and they gently rippled, sending slivers of light flitting across the opposite wall.

He turned down the hallway at the end of the living room, past an immaculately decorated guest room slipping into decay, a storeroom, a locked door, and a white-tiled bathroom utterly untouched by the elements. They had filled the tub with water at some point, but only the sinking rings remained.

He stood in the kitchen. A white wood table and white linoleum floor was coated with years of dust. He dragged his fingers along the counter, leaving trails in the dirt. He was drifting, feeling knobs on the kitchen drawers, glancing at the dishwasher, the stainless steel fridge giving off a horrible wafting stench.

A pantheon of companies and brand names lorded over the room: Plastered over toaster ovens and microwaves, over the fridge and empty baby food jars, across hand towels and kitchen cabinets. He couldn't look anywhere without seeing more names. Bredenbury was etched along a rotten carton of eggs and sewn across the front of the kitchen towels.

Again he felt a gnawing feeling like he was being watched by the house's inhabitants, like he was an intruder, a time traveller, knowing more than any of them could at this point in time. Who knew that these CEOs and companies would become the kings and queens of the twenty-first century? The monarchies the rest of the world bowed under.

"Wolfe?"

He leaned into the hallway and saw the rest of them trickling in. Unity touched the family photos on the walls while Brieux rested Lett on the floor. Scott made his way toward him.

"Did you find anything?"

"Oh. Um—I…"

"Oh, you're so ditsy…" Scott laughed, tossing his head back.

"Well no, I just—"

"Relax Wolfe, you take everything so seriously."

"I—" Scott swooped in and kissed him. Pulling the small of his back in and holding him there. Wolfe was perplexed, happy even.

He kissed him back. He tasted like spit, charcoal, and sand. Wolfe leaned back and watched his smiling face. The thoughts of his rude comments slipped away, lost in a blissful moment he had dreamt of just a few months ago.

"Right. This place looks virtually untouched." He pulled away again quickly, leaving Wolfe spinning as he pried through cupboards.

"I don't think anyone has been here, but Scott..." Wolfe had slipped out from under his spell, preparing to berate him for his comments as Unity lingered on the stairwell.

"Hey Unity, Brieux, come here!" Scott had spilled open a jackpot in one of the cupboards, and piles of canned goods came spilling out of a lazy Susan at the back of the kitchen.

A mountain of dried kidney beans, canned tomatoes, bags of rice, noodles, unmarked silver cans, coconut milk, half-eaten Halloween candy, and water bottles poured out. Cans of salmon and tuna, dried corn and dehydrated beans spilled afterwards, followed by mini cans of soda, and dried bullion containers.

In the excitement, Wolfe let his plan slip from his mind. "You guys can sort out what you find onto the kitchen table while I look a little more." And Scott disappeared into the bowels of the house.

—

When all was said and done, they had fifteen cans of meat, three pounds of cooking oil each, sugar, flour, and coffee, over a hundred cans of various dried vegetables, three cases of bottled water, one package of batteries, milk powder, seven flashlights, and three bags of dehydrated lemons, oranges, and limes.

Upstairs they had found a shiny new shotgun and boxes of ammo, brand new clothes, and in the garage, they found jerry cans filled with fuel. They searched every cupboard and drawer before stumbling across felt diapers and a box of medicine.

Wolfe walked through the upstairs hallway, and the doors were open now, footprints muddied the floor, noises banged up from the kitchen while someone rustled in the master bedroom. He glanced at the family pictures on the wall. From what he could guess, a younger family lived here, a youngish woman and her husband, with two pre-teen children and a baby girl.

He looked at their unsuspecting, naive faces. He leaned in close and saw glimmers of their eyes. The young girl had bright blue eyes, the same as her mother. The father and the son had brown eyes; the baby, who knew.

Wolfe formulated an idea about their lives:

Ken and Hazlet moved into her grandparents' house to farm and till the land at the turn of the millennia. Their daughter Alvena, seven, their son Mervin, five, and their baby girl Disley lived here until the oceans swelled, the sun burst, and the earth dried. The soft grassy hills became arid sand and desert. Alvena, Disley, and Hazlet were sold by their husband and father into slavery to the Valparaiso family to make ends meet. Ken, wracked with guilt, killed himself, and the son is still alive somewhere in the east, probably well into middle age. Born in two 2003, maybe later. He was currently dying due to some form of chemical poisoning near a silk factory. His sister had already given birth sixteen times, each of them sold to another buyer across the country. It didn't matter anymore.

Wolfe shook his head. *No.* No, he didn't know that was the case. He looked over their faces; he didn't want to do this to himself. They were okay; they were living in some house off the Mexican coast; they were fine.

There were pictures of them standing in front of their home. A date was scratched into it with a black ballpoint pen, but it was aged and sunken, and no one could make it out. From what Brieux guessed, they were in southern Oklahoma, or what would have been.

He passed the master bedroom while Unity styled sun hats in a splintered mirror. Wolfe smiled at her as they passed each other. He found himself in what would have been one of the children's rooms. A bright blue carpet obscured the wooden floor. Kids toys were sorted away neatly. A tiny plastic rocking horse, a set of Lego pieces, sat in a small multicoloured statuesque lump in the corner. This could have been his room as a child. Would the kids ever have dreamed of finishing their masterpiece?

Wolfe sat on a bed shaped like a race car, feeling the creaking and the shifting weight beneath himself. He rested over the cool sheets, laying over the jovial sea creatures printed on the blanket. He saw a blue-eyed tortoise, and he threw his head back on the pillow, watching the shadows swinging from the fluttering blinds towards the ceiling. A burst of cooler air breathed over him. He could smell rain in the air; the room grew darker with each outward breath.

—

The day had passed into evening. Wolfe woke up to the sun behind the hills that nestled the house, breathing in the smell of rain on the breeze.

God, how he wished life would go back to normal. It had to, at some point, return to a time where the colour of your eyes didn't matter or point your life in one of few directions. Wolfe's story was written before he'd even been born.

I am okay. If Wolfe told himself it enough, maybe it would become the truth. He knew that the colour of his eyes didn't make him lazy or stupid, but their constant demonization, the constant reaffirmation of their innate flaws, sometimes made him question. *Could they be right about me?*

Days would pass, and it all seemed so inevitable. They would get beaten, and when they stood up and threw off the abuser, they were the villains. *We get our faces blasted across screens day and night. Why is Mr. Bredenbury's face not up there?* Why, if God existed, pushing them to persevere, were they the ones running?

"Hey, what do you think of this Wolfe?" Unity said to him, spinning around the corner wearing a dusty red dress inlaid with sparkles, like glittering diamonds and frozen raspberries under an autumnal sunset.

Wolfe had spaced out completely. His eyes were blank, and he was staring at the ceiling painted blue. He wished he could just get up and go home without wondering who was watching him or what the next step was. He craved simplicity. To get up, eat breakfast at a table, live life, and go back to bed in peace and without a single thought of fear in his heart. *I could dream, hope, create, contemplate…*

"Look. Mulling it over isn't going to help you much, I can promise you that." She leaned against the wall. She was wearing heavy work boots she'd found in the attic and had tossed a sweater over her dress, so it spun and draped around her hips when she walked or leaned on the walls. Wolfe looked at her, actually looked at her for the first time. She had dark, loose hair that grew thicker at her forehead and above her bushy eyebrows. Her hands were more prominent than average, and her fingernails were torn. Her shoulders were broad and heavy, and at this moment, with the sun pecking freckles over her bronzed skin, she was the most beautiful woman alive.

"Get up and do something. That'll help. Come look through the closets with me." She stomped over to Wolfe with a smile on her face, a broad, natural smirk that showed all her soft yellow teeth.

"Look—"

"Look nothing, you're coming whether you like it or not."

She pulled him into the bedroom and tossed a large rimmed pink sun hat adorned with a yellow flower glued to its rim on his head.

"Stunning," she jabbed.

Wolfe laughed. He saw himself in the mirror and turned away. He looked skinnier than ever before. His cheekbones jutted out, and his jaw looked metallic. His eyes looked sunken and shallow like murky ponds. He turned away from the mirror, his head lowered. He didn't want to have to look at himself. He slipped the hat onto the bed.

"It's okay." Her voice was calm, friendly, with no venom, no malice. It was soft, like cotton and linen, like vanilla and meringue.

Wolfe looked up, and her eyes shimmered. They sparkled like cold frosty mornings, like delicate lace. Her eyes reminded Wolfe of the tinsel his family used to hang on their Christmas tree. Her body seemed to quiver, shimmer as if she was a vision, something spectral. Her gaze unravelled Wolfe. He was raw, naked, yet he couldn't find it in him to look away.

"It will be, anyway. Okay. Eventually," she said, turning her attention to Wolfe's discarded sun hat, which was crumpled on the patterned lace blanket on the bed. She fingered the petals of the small acrylic flower before she ripped it off, shaking a few damaged petals off and slipped it into Wolfe's mat of dark black hair that was coming down around his eyebrows.

"It makes your eyes look brighter." She smiled, and Wolfe expected her to hug him for a moment, but she patted him on the shoulder, crunching her lips together over her teeth with an uncomfortable smile.

"I'm sorry about Scott," Wolfe said.

"I don't need an apology from you. Trust me, assholes mean little to me." She smiled, looking out the window.

Heavy raindrops rattled the windowpane, startling Wolfe back to reality as the wind started howling and the curtains fluttered. He slid the pane open, savouring the cool breeze that ate through him. He felt the droplets touch his skin; the satin fluttering against his cheek, the scent of musty curtains overwhelmed him, and he stepped back, watching huge green clouds churn and undulate above him. The earth trembled with distant thunder, and when he looked back, Unity had gone back to the wardrobe.

Wolfe stepped down the stairs, feeling the stained wood slide under his fingers. The downstairs living room had been turned into a makeshift camp. The food was stacked against a wall, blankets and pillows from spare rooms had been strewn over the floor, and chairs had been lifted from the kitchen and placed around an empty fireplace.

Lett slept soundly in the corner, his hands clutching the pocket knife. Scott flipped through old magazines, and Brieux tossed books into the black fireplace.

"Wolfe, look at this!" he cried, flipping the pages around to him with laughter. He pulled out a fold-out page in a children's fashion magazine filled with pictures of blue tunics, blue vests, and blue dresses. Scott had spread them on the coffee table while he chortled.

"Yeah, that's wild," Wolfe grunted, staring at all the faces staring up at him.

"What is in your hair?" Scott glared up at him. He was wearing a long-sleeved shirt rolled up to his elbows, his hair was wet, and his smile had dissipated.

"A flower? You know, those things that grow out of the ground?" Wolfe snorted, rolling his eyes and turning around laughing.

"Take it out. You look so stupid." When Wolfe turned back to him, his face had melted into a surprised laugh and smile, an eye roll and a look of resigned indignation. Wolfe preferred the glare. Wolfe felt his cheeks burn. He ran his fingers through his hair and let the polyester daffodil slip into his back pocket. His ears burned with embarrassment. *How could I have been so silly? I knew I'd look weird.*

"Hey Wolfe, can you come help me?" Unity was standing in the kitchen, holding stacks of multicoloured candles in various shapes and sizes, with a box of windproof survival matches. She watched the entire display from the kitchen, and her face had dropped. She wouldn't even meet his eyes.

Brieux popped up and stretched. He pulled his arms up above his head, his white tee shirt lifted. He was wearing white athletic sweatpants and a pair of fuzzy pink socks.

He stepped over the blankets, grabbed a handful of candles, and hefted two under each armpit. He scattered candles over every table, desk, and chair around the room. With each window firmly closed and the broken ones nailed shut.

Wolfe watched her walk past him, and when he stepped forward to help her, he felt a hand wrap around the back of his waist, pulling him away from her and towards Scott. Darkness had settled in now, sparing the omniscient glows that seemed to seep into the walls, coating them in a soft glimmer.

Scott had slid his hand off him and moved to the fireplace beside Brieux. In a few minutes, the fire was roaring around them, casting deeply arched shadows against the walls. Wolfe watched Scott move across the room and beckon Wolfe over. He watched Brieux warm his hands in front of the fire, and it seemed to envelop him, a pillar of flame rising behind him like a dragon.

The house shook, and the walls roared and shrieked as a gust of wind threatened their sanctuary. The storms ripped through the southern half of North America, reaching as far north as the old states of Wyoming and Idaho.

Three dull, repetitious noises rang against the door. First a creak, then a thump, then a bang. It seemed a step removed from the clunking and banging of the wind, with the trembling walls and the dusty carpets.

"What was that?" Brieux asked, moving his hands to the hammer they had used earlier to seal the windows shut.

"Nothing is going to come out in this weather..." Scott said, sinking himself deeper against the blankets on the floor, pulling Wolfe closer.

"Scott, stop. Listen." Every few seconds, the sound would come again, randomly and sporadically, then, without question, it stopped. "Go look," Wolfe said, pushing himself off Scott and sitting up in front of the fire.

"Wolfe come on..."

"Scott." Brieux's face had grown dark, and he was holding his hammer out towards the door. Slowly, ever so slowly, and across the room, the door handle was turning at the front of the house.

"What the fuck is that?" Unity asked. Lett was awake now and scurried across the floor to Wolfe, holding his pocket knife out in front of him, trembling in his hands. Unity held a kitchen knife, and Wolfe held his empty gun.

Brieux moved closer to the door to investigate what was undoubtedly a figure gliding past the front window. Wolfe pushed himself up against the wall with Lett ducking against the wooden frame of the floor as Scott and Brieux moved towards the door.

"Wolfe, take Lett upstairs," Brieux whispered. It turned achingly slowly, and they had already slid the lock shut. The darkness upstairs screamed at Wolfe. There was no way he was going up there in the dark with BESNA guards creeping around, ready to kill them or worse.

"I—"

"NOW," Scott yelled. They were on either side of the door now. Wolfe saw their silhouettes, cold and trembling with fear.

"Come on," Unity called to him, grabbing him by the arm and pulling them to the bottom of the stairs.

The second floor was an obsidian void. The wind howled above them, shaking the fabric of the house. With its booming voice, the wind threatened to rip the roof off their heads and send them spinning into the night. The house howled threats back in response, sending blistering words through the chimney, whistling out into the night.

"Scott the back door…" Wolfe called back. And as they rounded the corner of the hallway at the top of the stairs, Wolfe looked back to see he was already gone. Brieux was crouched there with his hammer as the door rattled against the wind.

"Keep your head down from the windows," she said, pulling them through the darkness. The light still glowed up the stairs behind them. Then the sound of the wind grew louder. The door was open, banging against the wall inside the house, thunk after thunk.

"Brie—" Wolfe began. Unity threw her hand over his mouth, shaking her head slowly. The light of the fireplace crept suddenly out of existence.

"Wolfe? Brieux? I fo—" Scott had yelled before he went silent. The sound of steps creaking up the stairs followed them, and Wolfe fell backwards. The candles had gone out. The fireplace hissed and sizzled beneath the floorboards, plunging them into darkness.

"Unity?" He was alone now with Lett around his ankle. He groped the wall in the darkness listening to the creaking of steps in the hallway. A lot of them. His breath caught in his throat. He was in the bathroom, it seemed, and he slid into the tub with Lett, gently rustling at the curtain as he did.

The storm raged outside as the figures moved inside. *God, I wished I had bullets. I could finish it right now.* He would Lett close his eyes, tell him to think of his mother, and he'd pull the trigger. Then he'd think of all the faces he'd never see again, and he'd do the same to himself. Arcola. Scott. Brieux. Unity. Craik. *It's okay, you'll see them all again.* He told himself.

The bathroom door creaked open. Wolfe heard steps on tile and then rustling on the curtain. Wolfe held his breath. Then he heard thrashing and muted struggling across the hallway. He felt like dying as Lett whimpered into his chest. He could see Sandy, see her eyes, her last words.

"Keep my baby safe." And Wolfe knew he had failed her.

A man in black was towering over them in the bathtub, blinding them in light. He must have begged like so many before him, but he couldn't recall. Wolfe smelled something like rotten eggs and sickly sweet fruit. His senses fell away from him slowly: The movement of the branches cutting through the midnight air dissipated into silence, and the shifting sands and pounding wind were static against his brain, beating its relentless sounds against the dark halls inside his mind. His vision was gone, then the taste of rot and sugar in his mouth were gone.

He wasn't in the tub anymore; Lett wasn't against his chest. He was nowhere but everywhere, somewhere but nowhere, until finally, he was nothing. His last thoughts slipped into oblivion with him.

Sleep is okay.

Chapter 17

The Oasis

Darkness begets darkness. Wolfe passed in and out of consciousness for what may have been days. Indiscriminately, he'd feel warmth trace his throat, dripping down his chin and onto his chest, and then his dreams would claim him again. Worse yet, the demons he battled in his mind never let him rest. Familiar faces, distant as if through gauze, screamed and wailed, sometimes at him, sometimes for him. He saw faces he thought he knew, some he didn't, straining against the fog of his mind, twisting and contorting into vicious fiends.

He was standing in icy mud, breaking around him and sucking his feet out from under him. Snow was gently treading from the sky, swirling and dancing until it dissipated into the air above him. His fingers were numb, the wind stung his face, and his eyes were frozen solid.

He was in a yard. Abandoned sheds, houses, and barns stood silent yet shrieked in the wind. He turned to run, falling into the mud, his school uniform two sizes too small fought against him; his parents were going to kill him for getting dirty. He held their necks in his pockets; they were speaking to him, crying at him.

He tried to pull himself up, but lights flicked on in the burnt house on the hill. Men with guns, naked as the day they were born, ran out, covered in blood, laughing and crying. Twisting black bodies and charred animals gasped and giggled from the branches. They swung and flailed reanimated, trying to crawl their way back to earth, to scream without sound.

All the lights were on him. Lights from above, from the trees ahead of him. They were calling him names, screaming unintelligibly. His whole family was standing before him. Dark empty sockets cried for him, and when he reached for his family, they sank backwards. The mud pulled him back as he felt the sting of lashes in his back and smelled the combined reek of burning math books and wood polisher. The stench of spoiled lemons, burnt sugar, old sweat, and cinnamon billowed out of the muddy pit beneath him.

High above him, as he was pulled into the ground, a god made of eyes laughed at him. He went down a dark hole. His stomach lurched into his abdomen. He was in a scene from Alice in Wonderland, semi-trucks roared past him upside down, and a woman he knew but had never seen ate her lunch: A piece of peeled Italian pepperoni, a slice of herb and garlic cheddar, a raspberry yogourt, a salted almond chocolate bar, and a diet orange soda. She smiled at him, but she had no teeth, fingers crawling from her open mouth.

He stopped. Suspended in the air, he saw eyes he knew. Was he awake, or was he dreaming? His eyes were burning, but they were gone when he reached for them. Reduced. He was thoughts, a collection of memories and ideas floating in the darkness. No more dreams. No more stories. No more eyes.

———

He had no idea how much time had passed as he fell through time and space. A light appeared through the darkness, peeling through the corners of his eyelids. Silence surrounded him, but noises picked through the ringing: fabric dancing against sand, distant crying animals, creaking rusted metal. The light was scratching against the static of his closed eyes until Wolfe gathered enough strength to crack an eyelid open.

The light shrieked at him, blinding him, stabbing his eyes, and he snapped them shut again. He was fighting against caked-on sleep, which felt like too much work. He lay there, waiting for whatever may happen to happen, but curiosity was coiling inside him again. He moved his hands, letting his fingers move freely with no particular destination, and he rubbed the sleep from his eye.

He lay there, taking stock of his body. *Fingers? Yes. Toes?*

Yes. His feet were sticking out from under...*a blanket? Yes. Woollen. Am I wearing clothes? No? Yes. A shirt. What am I laying on? A cot? No.* He felt the frame of a bed underneath him. Not enough stuffing, smelling like rust. *Neck? Yes.*

His curiosity got the better of him. He felt his dusty fingers prying at the corners of his eyes, cracking them open by force. A sliver of light assaulted his corneas, and he let it. He broke open both eyes long enough to glimpse at the world around him: A crate, moving fabric, a woman bent over a man across from him.

Oh god, they caught me, he thought. *They need me alive so they can kill me. It'll be televised.* He knew he had to end it now; he had to deny them the satisfaction. He turned his face away from the beams of light drifting around the flapping fabric. A tent entrance. Through his squinted eyelids, he saw a few pebbles and the odd shutter of sand drifting beneath the edges of the tent. In the middle of the room, a table was resting with a book, a pen, a lantern, and a medicine chest.

He would have to grab the pen, stab the woman, and escape before being seen. *Perfect sense.* He thought of Scott, Lett, Unity, and Brieux, but the thoughts left him as quickly as they'd appeared. He listened to her footsteps approach. Her shadow hung over him, and she stepped across to the other side of the room.

He steadied himself. Wolfe made his move.

He scrambled out of bed and found someone had tied his left ankle to the corner of the frame. The glorious escape he imagined ended as quickly as it began. He flung himself through the air and fell flat on the floor, flipping the metal bed over onto himself with a magnificent crash that rivalled anything living or dead.

Metal and wood thrashed together, a dog somewhere barked wildly, and the woman screamed, waking other occupants in the building who cried along with her. Wolfe lay mortified, listening to others trying to get up, tripping, falling, and taking their bed with them too. The impending crashes and roars were followed closely by another poor soul trying the same thing he had done and failing miserably.

"What in God's name," he heard a man's voice from the front of the tent call over the sound of metal thrashing, dishes breaking, and people crying in distress. Wolfe elected to pretend to have been sleeping and fell out of bed during a nightmare. He felt the warm ground beneath him as he listened to footsteps drawing nearer. He tossed in a snore for good measure.

"Mr. Bredenbury I presume?" a low and grumbling voice said to him, a thick drawl pouring from his mouth like a meandering stream, each syllable a rock to be slowly crawled around and over. "Please, sir, I am well aware that you are awake. Come now," the man said. Wolfe gave up, and with flushed cheeks, he peeled an eye open. He was looking up at three men, none of which he recognized. Behind them, the woman cleaned people off the floor.

"Let's get you covered up now and we'll have a nice chat," he said, blinking his eyes away from Wolfe's bottom half, which he realized was naked from the waist down. The blanket was wrapped around his neck in the chaos, leaving the rest of him exposed and lifted off the side of the bed in an impossible position.

The two men rested the bed back on its feet and lifted Wolfe back into his bed, covering him with the blanket again. They propped him up with pillows and untied his ankle while he watched the floor with his eyebrows furrowed, his lips creeping over his teeth in a sheepish smirk.

"Now, do you need me to ask you why you threw yourself out of bed like that?" he asked. Wolfe went to respond, but no words came out. His words scratched each other. His voice was quick, thin, and watery, heavy with the taste of sleep.

"Mm. Water please?" the man asked the woman behind him.

Wolfe looked the man over from head to toe when he turned back. He was wearing a sun-baked plaid shirt, cuffed at the wrists, soft brown hair climbed over the backs of his arms, his skin was brown, kissed with black freckles and heat. He was wearing blue jeans that had faded into the colour of baby lace and soft diamonds, a rough red trucking hat pressed on a mat of roughly cut black hair with silver around the edges, and a golden cross around his neck, complimenting his brown eyes. His work boots were aged, crumbling along their seams like paper.

Two men stood behind him, but Wolfe couldn't escape the pants. They were foreign. Alien. External. Monstrosities. The blue-eyed men fringing either side of the man were warm, with heavy smiles across their faces. They were both wearing black sandals, pairs of gray sweatpants, and t-shirts riddled with holes, chewed by bugs and age. They were young, and their faces were still bright with youth, naivety, and belief. He both envied and despised them.

Wolfe sighed with relief as the water breached his lips, spilling down his throat as the rain washed the Desolation. He gurgled the water, letting it sit against the back of his throat. He pulled his legs closer towards him as the three men watched him.

"Are you going to kill me?" Wolfe squeezed out as daggers of thirst dug into his throat. The men smiled, chuckling to themselves, only making him feel worse.

"No. We're not going to kill you," the man said as they smiled. A glaze of suspicion must have slipped across Wolfe's face because the man stepped to his feet. "But of course, we can just show you," he said. "Alvena, could you find Mr. Bredenbury his things please?"

"I'm sorry," Wolfe interrupted as the nurse turned to find his pants, "but my name isn't Bredenbury." He felt his stomach clench each time they said his name aloud. He wasn't a Bredenbury; he would never be a Bredenbury.

"Of course. We have a policy of calling our defectors by their given names until they recall their former. Many can't. Some have never known another name."

"Defectors?" Wolfe heard himself whisper.

The man smiled at him again; yellowed teeth, nicely rounded and fitting his mouth perfectly, grinned back at him. "Yes, that gives you the idea of what we do here. Do you know your name? You can choose a new name if you'd prefer."

What could he possibly say? Was he even the same man, boy, that he was before? *Can I do my name justice?* Would they find him? Wolfe felt heat rise in his throat, felt his eyes flicker back against tears.

"Well, we won't need it now. Take your time. Your first name?

"Wolfe. With an E."

Mrs. Alvena tossed him his pair of freshly washed gray pants he'd worn for the past month. Then she heaved a torrent of knick-knacks into his hands: A crumpled polyester daffodil missing a handful of petals, a few broken pieces of an electronic chip, a single diamond earring, and a handful of crumpled paper. He held the past month in his hands, feeling their edges against his palm. She slid a tangled ball of chain and cord necklaces into his hands,

He crumbled it into a ball and shoved it into his pockets again. He slid the pants up underneath the blankets and around his waist. A pair of boots lay on the floor, the bottoms torn with sandpaper and studded with nails.

"And we can assume this is yours?" he asked as Mrs. Alvena held out a filthy, sunburnt gun towards him, still empty.

"Yes."

"We can find some bullets for you later I'm sure," he said, beckoning Wolfe onto his feet and towards the flapping entrance, letting the sun bleed into the room.

"Oh, and I hope you know they're no hard feelings over your disturbance this afternoon," he said as he beckoned out towards the front of the tent. Wolfe stepped over the scattered bedpans and smiled an apology at a nurse who glared back at him.

Wolfe stepped into the sun and felt his heart catch in his chest; his breath caught in the back of his throat. He was standing in the middle of what could have been his hometown, but it was hotter, dirtier, and sandier. Women walked along the streets wrapped in blue and red scarves glittering golden under the sun. Children raced sage bushes down the road with peeled sticks laughing and hooting.

He was standing on a cracked sidewalk, blustered with sand

and rocks. They had transformed the ancient relic of gas stations into barns, storage sheds, and stables for goats and sheep. Houses lined the streets without doors, cots hung in front of open windows, and people spilled in and out of doorways. He was standing in the heart of a town that had survived; against all odds, it was thriving in the Desolation.

Streams of horses drug wooden cisterns sloshing with water. Men and women worked and sweated, hauling and carrying, laughing, and talking in boisterous voices. Men conversed with women along the edge of the road, corralling younger children into bathtubs gleaming white in the sun, holding babies in slings over their backs.

"Welcome to our sanctuary." The man smiled, patting Wolfe on the back. "I'll take you to our main gathering area." he said, beckoning him to follow as Wolfe blinked the bright light and pain out of his eyes.

The long, spindly road led west, past crumbling fast food buildings and sunken semi-trailers under the imposing eyes of broken streetlights. They walked past the withering corpses of rundown motels; the metal signs along the side of the road were gone, and their green veneer had peeled and cracked, showing silver underneath. Yellow flakes dusted onto the ground like snow as they walked beneath a peeling McDonald's sign above them. An Exxon still sat proudly, redundant gas prices from a bygone age stared back at them as they walked, cars buried under the sand shifted in the hot wind.

"Where are my friends?" Wolfe pried, stepping over the long-unused hot metal train tracks, sizzling in the heat. Wolfe wiped beads of sweat off his face as the ground seemed to sizzle against his footwear.

"You mean the people we found with you?"

"Yes."

"That's where we're going."

The man pointed to a large strip mall. The building had shed its brown facade and was painted in brilliant orange and green hues in fat, irregular swatches. At the end of the mall, an oversized warehouse building sat. The mall had once been the home of a few clustered stores and businesses packed with cheap, tacky, 'in season' clothes that were all the rage, manufactured in sweatshops in third world countries. Then, the cheap, vulgar, 'in season' clothes found their homes in trash heaps when the slightly newer, more expensive version found itself on the shelves in their place.

As they walked towards the building, a few older men spoke outside its doors.

Wolfe remembered the men at the house in the desert, how they had moved on them, the stuff that had filled his lungs, how it had felt, how he felt now.

"Why did you guys act like that back at the house? Why not just knock?"

"Ah. Well, to be honest, we do that to everyone, and I'm sorry, it rarely hits people as strongly as it hit you. But it's for our safety. We didn't know your intentions, and you were on our land after all," he said.

"Your land? You can stake claim to whole areas of the continent now?" Wolfe felt a rise of indignation as the man had spoken.

"Every rich person in the world can lay claim to the land they can call 'theirs,' it's no worse for us to do I," the man replied, bored as if the entire conversation drained him.

"But doesn't that lead you towards a path like them? Having land you can kill people for being on, land you can charge people for stepping foot on. Does calling it yours give you the right to respond with violence?" Wolfe asked

"Maybe. But how can you fight the will of oppressing forces without something to fight with? Whether it be land, or money, or guns. Is it still anti-ethical to your beliefs if you use it to fight the oppression you want to throw off your shoulders?"

Wolfe fell into silence. He hadn't expected such a well-thought-out, carefully planned response. "Has someone said this to you before?" he asked.

"Many, many times." The man smiled. "Though if I'm being

honest, I'm paraphrasing my wife."

They were within earshot of two men outside the building now, talking back and forth, arguing over something in paint-stained clothes.

"I tell you it's the truth. A hundred and sixty of them, all full sized buckets."

"Nah, we've already been that far north, we've cleared it by now."

"Just you wait. We can head up there next time we're scouting, it's not far."

"Hello, Abernathy. Glen," the man beside Wolfe said.

"Hey, Chaplin," Abernathy responded

Wolfe smiled at them.

"And who is this?" Abernathy asked, squinting into the sun. The man was balding, his hair escaping off the back of his head, his skin peeling and flushed, and his neck was thicker than the rest of his body. The little tufts of dark hair that covered his body were losing colour.

"This is Wolfe."

Abernathy gave a toothy grin. "A defector? Where from?" Wolfe was silent in response. "Well, you'll fit right in no matter what."

Wolfe felt his lungs compress; his heart beat faster against his ribs. *I don't want to fit right in. I want to leave. Do they expect us to stay?* He smiled kindly, hoping his nerves didn't betray him, averting his eyes and staring at the sky. The man stared him down until finally, he gave up, turning back towards Glen to argue about paint.

"Follow me," Chaplin said, holding his arm against Wolfe's shoulder as they stepped into the building.

The warehouse building was unfamiliar to Wolfe: The metal racks, the iron shelves, and the overhead electrical signs had been pushed along the corners. Some lay in pieces; others were stacked against the walls. They had gouged large windows into the walls with saws and hammers, letting light stream across the yellowing epoxy floor.

Large, overhanging eaves on the roof connected to enormous metal tins and barrels that circled the room. On the right side of the building, giant blooming vegetables grew in raised flower beds, and large barrels of gathered rainwater fed into the earth in a contrasted drip. A few young women hauled jugs of water out the doors to a large fire outside, where it boiled in a copper pot.

A network of benches, chairs, and stools sat on the left side of the building, forged out of metal signs, melted plastic, school bleachers, and wooden stumps to form a cornucopia-style wedge around the walls. In the centre of the room, a cluster of people was gathered under the towering auspices of metal racks and teetering piles of plastic chairs and metal frameworks. In front of the heat stretched chairs sat his friends. His family.

"Scott, Unity, Lett, Brieux!" he cried out, his sandals padded against the floor as he ran.

"Wolfe!" Lett cried, his arms outstretched, running across the floor towards him.

"Hi, buddy!" Wolfe called out, crouching down on the balls of his feet to greet him.

He buried his face into Wolfe's stomach and was silent. A few moments later, Wolfe felt his body rising and falling with crashing waves, and he realized Lett was crying.

"Lett?" Wolfe asked, pulling himself away to see his face stained with tears. He held the tiny red pocket knife in his quivering hands, dirty with paint, bashed and scarred with damage.

"I'm sorry I didn't help you. I should have seen them!" he wailed, dropping the pocket knife and crawling back into his arms.

Wolfe felt his lip quiver, his throat tighten, and his eyes burn. He didn't know how to tell him.

"Kid I—"

"You gave me the best job, and I messed it up." He was crying out loud now. Wolfe could feel the rest of the adults towered above them, encircling them like animals.

"Look at me," he said, pushing him away and holding him squarely by the shoulders. Lett's face was red and splotchy, his nose was dripping, and he wiped it down his tan sleeve in a long trail. He dug in his eyes with dirty fingers until the tears were gone, replaced with bloodshot eyes.

"You did the best you could. *That* is what matters." He looked unconvinced.

"It was *my* job to start a fire but Brieux did it for me. It was Unity's job to find ammo, but I found it. It was Scott's job to tidy up the kitchen, and Unity did it. Sometimes, we need other people to help us, that's normal. It's okay."

"Well, I don't think it was—" Scott had begun to speak, but Unity must have hit him because he fell into silence.

Wolfe watched an understanding slowly creep across his eyes. They were a dark blue like Wolfe's brother's used to be. Like berries, like Neptune, like hydrangeas. His tiny nose contorted, and his eyebrows crinkled with questions.

"We all needed help, and we let you down. It's not your fault, I promise, we're going to be okay. I'm sorry." Acceptance seemed to sink its way beneath his skin. He beamed upwards at Wolfe and gave him one more hug, a few tears brewing in his eyes. Wolfe sounded like his parents consoling when his pet fish had died.

"It will get better from here, trust us." They had told him.

Wolfe stood, smiling at the rest of them. Unity was the first to step towards him, with a smile so wide it threatened to split the corners of her lips. She held her arms out, cutting the air into slices with her hands, sliding back and forth between beams of heat-soaked air and dust particles.

Scott pushed past her to greet Wolfe first as she stepped towards him. They connected, and Wolfe forgot everything about himself. He only knew Scott. He rubbed the back of his arm, down his elbow, over the crest of his back. He smelled him, lost in his touch, looking back at his smiling face.

Scott rested his hand beneath Wolfe's chin, pulling it up to face his own. Wolfe felt his rough, calloused fingers brushing over his stubbled face. He watched his eyes twinkle and hover over Wolfe's features, devouring him. Wolfe smiled back, pulling away to say hello to the rest of the group, but Scott was strong. Wolfe felt their chests pinch together. His necklace clung to the dewy flesh beneath his shirt, pounding his heartbeat back at him.

"Don't pull away, I haven't seen you for days…" He pulled Wolfe back in for another hug before flipping him around and holding him from behind. Wolfe felt eyes on him again.

"Days? Scott get off, people are watching."

"They don't care. And yes, days…"

"Scott."

"God I love you, I would do anything for you, you know that right?"

Wolfe turned around to look at him again, Scott's eyes seeming to scintillate with tears.

"Thank you for making sure he was okay," Scott said, looking up towards Chaplin, who was standing watching their display. Scott let Wolfe go, and he moved back among the group of stragglers around the room as Brieux smiled at Wolfe.

"Glad you're back Wolfe. Thought you might've died there for a bit." Brieux laughed, giving him a pat on the back, rubbing his knuckles into his shoulders like his uncle might have done years ago. Wolfe only saw the relief on his face.

"It's no problem. I mean, we did it to him. Like I told him, this rarely happens. It hit you stronger than anyone else."

"What do you use exactly?" Wolfe asked, searching the room for Unity, who had seemed to disappear.

"It's essentially just alcohol fumes. Homemade moonshine." He paused for a moment, no one knowing what to say next. "But you can come meet my wife and kids, it's almost dinner anyway," he said, pointing towards the doors they'd come in again.

Scott accosted him, scooping him under his armpits from behind. "Let go of me…" Wolfe grumbled from the corner of his mouth as Scott crushed him again in another hug, then a kiss. "Scott let—"

"Tell me, how did you organize such a wonder??" He asked loudly over Wolfe's complaints before he nudged Wolfe sharply in the ribs and shot him a nasty look, towering above him with dark brown eyes, his silhouette craning over him.

Wolfe ripped his hand off his side, swinging himself several feet away along the edge of the sidewalk. Scott wiped his emotions off his face, turning to the town leader, tossing his arms behind his back, and smiling instantly.

"Wolfe. Did you even thank Chaplin for saving you?" Scott called again, raising his eyebrows and grinning behind his back. Wolfe felt like he could cry, smiling at the men as his cheeks flared red with embarrassment.

"Oh no, don't feel you're imposing. We are glad to have as many people here and helping as possible. We're a family, we have to be out here," Chaplin said, smiling at Wolfe as they walked down the street together.

"Which raises the question, how do you survive down here? Everyone thinks it's uninhabitable," Brieux asked, walking beside Wolfe, looking towards Chaplin.

"Let me tell you, a lot has changed, that's for sure. It's hard to get people to stop worrying about money and just do what makes them happy. A lot of people don't even know what that is. It's a completely different life when you don't have bills to pay, and you're trying to figure out what you want to *do* with your life," he said.

"And how do you keep everyone's needs met?"

"We grow all of our own food, raise and butcher our animals, and share everything we can. Everyone does what they love to do, eats until they're full, sleeps until they aren't tired. There is no need for the government or BESNA."

"And what did you do before? Plumbing? Carpentry?" Brieux asked.

"Accounting."

"And no experience running a town?" Brieux joked.

"I don't run a town now," the man said. "We run the town," he said, gesturing to the houses and the women standing on the street corner as they walked. The older women were talking in the garden, their knees dirty with soil as they held pots of succulents in their arms. They smiled and spoke as they passed, waving to them as their lips still moved, asking each other questions about the newcomers neither could answer.

"That's amazing."

"It's been like that for a few years now. We have one extensive set of rules, but we need almost everyone to agree on a change before we make it, and everyone does what they want. There is always someone who loves to cook, loves to garden, loves to paint, why should they be doing anything else? And we had our power hungry tyrants, we ran out of food, water, disease was an issue, but we're here, what other option did we have?" Chaplin asked.

Wolfe fell behind them. They walked through a parking lot, it's yellow-painted streets had turned to shards, giving way to sand, then winking out of existence. Empty concrete planters sat sentient along the sidewalks. Most of the sidewalks crumbled, turning into gravel along the street corners, slowly becoming one with the earth again.

They turned down another street and made their way further along it. A large stone church sat on the corner of the block. Spindly glass shards poked out from the rim of one of the large, stained glass windows in the front of the church. The windows had been broken long ago, but he saw images of dancing angels in his mind, holy adorned figures glistening in pious light. The roof had collapsed onto the church, decaying into tinder. From the apex of the wreckage, small native grasses burrowed their way out from downstairs windows, the crumbling red brick melting back into clay.

"And you've kept your entire town running this entire time?" Wolfe asked.

"No. We've only been here about five years. When BESNA asked their members to start recording blue-eyed civilians in town and the government didn't stop them, we came south, away from their prying eyes. Our crops were dying and our animals were withering into racks of bone. We could have gone north with the money and the rain, but they were throwing blue-eyed families in camps up there and my wife and three of my kids have blue eyes as it is. I couldn't do that."

"You went further south?" Wolfe cried out.

"Yes. We gathered all the supplies we could in as many cars as we could fit and three hundred of us drove nearly nine hundred kilometres south from Kansas to Texas. The further south we went we saw more and more empty towns until finally, we found our miracle. Oasis, we call it. We built it up to what we have now."

"We passed hundreds of thousands of cars going north, their lives in the backs of their cars, but no matter where we went it wouldn't have mattered. It was all bullshit. It didn't matter who got in or what they promised, it just wasn't gonna happen. They needed cheap, disposable workers to meet their bottom line as the world got hotter. Money talks louder than words," one of the younger blue-eyed men said.

Kind words passed in the streets as they walked, dead trees craned over the streets, and wireless telephone poles stood vacant above him. They walked beneath an underpass while people talked and played games in the dirt with cards, pebbles, and sticks. Around a fire, people tossed unwrapped cans into a giant soup pot. A man was baking bread on metal sheets in the sun, the back of a route marker that read I27 on a silver backdrop.

"We don't know how long ago they abandoned this place, given the destruction of most of the town's buildings when we arrived. The rec centre was burnt to the ground as well," he said.

A wire wrought fence clung to aging green metal posts. Plastic swings swung with ghost children. Names and initials were permanently etched into the plastic and metal framework of the play structure. A spiritual breeze, hot and full of sulphur, dusted tiny bits of glass through the graveyard. Warped plastic bottles were caught against the fence, blowing in the wind. They walked for ages around the frames of long-dead trees ghosting between them. Their bark, hot and twisted. Stumps littered the ground with pale, exposed rings.

"Where'd the trees go?"

"Most of the dead ones had to be cut down, they were a fire hazard and all dead, anyway." He looked at the other trees, rubbing their bark before he sighed. "We've been trying to water these but I think they will have to go too." He watched the bark as they kept walking. They waddled behind him through the sand, careful not to step on cacti prodding through the cracks in the pavement. They walked past scurrying lizards that hissed and fanned out their necks when you noticed their stony visages scattered across the ground.

Lett pressed against Wolfe as they walked, dragging along with his leg. Wolfe knew that no matter what happened, he had to keep him safe. It was more than a promise; it was a duty handed down to him by celestial beings. Wolfe felt like nothing would spare him from the pressure, the guilt he had in his heart, bearing down on him.

Chaplin directed them to a small house, its curved domed roof reminiscent of a water tower. The windows were on hinges, so they swung open and closed for rainstorms and the hottest hours of the day. They were latched open, and men and women sat around the yard and house. Older children laughed and ran as the smell of cooking meat and herbs wafted to Wolfe through the open door.

"Let's get y'all some good food," he said, pointing them towards the door.

The walls of the house were cluttered with every object known to man: wrenches and screwdrivers, jerrycans and spare cups, knives and overalls, kitchen utensils and empty thermoses, cans of grease and paint, electronic components and pads of paper, books and pens. Huge nets swung from the ceiling filled with even more stuff, and an entire thrift store dangled from the ceiling. Along the floor rested car parts and gardening tools, old paint canisters and serving dishes, bags of animal feed and old yard signs.

The living room was loaded with card tables from wall to wall. Chairs were pulled up against every single wall along the length of the house. Every shape, size, age, and gender prowled the house with a plate heaped with food. They laughed at each other's jokes, spraying food across each other. A few people against the walls were plucking away on an untuned guitar while people stood talking in doorways, sat on the floor and rolled with dogs, or read books tucked against the wall.

"Where y'all from then? More escapee than man ey?" a stranger laughed, patting one of them on the back as they walked through the slim, crowded hallway and into the kitchen.

Men and women bustled around the loaded kitchen tables: Piles of chunky, roughly chopped vegetables steamed on large, mix-matched serving dishes in every colour imaginable. Thick slices of multigrain bread, dusted with flour and oats, were smeared with melting butter and slices of cold cut meats. Thick sauces swam in serving bowls along the length of the table beside large chipped cups filled with water that smelled vaguely of chlorine. Slices of what looked like succulents were fried in a strange coating reminiscent of dirt in strips across platters.

"Wolfe, Lett, Scott, Brieux…this is my wife. Tisdale, these are our newest defectors from the Bredenbury farms out east."

"Y'all are a while away from home." She laughed, turning around to face them. "How are you's doing? Hungry, I'd bet!"

She wiped her hands on a dirty, stained blue crisscrossed apron tied around over a pair of paint-stained overalls and a rolled-up denim shirt. Her hair was black, going gray at the roots, tied into a knot. The odd strand fell out of her bun and around her face. She danced around the others in the kitchen with heavy brown work boots laced around her ankles while carrying a tray laden with condiments; salt, pepper, and various other bottles labelled with white tape and a permanent marker.

"So we got fried horse meat, freshly baked bread, some goat butter, fried cactus, and mixed garden vegetables. Mostly root. Radish, beets, that sorta thing." She smiled, showing off a row of neat, clean teeth, her sparkling blue eyes lit like oriental glass. She heaped their plates, passing them each a glass filled with water, pushing them into the living room with the sound of banter and laughing.

Women sat haphazardly in the center of the room, strung around a wobbling card table. They threw down hand after hand of cards, sucking from bottles of brown liquid. They hurled insults with squinted eyes and roaring voices. People around them laughed and hollered with them, sucked into the fray. A few people in the corner eyed the new people curiously, elbowing their friends, family, and partners as they walked in. The uproar quieted for a moment as they surveyed them. Then, as if nothing had happened, it picked up where it left again with an explosive hand of cards.

One woman picked up her hand and chucked it at another player, bouncing off her head and landing on the floor in a plume of paper feathers.

"CUNT!" she yelled, storming into the other room, crying about lucky fuckers and cheating bastards. A man slid into her spot while they dealt again, tossing forkful after forkful of vegetables absently into his mouth with a plastic fork missing half its tines.

As Wolfe settled into a distant corner with Lett, he watched streams of women coming into the house with kids in tow, chattering with other women as they came. Across the street, other homes had come alive, with windows flung open and fires built on the lawn. A group of boys vaulted the living room window across the street, and the sounds of berating laughter chased them out. They ran back down the road as a bunch of girls watched them, pointing and eyeing them with smirks.

Hungry stragglers walked down the road, pulled left and right by calling voices. They hugged each other in the street, talked through windows, and hung in the shadows under trees. Children ran in circles through the streets. Their shrieks and cries sent chills down Wolfe's back. He had to remind himself they weren't being hurt.

To his left, a young man, maybe nineteen, only a few years younger than Wolfe, peered over the edge of his book and smiled a blushing, boyish grin. Wolfe looked away, looked back, and fell into his eyes. They were green like twisting ivory and like lush ponds, a green that screamed of life, that told him there were still sparks in the world. For a second, Wolfe forgot everything. He had only one desire on earth, and it had nothing to do with leaving.

"The food's good," Scott said, sitting down beside him, blocking his view of the green-eyed boy with the devilish smile. Wolfe was too busy watching another hand of cards explode in front of him to respond to Scott.

They ate until Chaplin crawled onto a stool and called above the clamour. His cheeks were flushed pink, and his eyes drooped more than before.

"I'd...I'd like to thank...equweg!...for being MORE...than accommodating to our...equweg!...fine...fine new guests and family members for the time being. Wolfe, Scott, Lett, Unity, and..." He tapered off, searching the crowd with a pained look of extreme confusion.

"Brieux!" Brieux called out.

"Unity...equweg!...thank you, Wolfe," he said, slurring his words. "And I hope y'all...equweg!...take a chance to get to know 'em. And—" He cut off the speech, slipping one leg off the stool and the other, then wandered into the hallway hiccuping. Wolfe followed him into the hallway with his eyes, and they fell over Unity sneaking into the house.

He tried to wave her over and her features melted into a smile. Wolfe hadn't even noticed she hadn't been with them. Then, when Wolfe looked back up from his food, she was gone. Scott pulled him closer and planted a kiss against his cheek. Wolfe heard a cough, eyes fell on them, but they disappeared into the crowd, and it was just the three of them again.

"We would make a marvellous family," he said to Wolfe as Lett pulled at a piece of meat with his fingers.

"That we would, but let's just go one day at a time."

"One day at a time," Scott agreed.

And Wolfe could see it when he closed his eyes. The three of them, living in some house, not having to be anything else. Wolfe closed his eyes and tilted his head back.

"And how're you guys getting on?" Tisdale asked, rubbing her hands against her pants and sitting down on the floor next to them.

"Good. Thank you. Dinner was delicious, it's nice to eat something not cooked in a can or roasted on a spit," Scott responded.

"If only I could eat something out of a can for once." She smiled, rubbing her legs up and down as she laughed. "Either of you want a beer now or…it's mostly paint stripper but if you like hard liquor it's probably best."

"I—"

"No, we're good," Scott said, interrupting Wolfe.

"All right then," she said, patting her knees as she stood, wiping her hands on her apron as she stepped away.

"Oh," she said, stepping back. "I'm going to let Chaplin sleep off some of his booze, and once a few more people leave, you and your friends can talk about your plan."

"Thank you," Wolfe said before Scott spoke.

"Don't mention it," she said again as she sunk into the kitchen, her arms laden with plates, and started scrubbing them in a large plastic basin filled with hot water.

"Why do you do that?" Scott said.

"Do what?"

"Talk over me."

"You talk over me, you just did it."

"Yeah, but I don't do it on purpose."

"And I do?"

"Whatever, Wolfe." And like that, Scott was gone, moving back into the kitchen. *What even happened?* Wolfe asked himself, trying to repeat what had just happened.

Outside, the sun was setting, and a soft breeze blew across the living room. Lett had fallen asleep in Wolfe's lap, and as he sat, his own eyes drifted. He took a deep breath and sighed, listening to the voices sink into a soft murmur around him until he couldn't help but smile.

He would have killed to get somewhere like this before, and now he just wanted to leave. Wolfe's heart pounded. *Run. Move. Go.* He was antsy, and his heart pounded. Wolfe was telling himself. Someone, something, anything might catch him if he allowed himself to stop. *What if?*

Chapter 18

Tales

The kitchen was ebony and darkness had fallen over them like a blanket. The soft pitter-patter of late-night rain disturbed the dust around them while salamanders and frogs hissed and croaked outside the window held gently ajar. Embers were trembling in the hearth, and candles lit the faces of the handful of them stuffed into the kitchen.

Wolfe hadn't meant to talk. He hadn't wanted to. He started simply enough, talking about his parents. He wanted to talk about the school, the camp, the rest of his family, his missing uncle, his friends he'd never see again, and the semi-trailers, but he didn't.

Wolfe was time travelling. He was in the ghetto. He was standing with Craik. He was meeting Scott again. He was hugging Arcola. He was watching the X's roll out of the darkness. He faltered when he mentioned Sandy and moved on again. The Midsummer Night's Festival. Craik's glass eye. Lett's bleeding knuckles. The burning plantation. Mr. Bredenbury's bullet in Craik's head. The church. The train. The weeks in the Desolation. Somehow, it hurt more the second time around. And when he stopped talking, he was staring at a wall of gaping faces.

"That's why we left," Chaplin said, pulling his wife closer to his side. She smiled, letting her eyes rest for a moment, tears forming in the corners of her eyes like dewy pinpricks.

It was hard for Wolfe to believe how strange the world had become. Ten years ago, he wouldn't have believed a quarter of this horror was even possible. It would have been, was now, unimaginable. No one else had spoken. They were still dark to Wolfe. Brieux sat with his arms pressed in front of him. Unity rocked back and forth on her chair. Scott pulled Wolfe closer in the dimly lit kitchen. Wolfe had torn open holes that had festered for years in his dreams. The nightmares would chase him back there tonight.

"And you all want to go back to that?" the same woman asked. Her blue eyes flickered with her own memories, her own fear. Her mouth was still open.

"Yes," Wolfe said again.

"Why?" a few people asked in near unison.

"Because. I can't sit here. I can't." Wolfe's consciousness objected. *But WHY*…and Wolfe cut it off. He refused to listen, refused to start the endless cycle of questions he would fall into. He was leaving, that was all there was to it.

"Yes, but why?"

"I know why I'm going. My sister is still in one of those city ghettos. I promised I'd come back for her, and I refuse to break that promise," Unity finally said.

"And do you know how dangerous it is? You may as well slit your wrists here and die with dignity," a man with a scruff of white hair around his face like a bear scoffed from the corner.

"I can't die with dignity without my sister. I told her I'd come back and I ain't gonna give up on that." Her voice was burning. She leaned against her chair and ran her fingers through her hair.

No one dared speak up against her. She rested herself, and she twirled her cup in her hand, watching the water swirl around her reflection in the bottom as the conversation resumed.

"And the rest of you?" Tisdale asked. She spoke into the silence. "If you don't know, all the better reason to stay until you're all certain."

"I'm certain. And if I have to go, I'll go alone," Unity said. She took a swell of water in her mouth, and Wolfe watched her swallow, driblets running from the cracks at the edge of her mouth, down between the valley of her chest.

"We have to at least try to fight them," Wolfe said.

"Fight them?" Tisdale asked. "We're never going to fight

them. You, me, us, all of us together can't stop them, everyone out there is fine with hurting us, we wouldn't stand a chance."

"There is a war."

"And wars have been started and lost since the beginning of time. Don't be stupid," Tisdale snarked.

"It can't be done," a man said.

"It has to be," Wolfe said.

Wolfe thought for a moment. His mind was stirring, and when he let his eyes flicker shut, his story played again instantly: The maggot filled carcass in the ghetto, the men and women who had been chosen to die in the fields for BESNA profit, the trigger pulled at his brother's neck, the people in the ghetto with PDT coursing their veins, the boys with their clammy hands wrapped together at the Midsummer Festival. Sandy. Craik. If all else failed, Wolfe would vindicate the broken, beaten, and bloodied people who never had the option. He would destroy everyone who let it happen, and he couldn't do it from here. He had to leave. He couldn't stay here while millions suffered. *Any action is better than none,* he told himself.

"You have never lived in the same world we've lived in. Blue-eyed people are just trying to keep their heads above water while brown-eyed people ignore us. Fuck. I would be quiet too if I could have lived a normal life, gone to veterinarian school like I wanted, and my parents got to live their lives into old age." Wolfe had everyone's attention now. He leaned closer to the light. His fingers felt the curve and creases of the table. "They will crush you eventually. Somewhere down the line, someone will decide you're costing them money and they will wipe you and your children off the earth. If I do nothing, if I sit here and pretend the world is fine, I'm condoning it. If I die trying, at least I can know that I tried to make the world better instead of having empty ended promises to fill my grave with when I die. If I did nothing, everything they say about us is true."

"So how are you going to do it?" Tisdale asked, looking first at Unity, then at the rest of them.

"One step at a time," Scott said.

"The Old Cobalt Historical Society, or OCHS is fighting BESNA in Mexico City. Most of the media is owned and run by people like the Bredenbury family, so no one ever gets to see the truth. If we can show the world the truth of what BESNA is doing, maybe people will turn against them," Brieux said, leaning closer to the candlelight.

"I love your enthusiasm Brieux, but BESNA has been telling brown-eyed people that we're stupid, lazy, and dangerous for decades, and people have been sopping it up. BESNA told the world that the reason our country was so shitty was because the enemy didn't live in Asia or Europe, weren't the poor or the rich, black or white, but *we're* the enemy. They told everyone that *we're* the ones working to oppress them, and they've taken it to heart. We can't change anything, it's too late," Unity said, leaning into her glass.

"How is that helpful?"

"I'm here for my sister."

"There are also rumours of a resistance movement pushing down from the Rockies into Old California. Maybe if the war finishes in Mexico and it doesn't go well—" Scott started.

"And if there isn't? Then what? Are you going to live the rest of your lives hiding in sewers and backyar—" started Tisdale.

"I don't mean any offence but I'd rather hide in sewers and backyards, gathering information, recording stories that would otherwise be lost, and helping anyone I can, than living a 'real' life that helps no one and does nothing," Wolfe said. The room fell silent again. The candles flickered as the rain fell slightly harder, pounding on the metal roof, dripping past the open window sills and pushing the smell of washed stone and disturbed dirt into the room. Their shadows were painted across the walls like sentinels.

Chaplin had barely spoken a word all night. His face was feverish, growing with emotion, flickering sharply between the candles.

"My family is doing lots. We're keeping ourselves alive, you can't help anyone if you're dead." He said it, but he lacked belief. His mouth tried to hide what his eyes couldn't as his lips shook and his fingers rattled on the table.

"You don't know who we could help. To one person, one word, one gesture, a few spare dollars might save their lives," Wolfe said.

"And what did we do for you?" Tisdale hissed.

The breaths grew hot and short in the kitchen.

"We thank you beyond measure," Scott began. His voice was soft like butter, his hands smooth, acting out scenes in a slow, silky motion. "And we are so thankful for your saving Wolfe's life. We all have parts to play, ours every bit as important as yours. One man does not overthrow evil, it is taken out by the roots with the mighty tug of all of us, together," he said, choosing his words carefully. He was playing the balancing act between both sides, trying to satiate the world.

The room was quiet, and Chaplin's weary face drew into a smirk. "You're right. That's why I'm going to escort you to Mexico."

"What?!" his wife screamed, leaping off his lap as she batted away his advances, her hands a flurry of dismay, her mouth hung open in rage. "You can't! You heard them, it's a war zone out there. You have kids to take care of!" Her eyes were steaming, burning like embers, hot coals, and heat cracked porcelain. She threw herself against the kitchen cupboard, swinging the door shut as a vicious wind tried to beat the house into the ground.

"Tisdale, honey, please."

"No. If you're content with leaving, refusing to raise your goddamn kids, so you can help…strangers! Fucking strangers, then go. What is wrong with you? You're old, be old!" His face dropped. He let his arms fall to his side, he turned on a heel, and his wife looked away, pretending to not see the pain in his eyes.

"If you need anything before you continue on your way, we will provide it. I suggest you stay for a few days, at least until the new moon, so you have a full lunar cycle to travel by. We'll all talk some more tomorrow."

"Thank you," his wife cried, wiping away tears with the tips of her fingers, and he dismissed her with a backwards wave of his hand.

"Hudson will show you to your rooms," Chaplin said quietly, gesturing his hands toward the blue-eyed man sitting beside him.

"Follow me," the young man said, beckoning Wolfe, then Scott further into the house. Another man directed Brieux, Lett, and Unity toward their rooms.

The room slowly trickled out into the storm. Some women comforted Tisdale, rubbing her shoulders and whispering to her.

"You spoke the truth girl, even if it hurt."

"You can't lose your husband because he wants to help some dreamers."

"You're right." The words 'you're right' struck terror into his mind. *What if we are wrong? What if we should stay?*

Hudson called them again, beckoning them up the stairs. Brieux waved them off in the stairwell. Unity and Lett stepped into their room and closed the door softly. The rain was magnificent. Men rushed through the streets with barrels and carts filled with bathtubs to collect the rain. Somewhere in the distance, thunder and laughter rumbled.

Hudson led Scott and Wolfe towards the second last door on the left. Before they could step in, he spoke to them both. "Chaplin wanted me to tell you the goat house needs to be re-shingled tomorrow if you feel up for it," he said, smiling an apologetic grin. "And for what it's worth, I'd want to go too if I were you." He smiled again as he sealed them in.

"Thanks…" Wolfe muttered to himself. His heart was mad; it wanted its opinions heard. The floor was wood, but a rug spun from plastic shopping bags ran against its length, rough against Wolfe's bare feet.

A queen-sized bed was resting under a sloping ceiling cracking with paint to their left. A few dressers, a desk, pens, paper, and a chair rested in front of the window that surveyed the garden. Tiny lights illuminated windows in the rest of the town, small kitchens, bathrooms, and bedrooms aglow with candles and lanterns. A fresh pile of clothes, pants, shirts, and socks was tossed over the bed's edge.

Wolfe flopped himself back on and watched Scott change into clothes on the other side of the room.

Scott pulled his sweater up over his head, wincing as it pulled over his gnarled, twisted shoulder where the bullet had entered and exited. The skin was still inflamed. Wolfe saw his back rippling with muscles beneath the skin as he struggled to undo his buttons.

"Need help?"

Scott scowled.

"Why not?" Wolfe pulled his pants down around his knee and pushed them onto the floor. He walked over, wrapping his arms around Scott and slowly undoing the buttons while smelling him up and down his back. They shared a moment of peace before Scott opened his mouth.

"You have to work on your temper. You were this close to costing us the most important allies we could have. Think before you talk," he said with a smirk, pulling Wolfe closer to him.

"When?"

"Five minutes ago. You can't insult the people we're staying with," he said.

"Why do you always have to correct me, can't you ever say something nice?"

"When are you ever going to do something right?" he said again, laughing out loud as he said it.

Wolfe pushed himself away. "Why do you always have to make jokes? You're such an asshole."

"Relax, I'm just teasing, don't overreact."

"I'm not overreacting. You're an asshole."

"And I didn't even mention all those times you made me look like an idiot today. It looks so ugly when you constantly undermine me." He ripped his shirt open, buttons falling to the floor. His pants slipped down around his knees.

"I do not undermine you." Wolfe pulled his shirt off and threw the blankets back, pulling his pillow away from Scott's.

"You do too. You make it obvious you like that woman more than me anyway, every time I try to show you affection and you push me off, everyone thinks I'm just a pedophile at this point."

"You're not it's just—Unity. She's not just 'that woman,' come on."

"It's just what? I am?" Scott said, throwing himself down on the edge of the bed, twisting the flame out in the lantern and rolling onto the bed. Their whispers stung back and forth like bug bites.

"No, you're not, I'm sorry!"

"Then why would you even have to apologize unless you were going to call me a pedophile? You always do this, you villainize me."

"Scott, that isn't what I meant."

They both lay in the dark, waiting for someone to argue again. A few more minutes passed, and still, neither of them spoke. Wolfe reached his hand over and felt Scott pull away. A snivel and a snort told him he was crying.

"Scott…"

"What do you expect me to do?" Scott cried out, sitting up again and flinging his feet onto the rug. Wolfe rested his arm on his back and felt his whole body heave with each weepy breath.

"I've done so much, and I always seem to fuck it up. I'm so stupid, stupid, stupid, stupid. I let down Arcola, I let you down, I let down everyone."

"Baby…"

"You don't even want to call me baby, it's forced, you don't want to take it this fast remember."

Wolfe's head was spinning. "What? When? Ho—"

"And have you seen how people look at us? It's a nine-year age gap between us, you know people think I'm a rapist or something. They probably think I'm forcing you to stay with me under threat. Maybe I am a monster, it'd probably be better if I kill myself. No one even loves me, you're not even wearing your necklace," he cried, looking away.

"I love you," Wolfe intercepted, pulling him back down onto the bed with his hands. He looked down at his chest, and it was bare. "I'm not wearing it because I was out cold for two days. Remember? Come on, don't be silly."

Sniffles.

"Come here." Wolfe wrapped his arms around him and pulled them together. Scott crawled on top of him, rubbing himself against Wolfe. Scott rubbed his hands over his neck, tickling his fingers down his spine. Their mouths connected, and the world froze. Wolfe could taste supper on his tongue, an alcoholic drink on his lips, and the smell of sweat danced on the whispers of his beard.

"What do you think we should do?"

"What do you mean?" Scott asked, whispering against his chest.

"Should we go?"

"Of course, I didn't even think it was a question. But would you wear your necklace, please? I don't want you getting hurt." Scott started kissing Wolfe's neck, outlining him with phantom touches.

"Yes, but…" He faltered. Scott eyed him like land to be claimed, an animal to be broken, a thing to be owned, and a game to be won.

"Yes?" Scott smiled, moving towards the front of his neck, rubbing his teeth against Wolfe's throat; his tongue moved in small circles over his skin.

Wolfe trembled, letting his eyes close.

"Nothing. Nothing at all."

"Boys, always taking it so fast," Scott murmured into his chest as he left sticky kisses down his chest, then onto his abdomen, running fingers down his side. Then his lips slipped further down above his hips, then further. Wolfe rolled his eyes at Scott's comment and forced a laugh as their bodies tangled together, their faces illuminated every few minutes by flashes of lightning.

Moments passed, then eons. Wolfe melted into Scott's hands.

—

Wolfe woke in the night, chased out of sleep by nightmares. The rain was hissing in rhythms over the roof. He craned his neck, listening to his neck pop and strain. *God, this bed is a rock.*

He pulled his feet out of bed and walked across the room to his clothes, sliding his pants up around him with two heaves. He rested himself down in the chair and looked out of the window over the sprawling town. Darkness had set in now, and the lights had burnt out of every window. The lightning was gone, so instead, he sat in complete darkness, his feet on the desk, his eyes closed, but his mind spinning.

Finally, he had let his heart speak; he let his mind and soul clash. *What should I do?* He tried not to think of the nightmares, chased in circles by faceless voices, flaming whips that smiled at him with venomous eyes. *How can I make everyone happy? Everyone wants to go, and now I'm just holding them back. But wouldn't we be safer here? Isn't this what Sandy would like for her son? But what about them?* Wolfe thought. He envisioned the men praying for death tonight; the children travelling without their parents to sex farms across the world tonight; the world crying out for help tonight while he was free.

What do you want? What was even the point in asking himself? Two different voices screamed inside of him, begging to be chosen. He would have to choose at some point, and he knew that. *What if you make the wrong one? Don't be selfish.*

A rogue beam of lightning struck somewhere in the distance, just enough to cast light over the room. It threw Wolfe's shadow beside Scott's sleeping figure sprawled across the bed. The smell of sex still clung to his skin, and his legs stuck out from under the quilted blanket. *Do I do it for Scott? For love?* Wolfe threw his hands into his face and leaned back, holding back tears. *Do you love him?* He was questioning everything tonight: the ground he stood on, the walls around him, the sky above them.

What about everyone else? His family lived within him, and it was the last place they existed. *How can I protect them? What would they want?*

Scott was muttering in his sleep. *Oh my god, will you shut the fuck up?* Wolfe felt a seed of rage grow in his chest. *I hate him. No, you love him.* Two opposing forces were fighting under his skin, threatening to break him into pieces of Wolfe across the bedroom floor. How could he hate a sleeping man? *He is just a man, as good or bad as the rest of us. He wouldn't be here if he didn't have good intentions.*

Wolfe pulled himself to his feet. Tilting his eyes back so the tears didn't fall. He had to get out of here. The sweat in the air was stifling him. He felt something sharp beneath his feet as he stepped back across the room. He pulled a pair of pants to his chest and dug through the pockets. He walked to the table and laid out a handful of garbage. The flower, the electronics pieces, the paper. He saw them again as lightning lit the sky. He felt the petals, ran his fingers along the cord of his necklace, and he let the tears run their course, burrowing in pools along his neck.

He pulled the necklace over his head again, resting his hand above the flower until he finally decided to leave it. He moved past the bed and to the door.

By the time he'd reached the end of the hallway, he had found himself against Unity's door. He listened and moved his hand to the knob. Then, deciding against it, he moved away again, standing at the top of the stairs. He watched Brieux's door, hoping it would fling itself open and call Wolfe in. *He would listen to me,* he thought as he started walking down the stairs.

The front door was closed, and the windows were shut. Then, Wolfe noticed the light shuttering from the kitchen, moving up and down the walls in arching waves. Someone fluttered in the kitchen as he stood there.

Fuck. Wolfe held his breath, trying to move backwards. If someone was down there, it was the last conversation he wanted to have tonight. He looked in the mirror hanging on the wall, pulling at a strand of hair bouncing near his eyes. *I need a haircut.* He flipped it behind his ear as he tried to sneak back up the stairs.

"Chaplin?" Tisdale called from downstairs. Wolfe cringed. That wasn't what he wanted to hear. He screwed up his voice, trying not to sound like he'd been crying, and called back.

"Sorry. No. Just me. Wolfe." He cringed again.

She was quiet. The movement in the kitchen stopped, and so did Wolfe. He was waiting for anything that would give him a chance to escape. He prayed she wouldn't call to him again.

"Thirsty or something?"

"No."

"I'll get you something."

Wolfe stifled a sigh. He turned himself back down the stairs and came down into the hallway, making his way into the kitchen.

Tisdale was standing in an empty kitchen. The table was cleared of plates, cups, and cutlery. Her hands were moving over vegetables and an enormous chunk of meat. The table had piles of clothes, neatly folded off the line, still damp after hanging in the garden.

"Coffee," she said, not a question, but a statement.

Wolfe sat in silence, the wooden chair creaking beneath him, sliding against the peeling linoleum floor. The windows were closed, and a sea of bugs battered themselves against the panes, trying to get in. She sloshed a mug filled with cold coffee down on the table in front of him.

Wolfe swirled it around in his mug, a chipped ceramic jug with eggshell speckling around the sides.

Wolfe let it run down his throat before resting it back on the table, letting the coffee churn in his gut. Before he could stop her, she had filled it again. This time, she tripped, sending coffee across the table, the clothes, and splashing it down the table and onto Wolfe's bare chest.

She flung the kettle back into the sink and whipped a towel off the counter. She tossed it over the table, and Wolfe watched the brown water seeping into the towel. He pushed his chair back, dropping to the floor beside her.

"I got it," he said, pushing the cloth back and forth. He rubbed until long after the coffee was gone, and the smell of burnt coffee hanging in his nose was the only evidence.

"Do you know what time it is?" Wolfe asked finally, gazing intensely at the diamond fractal pattern spreading across the kitchen floor.

"What?"

"Do you know what time it is?"

"About seven. Sun will be up soon."

Wolfe could tell her voice was strained from screaming or crying. He listened to the slowly timed slices of her knife against the cutting board. The darkness outside grew to a light blue tinge.

"So do you know what you're doing then?" she asked, letting the pace of her knife increase as she spoke. "Are you leaving soon?"

"Not sure. I want to talk to Unity first," Wolfe said, trying to make himself busy, staring in deep interest at the moving inches of coffee at the bottom of his mug.

"Oh? Why?" she asked.

Wolfe heard the anger in her voice. She attempted to cloak it in thick layers of interest, but it was pointless. Wolfe stared through her like she was made of glass and everything she thought was on display.

"Well...I..." Wolfe stopped talking. He didn't know, and they sat there together while she chopped. Wolfe sat, waiting, as the light slowly crept over the town. Wolfe could see the drizzle still; the gray sky hung over them. The branches on the trees outside jaunted back and forth, stiff in the wind.

"You don't know?" she asked, plunging her knife and board into the sink, startling Wolfe back into the present.

"No, I don't think I do."

She moved across the room with her back to him and sat across the table from him with dripping hands. Their eyes watched each other. Each of them waiting for the other to make a move, to say something, to set the tone. Wolfe looked down at her hands. Long and slender wrinkles formed around each knuckle, stained ashy from the root vegetables sitting on the counter.

She held a mug in one hand; the other was crossed in front of her, holding it back against herself. The steam from the hot water was rising in her face, and Wolfe followed the steam. Her neck muscles were pulled taut, and she was covered in sweat. A ring hung around her neck on a strip of leather cord. Her hair was pulled back with a band, and a few loose strands fell around her ears.

Wolfe's skin was shining in the flame's reflection. The candles cast a glow across Tisdale, and she shimmered. Wolfe saw her eyes, reflections of his own, alight.

"I want to know more," she said at last.

"About what?"

She laughed when Wolfe spoke, and he felt his gut curling inwards. It was a dark, cold laugh, and she flung her head back. When she looked at him again, her eyes were glinting, moist and dewy; the whites of her eyes were pink and glowing.

"I want to know more about the world out there. About you, about what it's like beyond the high-speed trains and the chips," she said, leaning back. Her eyes picked over Wolfe now, over his hair, his eyes, his stubbly chin growing fully into adulthood, over his bare chest, his tapping leg, and his bare feet. When she had finished, she started over from the top again.

"Well," Wolfe began, knowing she had heard him say this all before. "It's hostile. It's a dog eat dog world."

"That's bullshit!" she whispered furiously, dropping her hand to the table and leaning against it. Wolfe heard her voice echo against the walls, the reverberations of her ghosts in different universes.

"The world has always been like that. It's always about being the boldest, the brightest, the most successful, the richest. It didn't matter what you did or how you did it, but it's always been like that so don't tell me it's changed," Tisdale barked.

"I don't know what you want me to say. It's terrible, it's ugly, it's evil. What more do you want from me?" Wolfe felt his throat contract, the muscles in his arms and legs were shaking, and his stomach ran circles inside him.

She leaned back against her chair and nodded, pulling her mug to her face and steaming her skin.

"Where were you born?"

"What?"

"Don't play stupid. Where were you born?"

"I don't have to talk to you. I can just go back upstairs and pretend you never called me down, like I never sat here," Wolfe said, pushing himself back up against his chair, dipping his mug down to the table and mirroring her.

"If you're going to steal my husband away from me, my kids, and our life, show me how this isn't a suicide mission. If the world is hostile, ugly, and divided, if it's everything you say, then why should I send my husband out to win a war that can't be won?" She was standing now, crouched over the table. Two fingers were trembling at Wolfe, outstretched from the side of the mug, while her other hand shook behind the mountains of towels.

"Steal your husband?" Wolfe looked up at her.

She laughed, scoffing under her breath. She sat back down, looking through Wolfe at the kitchen table.

"Chaplin is coming?"

"Of course he's going. He listened to your drivel. He thinks he's doing it for me, for the kids. It's your fault, you tried to tell him it was possible."

"What do you want me to say? Do you want me to say it's going to be a vacation? That we're going to get back into civilization and convince the world that I, that you, that every blue-eyed person is smart and worthy of something? No! It probably won't work but...don't I have to try?" Wolfe was crying now. How could he argue something he was still trying to convince himself of?

"I see...you're a martyr. You have so little respect for your own life that you'd off yourself trying to feel important." She smiled, wiping away the blotchy specks from her cheeks, a wicked poison swirling in her eyes.

"You're a fucking bitch!" Wolfe yelled, pulling himself to his feet, throwing the chair back across the floor as he did.

"Sit down! A lot more than you have called me a lot worse," she growled, sipping at her drink.

Wolfe sat down again, glaring across the mountain of cloth between them. He rubbed at his eyes; his intestines were screaming at him, trying to make him do something, anything, to fight the war that was slowly falling apart inside him. *Why do I want to go so badly?*

Again, they sat in silence until she spoke, looking up over the clothing and at him with sad and threatening eyes.

"I've seen boys like you do this over and over again. They think they will be the one, the chosen one, the person who makes all the right choices. The one who makes life livable, the one they write stories about. And you know what?"

"They're always wrong?" Wolfe laughed under his breath, rolling his tear-coated eyes.

"Because they have to be. Heroes don't exist."

Wolfe listened, watching her come in and out of focus until she wasn't even in the kitchen anymore.

"Chaplin was one of them. He tried to fight everyone and everything that moved. He thought by pushing enough people to action he would change the world. He's too intense for me sometimes but god knows I love him..." She paused, thinking about her next few words while she sipped. Then she went on.

"He wants to be the hero. Like his brother had wanted to be, and our son wants to be. Everyone wants to do the big stuff, but who does the little stuff huh? Who keeps people eating, who keeps the kids safe, who keeps the water clean and the clothes dry? I will never save everyone, but I don't need to go to Mexico to save people when I can do that here. I can save you, I can save all these kids, I can save the old people down the road. All these people here need saving too and we can't all go and search for something that doesn't exist. Isn't saving people here enough?"

She looked away for a second again, catching her breath. Wolfe knew she was crying, but she didn't face him. She turned off her chair and stood in the entrance to the kitchen, soaking in the gray light that shone over her frame.

"I'll never be able to convince you to stay if you don't want to, but I hope if you're going to leave you're doing it for the right reason, whatever that is," she said. Her breath was ragged, and she sniffed every few words.

"And if you're going to go, please don't let my husband die in the process. I don't care how, but make him come back to his family. Don't let those same fantasies of valour and saving the world take him away from the people who *really* need him."

"I don't know how I'd—"

"Blow out the candle before you go back upstairs," she said, interrupting Wolfe. She had moved down the hallway with her back to him. Then, when she climbed the stairs, she spoke one last time in the brief splinter of light when they could both see each other through the banister.

"You don't need to run away to save the world. Goodnight Wolfe," she said before she climbed the stairs, creaking above him into her room.

And with Wolfe's ideas of his future muddled, he laid his face down on the table and cried until the darkness gave way to light, and his confusion gave way to restless sleep.

Chapter 19

Beetroot

Wolfe's hands were pink with juice as he stood over the stove. The heat of the day yawned above him, and through the closed windows and drawn shutters, he felt the heat eat away at him. He was standing at a sink, peeling beets into a bucket. He had filled it twice now, and the sound of popping and crackling outside the open door was audible.

He hadn't been back since that night. That dull, gray morning spent in Tisdale's and Chaplin's kitchen. He had tried to think, but it caused too much pain. So he walked, anywhere, everywhere, alone, until a woman on the street called him over.

"You alright love?" an older woman had asked, her hands rich with mud, her dress drifting over the dewy morning grass. Her knees were two muddy circles through her dress, and her skin was smoothed copper under the rising sun. He had nothing to say, and she called him in for a drink. And even then, he had stayed in silence. She had tried to speak to him at first, but now she left him to his silence.

He stood in her rose-tinted kitchen, the walls still dusted with yellow floral wallpaper, the white lace trim frayed and brown, the pink linoleum peeling in the corners. The old appliances still had their place on the counters, the toaster and the blender, both unusable without electricity as they gathered dust. The bowls were still painted with chickens, the walls still read "Give love, be kind, laugh often," "God is with you," and "Family is precious."

Even over Wolfe's last three days here, she hadn't tried to get him to talk. She had spoken of her family, her sisters long gone, her life before, her interests, and how to cultivate the best root vegetables. But through it all, she had let him smoulder.

Wolfe walked down the hallway to the front yard, his arms heavy with a giant metal bowl filled to the brim with ruby red vegetables peeled and gleaming with water and twinkling in the sun. Outside, a group gathered around an open fire pit, standing or sitting on stools and folding chairs.

Their fingers ran pink as they slurped down the roasted fruits, golden and dripping, running down their fingers in little rivers, soaking in the creases of their fingerprints, dying their skin. Juice ran down their lips, aching over their tongues. Wolfe smiled as the children in front of him pulled the bowl from his hands and rushed it over to the men sitting closest to the fire, stirring the vegetables around in the flames until a black crust sealed their juices in as they cooked.

At least ten dinners were cooked every night throughout town. All you had to do was walk up and down the street until a house beckoned you with its smell. Maybe there were roasted root vegetables at home; around the corner, there was stew; a little further down, they were cooking porridge; beyond that, perhaps soup. People would come and go as they walked up and down the street, tasting what felt good at the moment. Jokes were shared, and gossip about family members passed from lip to lip.

They were a band of nobodies crammed into this dying town in the middle of a burning Desolation, but everyone smiled. Everyone was always so happy. It boggled Wolfe.

Ernfold had no teeth, yet he was the one who smiled the most. He had lost all of his kids to the camps; five disappeared into the void. Regina had lost a leg during one of the many vicious beatings her owner doled out, but she still walked with her canes, talking to anyone who would listen. Kennedy had lost his wife in one of the camps. They had sold her as breeding stock to a man somewhere in the northern cities, yet he always had a positive twist to your problems. Glen was one of the men Wolfe had seen outside the shopping mall the day he arrived and now was stirring beets in the fire outside with the soft blue eyes people would have killed for a century ago; he was a defector from a wood mill up in the boreal forest. His mother, his last living relative, had died during some medical experiment in one of the hospitals. He had pulled his chip out with a pocket knife and escaped during one of their daily trips to the mines.

Borden and Traynor had green eyes. They had been shipped around in one of the travelling sex parties Wolfe had seen at the Midsummer Night's Festival. He and his brother had run when they heard their bosses were planning to kill them and boil their eyes into makeup for the rejuvenation properties found in green eyes.

Back in the kitchen, the woman was sitting at the table, wiping sweat off her face and nursing a mug of water. A dirty pile of beets was sitting in the sink, and an empty basket caked with dirt was at her feet. She smiled at Wolfe as he walked past, and he smiled back.

She was a short, delightful woman with eyes that shimmered with wisdom and hands that ached when the moon was full. She sat her elbows on the table, leaning forward. She was almost eighty. A wobble of neck swung below her chin, her hands were heavy with wrinkles, her white hair was loose around her face, and she always wore a warm smile.

"Doing alright?" she asked in her heavy southern drawl. She had milky almond eyes, like soft, creamy chocolate, swirling when he looked at her, flaked with golden stars.

"Yup," Wolfe said back. He moved his hands in the sink, flicking the buds off with a paring knife. He had rarely ever cooked, and they slid around in his hands. *I hate these slippery little bastards,* and he threw it, hard, against the floor in a moment of rage. It bounced three times, dotting the linoleum as it went.

"Have you spoken to your friends yet?" she asked, sipping from her water, watching the beet come to rest against the wall. It lay there sad and dejected, dented on its left side. A bloody vegetable trail slumped behind it.

"No," Wolfe said. A burning shame crept across his face as he swiped up the beet, resting it on the table and swabbing a towel across the floor. He wiped his hands off on the towel, stained shades of pink and sat beside her, a mug of water in hand. The rusty bucket sat in the sink, the knife balanced on the counter. They were free from the sun, and in the heat-hazed kitchen, they momentarily sat in silence.

"Well, the beets are coming along real nice is all I can say," she said. Wolfe knew this was a lie; there was a lot more she could say. "It's all in the amount of water you give them. Too much water and they are bland, too little water and they don't grow. Just the right amount and you get sweet little gems that melt in your mouth."

Wolfe wasn't listening. She was nice enough, but he didn't really want to hear anyone blather, not really. He was still too busy torturing himself.

That morning, two days ago, when she had called him in for a drink, the house was silent. Now the upstairs rustled, and people milled around the house before heading out into the heat for the day. She had offered him a room upstairs, and that's where he had spent the last three nights.

Over the last two days, he had helped her with everything around the house. He and a couple of men his age had fixed up her fence to keep the ground squirrels and the badgers out. Wolfe had weeded her carrots with her and fed the garden water by hand. He had cooked and cleaned with her, mostly in silence, but sometimes while she spoke.

"Momma taught me when I was a kid, god so long ago, granted I was the youngest of eleven sisters so I don't really remember that much, but the garden stuff really sticks with me, always been one of them outdoorsy types you know." She never took a breath while she talked.

Her 'momma,' as it was, had died nearly twenty years ago. Her daughters followed roughly the same path; they married once, divorced once, got married a second time, divorced a second, and never spoke to each other.

"And I said, I said that flu was a bad one, it was gonna take momma if we weren't careful and, well she's dead." Wolfe had heard this story too. She had maybe five stories she told to everyone, and she repeated and rehashed them every day.

"Everything affects us differently you know there ain't gotta be shame in that we're all gonna die may as well live a little that's why I got her dating again after Daddy died, celibacy ain't no way to live your life, and it was one of them young Mexican fellers you hear about in telenovelas, really handsome stuff." She laughed, spewing all her words together in a haze of spit. Wolfe looked at her when she'd spoken about shame. He wasn't ashamed of his thoughts or his actions. Why should he? *Did she mean me? What an old bitch…*He thought. His brow must have furrowed; his eyes must have crossed because she looked up into his face in the peace of the dark kitchen and continued.

"We've all had to make hard decisions before. Trust me. When I was younger, I made a lot of stupid, wild, decisions. Decisions I wouldn't take back of course, because that's why I'm who I am, but I might have tweaked them a bit if I'd thought about them first." She slowed for a moment, her words breathing with her.

Wolfe didn't dare dignify that with a response. How dare she presume to know how he felt.

"I've let my past affect my decisions. But you know what, I was always sure to do one thing first. At that moment, you have to be sure you do what feels right. I won't share an opinion on what I think you should do because my opinion is irrelevant. Even if it means taking no action, you should be a hundred percent sure that you do what YOU want. Not that I didn't take my share of wild leaps, but I was sure that I wanted to jump first," she said.

They sat in silence again as his rage simmered on. *Has she been talking about me behind my back? What gives her the right?*

"But you get on with it. I've gotta go search for a new trowel." She stood at once and left through the garden door, leaving Wolfe in the hot, dim light of the kitchen, one hand on a weeping beet, the other on a cup of water.

As he sat there in her absence, he started to think about what the world held out there for him, for them, for everyone. And as he thought, he realized he wasn't sure he wanted to leave. The external pressure was constant, but inside he was asking himself questions he shouldn't be asking if deep down he really wanted to stay. *Why leave?* He felt no desire to keep walking.

Wolfe stood and laid everything down on the table. He watched her walk around the edge of the garden, so he walked down the road in the opposite direction.

He walked the way he had come three days prior in boiling heat. He coughed, and a chunk of phlegm fell to the ground and sizzled into nothing. The air was dusty, and the sky, *god the sky,* was the purest, most brilliant blue Wolfe had ever seen. Not a drop of water, not a square inch of clouds. It was fleeting and stunning, enough to resolve a man to tears if the sun didn't evaporate them from his cheeks before they touched the ground.

He came around to Chaplin's and Tisdale's house. Chaplin and another man were smoking something that looked like a cigarette but stunk of dead leaves and skunk shit in the front yard. They passed it back and forth underneath the frame of a tree without leaves.

"Hi Wolfe, how's it going?" he asked, squinting into the street, holding his hand up to shield his view from the sun.

"Have you seen Unity?"

"Um…no? I don't think—"

"Okay, well, I need to talk to her."

"Is it about yous leaving and all that?" he asked, sitting up and letting the cigarette leave his lips and lay reeking on the hot pavement to his side.

"Uh, no. I—I just need to talk to her."

"Oh. Well, no, I haven't but I believe your…boyfriend?… wanted to talk to you. Brieux, too if that's as important."

"No. It isn't." Wolfe knew what they would say. They would remind him of their place in the world, their obligation to their people, to everyone dead and soon to be. He could do that himself. He didn't need to see their faces dripping with disappointment if he wanted to stay.

"Well, if you need something I'm here…" he mumbled, letting his eyes close as he passed the smoking ball of paper back to the other man.

Wolfe walked in another direction, slowly, without a definitive direction in mind. *Why do we have to run? Isn't happiness enough?* He asked himself, looking towards the sky for an answer.

Around the next corner, Brieux and Lett were standing around another fire with the smell of eggs crackling and sizzling into the limitless sky. Lett was already streaming across the pavement, arms open, smiling, voice calling.

"Wolfe, Wolfe guess what!"

"What?" Wolfe asked, crouching down beside him.

"Scott and Brieux said we're leaving tonight, when there's no moon, we can see the stars!"

"That's awesome!" Wolfe gasped, pulling him closer. He looked over Lett's back at Brieux, who was smiling at him, bouncing a baby in his arms he'd never seen before, his hair wrapped with a scarf as he handed the baby back to its mother. Behind him, a man Wolfe knew as Theodore beckoned them over for plates of eggs and goat cheese.

Brieux was making his way across the street.

"Come on Wolfe," Brieux said, holding his hand out to pull him off the ground. Lett ran towards the yard again and dug into his plate of food, grinning with the other kids around him.

"Wolfe, we need to talk—" Brieux began, but Wolfe cut him off.

"No, we don't. Have you seen Unity?"

"Wolfe stop."

Wolfe looked at his glassy eyes. He had never seen the beauty in them before. They moved and danced as he watched them, twinkling and exploding with different shades and layers, shifting and heaving like nebulae. They moved like galaxies as he fought Wolfe on the street corner.

"Brieux I…"

"We have to go. We've been here almost a week now and we're not getting better just sitting here. Scott is getting stir crazy, going for long walks in the middle of the night and talking to himself when he thinks no one is around. I want to leave. Lett wants to go."

"Lett doesn't want to go, you've pushed him into it. How would he not be happier here?"

"We have to go, please Wolfe, we're leaving tonight," he said, begging with his eyes, yet with his voice, he commanded him.

Wolfe felt his heart crack. He was ashamed, hating himself for speaking, for wanting to go, for wanting to stay, for being told what to do, for having to make his own decision. He wanted peace.

"No," Wolfe said. I'm talking to Unity first."

"We have to go. It's our responsibility. Think of Sandy, she would want us to go on."

"Go on where? No, Sandy would want her kid to be standing in the sun, smiling, without bruises and cuts, eating fruit in a garden with other kids. There is no reason."

"There is!"

"THERE IS NOT." The world paused for a moment.

"Last I heard, Unity was helping re-paint one of the houses around here."

"What?" Wolfe asked again.

"Go find her then. Talk to her. You aren't going to listen to me," Brieux said, turning his back to him. Wolfe's stomach turned with pain. He had seen it on his face when he turned. He heard Scott's voice just as he had rounded the corner onto the next block. *Thank god*, he thought to himself.

He could hear their excuses in his mind.

"Can we finally get back to real life?"

"Let's just go!"

"You're acting so weird."

He couldn't see Scott right now.

An hour later, maybe two, he saw Unity coming towards him.

"Unity?"

"Hey, Wolfe."

"Have you been avoiding me?"

"I don't want to fight."

"Who said we'll fight? I wanted to talk to you," Wolfe said.

"I know, that's why I said I don't want to fight. You don't want to go anymore do you?"

"I don't know…it's just…what are we going to find out there we can't have here?"

"Wolfe please I don't—"

"What?"

"My sister?"

"Yeah but—"

"But? But? Really Wolfe? I'm sorry I have people out there. You have nothing that you need to do anymore, so stay! If you are happy here, stay."

"But I'd be alone! Everyone else is leaving! No one will stay with me." He felt his eyes welling with tears. *Would I have to stay alone? Lose everyone all over again?* Why did no one want to stay with him? Would he always have to sacrifice what he wanted for everyone else's happiness?

"Wolfe, you're being selfish." She guided him onto the grass in front of a few houses with their windows shut.

"NO!" Wolfe cried out. "I have constantly tried to do what people want, go where they want to go, be where they want me to be. No one cares about me, about how I feel. They will be there for me until the second they need something else, and then they leave me here. Leave me alone with a town of strangers."

"Please…" she cried out, tears running down her cheeks. Wolfe couldn't even see straight anymore in a blur of tears.

"Every single fucking one of you would leave! You'd leave! Scott would leave! Brieux would leave! I thought you guys were my friends, my family. I thought we would stick together forever and now you're just leaving me? It's go out there and die, or stay here alone forever!?"

She was sobbing on the ground now. Only gasping breaths between sobs as Wolfe dreamt of yelling. *Just strike me down then, take me out, send me away then if I'm meant to suffer that much, kill me if you're going to drag it out much longer.*

"Won't you just fucking listen to me!" Unity yelled as Wolfe turned to leave. "I have to go. And I'm sorry that this is the place for you, but if you have to stay, stay. You have your obligations, and I have mine, but you don't get to be mad at me for them. My sister is out there and I told her I'd come back. Would you leave family out there? Would you really not even try?"

Wolfe sat down and listened, wiping his face in large muddy swipes. The pavement was boiling, but he barely felt it touch his bare skin. "I don't know Unity. I'm just tired of running."

"I know.

They rested for a moment in each other's presence.

"But that is why I wanted to find you. At the very least, you listen to me. Brieux and Scott just try and tell me," he joked.

"Men," she laughed.

"Men," Wolfe laughed back.

"What if I made you a deal, Wolfe? You come with me now, help me find my sister, and I'll come back with you. This place is…perfect, but I can't stay without her. Scott and Brieux can go find whatever they're looking for out there, but the four of us can come back and spend the rest of our lives here."

Wolfe thought about it for a moment. There was truth to it. He wouldn't leave Blaine out there if he could have saved him. *I'm a hypocrite. I can't abandon her while complaining about being abandoned.* He thought as emotions squirmed behind her eyes.

"We'll see what we can do in Mexico, then we'll go find her. I'm sorry Wolfe," she said, wiping tears off her face. "You don't have to come, but please don't hate me for going. Maybe the men have issues, but I'm going for the right reasons," she said, smiling up.

"Don't apologize. You've done nothing worthy of an apology," he said. "And yeah, I think you're right. Scott and Brieux want fame and something I don't think they'll get. But you're doing it for the right reasons, and if I help you, I'll be doing it for the right reasons too." He thought of Tisdale, her gray silhouette in the kitchen, beaded with tears.

"Thank you, Wolfe."

"You're welcome," he said. He crumpled his lips together and smiled. She was still sniffling, so Wolfe did the only thing he knew might make her feel better. He slid a few inches closer and awkwardly wrapped his arms around the top of her shoulders. They sat there frozen for a few minutes while her breathing slowed. She wiped the marks off her cheeks.

"We should get back," she said, then she leaned in again before they started walking and hugged him again.

"I'm sorry everyone was pressuring you Wolfe."

"It's fine. At least I know you have a reason to go. Scott just wants to get out of here, doesn't matter how or why."

"Can I ask you something, without you getting mad?"

"Of course."

"Why Scott? He…he acts like he owns you, like you're just another thing he has to corral. Why are you…with him?

"I know he can be possessive and controlling sometimes. An asshole too…but deep down he is an amazing man. I do love him, and he has his issues but…I love him," Wolfe said. It felt familiar, like he'd said this all before.

"And you're happy?"

"Yes." He smiled, refusing to let anything else slip through the cracks. He saw the green-eyed boy peaking over his book in his mind.

"Okay. That's all that matters."

"But he could never replace you, you're *rarely* an asshole."

"*Rarely?*"

The two of them laughed back to Chaplin and Tisdale's, where two boys were racing each other to finish their drinks, chugging amber liquid as it ran through the cracks of their lips and down their chests, puddling in the dirt by their feet.

Something had settled over Wolfe. Peace? Tranquillity? He didn't know. The silence he had wished for had come, and the voices in his head were finally quiet. This would be his last evening here. He smelled the dirt on the breeze, felt the stable ground, and closed his eyes. *I'll be right back.* He told the ground, the earth, himself. *I'll be right back.*

Chapter 20

Vows Against Twilight

"We'll go west through the night, then slightly south through the Desolation. We should find some form of civilization in New Mexico, Arizona at the latest," Chaplin said, holding out a map from fourty years ago that still had state boundary lines etched in fading ink.

"Not necessarily. The 'civilization' might be an army, the wrong one," Unity said, pointing to the map with a long finger, dragging out an imaginary line.

"The wrong one?" Tisdale asked.

"The BESNA army, they would shoot us on sight."

"Oh, god." She dipped her face into her hands.

Chaplin had already sent a few young men to gather supplies and take them to the edge of town. They talked around the empty dinner table in hushed voices. Chaplin and Tisdale, Scott and Wolfe, Brieux and Unity, the handful of strangers and the old woman Wolfe had spent three days with.

"Don't forget to take some bleach. You won't be able to take that much water, you'll have to find it out there," the old woman said, rubbing the tips of her fingers together absently.

"Thank you again," Scott said.

"We owe you our lives," Wolfe added.

"Is there anything we could give you?" Brieux asked, his leg crossed over the other.

"You can take this…" Unity said, pulling a bracelet off her arm and sliding it across the table. "It was Mrs. Bredenbury's, but she doesn't need it anymore."

"No, absolutely not." Tisdale reached down to the table and slid it back. "If anyone is going to need money on the other side it's you guys. What do we need it for? We can't eat it, drink it, or build with it, what's the point?"

"But—"

"No. Not for a second. Put it back." She shook her hands as she moved back to the sink. They knew it wasn't worth the fight, and she was right.

"Well, is there anything else we should think of?" Chaplin asked.

"Not until we're two weeks deeper into the Desolation."

Wolfe watched Lett drag phantom figures on the table with his finger. He traced the lines on the table back and forth, his face plastered against the sticky surface. Wolfe slid up in his chair and watched everyone eye each other.

"Well, if you're going to go you should get going, the sun is setting," the old woman said, gesturing to the golden light seeping in the window.

"I guess that's fair," Chaplin said, clapping his hands on his knees and standing up.

"Meet me down at the west side gas station? Bring the kids?" Chaplin asked, kissing his brooding wife on the cheek.

"In a minute. You go."

Chaplin and Brieux stepped outside and were already talking about the exact direction to go again, and the timing of the moon cycles. Scott waited for Wolfe, then he and Unity begrudgingly walked down the sidewalk together.

"Lett. Go with Unity. I'll be there in a minute," Wolfe said. The rest of them left until it was only him, Tisdale, and the old woman.

"Do you have everything?"

"We didn't come with much."

"Hmm."

Silence.

"I don't know how you think it's fair to treat me like this. I don't rank that high in terms of decision-makers here." She moved towards Wolfe, and he pinched his eyes shut, waiting for her hand to fall against his cheek. Instead, he felt a hand prying his fingers open, and she shoved the object between his fingers and left it there. When Wolfe looked down, he was staring at a silver ring inlaid with diamonds and encircled with words hanging on a thin piece of cord.

"What's this for?"

"It's the down payment on getting my husband back. Remind him of what's important. Don't let him go with you, promise me, make him come back." Wolfe could hear her voice cracking, but he pretended not to notice.

"Is this your wedding ring?"

She didn't answer him.

"He will come back."

"Just promise me you'll try."

"I will try. He will be fine, I promise."

Then, she smiled at him, and Wolfe tried to push the ring back into her fingers.

"No. You're taking it. If my husband doesn't come back, I don't want the ring," she joked, laughing out loud as they walked.

"Okay…" Wolfe pulled it over his head and yanked it down past his ears until it rested around his neck.

"That's a gorgeous necklace." She pointed to the cross that swung around his neck; shiny brown wood smiled back at her under the heavy orange sunlight.

"Thank you."

"I have to go get the kids," she said, excusing herself from the table.

It was Wolfe and the old woman again. He waited for her to speak, and she didn't.

"I should get going."

"Of course, I hope you're sure hun."

"I am."

"Then God is with you."

Wolfe smiled, stepping up towards the door before stopping outside the living room. He turned to her. "Why do you believe?"

Wolfe asked.

"You don't?"

"If God was real, why would he let all this happen? Why wouldn't he try to stop this?" Wolfe asked as Tisdale came down the stairs with a string of three blue-eyed children in tow, and Wolfe watched the eldest, the green-eyed boy smile at him. He felt his stomach lurch.

"Well, I don't accept the idea of an evil god. He ain't some big man watching over us either, he is all the energy, all the power in the world. God is humanity, luck, and creativity. There is no one without God, even if we don't know it yet."

Wolfe watched her, trying to understand.

"But, that's just me. I can't explain it as well as I can feel it, but I believe something is always trying despite a few people's best wishes. We will win in the end, we will," she said, standing and walking them towards the door.

"Hey, be careful! Go harass your father," Tisdale called after them as they ran ahead, turning the corner and racing toward Chaplin. Tisdale slowed, falling back beside the woman and Wolfe as they walked towards the edge of town.

Deep, arching shadows burrowed their figures against the sidewalks. Long slender shadows burst from hidden crevices and burrows, and the houses hung in shadow form against the ground. They walked up the road leading west, where a group was gathered in front of a burnt semi-trailer and a gas station. Backpacks littered the ground around ten people checking bags, watching the skies, making lists, and tying up boots.

"I'm glad you chose the dutiful option," Brieux said as Wolfe stepped up towards them.

"I'm not here for duty." Wolfe smiled. "But thank you?" Brieux beamed back at him while he strapped bags together. Wolfe didn't understand him. Maybe one day.

—

The sun kissed the edge of the horizon before they slipped into twilight. The dust shimmered on the horizon, giving the vibrant orange sky a green tinge before it eclipsed the horizon. Wolfe ruffled through his pack while Scott read out a list from memory.

"Dried food?"

"Check."

"Bleach?"

"Check."

"Bandages?"

"Check."

"Sugar and flour?"

"Check." As they went on, the sky grew darker. Chaplin cinched a shotgun over his shoulder and wrapped a bandana around his balding head. Wolfe slipped his pack on and readjusted his clothes, feeling his loaded gun lying stuffed in the back of his pants. He heard a cough behind him, and he turned to see Chaplin's oldest son, green eyes like acid, staring into his.

"I thought you might like to read something," he said, sheepishly holding out a dirty copy of Gulliver's Travels. Wolfe took it in his hand, admiring its form and shape, scribbled with notes and graduation dates, obviously from some school long empty. "I found it last year, it's one of my favourites."

"And you're giving it to me?"

"I heard you're coming back. Bring it with you," he said, smiling. Wolfe felt a twinge in his abdomen when the boy smiled.

Despite his age, the boy was almost his height. A mop of light, straw-coloured hair fell across his face.

"Deal," Wolfe said, smiling. He tucked the book into his backpack. "What's your name?"

"Fox."

"Thank you Fox, that's very thoughtful."

"No problem, Wolfe," he said, turning back towards his family to hug his father. There was life behind him and a life ahead of him, but Wolfe had made his choice, and he would be back. He thought of the daffodil resting on a table upstairs in Scott's and Wolfe's room. *I will come back. I promise.*

"Are you ready?" Unity whispered to Wolfe, waving her hand at Tisdale as she held back her children and her tears. Scott held the leash to a string of goats, and he eyed them with suspicion. They, in turn, watched him with more suspicion. They were more aware they would be eaten than Scott was.

"Why are they coming with us?" Scott hissed to him as they said their last goodbyes.

"I'm sure it's for the company."

"Why would we bring goats for the company?" he snorted.

"I love you," Wolfe said, the only thing he trusted himself to say.

"When is my mom coming?" Lett asked, clutching Wolfe's hand with one of his, the other holding his silver pocket knife dusted with streaks of red paint.

Wolfe wasn't strong enough. He couldn't tell him the truth. And so he lied again, trying his hardest not to show a flicker of weakness. "She will, just not quite yet."

"Oh. Are we coming back?"

"Would you like to?" Wolfe asked, staring down at him. Wolfe's fingers were softer than when he'd come, still stained around his nail bed from beets. Wolfe noticed he felt safe. He didn't question who around him was going to hurt him. He wasn't tired, he wasn't hungry, he wasn't thirsty, and he clung to that feeling.

"Maybe."

"Well, that's good enough for now."

He felt hope again. As they set off together under a dark sky, the empty moon crept its shadowed face over the edge of the Desolation beside them. The stars Wolfe had seen a thousand times watched them sink into the Desolation like ghosts.

Chapter 21

Desolate Lands & Caravans

The rain hadn't fallen in weeks. The sky remained stagnant, and the earth below it grew crimson and hardened. The clay earth hardened, pushing out the water that formed snaking ravines and trails, forging dark chasms for venomous creatures.

The night was dark. Tiny eyes pecked out from behind the vast sky; their twinkling stares blinked in and out of existence like children playing hide and seek. The moon was thin and spindly; its minuscule tips pricked the sky.

They had walked for nearly two weeks, maybe three, and the darkness had come and gone again, enveloping them with each passing day and night. At first, it was easy to manage the terrain, the boulders, tree stumps, and knee-high ravines in the earth, but the longer they went, the harder it got.

"I thought you said it rained towards the autumn months?" Wolfe breathed. His mouth was like clay, heavy and immovable. His throat was like broken ceramic, stabbing him with every swallow of sandy spit. His eyes burnt open and closed. His body stung and stretched with each breath of air, every blink, every swallow, every breath.

"And again, I said, it usually does," Chaplin answered. His throat was low like a dying stream gurgling death throes over jagged stones. He was trolling ahead of them as the moon passed behind ragged clouds, cutting out any light they may have had.

Lett still clung to Wolfe, but his tiny fingers felt like a sticky, sweaty curse that clung to him, exhausting his strength and stealing water from him. *A growth, an addiction, a parasite,* a — he resented himself before finishing his thoughts.

Unity, side by side with Scott and Chaplin, led the party,

fighting every few hours over which way they were going. They were lost, and the three were engaged in a feral battle, pointing to the sky.

"That's Saturn, which makes that Polaris, so if we continue due east," Chaplin began, pointing northwest at a blinding white star.

"Well, we wouldn't have to go due east if you hadn't taken the long route. We should have—" Scott started to speak.

"When we came around the southeast hills, we moved fifteen kilometres off course. We have to turn south again if we want to find a higher ridge," Unity said

"How would you know that?" shrieked Scott. "Besides, that's not even Saturn. That's Venus. And that's Polaris." He pointed to a star to the south, to which Unity snorted.

"No offence, but you wouldn't know Saturn if you had to take it as a suppository. That's not Venus or Saturn. That's Jupiter," she said, pointing to a white lump in the southeast.

"Ha. What would you know about planets? I live out here," Chaplin snarled. The heat, the thirst, and the hunger were getting to them as exasperation was setting in. The weeks were bleeding into a month, and still, they were walking.

"Yes, but—"

Both of them talked over her, trampling her into the dust. They went over her, under her, and through her, anything they could in a desperate cry to ignore her.

"You said you've never come this far west, so keep your mouth shut before you embarrass yourself. Again, *that's* Polaris," she said, pointing to the white dot to their right. "Saturn isn't even *in* the sky. And that's Jupiter." She raised her hand to the sky, and they all followed her finger. She rested on a large winking star, exactly fifteen degrees south. "We have to go towards Jupiter to head southeast and away from Redemption City. We're angling ourselves too far north; we're going to end up in Old California.

"Whatever," both men said in unison. Scott fell back to complain loudly about the conversation he just had, certain to make sure she heard him.

"Women are just impossible. You try to help them and—" Unity had already turned to defend herself before Wolfe spoke up. "Why? Is she impossible because you were wrong?"

Scott was flabbergasted. He sprawled, surprised by Wolfe's comment. Unity snorted in response, flashing her teeth and squinting at him. "Someone got told, didn't they?"

"Some days I could just…" Scott didn't finish, but his curled fists and pointed lips said enough. He instead redirected his anger towards Wolfe, hissing in his ear. "Why do you do that in front of other people? It wasn't your place, learn to respect me," he snapped.

"Whatever Scott," Wolfe said. He steadied Lett beside him, wobbling as he walked, trying to fight off sleep.

"Can we stop walking? My feet hurt…" Lett cried, looking up at Wolfe.

"Not yet. The sun will be up soon enough and we can rest," Wolfe said to him, tripping over a root peeking out of the sand.

Lett sniffled. "It hurts my nose when I breathe," he cried, pulling on Wolfe's arm. A wind froze Wolfe's sweat over his forehead, covering him with trails of goosebumps and a rush of heat. He felt nausea rising, spinning the world as saliva filled his mouth.

"I'm so thirsty!" Lett cried again. Wolfe stumbled over his feet, turned away from the group, and burped up a mouthful of stomach acid, foamy and white, onto the sand. The heat flushed him again, and he shivered.

"Wolfe?" Brieux cried, rushing to his side. "Guys wait!" he called, and Wolfe heard the rustling of feet on the sand. "Wolfe, are you okay?"

"Guys…I'm…I'm fine. I just got…a little dizzy, that's all."

"A little dizzy? Wolfe you threw up," Scott said, pushing past Brieux and helping him up off his knees, whispering unintelligible words in his ear.

"Guys…really I'm…" Wolfe retched another puddle of white,

foamy slime onto the dirt again. His eyes watered, and sand stuck to his pupils.

"We need to stop for the night," Scott said.

"We can't. We're already out of water as it is, and we'll be in dire straits soon enough. We'll all be in Wolfe's state if we waste two more days out here with no water," Chaplin said. Scott dripped the last few tablespoons of water into Wolfe's aching mouth.

"He NEEDS to rest," Scott said, flying into an angry titter.

"And we need to get out of the Desolation. If we walk through the day and night, we'll find…something, it's been too long."

"Are you insane? That won't help…" Scott whispered. He was holding Wolfe, rubbing his side with small thumbing circles. Wolfe's head was pounding, blood was pumping in his ears, and it felt like their voices were screaming in his brain. His thoughts seemed to yell at him as Scott nagged at him.

"Oh come here, poor baby. Let's get you some shade." Scott led Wolfe to the nearest stony outcrop facing north, away from the rising sun.

"It'll be crueller to do this to him. The next few days will finish him," Chaplin said. "I've seen this a hundred times."

"Brieux, what do you think?" Scott asked. Brieux sat on a nearby rock. His fingers running along the edge of his bag, his eyes flared when he looked at Scott, then softened when he looked back over at Wolfe. "I think you're right, Scott. We should rest, even an hour couldn't hurt."

"It won't be just an hour because he won't feel better. We should keep going before we all turn into him," Chaplin said again.

"Unity?" Brieux asked.

"I think Chaplin is right, he won't feel better to waste another day here," she said, looking towards the stars retreating into the sky. She grimaced at Wolfe as he retched again, not strong enough to wipe the vomit off his lips. Wolfe smiled as sweat dripped against his lips, and he tasted salt.

"Okay…" Wolfe began, all eyes trained on him. Somewhere behind him, the dullest beams of light softened the darkened landscape. A cold gray fog enveloped the land. The worst of the heat had barely begun, but the temperature had climbed probably two degrees. His brain pounded inside of his skull, trying to stage an escape.

"Alright. Unity and Chaplin are right. We have to go."

"Love you have to rest."

"Scott…let go."

"Come, let's go."

"Sco—"

"Now Wolfe."

"S—"

"Stop. Arguing."

"I said LET. Go," Wolfe squeezed out through parched lips and his burning throat, fighting off the latest rise of sickness.

"Scott just…get your shit together and let's get moving," Brieux said.

The earliest light beams fell across the Desolation, painting them orange. Wolfe could feel the eyes on him, but he didn't care; he wasn't going to die out here.

"Babe."

"No." Wolfe pushed past him towards the lane of hills ahead of them, identical to those behind them. Unity and Chaplin trailed behind him as Lett sniffled against his arm, dragging a backpack through the sand. Wolfe's headache grew stronger.

Unity smirked, wrapping her arm around his side.

"Scott looks like you slapped him or something. Thanks, I needed that."

"Save the enthusiasm for me."

———

Wolfe felt like he'd died and gone to hell for the fourth time in his life. His ankles burnt with every step, wobbling like jello back and forth until he was sure another step would shatter his bones. His eyes fluttered open and shut. Each time he opened them, they hadn't moved. *Maybe it all looks the same after a while.* He would let his eyes gently fall, his legs would stop moving, then an arm would lurch him awake.

"Wolfe, we have to keep moving," Brieux said, holding onto his shoulder, maybe to steady himself or keep Wolfe moving. Either way, he didn't care. He imagined it couldn't hurt to lie down on the ground just for a second. Just to rest his eyes and his boiling head. His ears were ringing, and sleep chased cold chills up and down his back.

They'd walked since the sun had come up and fallen again. They bumbled forward through the day as exhaustion claimed more of them. Wolfe dreamed; his hands could taste the air, hear space, and listen to the stars. His eyes felt like they were floating outside his head, and his thoughts were companions.

Even Scott had stopped talking, the comments had ceased, and silence was their only companion. They walked their funeral procession through the dunes, marching forward until they inevitably gave up, and where they sat to rest would be their graveyard. The fallen trees were grave markers; the cracks in the ground were explicitly dug for them.

"Wolfe?" It was pitch black now. He could make out faint outlines of carcasses glowing against a blinding light, and he stopped moving.

"You got it Wolfe, keep moving." He wasn't sure who was talking to him, and he forced himself to keep moving. The next time he sat down, he wouldn't get back up.

Wolfe was sitting. He rubbed his fingers along the warm stone, felt the sand built between his toes, and let the sand slide out of his boots onto the rock. Something stung his cheeks, and he forced his eyes open one last time before sleep took him.

"Sit down and open your eyes. Don't close them again, do you hear me?" someone said.

Wolfe felt something crusty, baked with sand and coated in a waxy finish, sliding between his fingers. He tried to focus on the object, rubbing it between his fingers, shaking it and listening to it flutter. He looked to his right and saw two lumps lying on the ground, lit by colours blurring behind them.

The colours floated like orbs, like flying stars in his vision. They started on his left, blinking, twinkling, multiplying, and jumping back and forth. Then, they shrunk into twins before flashing red as they came closer, then disappeared altogether. He looked down again, watched the dirty plastic bag between his fingers flutter into the wind, and disappear below him.

Wolfe pulled himself closer to the lights, and he felt arms on his shoulders. "Jesus Christ Wolfe, warn a guy."

It fell into place. Wolfe, Unity, and Chaplin were staring over the edge of a cliff, watching cars below them. They zipped by, tires kissing the sooty black highway, sand creeping behind each vehicle, and thrown back with the next. Along the strip of road, a sea of orange lit the ditches: fires broiled in pits, lights flickered in campers, and motorhomes lined the ditches. Motors hummed in trucks and cars as food popped and sizzled on electric stoves and over campfires. The strumming of guitars drifted through the open windows of buses, laughter and shrieks broke out above the clamour, and music pounded through rupturing speakers.

"Where's Scott?" Wolfe asked. Brieux flicked his head behind him, and Wolfe saw he was laying with his back against a boulder, Lett beside him. Brieux pulled himself back from the edge with Wolfe and spoke.

"Right. So we have two options. Someone has to go steal some supplies or we have to beg for it."

"I can go," Wolfe volunteered.

"Wolfe…you can't. This isn't the Desolation, they might see you."

He had forgotten his place in the world. It had been so long since it mattered. "It's still dark. I don't think anyone will notice, at the very least they won't expect it." He looked at Unity, who was trying to hold herself up. The light seemed to hover over her features, breathing over her in the glimmering light. No crevice wasn't bathed in red and white, softening her tired eyes.

"I don't think so, Wolfe."

"Scott has Lett, Unity and Chaplin are just as bad as I am. You shouldn't go on your own."

Brieux mulled it over for a few moments before finally sighing. "Leave your gun, no matter what happens we can't start shooting," he said. Wolfe slipped the gun out of his pants and slipped down the rocks after him.

They made their way towards the first set of cars and roaring bonfires. As they drew closer, the light grew with them. He could make out Brieux's beard, his stubble hanging around his cheeks and under his neck.

Wolfe dipped under the awning of the trailer as shadows pushed and shoved around him. He kept his head turned down, trying to follow Brieux's feet. Wolfe's head was still pounding, and when he moved too quickly, sparks erupted from the corner of his vision. He turned his face away from the campfire to his left and saw his reflection in the darkened window: the flames trickled around his face; a corona burst around him; stars twinkled above him. Wolfe looked miserable. His flesh was stretched like leather across metal supports, his lips flaked and peeled, and his eyes glared back at him.

"—et me tell you, those bluies are fixing to get found I'll tell you that." A group of young men were gathered around a fire as Wolfe and Brieux walked by and caught their conversation. Wolfe pulled at Brieux's shirt and flickered his eyes to the left.

"I've seen them ads, haven't you? It's sick." One of the scraggier-looking boys leered at the rest of the group. The harsh light of the fire transfigured their faces into sharp, ambiguous shapes. Wolfe and Brieux slid behind the hitch of another trailer, crouching in the dead grass to listen.

"No, no, here's the thing. I don't think they're ever gonna be found. They kept saying they went into the Desolation right? Who would survive down there for two months? Why do you think so many of us are moving north, huh? There ain't nothing left down here."

"That might be true and all, but Mr. Bredenbury said he was going to bring them ALL to justice, every last one."

"He'd be the first to know, he lost his entire family."

"I still can't believe they killed them like that. The fucking savages, they truly are inbred monsters," one man said. "I mean, hanging his family up in the trees like that right in front of him? That's true evil right there."

"Mhm." The other men nodded in unison.

Wolfe could feel his heart pound in his throat. They'd willingly waltzed into enemy territory. They were the sheep among wolves. People stumbled by, some with glass bottles in hand, some drug children, but the one thing Wolfe noticed was the absence of colour. Everyone had dark eyes, and he was sticking out like a sore thumb.

He felt a rush of heat in his chest. *How can we escape this? What if the entire world is like this? Escape to where?* Brieux gently touched Wolfe's shoulder, and they listened to them talk again.

"Let me tell you, I'd kill any blue mutation, bluie, mutt, whatever you want to call them, before they came near my family. It's us versus them and I will not let some violent terrorist hurt anyone I know…I think we have to put our people first for once, what's wrong with that?"

"It's perfectly equitable to flip the scales back in our direction again. My brother just got a job as a BESNA officer out east, and his boss says they're all so bitter about it. I'd be *happy* to get a job, get credits, and so on. At least they are guaranteed work!"

"Fucking right."

"Didcha hear? Mr. Bredenbury is running for prime minister, just hasn't chosen a vice to run with him."

"Shit, I'll vote for him, it doesn't matter who he drags along with him, they'll win by a landslide."

"'Bout damn time. There ain't nobody in this goddamn country with balls that'll say what needs to be said. It's all liberals and snowflakes as far as the eye can see, and no one will stand up and end this violence from bluies. Don't get me wrong, Prime Minister Windthorst was one of the best, he did all of this and got bluies to learn their place, but we need someone who will keep the ball rolling now."

Wolfe slipped over a hitch and came out near the road. He stopped for a second. Even when he closed his eyes, he saw the blur of lights tear past his face. The dirt filled his lungs, but he didn't care. The gravel stung his face, but he didn't care.

He felt an arm on his back, tugging him back from the road.

"We aren't even going to talk about that?" Wolfe whispered.

"What's there to talk about?" Brieux whispered back.

"Mr. Bredenbury is alive."

"That's what you took out of that?"

Wolfe felt a pang of irritation. Before he could talk, Brieux spoke over him.

"If they're all moving north, the army must already be into Mexico, or further. We need to hurry."

"We weren't already hurrying?" A wave of nausea overcame Wolfe again, and he steadied himself on the rusted metal of a cattle trailer.

"We just have to keep moving."

"Brieux, I'm tired of moving. I'm tired." Wolfe let himself slide to the dirt beside the trailer. The voices of the young men were gone into the melee, drawn into the sound of passing cars, lost under the chatter in the air.

"Are you okay?" a woman with a tart, sharp voice called down at them from the path. "What are you doing down there?" she asked again.

She clutched her knapsack with one hand; it jostled with the sound of metal and sand. She had a glint in her eyes that stung with apprehension. Loose hairs were glued to her forehead with sweat, but the rest of her fraying, stark white hair was tied into a ponytail.

"We're um—just..." Wolfe eyed her hands as she rustled around in her backpack for something. *This is it.* He looked at Brieux, and fear flashed across even stoic eyes.

"Ma'am, let me explain," Brieux begged as she pulled something small and black from her bag. Wolfe scrunched his eyes shut and held onto him, aware of every minute detail. How dirty his shirt was, he could feel his breath whispering over Wolfe's head, their hearts pounding under their shirts, their chests rising and falling.

Mr. Bredenbury is alive.

They waited. Still nothing. Wolfe cracked open his eyes and saw her fiddling with its back end. When he looked down, he saw Brieux's arm around his own waist. They were sitting in the ditch, and his eyes were wide open, staring up at her. He had wrapped himself around Wolfe, preparing to protect him from a gunshot.

"Eh, this stupid thing. If it ain't gonna work, I may as well not waste my batteries." It flicked to life, and soft, warm, yellow light filtered through the dusty air. She shone the flashlight into Brieux's face, who squinted up but tried to keep his eyes open towards the woman, hands and hair falling over Wolfe.

"I didn't think so…" she muttered as the light flickered off. "There ain't any bluies going to take a chance on coming down into these parts. Simply ain't worth the risk." She rustled it into her pockets and stood there staring at them. They stared back.

"Well? You're both gunna just sit there like a pair uh dummies?"

Wolfe pulled himself up and was surprised at her height. He easily dwarfed her by six or seven inches. Brieux by twelve.

"Sorry umm…we just, ah we…"

"Do you have food?" Wolfe interrupted. He watched the ground, trying to stick towards the shadows.

"Wolfe you can't just…"

"My lord, look at you both. You look like death. There ain't gunna be no good in this world if we ain't help each other when we're down on our luck." She patted herself on her hips and started waddling back down the side of the highway.

"Well come on now, I'm not waiting up all night for you."

Wolfe pulled Brieux up by his sleeve, and they set out after her. Wolfe's ankles burnt with each step, they'd rested for those few sweet moments, and even that wasn't good enough.

The woman was wearing a long-sleeved dress brown with dirt, and it was cinched up past her knees over a pair of tan jeans with initials bejewelled over the back. Over it, a dirty, once pink bathrobe had the letters B&B on its breast, and it was tied shut with what looked like a yellow stuffed flamingo leg.

The air was festive. Bottles clinked. A breeze blew off the highway carrying hoots and laughter. Food passed between dirty hands, drinks between the crooks of elbows and off the ends of fingertips. Bodies swirled around them: men with missing teeth and scarred faces, women wrapped in scarves as strands of dark hair bit against flames, children played in the dirt, smears of dried snot stretched across their grimy faces.

They just looked like people. They could have been in another town in the Desolation. They were just as filthy and ratty as he'd seen at the camp all those years ago. The same laughter, the same figures slipping behind rocks with tongues slipping into mouths, the same gossip shared around a smouldering fire.

They were vagabonds, wanderers, travellers, escapees from their own lives. They were all running like them, searching for the best they could find, looking for something that might not exist. They were all identical, like Scott, like Chaplin, like Unity, like Wolfe, like Lett. Yet, he knew, and if they knew, they would agree with him; they couldn't be more different if they tried.

Nobody stopped, no one looked at them, and no one acknowledged their existence. They stepped around a campfire and through a line of bushes with the woman.

"Right in 'ere." The woman pointed at a metal trailer hitched to an SUV, the edges rusted against the rims of the tires. The fire was brilliant, casting an aurora of light across the walls, refracting around them like a crown of sunlight. A few tents were scattered around the camp, and a circle of old stumps acted as chairs for the mix of faces around the fire, shrinking back from the light into shadows.

"This is it," she said as she turned back around to face them. "What little we got, we got it here."

A young man a few years younger than Wolfe popped up

immediately. An older man, an older woman, a few kids, and a middle-aged woman looked at them with suspicion, concern, or even anger.

"This is my son, Jansen," she said.

"Here. Take something to eat." He stood; his mop of strawberry red hair hung past his eyebrows, but he pushed it up past his face and above his head. He had large scars across both of his arms, and a dirty sweatshirt was pulled up towards his chest. He handed them bowls of lukewarm soup with a few chunks of bread he had ripped off a small loaf with his hands.

"I ain't mean no offence but you both look like shit," he said.

"Eh, maybe they are shit," an old woman crowed up from the back, tossing her hands in the air.

The woman in pink spoke up quickly.

"Now you just wait one goddamn minute Beatty. You may be blood, but I could end that right now, you know!" She brandished two fingers at her while she chewed on her bottom lip.

The other woman dismissed her with a flip of the wrist and swung open the door to the trailer. She yelled out of the metal tin behind her as she went, "There ain't enough food to keep us alive. Never mind the trash you find and pick off the side of the road, Zelma."

"You can be the next person someone finds on the side of the road if you keep testing me you fat cow," Zelma said.

Wolfe hid his smirk in his bowl of soup. It was thin and watery, straight out of a can, but it was the best thing he'd tasted in over a month. It was like heaven, churning against the vacuum in his stomach.

"Why do you look like that?" a little girl spoke from behind a woman's dress. She had moved into the light of the campfire, and her dark brown eyes shone.

"Little miss, don't you get into the habit of going 'round and asking lord knows who every question under the sun. These people are trying to change their circumstances, just like us." The woman smiled up at them.

"My name's Vista," the little girl squeaked from behind her mom.

"Beautiful name," Wolfe said.

"Rose." The woman smiled and nodded at them both.

"Wolfe."

"Brieux."

"A pleasure," Rose said, looking over them to the rest of the group. "That's my uncle over there, and the woman who brought you here is my aunt. A heart of gold that one."

"So you're cousins?" Wolfe asked. Jansen stirred the coals, and Rose fed a baby in her arms.

"Yeah," he said. "She's *only* a couple of decades older than me. She practically saw the fall of the Twin Towers," he joked.

"Seven years. Tops," she rebutted. She cradled a small boy in her arms and rocked him gently while smiling. The shadows almost hid her face.

"Pa, say hello."

"Ghmm," he grunted in response.

"He doesn't think we should help as many strangers as we do, but he ain't gonna voice no opinion, that's for darn sure. Would you be surprised if we told you you're the twentieth pair to come through here? I swear she goes scouting out for people to bring back," Jansen said.

"Well, I don't know how we can thank you," Wolfe said.

"You're very welcome. You both look like you could need some extra energy. Whereabouts are you headed?" Rose asked. Wolfe could see the genuine curiosity on her face. Her features were soft and sandblasted. She pulled herself closer to the fire, and her complexion shone, her pale hazel eyes coming out of the darkness.

"We're going south."

"South!" Rose cried, and the group fell silent. The only noises were metal creaking in the wind and the gentle popping and hissing of a kettle resting on the coals of the fire.

"Do y'all even watch the news? Why do you think we're all

fleeing north, there isn't anything down there for us," Jansen said. Wolfe saw his reflection bouncing back in his dark, obscured eyes.

"Well…we…" Wolfe stopped. He didn't know what to say, so he looked to Brieux for help.

"Are you guys going to fight in the war? That's so cool!" he said, dropping his stick into the fire, crawling with embers.

"Well…" Wolfe began.

"I'm a front line doctor and this is my husband." Brieux pulled Wolfe closer.

The old man snorted. "Woman, ain't that just your luck, you reeled in two government workers and two fags."

"HEY!" Zelma roared, jumping out of a fabric chair, missing both arms with her flowing pink bathrobe slumped over her hips. "Don't you ever open that stupid maw of yours again if idiotic shits gunna keep coming out," she cried, dropping her drink to the ground and ripping off a sandal.

"Get off me you fat cunt!" he yelped as she smacked him around the head with her sandal and berated him with every smack. "If. You. Weren't. A. Rack. Of. Bones. I'd've. Boiled. Your. Carcass. For. Lard. By. Now. Go in with your hag of a sister and leave the rest of us decent folk in peace," she cried again as he stormed off to the trailer, slamming the door shut with enough force to shake loose caked dirt around the wheel wells.

"I done knew it, the way you were holding each other in that ditch I could tell you were in love." She smirked to herself, dipping into her husband's absent chair.

"Why aren't you in all those government conveys going south each day?" They watched as a long trail of slithering black cars and army trucks crawled south on the opposite side of the highway, rolling in mournful, electric silence.

"Umm…"

"You ain't no doctor then," Zelma said, leaning back in her chair and holding a bottle of beer up to her lips. Jansen tossed one to each of them. "Go ahead now, fess up, we ain't no snitches." The three watched them, waiting for them to start speaking.

"We are!" Wolfe cried, pulling Brieux closer as he took a swig from his bottle. The flavour hit his tongue, and it was nirvana. It fed his soul; an invisible hand poured PDT directly on his brain.

Zelma saw no need to believe them or take them at their word. They rattled off lists and ideas, all of which weren't anywhere near the truth.

"Government defectors?"

"War junkies?"

"Documentation folks?"

"Well. We. I." Wolfe started to think. Would it be that bad to tell them? They would need a lot of food and water for the rest of the group shrivelling into husks on the hills behind them. They would cause a scene if they tried to take it.

"Oh, good lord, just spit it out already!" She tossed her empty bottle over her shoulder and into the sand.

"I'm Wolfe Bredenbury." The camp went dead silent. It was like the air was sucked into space.

"Bredenbury? The workers…but your…your eyes?" Jansen leaned in, and Zelma and Rose arched their eyebrows. Wolfe watched them all closely. No one moved for a gun or a tablet. No one looked like they were about to scream for help.

Brieux was lost for words. Nothing but wheezes of air slipped past his lips. His eyes darted; he looked like he was ready to bolt. Wolfe stood, pulled his lump of wood closer to the fire, and let the flashes of light sparkle across his eyes.

"HOLY SHIT! I mean…holy shit!" Jansen said. "I knew you looked damn similar, how'd you get this far? Did no one recognize you?"

"Why are you going south? There ain't nothing down there but brown-eyed people. You'll get turned over to them in seconds," Rose said.

"Didn't you torture the Bredenbury family?" Zelma asked, nursing another glass bottle and staring into the sky above them, misty clouds reflected in her tired eyes.

"We didn't torture anyone. I didn't."

"But you egged them on, you pushed the workers towards violence," Zelma almost whispered.

"We didn't do anything the Bredenbury family didn't do to us."

"Really?" Rose asked.

"That family beat a pregnant woman so badly she gave birth in the gravel dirt and they fed the baby to the yard dogs. They whipped me for serving them, sometimes they made the kids eat out of the trough with the yard dogs…" Wolfe begged them each with his eyes.

"Violence is violence."

"So you're going to turn us in?" Brieux gulped.

"There is a bounty out for each of you for millions of credits. Each," Jansen said, refusing to look up at them. Their voicelessness was ringing in Wolfe's ears. His heart twittered against his ribs, and his fingers trembled along the wood.

"Where are you going, then?" Zelma asked. She looked like she was in pain, and it hurt her to ask. "There is nowhere you get to be normal anymore. What are you going to do?"

"We're going to try and show the world what is out there. Show them the truth," Wolfe said, pausing for a moment.

"You can't change an idiot's mind, you have no proof, nothing to show for it," she said. Wolfe went to lift his shirt and show the marks along his back, but she waved him down. "That can be excused away, you can't make people believe, no matter what you show them. Most people would do worse to you if they caught you."

"We're going to go fight in the war, help how we can."

"Ha!" she scoffed. "The war will be over by the end of the week, it's suicide."

"Well, you're lucky, you have a choice."

"We're lucky? Half of our family didn't get to escape like you. My mother is in a 'hospital,'" she said, making large exaggerated marks with her fingers. "It divided us as much as you. You are the people we lost in our families."

"He's right, I want to fight too," Jansen said.

"Like goddamn hell, you will!" Zelma hollered, throwing her bottle back in the chair. Her face blushed with rage. Jansen was a ball of gas and fire. A floating eye of methane and flame, hanging in time and space.

"Momma, I gotta, Leo would want that!" he cried, his eyes dripping onto his cheeks.

"Are you stupid!! You want a bullet like your brother? Would he want that? Would he want you to die for him?" Zelma yelled. For a few moments, she towered above him; her stature and voice dwarfed him five times over. She was a statue, a monolith against him. He was a wave, beating and begging his relentless pressure against her like the sea against the shore.

"Momma please," he whispered. Stamping up and down like a petulant child throwing a tantrum. He was on the verge of tears. He was the hurricane roaring. She responded with a bitter silence for a few seconds before she broke.

"No."

"Momma, please!" he begged. This time dropping to his knees and pulling at her hands, dancing along the edge of the bathrobe with dirty, crummy fingers. He was digging into the dirt with the downward force of gravity. Now a gentle sea, swirling knee-shaped holes appeared in the soil beneath him. She spoke again.

"No."

"Momma, please…" he cried. At last, a puddle. Weeping into her with rage and contempt, this time with eyes that were gray and despondent with emotion, she dragged him into the cabin by the scruff of his neck.

"No!"

"Momma plea—" was the last thing they heard as she slammed the rickety metal door shut with a snap. Leaving the sound of the cars on the billowing freeway to fill their ears.

"I guess you're going to need something to take with you. It's probably…a few thousand kilometres south of here."

"Where is here?" Wolfe asked as she shuffled around behind

her in the dirt. The curtain inside the trailer had drifted, maybe a touch, a brush, but it still swung in a phantom breeze. Vista crept in the dirt behind her mother, the baby in Rose's arms unlatched from her weeping breast.

"Not sure. I'd guess somewhere between New Mexico and Utah? Maybe Arizona. California?"

She fluffed out two bags and stuffed them with silver cans, clunking and jangling together in the bottom. They sat there in silence, Wolfe and Brieux listening to the crinkling of plastic and metal touching and rubbing together.

"Here. Take these." She handed them a bag of food each. Maybe three days worth. "It's not a lot, but it will keep you on the road longer."

"Thank you."

"I hope you both do well...wasn't there a lot of you?" Rose asked. "I can't help but feel that there were more of you on the screens and the billboards." She screwed up her lips over her teeth as she said it, tilting her head back and forth like a lost dog.

"That's true. We have three adults and a kid up on the ridge just back that way." Wolfe pointed to the rocky ridge swung over the highway, now dusted in golden light hidden by the cliffs beside them.

"Jesus Christ...and are they all in just the same state as you both?"

"Just about," Brieux said, pulling his bag closer, looking down at the ground, not wanting to ask for more.

"Lord above..." she whispered, looking around for an answer. She thought long enough for spare beams of light to trickle over the hills above them. She pulled four more bags out from behind her chair.

"No, we couldn't—" Brieux started to say.

"Please," Wolfe asked.

The door to the trailer creaked open achingly slowly. Just long enough for Jansen to stick his red, puffy face out, stretched with tears and snot. He pulled himself out, rubbing his face with his sleeve, dragging his face clean.

"Go grab that cooler," Rose called towards Jansen. He did, slowly, and tried not to meet anyone's eyes. Trying not to show them he had been crying. She riffled through it, and then with four more bags in hand, she heaved them onto the ground by their feet.

"This is better."

"Thank you so much," Wolfe said.

"Where are you going then?" Jansen asked. He looked towards the rising sun, his back to them, rubbing his face with his sleeve again.

"Don't harass them."

"I'm just curious," he muttered, walking the long way around the now-dead fire, tossing his hands behind his back.

"Down to Mexico city."

"And how are you getting there?"

"Jansen, I—"

"Walking I guess."

"You won't make it. I can help!"

"Your mother needs you, you're staying," Rose said.

"I want to go."

"Absolutely not," Rose snapped back, refusing to say anything more.

"That weird man, right across the way." He began pointing across the highway, ignoring her. Between the blur of cars, they could make out a sickly lime green van with no lights, rusting along the edges, sitting on the road's edge.

"A van?"

"I heard a few people talking about it when I went to get water. The man goes back and forth between Mexico and Wyoming for family members."

"Jansen, now you're just talking out of your ass."

"It's true!"

"Just because a few idiots can't tell the difference between their asshole and their mouth does not make it true. You heard your mother and I think she's right. If others want to throw themselves away for a hopeless cause so be it, you don't have to, you're as brown-eyed as the rest of us." Rose looked up guilty at them as she said it.

"Fine. You can argue six ways till Sunday but I'm going to help them get over there. It'll be dangerous for bluies."

"Wolfe, we should get going," Brieux said, grabbing him on the shoulder.

"I'll help you carry your bags," Jansen said.

"Jesus, Mary and Joseph, if you don't come back…I will not be the one who let you slip away," Rose snarled.

"Relax Rose. I'll be back. Besides, I have Momma's blessing." He smiled at her. His face was almost back to normal, sparing the rim of puffiness around his eyes.

She glared at him as she watched them go. Vista, the little girl, shrunk out of sight as she waved. They duck and dove around the last of the late-night strangers. The world around them sank into a lull, and even the highway was empty.

"Ain't no soul alive is gunna be driving around during the day. It's a fine way to have your car explode," Jansen said, watching a handful of cars race by on the highway. Most of them had pulled off to either side, and the ditches were even more crowded with metal and wheels. People all around them were putting out their fires, packing in their food, and hiding in what shade they could find for the hottest parts of the coming day.

A few people still milled around. Wolfe watched a man, drunk off his mind, stumble into a pair of wiry bushes. He turned around to face them, pulled out his cock, and started pissing. An orange stream that reeked of onions and alcohol, mixing with the muddy red earth into a boiling stew, wafted as steam over them. They stepped over the young men who had been talking before. A few of them still shifted, but the rest were snoring under cots and tarps as the chill of night crept away.

Mr. Bredenbury is alive.

They walked in silence. Wolfe felt his eyes drifting. The food and water in his stomach would pull him into sleep again; the exhaustion was creeping over him again with waves of nausea. He just needed rest.

They climbed the hill onto the outcrop, both steeper and slicker than it had been on the way down. Wolfe's legs quivered. At the top, they found the rest of their group piled together under the shade of the boulder.

"Guys. Guys. We got some stuff," Wolfe said.

Scott popped open his eyes immediately and panicked upon seeing the strange young man. He leapt to his feet, lunged at least five feet, and landed with a dense thud on the dirt several feet away from Jansen.

"WHATAREYOUDOING!" he bellowed, scrambling on the dirt towards him as spit danced off his tongue. Sweat leapt onto the earth as he slithered along the ground. Jansen danced back in horror, dropping the bags at his feet. He let out a piercing scream that echoed across the canyon walls.

"SCOTT!" Wolfe yelled.

The early morning light painted them all in grayscale. Lett, Brieux, Unity, and Chaplin were shadows. They all watched in silence.

"Pull your shit together," Wolfe said. "You're an adult, act like one."

Scott tripped and spluttered over his words as he tried to stand. Wolfe walked past him without a second's glance. "Bitch me out later," Wolfe called over his shoulder.

"Lett come here," Wolfe said, dropping to his knees. Lett crawled across the rocky earth to him as he pulled out a cup of cold soup and stale crackers, letting him sip on a bottle of soda.

Both Chaplin and Unity slurped at cups of water. Nausea hit Wolfe again like a cold stone against his stomach. He knelt over, blood pounding in his ears, trying to keep down his breakfast of watery soup and alcohol. "Right. See that van over there? He is going to Mexico, and he is going to take us with him." Wolfe pointed to the large black lump down on the side of the road. It was the only van for maybe sixty meters.

"He is?" Chaplin asked.

"He is. He just doesn't know that yet," Wolfe said.

"You need to get back to your Mom now," Wolfe said, pointing towards Jansen and flicking his head in the direction they had come. "And you," he said, looking at Chaplin, "you need to get back to your wife and kids."

"I'm in no state to walk back through the Desolation. It would be suicide. I'll leave when the sun goes down again," he said, shielding his eyes from the ever-rising sun.

"Fine, but—"

"I still have to take you to the van. It's dangerous," Jansen said. He was nibbling along the edges of his nails, leaving frayed, inflamed skin along his nail beds. His eyes kept creeping over the edge of the rocks, down to the road below as another train of trucks and vans tore south.

"But…"

"Wolfe would you just leave people alone for over three seconds? Jesus, are you trying to get rid of everyone?" Scott yelled. Wolfe felt his throat tighten; his mouth drew into a hard line.

"Sorry, it's just—"

"Come on Wolfe—" Brieux began to say, pointing down the rocky path across the highway.

"Mr. Bredenbury is alive," he said, interrupting Brieux.

"What?" Unity asked, her eyes widening like discs.

"He's going to run for prime minister. He hasn't chosen a running mate."

"What? How…I…"

"I heard some guys talking abut it. He must have survived at the manor. He must have escaped somehow, he must have…" Wolfe stopped talking, it made no difference. *Mr. Bredenbury is alive*.

They sat in silence for what seemed like ages, grappling with the impossibility of it, before they finally lifted themselves off the sandy floor and began making their way down the hill across the other side of the highway. Wolfe kept one hand on the rocks; the other held the cross and the ring around his neck. He felt the rough surface of the cord and the smoothed surface of the necklace, and he felt them both tighten.

Chapter 22

Sunbeams

Wolfe thought himself into such a stupor, that in the hour it took them to navigate themselves to the ground, he wanted to strangle everyone who dared to cross his path. The sun lashed them as they walked. Wolfe's eyes burnt, his ankles were swollen, and deep bags sunk under his eyes like ravines.

"That's it," Jansen spoke up at last. They had walked for ages under the sun. Wolfe felt the wrinkles deepening on his face as they had walked. Maybe stress, anger, or fear; it all blurred together into a murky, unnameable stew.

The van was parked north of a tall rock wall to the right of a long, dwindling tunnel. Its dark gray blinds were drawn shut, and it looked like it had never moved from that spot. They sat for a moment behind a snoring R.V., rumbling up and down while they thought it over.

"All right. Does just one of us go, or do we all go?"

"Well. We have to look at all the options."

"And what are those?" Jansen asked.

Wolfe could see the apprehension dripping off his features. A face of youth intertwined with fierce excitement and tension. Nuts and bolts screwed his face together like a mechanical creature. Wolfe could see the emotions ripple and change across his face like sinking and rising tide pools. First fear, a tightness in his eyes, sucking his skin taught against his bones. Then excitement snapped against the harsh exterior, and his eyes grew bulbous and sheeny. Wolfe peered across the road, where he thought the woman and her family were parked. Nothing but embers floated up from the open campfire.

"Well, he is parked far away from everyone. That doesn't

make you think he likes to be bothered by people," Wolfe whispered, feeling the cold metal of his gun against his back.

"True. But I doubt he would try and take all of us at once," Chaplin muttered, pulling his hands at each other.

"Fair. However, I don't think all of us trying to crawl into a van in the middle of the day is best," Brieux reasoned, looking to the others for support.

"You're not wrong. Still, I think we have the element of surprise," Scott said

"Wrong. We have to move at least a hundred feet to get there. If anyone is watching, they are going to see ten people moving towards the van. I'd be out of there here faster than anything if I was in that van," Unity said.

"Oh, of course, here I am, always wrong. Why didn't you pipe up for anyone else? You obviously have something against me," Scott snarled.

"Or. Maybe you're just fantastic at making stupid comments," Unity bit back.

"What is your issue, were you born a bi—" Scott was cut off.

"GUYS!" Wolfe yelled. "Would you stop, please…Scott? Come on." It stunned Scott into silence. The air was hotter. The sun was higher.

"Okay. If we all go, things could go badly. If only one of us goes, it could go badly. It does no good to just stand here. Either way, you can't tell me he hasn't dealt with his fair share of people trying to mess with him at this point," Wolfe noted to the group, all of them rooted in silence.

A few dirt-coloured government trucks flew south, leaving plumes of swirling dust behind them. They caked the air, lights radiating in the tunnel behind them, shining like diamonds buried deep within the earth. Jansen was standing at the back of the group. The world was rumbling; tiny rocks and heavy layers of dust levitated off the ground as the trucks ran towards them.

They looked between each other, and in the split second it took them to look away from Jansen, he was gone. He slipped around camp stoves, scurried over a long hanging R.V. awning and behind a pile of trash before they lost sight of him. All the while, they could hear his screams above the roar of the trucks echoing through the tunnel.

"HELP! HELP! MUTTS! THERE ARE BLUIES HERE!" he cried at the top of his lungs as he ran north. Wolfe could see the tunnel lit against him, the glimmering lights growing second by second as if the throat of a stone monster was lit aflame.

Wolfe was standing alone in a tract of dust. The rest of them ran towards the van, calling back to him, falling on his deaf ears. Wolfe turned on his heel and ran away from them, barrelling straight towards the glimmering lights and Jansen.

Jansen ran fast, but he slipped and tumbled without thinking, squeezing through the tightest holes in a desperate attempt to escape Wolfe. Whenever Jansen was confident he'd lost Wolfe and stopped to breathe, Wolfe would see him around a corner, forcing him to run again. Wolfe was alive with energy, irradiant, glowing with heat, slipping in and around trucks and campers, moving as cautiously but as fast as he dared.

Lights flicked on as he ran. He watched Jansen merge out onto the highway, waving his hands above him when Wolfe knocked him down into the ditch again. They were lying on the ground, tussling on the steaming pavement.

"HE—LLP! The'rye…" Jansen tried to gurgle as Wolfe pushed dirt and gravel from the road into his mouth by the fistfuls. Jansen was hysterical, his eyes dark pools as he choked on the dirt spiralling in and out of his mouth, grinding against teeth. He was still waving and struggling, but he was no match for Wolfe in size or rage.

"What's going on?" someone cried to their neighbour.

"Did you hear that?" someone called back.

There was a pile of black trash bags off to the side of the road, and with the lights bearing down on him, Wolfe pulled him off the ditch and into the pile of garbage. They would have seen him on the road, the waving, the screaming. In his mind, he could hear their tires on the pavement spitting up gravel as they came to take him away.

"You asshole," Wolfe whispered.

He was vibrating with blind, volcanic rage. He had never felt anything like this; claws of fire were ripping at his stomach, and it felt like he could scream until his vocal cords snapped. His hands shook with such ferocity he almost dropped Jansen as he dragged him off the road. Jansen still fought. Their skinned and burnt flesh was stinging as if someone had dipped them in acid.

He could hear voices calling and dogs barking. Steps were brushing past metal, and fingers opened and closed gates, there one minute, then gone the next. Wolfe listened to curtains sliding on metal racks, open, closed, open, closed.

"Give me something for trying." Wolfe looked down at Jansen, and he was smiling. *The dirty fucking bastard is smiling.* Jansen beamed a wide grin with mud and gravel-caked teeth. A cut above his eye filled with dirt and sand. Tiny white scratches covered his face, looped in winding patterns.

For a second, Wolfe saw Mr. Bredenbury. Despite it all, despite himself, he couldn't see anything but a villain. No better, no worse than those guards, the officers, or any brown-eyed people in between. He saw evil in Jansen's eyes, real or imagined, no better, no worse than the Bredenburys. *Mr. Bredenbury is alive. He killed Craik. I'm going to kill him.* Wolfe didn't stop to consider.

"It still might have worked…" he mumbled as Wolfe wrapped his mouth with a willowy blue garbage bag that reeked of fermented juice and alcohol, like the inside of a recycling plant.

Wolfe pinched his eyes shut but didn't dare lower himself closer to the ground. Wolfe kept his full weight pressed down on Jansen's hands and face, crushing them against the rocks. His body was resting near his pelvis, and Wolfe was pushing his legs down with the rest of his body, spread like a spider across him.

The rumbling grew louder as Wolfe crouched, listening. He could see it all: The sound of tires on gravel, the yell of guards, the pelting of bullets. Bullets. Wolfe felt the gun against his back. If they came, he would shoot them both. Then maybe the rest would be safe. He would exist only as the visions people held of him, all a million different versions of himself.

What about the rest? Did they even make it, or are they waiting for the guards to scoop them up? Would he hear the gunshots from here? Would he listen to them die?

The earth trembled as the trucks broke into the placidness hanging around the tunnel's edge. One blinding roar after the other. One. Two. Three. Four. Five. None of them stopped, and none slowed. They were gone, tearing down the highway.

There was only silence between the two of them.

Wolfe pulled the bag off his eyes and looked at him. He was a kid. Maybe as old as Wolfe when he was in the camp. *How can I trust those shitty brown eyes?* How could Wolfe have been so stupid?

"Look I—" Jansen began. Wolfe threw the first punch. It hit flesh, but his skin was hard enough to send shocks of pain up Wolfe's arm that didn't faze him. He felt nothing. He struck again, and again, and again. When he pulled his hand away, blood ran down his fingers, trickling between his knuckles and dripping down the lines on his palm. Wolfe felt a power filling and swelling in his chest with each touch. Nothing and no one could stop him. He held Jansen's life in his hands.

Jansen reached his hands, barely extensions of himself, towards a gap in the garbage bins as he managed to kick Wolfe off. Jansen kicked a cloud of dust into Wolfe's face, choking him.

"Hel—" he went to yell again, and Wolfe pulled his legs out from under him. "Fuck. You!" Jansen made a strangled cry like breathing caused him pain as they grappled in the dirt. Jansen climbed on top of Wolfe and tried to beat Wolfe into submission. Wolfe tasted a glob of Jansen's spit enter his mouth. Wolfe tasted his own blood.

Wolfe rolled over him again and pinched him between his legs. Wolfe used both hands to attack him again, spurred by the pain in the rest of his body. A string of mucus was hanging across Wolfe's fist, and he was aware of blood dripping from his forehead as he paused to breathe. Jansen's knuckles were skinned down to stumps.

Wolfe followed his eyes down to the ground, where Jansen's foot rested on his pistol. Wolfe looked up at the sky, then down to Jansen, his eyes shining in the rising sun. An eclipse inside his pupils pivoted lights back down onto Wolfe's hands. Both of them were tangled under the eyes of the sun.

Darkness swelled over the valley, the gulleys, and the depressions that swathed the country. All the darkness hidden in locked boxes in attics and hidden in the backs of closets lifted from their homes around the world and swooped towards Wolfe, riding like an army of black knights to kill him with despair.

Jansen closed his eyes as Wolfe pulled the gun up, and he clicked his nail along the length, crouching down on both knees. Birds called somewhere above him. He looked away, finger on the trigger.

"I'm sorry. Do you have to?" Jansen mumbled, tears washing the wounds on his face. Wolfe couldn't see his face through his own tears. Two trails of snot ran down his face.

This is humane. This is survival. This is humane. This is survival. Can you do it? Wolfe shut off his brain. This time, the gun wouldn't go off. He'd have to pull the trigger.

—

Wolfe pulled himself out from behind the trash cans dragging Jansen behind him. They crawled around a long stretch of parked cars with strips of fabric pressed into the windows to blot out the sun. They were chased by the boiling heat, dripping into the ground as Wolfe semi-walked, semi-dragged Jansen behind him. The van was still parked in its spot in the shade. Still rusty, still abandoned, still an acidic lime green. Wolfe stepped up to the door and rapped his fingers against it, leaving a smear of Wolfe and Jansen across the paint.

Brieux was standing in the door with wild eyes, pulling Wolfe in by the scruff of his jacket, and Jansen by the torso. Wolfe slipped and landed on the floor, panting and revelling in the slight coolness of the van.

"Wolfe!" Scott wailed.

"What did you do?" Brieux yelled, turning to a terrified

Jansen.

"He started it! It's not my fault! I—" Brieux threw Jansen to the floor and turned to Wolfe for the gun.

"Wolfe, give me the gun," Brieux yelled.

"Wolfe? Are you okay? Did anyone catch you? How did you catch him? Are you okay? That bastard." Everyone spoke all at once, and their voices were indistinguishable from one another. All their voices swam together in a medley around his head, bashing themselves against his ears. Wolfe's head was pounding.

He pushed himself off the floor and onto a dark purple sofa. Its length ran with light tan stripes and silver polka dots. It crunched beneath him when he sat, coated with fraying plastic and wax. It was short and dumpy, crumpled along the van's edge, pulled taut over metal and wood.

The walls were sparsely decorated. A decorative plate with a large fish on it swung with the word ALASKA printed in bold red letters. A tiny cross made of wrapped wire hung above them, cut by beams of dusty brown light flickering in through the dust-caked slats of the window. Little wooden trinkets carved by hand lined the windows, stuck with chunks of glue.

Wolfe watched the light dance. Move. Flutter. Tremble. It seemed to ache back and forth, growing tense and rigid, hovering between space and time. The next moment it seemed to ebb and flow, pouring and lurching around the room. Wolfe let his eyes close as the voices kept muttering in his ears.

"He almost gave us away. He tried to turn us over to BESNA. I should have known, Zelma and her whole crew had packed up and left. They just wanted the credits," Wolfe finally said, and the van roared.

"You're an asshole!" Scott said, "I knew we couldn't trust you."

Chaplin stared out the window in silence.

"Wolfe, are you okay though? If BESNA caught you…" Unity said.

"We have to kill him," Chaplin finally said.

"WHAT? Please, no, don't I—" Jansen started crying, and Wolfe felt rage twisting in his stomach.

"I could have killed him back there and not had to drag him back here. We can't. He's not even sixteen."

"Are you stupid? His entire family is going to be after us now. We have to kill him and save ourselves," Brieux yelled, raking his fingers through his hair and panting.

"Stupid? Really? I don't remember any of you running off to stop him. I'm the only reason we're not in the back of a BESNA truck right now. We have to take him with us. I'm not killing him."

"Check him for a tablet, something that might track us," Unity said, and Brieux pointed Jansen to his feet.

"So you're just going to take me down to Mexico city? It's a warzone down there," Jansen cried, wiping his grimy face with the back of his arm.

"Are you happy to be alive? I could have killed you, you'd have deserved it too." Wolfe winced as his knuckles brushed the back of the sofa. Brieux rubbed Jansen down from head to toe twice. Unity came and inspected the bleeding cuts on Wolfe's face.

"Now let me go. I won't tell BESNA. I won't tell anyone. I promise."

"I didn't think you were utterly fucking stupid. We can't trust you!" Scott yelled.

"At least if he's with us, we don't have to worry about him waving down the next BESNA truck he comes across," Wolfe said, turning to Brieux.

"We wouldn't have to worry if we…dealt with him."

"If you want to kill him, say kill. Own up to it Brieux."

"Where is your family going?"

"My family? They…oh, they're…going to contact BESNA if they don't hear from me within a day."

"He's bluffing. By the time BESNA knows anything, we'll be in Mexico City," Chaplin said.

"So you're kidnapping me?"

"Join the club kid," a voice said.

Chaplin had his shotgun trained on the voice. A figure was sitting in a chair beside the sofa, watching them all. The man was in his mid to late fifties, though he could have been younger. The man had long grayish hair that hung past his neck and was tied into a greasy ponytail. He was wearing a moth bitten t-shirt, riddled with holes that gaped through the faded Metallica print. He was wearing grease-stained sweatpants and stunk of pepper, diesel, dried lemons, and cigarette smoke. His face was rough cut and icy; sharp peaks formed where chin and jaw should be.

"Well, how is this going to end? A bunch of outlaws, theives, kidnappers, and literal murderers in my van. How is this going to end?" he asked. Gently letting his hands drop to his side, eyeing the gun barrel up and down.

His voice wasn't the rough and tumble, dwarven drawl he expected. It was sweet, airy, and laced with the lofty threads of carelessness.

"Hostages, that's the word I was thinking of. We haven't been kidnapped, we're hostages."

"Don't get smart or we'll just kill you," Brieux said, Chaplin's gun cocking up in response.

"How does this thing drive?" Scott asked, sitting up in the chair, hammering away at the petals, and ignoring the rest of the conversation in its entirety.

"With the gas pedal," the nameless man said. "Besides, why don't you kill me, regardless?" he questioned, leaning forward in his chair.

"Would you like it to be arranged? You ain't the person with a gun atchyer head," Chaplin snapped.

"Touche," the nameless man whispered with an air of resentment. His voice was coated with sticky, sweet bitterness. Behind the man's eyes, you could see the narrative shift and swell. He was less human, more fae.

"Do we have to jump straight to killing everyone?" Wolfe asked.

"If Jansen is coming he may as well too," Unity added.

"Could you let me be the adult for ten fucking seconds Wolfe?" Brieux snapped, and silence washed the van.

"What?"

"I have to agree with the lady. You won't know where the key is, and I guarantee you won't find it. I was going to Mexico anyway, and I might have taken you all if you'd knocked…" The man smiled.

"Or you can tell us," Scott said.

"And die?"

"Couldn't we kill you after we have the key?" Chaplin asked.

"You could. Or you couldn't."

"Who cares if he comes or not. Chaplin has to leave," Wolfe said. The ring around his neck tightened again.

"Why do you keep trying to get rid of me? It's the second time you've mentioned it in the last two hours. You owe me your LIFE!" Chaplin cried so loudly his voice hung in the air.

"No, we don't. For all your guys talk about killing rather than taking hostages, Chaplin gassed us and dragged us to a town in the middle of fucking nowhere."

"That is not the same."

"Yeah, you're right. As far as I know, you didn't consider killing us. I don't care if you're here, there, or dead." Wolfe pulled the string around his head and chucked the ring at him. "Your wife wants you back."

"How do you have my wedding ring? Did you steal it?"

"Chaplin…" Brieux said.

"Why would you defend me? Be an adult for ten fucking seconds, Brieux and keep parenting us like you'd like," Wolfe snapped.

"I was just saying that—"

"And as if you have a leg to stand on. You had a horrible reputation at the Bredenbury plantation. You want to lecture me on what being an adult looks like? Fine, but you played a monster a little too well," Wolfe said, driving the last stab between his ribs, aiming for the heart.

The van fell into a final, resolved silence.

Chaplin tossed the necklace back at Wolfe, and it hit the floor by his feet. Wolfe screwed up his foot and kicked it, spiralling it under the driver's seat.

"Get changed, Wolfe," Brieux snapped. Pointing at a folded lump of clothes that smelled overwhelmingly of alcohol and dried dirt. Everyone retreated to their own areas of the van to sulk: Brieux in a bunk above the driver's seat where he intended to sleep until sunset, Unity and Lett on the purple sofa, Chaplin as far away from Wolfe as possible with the gun trained on both Jansen and the nameless man.

Wolfe felt a glimmer of guilt flash through his mind. He hadn't wanted to hurt Brieux. *Well, I had*, but now he was asking himself if he'd gone too far. Scott squeezed him on the shoulder, and they waited for night to fall.

Chapter 23

The Exodus

"Is that it?" Scott asked, peering over the windshield towards the road ahead of them.

"Why even keep asking?" Brieux said, piloting the vehicle down the endlessly black highway. A black snake shone through the hills ahead of them.

"Just anxious I guess."

Wolfe laid on the sofa, trying not to expire. The temperatures had gotten nearly unbearable at night, never mind the day. The sand seemed to boil and shrink into diamonds as the sweltering winds bolted around the van.

"Where are we then?" Wolfe called from the sofa with eyes closed, focusing on the constant throbbing beats pounding against the inside of his skull. The gashes on his face had shrunk into lines of scabs and were falling to the floor.

"Somewhere in Mexico," Brieux said, watching as a silver sign with the words long melted away slipped past them. Scott pulled a crusty faded map out from the dash, lit by stale white lights, flipping bitterly through its light blue and green pages.

Wolfe sat up, scratching at his scalp, and watched tiny curls of dandruff drift onto the ashy gray carpet. He didn't dare open the blinds and let a degree of heat rise in the van. Wolfe stared at the ring, gleaming under the sofa opposite him, twinkling back and forth in the beams of moonlight flashing through the drifting curtains.

Wolfe listened again to his stomach churn like thick, black waves on a stormy sea. They had stopped once, and they had pushed an emerald necklace on two dirty vendors for a bottle of water for each of them and some turning produce that they had devoured before it could shrink into shrivelled images of itself overnight.

"Why do you think we're in Mexico, big boy?" The nameless man leaned back, smiling at him through the hole in the back of the passenger seat. He blinked dramatically with a pair of long eyelashes and made a stupid pouty face. He had been at this for the past two days, a constant barrage of quips and comments.

"Why are you like this? We have to be in Mexico. It's been three days," Brieux said.

"Well, I'm bored…" he said, taking a long drag off an expired cigarette and tossing the empty carton under the seat, looking out towards the Desolation. The hills and vales spread out into a shrinking, dancing expanse as they drove through an interminable, sterile expansion of the earth. Clusters of ramshackle houses trickled down the hillside, ebbing and flowing like a giant web across the Desolation. Maybe once protected by trees, now mercilessly pummelled day in and day out by the unrelenting elements.

The farther south they drove, the fewer cars passed them going north. The first night was an endless stream of red and white, faces lit inside vehicles by orange and yellow lights, their homes on their backs as they rode north for a better life. The light drew to a trickle over the next few days. The brilliant flashing, the blur of colours new and old, became a drip. A car here, a car there, until finally, nothing but pure, inky night enveloped them. Their van, shuttling along through the darkness, was the sole strip of light for miles. The houses grew denser and denser, yet emptier and emptier, like ghosts; the ancient monuments to lives once lived, stories once shared between someone.

"Have you seen a sign that says…" Scott began before falling into silence and staring back over the map.

"No. I haven't." Brieux smiled as they watched a silver sign pass, warped with heat.

"Ha." Scott grimaced.

Wolfe didn't listen to them talk. He picked at the skin around his fingernails until they stung like fire and dripped tiny drops of blood onto the carpet. His lips were frayed and tasted faintly of metal. His nails were broken stumps. He had tried to read, but he couldn't get past the first chapter. He had dreamt of the green-eyed boy. The book sat on the nightstand, and he picked at it, flicking to random pages. They had all silently agreed to ignore the argument days ago, but Wolfe felt both conflicting waves of guilt and annoyance.

"What's your name?" Wolfe asked, looking past Unity and Chaplin at the man in the chair, leaning back, dreaming of a cigarette. The nameless man didn't answer at first he just looked at Wolfe. The smoke on the walls still stung Wolfe's throat.

"I'm a dead man walking as they say." He smiled, leaning back to stare into the night. The road rumbled underneath them; broken pieces of pavement, melted and regrown, churned against the tires.

"That's not your name," Wolfe said, absently bringing his fingers to his mouth, staring him down across the dimly lit van.

"You don't need to know."

"Hmm," Wolfe said, leaning back again. "Do you have more smokes?"

"Maybe. Do you smoke?"

"Not yet," Wolfe said.

"Third cupboard by the sofa."

Wolfe leaned over, counting third from the left, and pulled at the sticky metal handle. He pulled out a white carton, dusty, its back painted with a picture of a woman with a hole in her neck. He ripped the plastic off and pulled one out with his teeth. That's what the older kids in school used to do.

"Gonna share? I have the lighter after all…"

"Can I have one?" Jansen asked, peeking his head from behind the nameless man.

"No."

Wolfe flipped one to the nameless man, and he caught it in his hand, startling Chaplin from the edge of sleep.

"Hands out front." He pointed a finger at him, shotgun resting at his side.

"Relax, Chaplin."

"Wolfe you…" Chaplin began.

In the time it took for Chaplin to complain, the nameless man had already pulled the lighter out and flicked it to life. Reducing the cigarette's tip to smouldering embers, glowing blisteringly red and hot.

He tossed it to Wolfe, who let Chaplin's complaints fall on deaf ears. Wolfe took a long drag and choked on the bitter smoke. It felt like it was feeding his brain, sending currents of soothing electricity down the rest of his body as it suffocated him.

"So. What do you do? What *did* you do before all of this?" Wolfe asked the man.

"Doesn't matter."

"I know it doesn't matter, but I'm curious."

"What did you do?"

"I asked first. But if you must know, I was in high school."

"So you're a baby?"

"Something like that."

The man thought in silence for a long while, letting himself take several long drags before speaking again.

"I'm not that interesting."

"I digress."

The man was silent even longer this time. Taking down the cigarette to a tiny nub until it smouldered and burnt heavily with smoke, letting out a final puff before extinguishing itself in an ashtray as he grabbed another from the carton.

"I guess somewhat of a carpenter, but not really. Anything that made money, to be honest."

"And your family? I heard you're going south for family members."

"Kinda true. People pay me money to drive back and forth with their family members. I don't have a family."

"No one?"

"Not anymore."

"Oh?"

"I had a kid before. Just one…knocked up some chick and she…well, they…he's an adult now. Shit, that had to be back in the forties already," he said, puffing on his starched cigarette, emitting puffs of blue haze that encapsulated them in grime.

"Brown or blue?"

"Don't know. Never really met him, a couple of times as a baby but…"

Before Wolfe responded, Chaplin spoke out of thin air. "Y'all smell that?" he said, holding his nose up to the air. The van rumbled along, and they sniffed together. Sniff. Sniff. Snort.

"What is—" Wolfe began.

"Shh…" Scott whispered. Peeling his eyes at the road ahead. The air around them seemed to grow grayer and grayer until the scent of smoke was unbearable. They cut in and out of the dense fog as they steadily climbed up the winding roads. The smoke trailed off to the right a few moments later, and the road veered left.

"A wildfire you think?" Brieux asked, peering through the cracked windshield spotted with bugs.

"I doubt it. It wasn't wood smoke," Scott said, peering out the window.

"What was it then?" Unity asked and only got silence in return. She was sitting on the floor, her head back, Lett curled around her stomach.

Wolfe didn't see how it could be a forest fire. He peered out through the window behind him: A few dying trees, dead bushes, and dead animals watched them as they drove past glowing houses, a few people living out their lives in the Desolation.

"How do people still live out here?"

"Stubbornness," the nameless man said. "So now you have to tell me about yourself."

"No, I don't," Wolfe said, putting out the cigarette and standing up to stretch his arms above his head, brushing his fingers against the fuzzy roof of the vehicle as the smell came back again with a bitter vengeance. It was fiery, spicy, and acrid, burning out Wolfe's nostril hairs like burning battery acid or snake venom. It reeked of burning hair, burnt tires, and plastic.

The van filled with smoke so dark it blinded them. Through the eye-watering, greasy film, Wolfe peered out the window again, catching sights of flickering shadows cast across the top of the van.

"Guys, look!" Wolfe called out as he stared out the window. On their right, over the heads of a towering hillside, over the dead silhouettes of spindly trees standing jagged out from the hillside, sunlight flickered.

Somewhere behind the mountain, millions of trees were lit from behind, and it was giving off a terrible stench. A reek rolled over the valley and snaked down around them, crossing the road and pushing deeper into the valley to their left.

Brieux screeched the van to a halt and leaned across the dash, staring through the cracks over the hill.

"Fire?" Unity asked, pulling herself up for a look

"What if it's our city?" Brieux asked.

"It sure ain't moving like a fire," Chaplin added.

Jansen eyed the hill with waves of horror, and he looked like he was going to burst into tears again. Even the nameless man was leaning back in his chair, looking west up the hill with the rest of them, pulled out of his blasé demeanour.

"Wanna find out?" Brieux asked and pointed to a snaking dirt road, barely large enough for the van, that crawled around the twisting roots of trees and up the hills towards their right.

"Guys, that's a terrible idea. If we get caught in a fire, we'll burn alive in this tin death trap," Wolfe said, watching the lights ebb and flow over the hillside, painting the skeletal trees in visions and shades of light.

A moment later, they were trickling up the hill, the van straining over twisted, gnarling roots. She climbed the mountain in silence, the exhaust sputtered, her wheels moving slower and slower. The lights grew brighter then dimmed every few minutes; the air seemed to tremble as she cried underneath them.

"The fuck is going on up there?" Chaplin's gun was lying on the sofa alone while he peered between the driver's and passenger's seats, staring out the cracked, bug-splattered windshield. A dusty margarita plush, a pine air freshener, and a pair of dollar store sunglasses swung back and forth in the rearview mirror.

The stench was nearly overpowering as they crowned the hill. They stared into the misty abyss as heat and smoke barrelled toward them. During their ascent, the sun seemed to have risen. It flickered through the dense clouds and fog. The heat threatened to press in on them, melting the glass, popping the tires, pressing the vehicle's walls until they were nothing more than piles of scorched atoms. But it didn't happen, and they slid down the other side of the hill beneath the hazy, smoky air.

The trees on this side of the mountain were white and bare; their bark had been peeled off them, sagging like burnt skin, falling off in rings. The trees hunched over across the road, hanging precariously overhead. Their corpses were burnt and forgotten.

The sun seemed to grow and shift, sinking and fluttering along the edge of the hills before it would rise again, and waves of heat and burnt light enveloped them. They drove to the edge of a plateau and began down it, coming to cross a small bridge formed of wood, cement blocks, and melted plastic that would once have crossed a stream.

A stream of semi-trucks were moving down the highway opposite them. Each semi-truck was black with a large metal box on its back, the colour of burnished leather. A tiny golden eye was printed on each semi-trailer in the top right hand corner, and the name *CHAMBERLAIN* was pressed into the metal. Hundreds of BESNA trucks moved past them in a roaring procession. A symbol was painted beside the golden eye in the corner of each truck, hinting at what precious cargo they might hold. Red eyes. Green crosses. Pink fish. Silver forks. Simple X's. Some were for breeding, some were to test developing drugs, others could be workhorses, some to be castrated, some to be farmhands, some to be house servants for those who could afford them.

The trucks piloted past them on a trail that stretched beyond the horizon, one after the other. The words BESNA PROPERTY TRANSPORT were spliced across the backs in golden paint. Tiny black grates were stuck in the top left corner, and in one of them, a face was pressed against it. Wolfe watched them pass with mouth gaped; the towers of trucks roaring past them paled the van in comparison, aged and sunburned, rumbling with weight.

"What are those?" Chaplin asked as the last of them went by, maybe two hundred in total.

"Those are…" Wolfe began but fell silent. No one had the strength to go on. Wolfe felt as if he were inside their bodies, hands burnt and raw, bodies covered in blisters from burning metal, piss and shit fermented in the fetid greenhouse they were sealed inside.

"They're slave transports. They're everywhere. You see them all the time," Jansen said quietly from beside the nameless man. He was inspecting his half-empty bottle of water nervously, looking between them and the sloshing water with one pale brown eye.

Jansen went on. "My grandparents' farm was just off one of the main highways over in Florida, and an internment camp was only a few kilometres down. They drove day and night. Every day. Up till the day we left." His fingers jolted over the edge of the chair, and his eyes drifted as they passed them. Jansen forgot about his nerves.

"Once, one of the trucks stopped on one of my shifts at the old gas station I worked at when I was thirteen. They flung those big metal doors open and shuffled all of them out. They tossed the dead into a giant heap and poured gasoline on the bodies. After the fire was raging, they tossed the sick and dying into the fire." His voice dropped to nearly a whisper.

"The officers didn't say a word. All with those black, faceless, helmets and golden eyes they just…stared as it burnt. One of the other gas station attendants clued me in to the secret, 'They just aren't people, they don't feel pain like you or me.'"

Unity sat in the back of the van, looking through the trucks, gray and unseeing. Wolfe moved to her, stepping over Lett, playing with his fast food toys on the floor. Wolfe sat beside her in silence as they watched the sunrise flicker between the trees.

When he looked back, her face was pocked with tears. She was like an unyielding marble statue, yet beneath the marble, cracks were showing. Wolfe had never seen this much emotion from her before.

"Wanna talk about—"

"No." She pulled herself off the sofa and scaled the side of the van into one of the bunk beds, yanking the curtain back with a muffled sob, and was quiet.

"How—"

"Let her relax Wolfe," Scott called back to him. Scott had leaned back and had a foot on the dash, watching the sunrise outside the window. The lights flashed past them from the trucks beside them. Wolfe tried not to think about it, choosing instead to stand behind Scott, resting his arms on either side of him, letting his hands dangle down over his chest.

"She—" Wolfe said.

"Just…let her breathe." Scott sighed. He sounded exasperated. Wolfe felt Scott's hands go slack around his wrists. Immediately Wolfe felt a twinge of fear. *How can he give up on me? Does he not care anymore?* Wolfe leaned back again, pulling his hands down to his chest, head resting against his face.

"Want me to drive, Brieux?" Scott asked, stretching his arms above his head and cracking his neck left then right.

"No…I'm fine." He yawned.

"Brieux." Scott shot him a glare as he steered the van against the gravel at the edge of the road.

"We're going to need to get gas soon." Brieux yawned, stretching his arms over the steering wheel.

"If this thing leaves us stranded, that might be the final straw."

Scott laughed as he slid into the driver's seat while Brieux crawled into the bunk above them and started snoring in seconds.

"Sit?" Scott gestured to the empty passenger seat.

"You sure?" He looked behind them, and Lett played in silence. Chaplin fought sleep, Jansen fiddled with the sofa cushion, and the nameless man read a dusty cowboy erotica novel frayed with tattered yellow pages, one hand resting over his pants. Wolfe shuddered.

"I know…" Scott whispered, pulling out into the road and heading off again, a smile teasing across his lips. Wolfe stretched his legs and looked around. The sun flickered through trees, sending cold and translucent rays through the cabin as the road dipped into the long-dead forest. Wolfe popped open the glove box: spare erotica novels, used floss, melted chocolate mints still wrapped in silver foil, and a handful of condoms that expired fifteen years ago.

"Not much use for these, I'd imagine," Wolfe called, smiling, holding up a string of purple ribbed condoms behind his head, waving them to the rest of the cabin.

"Please, this is my friend's van. You should see *my* van, loaded to the brim with condoms, used and ready to be used," the man said, not even looking up from his novel, catching a flash of purple from the corner of his eye.

"Mm," Chaplin snorted, rolling his eyes.

Wolfe felt himself laughing. He looked at Scott, and he was laughing, too. His eyes swam, his lips curled up in laughter over stunning white teeth, and his hair was longer than he'd ever seen it, wrapped around his ears, hanging over his eyebrows. Wolfe reached his hand over and touched his leg, feeling his thigh through his beaten pants, breathing in the fresh air coming in through the broken A.C.

They had come out of the trees, and the sun was on the horizon again, flickering and blinking without the trees. Wolfe looked around at the van. They weren't scared. They weren't cowering, the scars on Lett's hands had healed into thin white lines, Scott's gunshot wound had healed and life was good for the moment. A thousand possibilities laid ahead.

"We're going to need to stop soon and wait out the day," Wolfe said.

"Mhmm," Scott murmured in agreement.

They had come down the side of the mountain and had come full circle around the globe. The earth had changed its rotation, and the sun was now rising in the northwest. They had come down onto a flat stretch of land stretching past the horizon. It was flat enough that Wolfe could see the twinkling of golden stars crowning the night sky. He pushed himself up, pointing to the sky.

"Scott. Scott, look! There are stars! How are there stars?" Wolfe asked, realizing it as he said it. Scott didn't even look. He was too busy staring out towards the sun.

"Ohmygod…" Scott breathed, faltering for a second.

To the northwest sat what was once the biggest city in North America. And what they once thought was the sun, they realized now was the entirety of Mexico City being razed to the ground.

Chapter 24

Ashes to Ashes

They sped towards the city, kicking up dust behind them. Wolfe, when he blinked, imagined a different city. The normally glittering sea of glass and plastic, nestled against the rivers and swollen ocean, was empty. The plastic skyscrapers usually vibrating with electricity were dark. Wolfe could see the air was filled with helicopters and planes, hanging in the air like gnats while fireballs, numerous and heavy, leapt from their faces like the tears of a hydra, trailing to the ground and exploding fire and death over the city.

The city reeked of burnt rubber, pulling and yanking at his lungs. The fireballs gnawed through plastic, turning the city into molten fire and extruding bouts of toxic gas and chemicals into the air.

"Mexico City is the pinnacle of life around the globe." Wolfe could hear news anchors in his mind lamenting about the most prosperous city of the twenty-first century. They formed plastic waste from first-world countries into towns, houses, hospitals, skyscrapers, and metropolises. Mexico was the centre of innovation, a thriving spider web of millions, each snaking through their own city of wonders, searching for their stake to claim.

The bombs shook the ground, vibrating into Wolfe's teeth, followed by uncomfortable silence and a flash of light brighter than a thousand suns. The moment was bright enough to etch the world into their closed eyelids. A cool night became a boiling day in a second, eyes opened or closed.

The world grew dense, hotter with each passing car, each silent ranch, and whispers of homes sitting abandoned. The highway was an unending stream of cars heading away from the war zone, loaded with belongings, teetering above the cars wrapped with ropes and held by arms in the backs of trucks. A woman and six children walked alongside the road opposite them. Her face was impassive and blistered with heat. Her children were bloated and fat, and she was a rack of bones. *They won't be alive in a week,* Wolfe thought, and her face held that understanding in the shadows and wrinkles along her cheeks and under her eyes.

The traffic grew denser as they drove past dust-choked rivers crammed with the new blue boats, a heap of honking cars and screaming voices crowded around the van as the temperature climbed in the night lit alive by bombs and fire. The artificial sun never set, the eclipse of light and darkness had lost its cycle, time was unending, night and day lost meaning.

The closer they came, Wolfe could see the city of plastic, a broken figure of what it once was. The multicoloured plastic windows dripped and bled down the skyscrapers, and ditsy spires seeped upwards, fighting gravity into thundering gales of black, windblown smoke. The city trembled again, rising and falling like the roars of a terrible dragon. The spires were teeth, the bombs were fire, and the people were blood trickling from its wounds away into the countryside.

The closer they got to the city's heart, the smaller the houses became. Along the edges of the city, people were squeezed among millions, tossed together in hovels, strung together with hemp, concrete, and metal. The thriving gardens and illustrious penthouses of the inner city were a cruel joke to the millions living in squalor. The only food to be found was the refuse of the inner city citizens. An entire different city lay ahead; a world within a world.

The fields this far out were bare. Expansive watering and cooling systems, each stamped with the Bredenbury family symbol of golden wheat on its frame, hung above the fields. The bare ground was covered with plastic shielding. The lush, brown soil was moist, and water dripped off virgin plants as they were tended to by Mo after Mo. A boiling, heat-cracked landscape, infertile and unfathomable, lay beyond the Bredenbury's high-tech, fertile nexus.

Men led menageries of animals bawling and crying through the streets, women carried their lives on their backs, men lay on the road, eyes blank, hands burnt, blood boiled inside their skin. Somewhere children were screaming. The sound of the end for thousands. *Thousands.* Wolfe would never even know they were missing from this earth. Nothing to some, quickly replaced by the children born halfway across the world in luxury, sterility, silence, and love, oblivious to the world between him and them.

"Scott look," Wolfe said, pointing to the faces of the men and women rumbling around the van through the fog. Wolfe saw ordinary brown, green, gray and blue eyes wobbling around them. No one met his eyes, but Wolfe saw souls, entire lives inside those eyes. Here one second, gone the next, and then a whole life would pass before Wolfe saw them again.

Wolfe watched a family of five children get dragged by their parents toward the city's heart. An entire family of blue eyes worked their way through the sea of people towards the BESNA army. If only Wolfe could tell them they're going the wrong way. *They will kill you; they will kill you.* He wanted to scream, but they were gone before he could look again.

The sky was black and thick with grease without stars to paint it. A greenish luminescence plunged them further and further into light beneath the sky, sealing in the morning. The earth shook enough to pull Chaplin off the sofa and onto the floor. A few people screamed outside as tiny flecks of gray snow fell from the sky. Plumes of paper and plastic flushed through the van in waves.

"We're almost out of gas," Scott said, grimacing at the meter. His features were taut. He'd aged fifteen years in the last hour. He tapped the wheel, his eyes darting across the scene outside, back and forth in tiny beading motions as he pulled at his shirt, and Wolfe caught sight of another cross like Wolfe's own dangling against his chest.

"What's going on?" Brieux pulled himself out of the bunk, and his hair was pushed up against his head, caked with sweat. He rubbed his eyes while he slid his hand over his face, leaning up against the back of the chairs.

"Jesus."

"Yeah."

"We're gonna run out of gas, aren't we?"

"If traffic stays like this? Probably," Scott replied as he touched the brakes again. A large truck filled with lumber and rusty tools was swinging back and forth in front of them. A sizeable greasy man was screaming out of his window, slamming his horn as the car in front of him stuttered.

"Right then." Wolfe pulled himself out of his chair and yanked at his jacket, sliding it down with a large knot around his waist. He slid his gun into his coat pocket and a kitchen knife into his boot. He tossed a scarf around his face, wrapping it around his nose and mouth. "I'll be back."

"You can't go out THERE," Scott cried, jumping out of the seat and leaving the van unmanned.

"Why not? Drive until you find gas. I'll be at the next gas station. If you run out of gas, I'll bring back a can. I'll get there before you guys, and if not, you'll find me there."

"We don't even have any money. How are you going to get gas?" Scott cried, pulling at Wolfe's shoulders from behind.

"I'll figure it out," Wolfe said, knowing he had no plan. The gun in his pants whispered plans to him.

"I can come!" Lett cried, pulling out his pocket knife and hopping to his feet. The vintage fast food toys lay on the floor, forgotten.

"Not a chance," Wolfe snarled.

"You can't go on your own," Scott yelled. "You're not going."

"Wolfe, please! I can help you, I won't get in your way, I promise." Lett was holding back tears now. His throat was throbbing, and his eyes grew glassy and wet.

"No, Lett. Scott, I'll be fine."

"I'll come."

The van turned in slow motion, and Unity pulled herself out of the bunk with two knives and a wrench in hand. As she walked, she slid the weapons into her belt. She slid her boots up her legs and laced them twice, tying them snug in complete silence. She slid a golden bracelet off her wrist and passed it to him.

"We'll get gas with this."

"Alright," Wolfe said, moving towards the door.

"It's too dangerous," Scott said, stepping in front of them. "I won't let you go."

Unity stepped in front of Wolfe and smiled into Scott's face. He was six inches taller than her, but she was baring her teeth and her eyes were pulled back in rage.

"You're going to step out of my way in three seconds, got it?" she said, pulling her hands up and pushing her hair into a ponytail while he watched. "Or gas is gonna be the least of your issues," she snarled.

Scott held his ground with a smile of contemptuous glee at the thought. *Sure...*he whispered in his mind undoubtedly as they eyed each other.

"Scott move. Come on," Brieux called back. The nameless man eyed them up and down with glee.

"Who doesn't love a fight? Fight! Fight! Fight..." Unity shot him a glare that could have turned him to stone, and he dramatically sighed, rescinding into silence again.

"Now..." she began. "One." The room was silent. The tension was just simmering. Scott's cheeks were glowing, and his smile slipped off his face. Wolfe could see her body shaking with rage, her hands working a bandana over her hair and out of her face.

"Two."

"Come on. Stop!" Brieux yelled. Her leg was bouncing now. Chaplin and Wolfe looked back and forth at each other. Jansen was panting beside Lett. "Scott, please..." Wolfe begged, "...just move." Concern occupied his face, and his eyes were vast. Her eyes had dropped, and for the first time in weeks, Wolfe saw a grin crawling across her lips, wrench in hand.

"Three—" She bounced forward and raised the metal above her head, but he stepped aside before she could hit him. His cheeks were burning, and he flicked his middle finger at her as she walked towards the door. The smell of burning plastic rushed into his nostrils as they stepped outside into the boiling stench, and she stopped outside the door, curtsying as she went.

"Your majesty…" She smiled, stepping out of sight.

"BITCH!" he yelled down at her, and she bared her teeth at him in a wide smile.

"Pussy!" Unity yelled back into the van. A glob of spit flew out the door and hit the dirt. Someone rushed past them and stepped in it, spreading it through the dirt with their heel.

"Wolfe?" Lett was standing behind him with an outstretched fist. He opened it and held it out towards him. "Don't get hurt." He was holding his now silver pocket knife with the paint flaked and rubbed off in his hand. His hands were shaking, and he didn't meet Wolfe's eyes. Wolfe dropped to one knee as he felt a hand on his boot from behind.

"Promise buddy." And Wolfe hugged him. He smelled like old cigarette smoke and dirt. Wolfe could feel the sadness in him, weighing his body down. Wolfe knew it by heart; an age-old friend and enemy.

"We'll be back." And they slipped out the door.

The air scratched at his lungs, and they curled inside out. A zoo within him was clawing to get out with every breath. One breath lions, the next the claws of an emu, after that, an elephant was fighting up his throat.

The van disappeared behind them as they weaved and dipped around people. Wolfe was in awe. A kaleidoscope of colours swirled around him. Dusty, red earth, and smoke mingled around the ebony black bodies of lurching tires. Eyes glimmered around them like bits of glass: a hint of silver, a splash of ivory green, peacock blue. Voices shouted, and some cried like angels, lusting above their heads; a deep riveting pain chewed through Wolfe like cold steel.

Some voices were deep, whispering careful exchanges and

secret meetings. Others were childish and playful, maybe a joke passed between siblings. Others were cold and biting, a snark of hatred between people trapped with needy children. Either way, the long night was hot and foggy, long coats swirled through dirt, and the trail of cars was lurching along like molasses.

They were into the density of the outer city, where the dense hovels had grown above them. The teetering towers of tossed-together homes and shelters weaved and danced into the apex of the sky. The city was trickling out into the country: clothes were being ripped off lines stretched between windows, suitcases flew, bodies shifted and amassed together, rippling and throbbing with the movement of the streets. Mountains of people were piled in the back of wailing trolleys, roaring under their weight. Most citizens were on foot, rushing out with children in hand, and bags on their backs, sometimes running barefoot over broken stones and chunks of burning ashes. A boy was crying, trying to pull his dead mother to her feet, snot staining his cheeks while his wild eyes tried to pry someone to their aid. Wolfe went to reach for him, and then he turned away. *We don't have time.*

Wolfe looked up and down the monstrous plume of the city as tiny drops of burnt and melting plastic floated down from the sky. The night grew darker as they drew closer, and the street lights flickered to life. Lights in homes and boarded-up shops flickered as street lamps sparked and sizzled, popping out of existence as the power shut off around the city in swathes.

Wolfe heard the screaming first. People scattered like rats off the street and into alleyways, crawling over fences as fire rained from above. Six planes hovered above them for a split second before darting away again. The houses, the apartments, and the street corners burst into flame around them, pushing waves of heat over them as blackened chimeras roared and bellowed fire.

The buildings melted. The plastic sizzled, releasing greasy black smoke that hissed and howled, blooming out into the street. Wolfe watched the inhabitants spill into traffic encased in the molten plastic, pulling their hands for air. They were already dead, and the plastic had hardened again; their clothes were reduced to razor-thin, melted strands over their naked bodies, their eyes drifting listlessly without eyelids.

A second later, another plane was overhead, drifting and lagging in the sky above them. It stopped for a moment, then continued. Somewhere high above the sounds of misery, gunshots rang out.

Wolfe and Unity ran. They ran as long as they could until they came into another throng of bodies walking over hardened plastic in the street. The lots around them were empty; the apartments long ago melted.

"Let's try to go around," Wolfe yelled over the roar of people as they dived into an alleyway. They crawled over large metal garbage bins, crawling with maggots and emancipated dogs digging into corpses. They pushed past a family, trying to rip a weeping elderly woman out of her home, her arms wrapped around the door frame. A flurry of words, crying, begging. Gone. They scrambled over a low-hanging wall and onto two girls lying against the wall. Wolfe saw one of them was missing a leg, and a trail of blood was running into the gutters. The gnats and flies clung to them.

"Please, please, just try for me…" one of them cried, dragging bloodstained fingers up and down her face. The girl was dead, pale and gray. Wolfe looked between them and saw the pain. She looked up and started begging.

"Please, oh thank god, please help us," she cried. "My…she… my friend…she…I…" She tried to get her words out, but she was a blubbering mess. Wolfe felt his heart clench. He saw himself in those blue eyes,

"You have to leave!" Unity cried over the sound of bombs exploding nearby, followed by the silence of death.

"She's fine. She's fine, trust me, she's just…she's fine." She trembled when she spoke, pulling at the other girl's face in slow, methodical motions, trying to bring life back to her cheeks. Wolfe saw both girls were covered in burns, their blue and green clothes were singed, and their skin was stuck with pieces of melted plastic.

"LEAVE! GO! SHE'S DEAD!" Wolfe yelled. Gunshots rang out, and the sound of a gutted engine roared.

"No, I…" she began.

Wolfe could feel Unity's hands on him, pulling him away. The sound of a plane above them drowned all noise. The girl's lips moved.

"Please. Please. Please." Over and over again, reaching out to Wolfe. The planes were right above them, their holds opening, shots ringing. Wolfe felt his own feet moving, and the girls were gone. The fire was everywhere again. When he looked back, they were a motionless ball of flame. They still held each other even in death. They were okay now. No more pain. No more sadness. Peace.

Two blocks down and over another fence, they found a medic station. The sea of people was weaker here, but shots were louder. The skyscrapers swung above them, tall and menacing, like knives in the earth. They were flaming, and bits of plastic and ground glass fell periodically, tinkling in cascades down their bodies. A tall woman was barking orders at the medics, covered in blood and bruises. The men and women lying over the parking lot were missing limbs, faces, and souls. Dead, dormant eyes stared into space with smiles or screams frozen on their faces.

Wolfe ran up to her, stepping over bodies on the ground. She was trying to speak to a young woman in Spanish and failing. The woman ran away, only to be blown to pieces by a riddle of gunshots. Behind them, towards the city centre, a wall of metal and guns towered. Distant bodies dressed in blue and green fragments scattered their shots towards the base of the towers while hell rained on them. Chunks of the wall were crumpled like pieces of paper; rains of bullets pierced white holes in the metal as flame and tires fought to crush the officers.

They were shooting away from them, but bullets rained towards them, sometimes catching people in rows.

"Hello? Hello!" Wolfe cried.

"I can't help you!" she cried, swivelling around to meet them. She was pointing with her hands, yelling directions to her men, ducking and shielding away from hails of bullets as a wall of BESNA officers began to spill over the barricades, lighting the streets with a black blizzard of bullets.

"We're looking to fight!" Wolfe cried.

"The war is over. There won't be anyone left alive in the inner city by tonight. Get out while you still can!" she yelled, pushing a man into a van laden with moaning bodies, reeking of blood and piss as gas stations exploded and storefronts were torn from the earth.

"We didn't come here to leave, we can fight," Unity cried.

"I don't know what to tell you! Then you came here to die!" she yelled back.

The last of the wounded were loaded into the vans as the distant sound of gunshots roared above the flames, and explosions lit her haggard, emancipated figure. She was dressed in muted blue and green stripes, with the letters OCHS spread across her wrists in silver.

"There is space if you're coming!" she yelled again as the perpetual day roared again, and chunks of fire rained down from above. She was holding open the door, and there was space for maybe three more people, including them. "You coming?"

They looked at each other, and Unity paused.

"Fine. You're on your own then."

"Wait!" Unity flew towards them and held the door open.

"Who cares?! It's all over. It's over! We're fucked! We're going to just have to lie low, live the best life we can after this. You're stupid if you think there is any future for us!" the woman yelled, sucking her lips against her teeth.

"That's what we're fucking trying to do, you dumb cunt!" Unity shrieked at her. Unity banged her hands against her own head, digging her hands to the roots and kicking the van's side. Spit flew from her mouth as she screamed; her hair escaped her ponytail and was sticking against her cheeks, caked down in layers of ash.

"If you want to do something, there was talk of a man on the north side who sold contact lenses. There were whispers he could change your life, but…it's all gone, it's empty. It got annexed last night. There won't be anything left but you can try. That's all that's left," she cried over the roar.

"Thank you!" Wolfe yelled, but the door was already shut. The fleet of vans shuttered off and tore towards the slums, away from the city with her cadaverous figure drifting in the window. Unity collapsed against the abandoned gas station. Medical tents were empty and heavy with dust, abandoned stretchers painted the ground white, and the earth trembled as the gunshots grew closer. They could hear the screaming and yells of retreating forces.

She pried hair off her face, and Wolfe closed his eyes for a second, pushing his head against the wall.

"We're fucked," Wolfe whispered to her as they sat there.

"Pretty much."

Wolfe tried not to cough but spewed black spit into the dirt beside him. His face was black with ash, and his mouth was metallic with the taste of blood.

"I've never spoken to you about my family have I?" she asked.

"No."

"My sister's name is Liberty. She is so pretty, much prettier than me, smarter too, she has better control over her emotions. She's more like Mom. I'm more like Dad. I had a brother too but it was just Mom, Dad, Liberty, and I after BESNA brought us here from Europe. They shot Dad at the Worker's District in Redemption City during one of those selection days. They forced the three of us onto one of those semi-trailers, and we were caught in a sandstorm on our trip. We were there for two and a half weeks. I never saw my sister after that."

Wolfe didn't know what to say, so he was silent.

"You know, my dad, brother, and I used to stargaze. We'd drive to one of the darkest mountains in our country every father's day, and we'd spend the night watching the stars. He showed us every constellation, told us all the mythology, and how to tell the time with the stars. I miss them both so much. My brother fought when they came for us and he's gone. He taught me to fight, and Dad…he…taught me everything I know."

They listened to the roar of war behind them. A gale of bullets pierced the burnt frame of a truck in the street. The voices were getting louder; the sound of tires crunching over ruin was ringing in his ears. Wolfe closed his eyes, knowing this was the end.

"I used to think fighting was my only way…maybe it is… but…" she looked at Wolfe, and he tried to read her face. "I'm so tired of fighting. I'm tired of nightmares, guilt, and fear. I don't want to fight anymore."

Wolfe couldn't look at her again; he knew he'd feel something if he saw her eyes.

"Trust me. I know what you mean. I lost everyone too." Everything he'd held back came out at last. "BESNA came for me at school. Even looking back I can't figure out why it was just a random Thursday in March. They came, they killed, they beat kindergarten kids into the dirt with their boots. Kids Unity, kids. They sent all of us to a camp in the middle of nowhere, and I met my family again. We spent the summer in that camp, and at some point they took Mom. I had friends there, I thought I might fall in love there, oddly enough, and I know it doesn't make sense, but I thought I might get used to life in that camp," Wolfe said, willing the tears to come, but they wouldn't.

"But, they picked us at random one night long after curfew, and just…I was sixteen when I watched a BESNA guard shoot my brother in front of me. Dad is dead. Mom is probably dead too. My aunt is dead, my uncle is missing, Arcola is probably off in some 'hospital' somewhere. You guys are the only family I have left. BESNA has taken everything from me. Everything. And all of it was for…*nothing*. There was no *reason* to do what they did."

"It's not our fault for trying to survive. We're fighting, and if we fail it's not our fault."

"Whose is it then?"

"Every single brown-eyed person who stayed quiet and told

themselves that the riots and protests were too dangerous or weren't worth their time are to blame. Every brown-eyed man, woman, and child, who told themselves they didn't have the time or energy to fight with us, didn't argue when they heard those lies, are to blame. Every doctor, teacher, politician, farmer, nurse, social worker, lawyer, service worker, employee, employer, executive director, gas station attendant, and homeless person let BESNA build this new world on their silence."

"My aunt told me something the night before she died. Something about…responsibility, staying united something…I—" Wolfe began.

"Our individual responsibility to humanity is to stand united when we'd rather tear each other apart. An overzealous desire for conformity is more dangerous than a forced, willful togetherness." Unity said. "N.B. Hanley, the Order of Truth and Justice," she finished.

After what felt like an eternity, she finally spoke again. "We have to move."

Wolfe still didn't speak. He felt nothing. He didn't care if he lived or died; if Lett lived or died, he couldn't bring himself to care.

"Wolfe?"

"What?" Wolfe opened his eyes, and she was crying. Even through the fog, he could see her. She was bleeding, dirty, and slashed, but she was crying, and her hands were trembling.

"Will you promise me something?" she whispered against his ear. Wolfe could hear her voice thick with emotion, rising and falling in ragged breaths.

"Yes."

"If I die, you'll find my sister. If you die, I'll take care of Lett. They matter more than us."

"Promise," Wolfe croaked.

Wolfe felt her hand in his, her arms around him, burying her face in the crook of his neck. Then she was smiling, pulling him to his feet. To their right, the army of blue and green suits was moving backwards, overtaken by BESNA.

The whizzing of planes above them made the air tremble. They moved back over the OCHS soldiers fried in the street. They moved past the house; the old woman's handprints were still streaked across the door, past the garbage without bodies or dogs.

They came out in front of the army. The receding military was behind them and further back, a sea of guns, bombs, and bodies. Tanks larger than houses crushed semis burning in the streets as BESNA officers crawled over the walls and butchered the muted OCHS military.

Wolfe was enlightened. Time didn't exist, and neither did he. He ran like he was dead, and he was nothing: past the sounds of begging, of cries, through the throng of bodies trying to escape the city.

The BESNA army marched down the centre of the city, tearing the fabric of the capitol apart. Dead trees with purple leaves leaped to flames, and the old capitol building was bombed into the ground until only coloured glass and angel statues peered out of the earth. The army turned entire blocks into gaping, burning craters.

People were robbing each other in the street. Wolfe was pulled aside by a muscular arm, and a moment later, a truck roared past, crashing into two elderly men on the street, creaming them against the curb.

The world shook and froze. There was no sound, no movement. The world was staring at the buildings behind them, and even the gunshots had stopped. The planes stopped firing. The army stopped marching. Wolfe looked back and froze too. The tallest building behind them crumbled like a paper bag in the city centre. A plume of dust, higher than the obelisk itself, tore towards them, turning the windows between them to dust, the street to gravel; a hurricane of twisted metals and broken plastics ravaging the city. Wolfe threw himself against a building as the wave passed, painting the world white.

The gas station across the street was dusted with snow. Not snow; ashes an inch deep settled across the street. All at once, the world resumed rotation, but no cars moved. Unity and Wolfe blinked, and they were alone. The masses had abandoned them; their cars were still running, and their belongings coated in plaster and paint were still strapped to roofs and laid in the streets.

The gas station still stirred. A family inside cowered behind the counter as Scott brandished a shotgun at them. Wolfe slid across the road. The ashes held out the sounds and basked them in silence as his ears rang.

"Jesus Christ, guys, where were you? This fucker wouldn't give us gas," Scott said. A bullet flew through the air, piercing the window and sending spider cracks across it.

"It's over, the city is falling," Unity said.

"Do you know who sells contact lenses?" Wolfe said to the gas station attendant. He could hear the sound of buildings falling and a city on the brink of capsizing.

"What?" Scott asked, "What does that have anything—"

"Sshhh," Wolfe hissed.

With a clammy forehead and thin wisps of graying hair over a fat, egg-shaped head, the man stuttered in Spanish. He held up his hands, gesturing towards his kids, clutching his hands together, and repeating the same words in Spanish.

"Scott! Leave me for a minute," Wolfe said, pushing his way in front of him. Unity was pulling bottles and packages off the shelves. The store itself was almost empty. Thin metal stands were pressed against broken windows caked with ash as the air shuttered outside. Another rush of officers passed them, firing back into the void as they were cut down.

Wolfe reached across the counter and pulled a magazine off the shelf. The front page showed a brown-eyed family lounging on the grass, eating sandwiches in hemp clothing. Wolfe ripped the front page off, and with heavy-handed tears, he pulled the magazine to shreds. Then, he held the picture of the family up against his eye. Slowly, Wolfe pointed one dirty finger to his eye. The man watched him slowly as Wolfe pulled the family picture against his face. Then, he pointed between the eyes of the family, then to his own blue eye.

The man shared a look of understanding between them; as if a light bulb had come on, he cried out. "Address. Address!" he screamed, pulling at the magazine and with the pen behind his ear, he scratched words onto the shiny, opaque paper.

Unity filled her bag with water bottles, chip bags, and watery fruit. Wolfe yelled over to Scott, glancing around at the flickering lights and empty shelves. The family was already gone out the back door, stepping over the broken plastic windows and across the speckled ground, delving into the smoky night.

"Right. This is where he said to go," Wolfe yelled over the screams of the approaching army. "One seventy six Calle Aremerinto,"

"For what," Brieux asked. "The war, we need to—"

"We met a medic and she said the north side is completely annexed, and the west is falling back through the city centre. The city is going to fall. The war is over. But, she said there was a man who sold contact lenses in the north, and that she heard he could 'change your life.'"

"How're we going to get through enemy lines? We'll be caught for sure," Chaplin said to the group, holding his finger up to his head and pretending to pull the trigger.

"We have to leave the van," Wolfe said. "We could probably just hide and the fighting will pass right over us."

"Like fucking hell we will," the nameless man said, finally. He had dropped his book and his demeanour. His nose jumped and flared, and his lips shook. He watched the wave of fighting move ever closer through the streets.

Another line of hovercraft materialized over this side of the city.

"Fine. We can drive it as far as we can, then we will park it down some back alley and go on foot from there. After we have —" Wolfe was interrupted again.

"No."

"You listen to me, you're here because we don't want to kill you yet, but I'll do it if it keeps the people I care about safe, so you can keep your mouth shut. Move," Wolfe yelled, pushing up against the van with his finger up. "I will do what is right."

"Right for who?"

Jansen materialized beside the nameless man.

"Let us go. Please. My family is going to be worried sick." Ashes landed in his hair, and his misty eyes shone up at Wolfe. But the swathes of BESNA officers came closer, and he'd just told them their plan.

"In," he said, pushing the nameless man in, then Jansen. Wolfe hacked his lungs onto the floor, breathing in the welcome smell of cigarette smoke and pine air freshener. In front of him, glittering under the steps, was Tisdale's wedding ring, shining against black metal. Wolfe snatched it out, pressing it between his fingers, watching the city collapse around them.

The van was moving without words, north, away from the army and towards another. Millions of displaced people ran barefoot towards a world ready to turn them away as their city fell into irrelevance and the night slipped into the morning.

Chapter 25

Dust to Dust

They had abandoned the van six blocks ago, and now they were lying in the shell of a house, listening to the sound of war above them. Wolfe felt the explosion in his bones, felt the walls tremble and cry out above them.

They were lying in a crawlspace, open and exposed on one end, sealed with collapsed dirt on the other. Wolfe could feel Lett digging his face into his chest and his hands into his sides. The earth shifted with another explosion, the voices of men screaming out orders and commands, their voices cut off as they fell on flying bullets.

The city had fallen while they lay there. The fighting had stopped, prisoners taken, slave transports filled. All those people running on bare feet out of the city were dead or worse by now. This was the end of an era, the start of a new epoch. God was dead. The fires had been put out, and the spires of plastic and metal still seeped into the earth. The fire and brimstone were gone, and only the ashes and dust remained. The rapture had come.

There was nothing but stillness. The stale wind sounded like screams brushing through the burnt skeletons of things once living; the walls of houses, the frames of cars, the bodies of people and family pets littering the streets. The streets had stopped breathing. A gentle rain of ash dusted the roads; the suburban sprawl with its manicured lawns and perfect houses were blackened and hollow, buried in their tomb of chemical snow.

An indiscriminate house had caught flame every few blocks, and its charred corpse sat sunken where a home once was. The houses were empty. Their windows were dark and cold, their frames shallow. They walked past a melted stop sign and a car parked in the street. Its tires had been popped, its windows were broken, the entire frame was charcoal, and the metal was ribbed and fluxing. Seldomly, Wolfe would swear he saw movement around the houses; a family fleeing towards the front lines or away, BESNA here to kill them, a wild animal scrounging the wastelands for dinner.

"Where are we?"

Wolfe squinted, trying to see the sign even though the words had peeled off. Its black words slipped off the sign.

"That's Calle. Maybe…" Wolfe pointed at a sign melted and bent halfway along its length. They turned down a boulevard with shrivelling trees. They left white footprints as they walked in the chemical ash, past empty shops, and abandoned cars, past the ghostly frame of what was once a city. They walked past cathedrals and black metal gates, they walked past bright blue walls hastily covered with boards and black paint, they walked past blue-eyed couples in ads on windowsills with their eyes cut out by terrified shop owners.

The soft morning light seemed lost, fighting its way through the same hallowed streets as them. Even though the sun was rising over an unchanged earth behind the smoke, the same world it had risen over forever; from their side, the world had been reborn in hell's image.

"What do we do if we get split up? Where do we meet?" Unity finally spoke into the silence, her voice soft and muffled beneath her scarf. Chaplin grunted. Walking with the gun at the man's back, they trudged on.

"Back here?" Scott suggested, pointing his thumb over a gray, bleak building, the same gray facade as the rest of the surrounding buildings. Beneath the thick dredge of ash and dust, the words Carmen's Delicatessen was written above a jagged window, broken like every other window, every other house within sight.

"Too obvious. You could follow the tracks right back here."

"We could say the same for wherever we decide to pick," Unity said.

"Okay then, where?" Wolfe asked.

"The capitol building," Scott said, pointing a dirty finger across the road.

They all stared across the extensive garden in front of them. The capitol building sat across a network of cobblestone paths, empty fountains, and shattered benches. A dead flower garden was choked beneath the ever-falling dust. Stunning granite arches and staircases led to the structure's apex, a heavy set dome with thousand windows for eyes, its snaking tendrils of staircases for legs. It was built into the side of a hill so that the rest of the building came out a thousand metres high above Mexico City.

A hundred flagpoles stood somberly at its base, each decorated with the golden BESNA eye. One flag on each relentlessly beat the silver sky. The building was dead, a drifting watcher over the land, the yard, the streets, and the world.

"How about somewhere else?" Wolfe asked, watching the dead eyes move with him, watching his every step.

"Like?"

"Here, down this back alley," Wolfe said, pointing towards a line of green and black dumpsters. "Then, if something goes wrong, Chaplin can go home, our friend here can go find his van, and the rest of us can go find Unity's sister."

"It doesn't really matter. I can handle that, I've done my part," Chaplin said, looking over at them with a scraggly beard and warm eyes. "I'm sorry for what I said in the van back there. Maybe you're right, Wolfe, maybe there was nothing to be done."

Wolfe glanced a smile at Chaplin before looking up the hill to the left of the capitol building. Snaking up the side of the mountain was a network of houses and roads crawling back and forth like ribbons. Lights appeared on the hill, blinking, flickering, then disappearing.

"Think so?" Brieux asked, squinting to read the signs beside them as Wolfe stared up at the hills above them.

"We're on Calle now, so possibly."

"Okay," he responded, and they set out again.

They moved at a soft gallop, quickly and as quietly as they could, with the ash breaking their footfalls. Wolfe watched the tracks slowly disappear, dusted again with ash as the light forced itself through the fog.

They scuttled across the plaza and down the street. The roads grew steeper, and the thin dusting of ash made the ground slippery beneath them. Wolfe listened to their feet echo against the disquieting tranquillity. *Maybe, after all this, the city is just sleeping, just...resting.* Wolfe thought. And the sun would rise, the clouds would leave, the people would come back, and tomorrow the same days would play a mirror of the days before and after for eternity.

The trucks rolled by in silence below them, their tires whispering against the pavement. They rolled over something hard every few moments, and it would shatter, subdued beneath their tires. Their torches would slowly search over what houses remained, searching for the people hiding in piles of bricks and wood, their roofs caved in, their entire frames slipping down the hillside into the homes below.

They were nearly level with the top of the flagpoles, and they could see most of the city. The once glimmering city of the future, Mexico City, had been brought to its knees. Half the city was a gaping hole, and the south side was still burning. Aircraft gently hovered, shining lights out over the debris. Towards the city's epicentre with its fiery stumps and its black, charred face, hundreds. No. Thousands of trucks rolled out in every direction. If Wolfe closed his eyes, he could hear the crying. The screams of lives ended and torn apart. If he listened, he could hear the gunshots.

Lights shone from below this time, sending beams of sunshine over the hillside, painting the gray grass and flowers bright. A second later, a man yelled in an unfamiliar language and masses of bullets rung through the air. The screaming died with the wailing of children. It clung to Wolfe's ears, sticking onto the memories of the hillside, their spirits etching their final breaths in the earth forever.

Wolfe clapped his hands to his face. His legs trembled. This was too much. He couldn't go on. He couldn't. They could do what they wanted with him, but he would never move again. This had to be the end of the line. The misery clung around his heart, clogging his arteries, turning his heart into useless muscle.

"Come on Wolfe, we can't help them."

"We can't...I can't leave them," Wolfe said, stepping against the edge of the road. He watched them disappear into black nets and trucks. Karma would come for him eventually. All the people he ran past, all the people he never tried to help, all the damage he'd done.

"Don't worry about them. We can't help them."

"Are we ever going to?"

"Please Wolfe. I just...come on. We're almost there," Brieux said.

"Why?"

"For me?" he asked.

Wolfe sniffed. Brieux rested an arm on his shoulder.

"I know how you feel. I do. You want to give up. You're tired of fighting, of arguing...I know."

"How? I didn't want to come. I would have been happy to stay in the Desolation." He turned, looking at Brieux's rippling face.

"I know. And I'm sorry. Maybe you were right, but I haven't always been a doctor you know. I had a life before this."

Wolfe fell to the ground and sat in silence. They all slumped on the hill together, watching the sunrise. Wolfe. Unity. Brieux. Lett. Scott. Chaplin stood behind them with his shotgun as Jansen, and the nameless man stared over the city. They breathed together, and Brieux started to talk.

"When I was born my mom was alone. She had been raped, didn't know my father, and she had to make it work any way she could. To say we struggled through life is an understatement. She danced, I worked every job I could get, she tried to put me through school but…there is only so much money out there. I robbed, I stole, I did everything to keep me and my family from running out of food. I'll be damned if anyone gives a fuck about kids starving on the street. 'Life is precious, save the children' they say, until you're trying to survive in the world they built. Then you're a thug, a criminal, a danger to society, useless, violent, unnecessary."

He paused and collected himself, sucking in the shimmering white air.

"The crime didn't last for long though. I got a few years in prison, came back out, and fell right back into the habit. There is nothing to do, the world set me up for failure. No one would give me a job, I couldn't go back to school, but…you gotta eat. I got seven years for intent to injure and attempted theft, by the time I got out again, Mom was gone. She took my brother with her when she went. I didn't know what to do, I was angry, I was scared, the only people I'd ever known did drugs, stole, it was a way of life. I didn't know how to escape it."

"Brieux I—"

"Please, Wolfe, just…" he began, faltering. "When the BESNA movement started, I played it off. It can never happen; people aren't hateful, people aren't like this anymore. Not this time. Not these people. I was going to organize a counter-movement with a few other friends, but I ran when they started handing out prison sentences and hundred thousand dollar fines. I was scared. I saw the terrorist bills, the anger, the violent riots and…I should have fought, rather than now, but…how do you know? How did I know it would be like this? It was in every house, every store, every church…"

The silence grew between them. The world was against them now. *Who is the world then?* Wolfe asked himself, *who are they?* And he laughed inside because he already knew.

"It happened so quickly. The camps. The bombings. The elections. For a split second, it all felt justified, civilized 'people' don't act like that, terrorists walked the streets. It was so easy, promises of cheap college, more jobs, more money. Make the world great again, and I just accepted it. I got a degree, my prior charges were wiped…it felt like a new world, a world I might have had the chance to been on top of. Everyone justified it:

'BESNA just needs workers. The discomfort of a few for the joy of the many.' They said. It felt like such a small sacrifice, a few innocent people work for a few companies and everyone had a chance at a good life again…but…I started working for the Bredenburys and the rose tinted world I'd thought I understood fell apart. I woke up every night wracked by nightmares and guilt about what I had to do to the night before to stay alive: forced abortions, skin transplants, shipping kids away from their parents, chips… I…I67879 felt like the villain. I was the villain. So when I had the chance to help them, help people like you, Wolfe I took it. One of my biggest regrets was not doing enough, not fighting for what I thought was right when I should have, only looking out for myself. It was like a death sentence, divine retribution. A chance to break you out, the entire plantation…it fell into my lap, I had to do it. It felt…I don't know like I was making up for all the pain I let happen, all the suffering I never tried to stop."

"I didn't ask you to do that, Brieux, just let it go. It's over," Wolfe said, wiping more dark smears across his face.

"But that's why we're here, and that's why I need to keep trying. And if you have nothing left anymore that's fine, that's okay but…if you have anything left, even just a smidgen, can we at least try to finish what we started? Can we try and change what I should have stopped before it was too late? Please?"

"You risked your life for nothing," Wolfe said with dead, cold eyes gazing over the ruined city.

"Not for nothing."

Brieux hugged Wolfe. His entire body stunk of burnt hair and singed eyebrows, sweat and blood, exhaustion and tears. Wolfe just sat there, arms draped around him for a minute.

"You're not guilty Brieux. No more than any stranger on the street, any brown-eyed person in the world," Wolfe said. Wolfe pushed himself onto his knees, then onto his feet. He held his hand out, the other hand on Brieux's shoulder. "We're gonna be okay. Somehow," Wolfe said. He nodded at Brieux, barely more than a tremble, and all of them slogged their way higher again, past what they left of the houses.

The trashcans rattled with the emaciated frames of coyotes as a stale wind stirred, whisking off the last of the powder and wiping the hills clear. The sun was kissing the horizon as they watched the numbers on the houses. Eighty-five, one hundred and six, one hundred and fifty-three, one hundred seventy— "This is it," Wolfe said, eyeing the paper in his hand, the scratchy handwriting reflected clearly on the house in front of them.

The house was dense and squat like all the others. A brick wall around the house had been destroyed, and the blue bricks and trash cans were scattered through the yard. The rest of the valley behind them had opened up into a network of suburbia, and Wolfe saw glints of movement in the back alley. They stepped over the bricks and walked up to where a door would have been. A dark, mushroom brown door was thrown aside, ripped off its hinges, opening into the rest of the home.

Wolfe was the first to step across the threshold, his foot catching on the torn-up carpet, once white, now gray, revealing century-old hardwood floors.

"This is a beautiful house," Wolfe said to himself.

"At least a hundred years old," someone else responded.

They walked in, staring at the walls where pictures once hung. Broken photographs of a smiling family were cluttered on the floor along the wall. The house stunk of mildew and mould, the ceiling slumped in the middle of the room, dangling against the top of an eggshell and charcoal-coloured fridge.

A flat-screen had been ripped off its walls; tiny black shards of glass twinkled in the dull morning sunlight. The metal chassis of the couch was exposed to the air, and its stuffing was strewn across the living room like confetti. Metal shelving units were flipped on their sides, and papers were thrown across the room. Pots and pans were ripped out of the cupboards, and rusty cutlery and broken plates were strewn across the kitchen floor.

A large glass window was sitting just to the right of the hallway when they entered, although it was shattered. The stillness was unsettling, a cold, damp quietness that sucked at Wolfe's ears, making it quieter than it even could be. Wolfe heard a faint cry and the soft, fleshy sound of bullets hitting their target.

"Everyone, go check a room and see if you can find anything. Contacts, lens solution, even better, a living person," Scott said, pushing past Brieux to dig through the kitchen cupboards. Chaplin and the nameless man dug through the remains of couch cushions and under rugs. Unity sank down the hallway to their left, and Brieux after her. Jansen stood in the living room and refused to move.

"Why would I help the people keeping me hostage?" Jansen cried, and the nameless man shot him a fleeting glance when he thought no one was looking.

Wolfe followed them down the hallway with Lett at his side. He and Wolfe entered the bathroom to the sound of sloshing water. The green and brown faucet was dripping and had filled the cement dusted tub with soup; it had filled the bathroom floor, causing it to give out into a watery basement. Wolfe opened the cabinet above the sink, finding nothing but empty toothpaste containers, expired pill bottles, and a collection of faded rubber ducks.

"I don't think anyone has been here for years," Wolfe called out into the living room.

"Found anything then?" Scott yelled back.

"Some painkillers, that's about it. You?"

"A World's Best Mom mug." Scott laughed, holding up the chipped pink and white mug off the floor.

Chaplin glared at him, flipping a cabinet right side up. "This was someone's whole life."

Wolfe picked up one of the broken photographs and let the glass dribble to the floor. He slid the picture out and eyed the family up and down. A smiling couple with their four kids. Wolfe shook his head.

"Two blue, four brown."

"Goddamn shame," Unity said, shaking his head.

Wolfe slipped into the office, and he heard the lofty voices of men and a woman speaking in Spanish in hushed whispers.

"Anything?" Wolfe asked, and Lett pointed to a computer smashed into smithereens. Keys were strewn across the desk, broken, delicate metal chips and pieces were snapped in half, and lights shone through the windows as Wolfe dug into the pile, letting metal instruments and parts trickle through his fingers.

Brieux stepped into the room behind them as the whispers grew louder, and he held up a pink children's blanket soaked with blood and torn to shreds.

Wolfe turned Lett away from the blanket and directed him to stay quiet with hand movements. Wolfe looked at Brieux for a few moments and held a second between them. Just a parting glance, a flick of the eyes told him a million stories. "Come with me, I'm sorry, let's leave, I love you..." All in the blink of an eye. He looked away again. Wolfe wanted to say something but fought against it. He promised himself he would later. There would always be more time.

The voices subsided, and the lights disappeared. Brieux waved out into the rest of the house, beckoning them into the hallway, crowded together face to face.

"They're dead. Seems to be a while too," Brieux said.

"Now what?" Unity asked. "There isn't anything here."

"So this was all for nothing?" Scott asked, rolling his eyes. "If we leave now, we can get back to the van before it gets too bright." He watched over his shoulder as he said it.

"Well, this has been fun. Do I get my van back yet?" The nameless man smiled.

"Can I leave?" Jansen asked.

"If we're all going our separate ways...we can't keep them here forever." Wolfe looked back to the rest of them.

"Did anyone check that door?" Chaplin asked from the hallway, pushing the nameless man and Jansen further down the hallway.

"It's locked."

"And?"

Wolfe jiggled the handle, and it barely moved. Brieux smiled, shrugged, then kicked with all his force against the door. Then again, and again, until finally, it cracked open, splintering along the handle, falling open into darkness. The basement was filled with water, maybe waist or belly button high. Large plastic containers floated through the churning, rusty brown water while limp cardboard boxes sagged. Brieux stepped down into the water, then Wolfe followed, drenching his shoes instantly and soaking him up to the calves as he stopped on the stairs.

The voices had come again, hovering near the front door.

"Hola?" a shaky voice whispered into the entrance of the home.

"Hola?" A few other words jumbled out after that, but Wolfe didn't make them out. Brieux, already up to his waist, wadded over to a large cabinet and pulled a metal case off the top shelf. He rooted through it and found two small flashlights, tossing one over their heads and into Unity's hands, who walked over to the nearest tub and popped the lid open as quietly as possible.

The tub hissed as it opened, and her face lit with surprise. She tilted the box forwards, and pile after pile of brown contact lenses leaned towards them.

Brieux lifted a pile of soggy cardboard and found plastic bags filled with contact solution.

"What about the man who was supposed to be here? What now?" Wolfe whispered.

"I don't know," Brieux responded, his voice dusting across the stale air towards them. "We have something though, it's better than nothing." He tossed them each a handful of contacts and solution. Wolfe filled his pockets until little white bottles bulged from his pants, slipped from his fingers, and bobbed in the water like ships.

They all stopped breathing. Steps creaked through the hallways above them, coming up to the door. As quiet as they could, they moved back towards the stairs, lapping water sloshing up the cold cement stairs and into the rest of the house.

Words slipped back and forth above them in the darkness. Wolfe pulled at the knife in his boot, holding his gun in the other. He listened to the sound of a flashlight slipping from Brieux's fingers, clinking down the cement steps and waving away under murky brown water.

Unity flicked on her flashlight just as three faces rounded the corner of the hallway. Six blue eyes stared back like bats.

"Hola? Eres buena?"

"I don't know. We're not going to hurt you. Blue. Blue."

"Azul?"

"Where's Jansen?"

"HELP! HELP! BLUIES! BLUIES! MUTTS!" he cried, his voice shattering the dull silence of the morning and drawing the sound of tires and calling BESNA officers.

Wolfe ran, slipping on the cement and smashing his knee into the stairs. He crumpled in on himself and listened through a haze of pain as feet rushed over him.

Two men and a young girl were racing into the street, their voices high above the weeping night. The brilliant sun was bathing them in halos of yellowed light. By the time Wolfe had lagged down the hallway, wet fingers dragging trails across the wallpaper, he had heard the sounds of cries and gunshots.

Brieux was behind him, hand on Wolfe's wrist. When he looked back, his eyes were wide, lights flickered over him, his eyes flashing like a cat. He was tugging on Wolfe, dragging him back away from the living room washed out with light.

Lett was standing in the kitchen, eyes aflame, body frozen like a deer. Wolfe ran and held him, slumping them back between the wall and the fridge. The sound of screaming.

He saw Chaplin pushing the door shut. Then he heard crunching gravel, the glints of black beetle bodies outside, reaching their guns around the edge of the window. Wolfe closed his eyes.

Wolfe felt a hand on him. He opened his eyes and watched Brieux duck back from the bullets, clinging to the ground in front of him, holding his hands in his. He was saying something, mouthing something, but he was deaf. Drywall was raining on them from above. Brieux was pulling at his legs and arms, ducking towards the hallway. Outside, Jansen was pinched between the road and truck tires. Blood leaked from all of his orifices as a BESNA officer raised his gun; Jansen pulled his hands back to protect his face.

—BANG—

One down, seven to go.

Wolfe watched the dust glimmer in the air, sinking to the ground. To his right, he saw the base of the fridge. Against the side, between the back of the wall, a small roll of tape was clinging to the elements with magnets. Wolfe watched it in the murkiness. The roll of tape that matched the wallpaper drifted in and out of his vision. He plucked it off, holding it in his hands, watching the roll of words and numbers.

He looked up and saw the nameless man bathed in light. He was standing in the window, one arm up and behind his head, the other pointing towards the hallway, screaming and pointing, squinting against the light. A moment later, the sunlight shone through him. He was a ball of muscle and blood, sinking to the floor, leaking out into the carpet.

Two down, six to go.

Wolfe started crawling behind the counters, dragging a crying Lett underneath him like a lioness with her prey. He slid down the hallway with bullets behind him, shattering the walls. He blinked and saw Chaplin back against the wall, crimson dripping down his body as bullets riddled the door. The beetles were crawling through the door behind him, and he ran. One stumble, two. Then he was towering over Wolfe in the hallway.

Wolfe swerved down the hallway while Unity was screaming with bloodshot eyes. Spit clung to her mouth as she screamed something unintelligible to him. Her eyes were bleeding white. Tears clung to her cheeks. She was begging him for something, but a crown of fire stuck to his scalp, searing him.

He turned and looked behind him. Lett was gone; his hands were empty, spare the roll in his fingers, sweaty between the lines on his hands. He and Chaplin looked at each other; Wolfe felt Tisdale's wedding ring burning circles in his chest as he looked at him. Chaplin held his stomach, red with blood, dripping out between his fingers. His legs shook back and forth. His face was a blank canvas; his eyes trembled back and forth. Chaplin opened his mouth, and his head exploded.

—BANG—

Bits of Chaplin littered the walls like a Jackson Pollock painting. The wall was painted red.

Three down, five to go.

A tall, black beetle, maybe a few inches taller than Wolfe, dropped over what they left of Chaplin's body. Bullets came from behind Wolfe, destroying the black shadow towering over him. The walls behind him were littered with holes. *Were they there before?* Wolfe couldn't be sure.

Wolfe knew he was screaming for help, knew his feet were moving, but where was he going? He came down to the end of the hallway, to a dead-end, searching aimlessly for Scott. There was nowhere to go but back the way they came towards the rain of bullets. Scott was gone.

Four down, four to go.

Wolfe was running through gauze. Each step sunk him deeper and deeper into the heaviness around his crown. He felt something soft and squishy beneath his feet, but he kept running, falling over the uneven carpet and feeling hands pulling him up and pushing against his shoulders.

He was looking at Brieux. His mouth spelled run. Run. Run. Run.

"RUN!" he finally heard.

The words tore through his mind as he saw another dark shadow slip and tumble over Brieux on the ground, and he was lost. The sound of gunshots brought blood to his ears. He felt an arm pushing him up through the window at the end of the hallway, scrambling off a metal file cabinet and landing on earth.

Five down, three to go.

Lett was pulling at him. Wolfe's head was bloodstained and raw. He heard someone calling while shadows danced around the corner of the house. A steep incline behind the house filled with roots and sharp rocks loomed, and yelps hung in the air behind him. With Lett on his shoulders, he scaled the hill, jumping over a metal wire fence on top of the hill. He felt something rip, then a fire tore along the length of his thigh. Unity was squeezing out of the window. By the time she landed, more officers had come around the side of the house and tussled with her in the dirt.

"You bastards, you bastard!" She looked up and met Wolfe's eyes. She was reminding him of the promise made a few hours ago. She didn't say a word, but there was something in her eyes. She was crying, and blood was pouring from her nose into her mouth, staining her teeth. She wanted to tell him something as she convulsed with rage.

"He's—" a sharp smack cut her off as a pointy metal lance connected with her cheek. She was rooting for a knife and had pulled it to her throat. It was knocked aside before she had a chance, and the punches kept raining down. He saw inside the house: Brieux was gone, Unity was gone, Scott was gone.

Six down, two to go. No. The tally in Wolfe's head stopped. He wouldn't count another. They would not go like this.

A guard yelled, and a bullet whizzed past them. Wolfe had gone up another incline, around the ruins of houses, through a fence, and down another sharp hill. He could hear voices calling out, the sounds of sirens, and boots on pavement and dirt. This was all a dream, he told himself. He would turn back, and they would be running behind him, fighting, bickering, laughing, and smiling. He could see Scott's dimples, hear Brieux's accent, smell Unity's hair, hear how Chaplin spelled out his R's. He and Lett were alone, and there was nothing but them and the pavement.

They ran.

They ran until they couldn't run anymore. Wolfe and Lett lay unmoving behind a bright blue brick wall, gasping for breath.

Voices screamed and bellowed somewhere in the distance, and the sun dawned in full force over the hill towards him. Lett kept peppering him with questions that only aggravated the burning pain around Wolfe's head. They ran again.

They moved through yards into dried pools and dead shrubs. They crossed roads, through boulevards, around stores and down back alleys. They passed back in front of the capitol building as light trickled back across the gardens towards them.

Wolfe saw the deli from before, their footprints long-buried in ash. Splashes of turquoise were spinning in the sky again. A hot orange light was shrinking across the bronzed ruins of the city. Lett was bawling. Broken glass was stuck in Wolfe's skin, muscles were torn in his side, blood was weeping down his back, and his knees were skinned. The adrenaline was wearing off, and the pain was coming. Wolfe saw the line of garbage bins, a solace among the anarchy.

He lugged himself over the side, heaving Lett in with him between his pounding sobs. Wolfe would have prayed, but if there was anything he hated, it was God. This was all a nightmare. So Wolfe wouldn't pray. If God knew he wanted something, he'd probably take it all away from him.

Their deaths were false on his tongue. He didn't believe it; he couldn't believe it. He refused. Unity's sister and Chaplin's kids wouldn't know tonight. Wolfe would never see Brieux's starry eyes again. Scott and his future no longer existed. Zelma would wait for a son who would never come home. He held the ring and the cross against his fingers, thinking of their faces. Wolfe never wanted to forget. He refused to ever let them slip from his mind, even if they were...*No. No. It's a dream. A nightmare. Wake up. Wake up.*

He waited for the dream to end, but it didn't. He waited for the lights to go out and everything to end, but it didn't. So instead, they lay in wait, waiting for something that might never come. They might have laid there forever had someone not flung open the garbage bin a few minutes later, crying out Wolfe's name.

"Wolfe! Oh thank god, I thought...oh my god," the man

towering above him pulled Lett out, then Wolfe.

"Are you okay? Oh, my god." Wolfe looked him up and down and couldn't even help but feel his stomach twist into a slimy knot.

"Scott? I—"

"I know, baby…" Scott reached his arms covered in peck marks from gravel and blood. Wolfe felt his mouth flood with saliva, his throat kept constricting, and he pushed Scott away. He squinted his eyes shut and still couldn't force the tears to come.

"How did you find us?"

"I followed your footprints. Oh, baby." Wolfe's limbs rattled and shook, banging against the metal. As he landed, something cold and metal stuck to the side of the garbage can. He reached inside his pocket and pulled the small roll of tape up to Scott's face.

"What is that?" Scott said, leaning in, pecking him on the forehead.

Wolfe shrugged, wiping his forehead with his sleeve and peeling off the tape. Once he'd finished, he found a small black case that slid open and closed with a snap. When he popped it open, a slight curl of paper came out. Wolfe unfurled the yellowed paper with shaking hands. Pulling it close, he eyed the greasy black streaks across the lines.

He opened it and read out its contents shakily.

~~"Catty Ave, Penn. Clock. Wall. Consider twilight hours."~~

~~"Lip Station, NV. 'For Your Consideration.' Complex. Tree."~~

~~"R.E.D Ghetto, Alison. Tied. Bone. Nine."~~

~~"Dr. Glaslyn. Greenhouse. Seventeenth Walmart. Northwest."~~

~~"At the edge of the world. Red brick. Eleven. Sunset."~~

"Tower fourty-two, Old NY. Phoenix. Gang. Seventy-three."

"Nationalists. French. Eighty-ninth to Albert."

"Are these locations? If the rumours were true about this man, could they help us?" Wolfe asked.

"I hope not," Scott said. All but two had been struck with black dashes. If those were contacts, there were only a couple left.

Wolfe tried to smile, but the memories of just a few minutes ago flashed back to him. Brieux. Unity. Chaplin. Jansen. The nameless man. Dead. All of them were dead. A day ago, Wolfe was sitting in the van, dreaming of possibilities. There were none.

"No, no, no. Look," Scott said, pulling Wolfe's face up to his. "We," he added, pulling Lett in close between them, "are going to do this. Together."

"How? How am I even supposed to keep going? How am—"

"I don't know, baby. I don't know."

Wolfe stared into the void. His heart didn't want to beat anymore; his lungs didn't want to keep breathing. With every blink, he saw a moment in time shattered: those hours in Scott's cabin imagining a world where they could be free, the train out of Landia when they screamed into the night, Unity telling Wolfe they'd come back to live their lives in Oasis. Chaplin's kids would never get their father back; a promise was broken. Unity's sister was the last of her family, and Liberty was alone. Jansen's family would never know what happened to him. The nameless man would never get a chance to see his kid again. Only Scott's footprints marked the ashy ground as he clung to Wolfe, his chest rising and falling, listening as the birds began to sing.

Chapter 26

The Metropolis

It was October, and the streets were cold and murky. Slimy brown water ran through the streets, wiping grunge, dirt, and grease off the sidewalks and into the pools of dirty light where drains should have been. A sickly gossamer green slid over the water. Wolfe and Scott were walking in silence, chunks of grass and mud clung around their swimming ankles, pulling them deeper into misery.

The rain soaked them as they walked. The van was gone when they went searching for it back in Mexico, they had no money, the car had run out of power, and it was too risky to steal another one, so they walked: past the blur of cars, past the roar of hovering trains glittering along black metal, past puddles that reflected the suburbs of Old Pennsylvania back at them.

Scott took the lead, followed by Lett, sandwiched between Scott and Wolfe. Wolfe rubbed his pruned fingers along the rim of his heavy, waterlogged sweater Scott had bartered for in Old Wyoming. Water was wrapped around his head, a cascade of water droplets sinking past the periphery of his vision. The streets were almost empty, nothing but the blur of lights behind his eyes.

No one in the world even noticed them; they ambled past a few people here and there, but everyone sloshed past them without a second glance.

They were limping through some soggy suburbs in what was once Pennsylvania, now just province seventy-five out of one hundred and thirty-eight: past dollar laundromats, massage parlours, and empty strip malls lined back and forth, up and down either sidewalk. Every billboard along the road shone with Mr. Bredenbury's face. "Join Mr. Bredenbury in York park, October

3rd, 2068, as he announces his running mate for vice prime minister!" The golden eye hovered beneath him.

Wolfe looked away.

The three of them dashed across the street as the light turned green behind them, and cars hummed forward, shimmering into a blur. A hovering train merged onto a track above them, and they moved together beneath the black stone monolith of a train station. The glow of the surrounding suburbs reflected light off the shimmering black stone, humming with electricity. The lights seemed to hover in the air around the three of them. The raindrops reflected light, and the world spun, a glittering disco ball suspended in twilight.

"How are we going to find this place?" Wolfe asked. They had picked the first one that wasn't scratched off, and they were working their way towards York. He had written it on his arm. *A wise decision,* he thought to himself as the paper had dissolved into nothing in his hands. Fat, inked blotches slid across his hands, and yellow blurs slipped up his arms. He flicked yellow stubs into the grass as they walked.

He repeated it in his mind. *Tower fourty-two, Old NY. Phoenix. Gang. Seventy-three. Tower fourty-two, Old NY. Phoenix. Gang. Seventy-three.* It was the only thing he could think about, the only thing he wanted to do.

"What are the chances, though, Wolfe? If they killed that man, who is to say this person is alive either? If that man was dead, what makes this one any different?" Scott asked as tires hissed through puddles, forming clouds of mist around them.

"Maybe they killed them, but do we have a choice?" Wolfe asked.

"I know," Scott said.

Wolfe glanced up at Scott. His face seemed to glow with light; his rough exterior melted away as water pooled in the bags beneath the eyes. His broad, owl-like eyes dazzled as the cars drove by, sending sparkling coloured droplets over them. Scott met his eyes. The hints of a smile played at his lips, but Wolfe watched guilt filter across his eyes in the dim light when he looked away.

Wolfe looked away, smearing a few hair strands out of his face. "You need a haircut." Wolfe smiled, pulling the hair back over his head.

A man moved by them, muttering, glancing up as he passed. Wolfe felt his head explode, burying his face in his elbow to cough. The man brushed past them without a second thought. Everyone was invisible here, a giant shifting mass of shadows moving, drifting, and transforming. The world was ethereal and shiny. Nobody stopped, nobody listened, nobody looked up from their tablets.

Yet Wolfe still felt like he was in the lion's den. One wrong word to one wrong person, and it was over, just like *them.*

Wolfe had to jog to catch up with Scott. He climbed dark marble stairs three at a time, leaving Wolfe and Lett to scamper up the steps, through and over the lakes and rivers growing on the stairs. Wolfe walked by people only seeing shoes, only hearing the buzz of their feet against watery stone, only listening to the incessant buzzing of their voices against tablets.

Black strapped velvet shoes slid through the water, splashing water up the side of skin tone stockings. Hard, cold, pressed brown shoes shone like freshly baked cakes under the bright white streetlights that caught the drizzle. High heels shining like jade descended opposite, brown soccer shoes trailing behind her.

They moved up to the platform and stepped up to the doors. Before Wolfe had a second to touch Scott's shoulder, the doors glided open, and Scott stepped inside without hesitation. Wolfe watched his shoulders straighten, the wrinkles around his eyes disappear, and his teeth grow tighter. He wasn't a man fleeing Mexico with his lover and a child; he was a father who lost his keys, a financier lost in a strange city before a conference, a political campaign manager running late for an important meeting.

"I'm so sorry to bother you, sir, but do you know where this address is?" Scott said, striking up a conversation with a balding man who gazed over sparkling glasses with sharp hazel eyes, a soft gray trench coat swinging against the edges of his seat. In his hand, a sparkling silver tablet hummed, shimmering with light. It was rounded, hovering above his hands, pulling in the light and turning the air into electronic fuzz.

"Yes…" He leaned back up against the window, letting his eyes flicker between them with a hesitant glower. "That would be…just outside Fulton station and a few buildings over."

"Oh, thank you. I was worried I would miss my appointment, and in the middle of weather like this!" Scott laughed, gleaming at him. "Anyway," Scott said, smiling at the man who refused to take his eyes off the two dripping men and boy. Scott had already collected Wolfe and Lett and walked them away, muttering nothing of substance in Wolfe's ear while flicking his eyes towards the man.

"Where are you from?" the man asked.

Wolfe saw a glimmer in Scott's eyes before he turned around. *Got him,* they said. In a split second, Scott walked up and shook his hand. He had glanced at the make and model of the tablet, freshly bought. The state university on the lapel of his coat, his accounting firm on his briefcase, and he guessed his age on a whim, born in the late twenties.

"Oh, I'm from some small, puttering, ditty of a town in old Michigan. You've probably never heard of it," Scott said, rolling his eyes and leaning against the wall, shaking his head in fake sincerity.

"Well then, you'd be surprised. I'm from old Michigan myself." The man's eyes lit up. Both with realization coupled with the smiling relief of familiarity.

"Really?!" Scott cried out, shaking his hand again. "I'd've never guessed. Did you go to university there too? Not Anderson State by any chance?" Scott roared, nearly shaking with excitement, lighting the coals in the eyes of the gray-haired man on the bench.

"Both of my degrees, seven years, Anderson State." The man smiled.

"You're kidding!"

"Lies!" the gray-haired man joked as they dissolved into an

intense conversation about the university. They always had the best meals, worst teachers, best classes.

"Then there was Mrs. Belle, What a piece of work. I can't believe she is still working."

"She had such a reputation on campus. She failed me because I forgot to cite a single source!" Scott said. "Then the food…"

"I swear, they were trying to kill us." The man laughed.

They were a few moments into a passionate conversation about the best bachelor's degree to get into the law program when the train walls lit, requesting the scanning of tickets.

"Well. It was nice meeting you." Scott jumped up and bustled for the door, not giving the man a second to respond.

"You aren't taking the train?" the man said, pushing his glasses up on his nose and tilting his head towards the water pouring down the window across from them.

"Ugh, and that's where my stupidity rears its head. I locked us out of my brother's car and subsequently our wallets and tablets, and we're walking back to my apartment to get the spare keys. All before I have an appointment to get to."

"Where do you live? In this weather? That's silly! Please, come sit!" He beckoned enthusiastically for them to come, holding his tablet up to the wall and three extra seats lit beside him.

"Oh, we couldn't," Scott cried. "I'm not near greedy enough to let you help us like that. You don't know us, sir," Scott said, dragging Lett over and plopping him in the seat beside Scott and the man.

"Nonsense. What's the point of having all this money and not being able to help a fellow Anderson State brother?"

"You're too kind."

"Ah, it's my good deed for the day."

Wolfe watched out the window while Scott and the man spoke, and the train started moving. Outside the window, the neighbourhoods melted together. Thousands of tiny orange lights twinkling and flitting outside swirled a burnt, rusty orange in black, icy darkness. Every once in a while, a pop of neon yellow, a bite of green, a splash of a faded pastel purple. Wolfe tried to follow the colours from left to right, but they were gone over the horizon before he had a chance.

Brieux would have loved this, Wolfe thought to himself. He would have smiled that same half-smile when he got excited and didn't know how to say it. The pain returned, and the thoughts and memories he had been trying to bury for the past five days came back. He tried to pretend the nightmares didn't come, that he didn't see their broken faces chasing him in his dreams, tried not to think of Chaplin's family moulding without him, the ring around his neck choking him.

Wolfe heard Unity in his mind, her voice clear and concise. "Promise me Wolfe. Promise me." He thought of the lights, pulling him in the wrong direction, away from his promise, away from them, from their bodies.

The men talked about politics and their family history, chasing each other in circles with their words. One second they were coming over the hill towards a town, a flash of light, a second slipped by and they were in darkness again, rain and wind pushing the train forward. They were wrapped in light the next moment as they grew closer to a city centre, and before Wolfe could think about it, they had ripped into Manhattan: lights flew above them, below them, and around them. Lights of all colours and shapes were blurred by the wind as they battered the train walls.

"And—"

"Wow. It really is something, isn't it?" the man said.

"Always has been, to me anyway," Scott said.

"Well, you probably don't remember if you're a 2030s baby, but back in the early 2010s, this upper New Jersey nonsense was so ugly before they built all these trains. Boring, 'chic,' and monstrously hideous."

Wolfe had never seen towers this tall before. They were built on top of the water, drawing violent, icy perforations in the blackened clouds, steeples of twinkling glass that went higher than the eye could comprehend. In the other buildings, the older ones, where streets had once rushed with cars and people going from job to job, home to shops, back to apartments barely affordable, water stood stagnant around their bases.

A network of bridges, floating buoys, pathways, and boats motored around the base of the buildings like ants around giants. The train whipped around the city, past the golden spire landmark built after the sickness, and on top of a flat square building where the water was a few feet from the edge.

The rain was just spitting here. The lights from the city showed a gathering storm as they came to a stop.

"Ah, that's about it," Scott agreed.

"Still so stunning." The man smiled as the door opened, and a mill of sweaty stragglers came aboard the train.

"Well, that's us." Scott smiled again, popping up off his seat.

"Oh!" the man cried. "If you're ever near Soho, drop in and meet the wife and kids." He smiled again, scribbling out a note on the edge of a spare flap of paper.

"Thank you! I'll talk to the wife and twist her arm into it," Scott said.

The man nodded, and as the green lights flashed again, they stepped outside onto the roof of a building, water lapping along the white concrete paths rimmed with glass walls. The train shuttled away a second later, leaving them staring at plastic tunnels in every direction, a spiderweb expanding outward like hamster tubes. At the corner of the station, a small black box whispered quietly about weather bulletins and news anchor opinions:

"Well, let's hope this weather clears up for Mr. Bredenbury's hotly-anticipated speech in York park tomorrow night. Reports say that Mr. Bredenbury will announce who is running with him for prime minister in just a month's time."

Scott tossed his hand up behind him, and the piece of paper unfurled into the darkness outside the station's light.

"Oh, my god, that was amazing. How did..." Wolfe tapered off.

"Well…it's what I'm good at."

Wolfe looked to his right and saw a towering complex beside him. The entire side was made of glass, hundreds of lives milled inside, oblivious to Wolfe watching them: a woman bounced her baby as she wandered in circles, a woman was typing away at her desk, crunching down chips one after the other, a man walked around wet in a white towel.

"If you knew this was how it ended, would you change anything?" he asked suddenly, staring out over the buildings.

"What do you mean?"

"Like, in general. Would you change anything?"

Wolfe didn't know how to answer.

"That'd be the south side," Scott said, ignoring Wolfe's silence and pointing to a bridge that crossed the river to their left into the base of a tower. The lightning was sporadic. Somewhere ahead of them, the roar of boats ripped over thrashing water.

"Remove yourself from the station floor." A glacial voice cooed through a speaker. Water lapped up over the glass walls onto the floor like a giant fish tank. Ten seconds later, the rain came, pelting them as the next train arrived, then disappeared into the night again. "Last train in fourty-five seconds," it said again.

The wind roared again, and another wave splashed against the glass, shooting fifteen feet in the air, smacking against the floor. The doors onto the bridge hissed open, blowing water backwards out and drying them. They moved across the glass walkway as the last train departed. A minute later, the train station was invisible under rising brown water.

The building would have once been an office building years ago, but it had been transformed into a shopping centre, unlike anything Wolfe had ever seen. Each level was a new store, a new world entirely: candy stores spilled their sugared scents and bright pink rot into the stairwell, clothing shops spun with the latest styles in shades of brown, red and yellow, and electronic stores laid their freshest tablets on tables, surveyed by pretentious looking men in black and brown suits.

A filthy, brown-eyed man parted through the sea of grandiosity, dressed in sordid black rags and a mouth full of rotten, putrid teeth. BESNA officers in black watched him stir around the tablets. He lurched forward and clung to Wolfe's arms, begging for spare credits. They grabbed him, but he slipped through their arms and darted, shaking and trembling, up a staircase winding kilometres above them.

"Right. So tower fourty-two would be…" Scott paused to think, looking around at the walls and numbers around them.

"Up to the eighteenth floor and six buildings over," a woman at the security desk said, not even looking up. She was a large, brick-shaped woman tapping furiously on an old tablet. "Stupid son of a—" she grumbled as she tried to balance it over two stacks of paper and a water bottle, charging precariously.

The wind was battering the buildings harder now. The lights flickered every few seconds, and waves crashed into the glass, throwing the room into shadow. Churning black water pushed in against the windows, bowing them, then when the water retreated, it pulled the glass back.

"Ah, don't worry, we just had the glass changed in ah…ten years ago?" the woman said again, looking up at them standing in the lobby.

"Ten?"

Scott pulled Wolfe up the stairs by the crook of his elbow as another wave sent the room into shadow before she could respond. The stairwell reeked of cigarette smoke and weed. People clambered around them: moving, talking, mumbling to themselves and others as they climbed. Wolfe pulled Lett along as they climbed two steps at a time.

They passed a thrift store; the malodorous stench of mothballs, secondhand smoke, and stranger's sweat followed them. They passed a pawnshop with piles of old electronics teetering against the dim light bulbs, guns lined the walls, and glass cabinets, grungy with greasy fingerprints, ran along the wall in a semicircle. A gyro restaurant leaked the soft, savoury scents of roasting meat, yogurt, and herbs into the stairwell, and a lineup snaked around two levels. Three levels of apartments, a shop that smelled of plastic, oil and burning rubber, and three more levels of apartments. They slipped past a bank with armed security guards at either side. A sex store shone beside them: huge, full-sized prints of nude women, huge pink X's covering pictures of spread thighs and weeping lips. The last levels were one big box store, with everything you could ever need stacked on shelves higher than Scott and Wolfe combined.

They crossed over another glass walkway above the black Atlantic ocean. The boats were gone, the waves battering thirty feet against the edge of the skyscrapers. The wind moved through the windows in the glass walkway, billowing their clothes and hair around them with the salty breeze.

In the next building, golden walls and white stone floors shone. A sign hung on the wall, pointing them toward seafood markets and medical cannabis dispensaries along with lower floors. A staircase up, they heard the sound of tinkling dishes and laughter, the stairs guarded by more men in brown suits.

They crossed another large glass bridge to their right, across the streets below them, looking out towards the churning black ocean where parks and outdoor concerts would have been once held. The other buildings disappeared into the fog of the storm. The bridges moved back and forth, and the buildings creaked like cold steel. Thousands of people moved between the bridges below and behind them.

Wolfe noticed that fewer lights flickered in the taller, newer buildings built on shiny metal platforms above the sea. He could see ebony curtains and heavyset oak armoires against walls, glass chandeliers and golden wallpaper. Below them, a middle-aged man, bare-chested, was sitting against an open window, his drenched arm feeling the rain between his black fingernails, rain trickling down his arm hair. The other hand drew close against his bare chest, a cigarette between his fingers, smoke pouring from his nose and open mouth rimmed in shamefully red lipstick.

The next building read 'Lower York BESNA Community Centre,' and Wolfe felt his stomach open up into a pit.

"Scott, I—"

"Lower York BESNA Community Centre. Yes?" a woman asked Wolfe, and he felt his heart stop. He looked away from the desk and pretended to admire the picture of a man on the wall, his dark chestnut eyes looking black against the white wall.

"Oh, we're not—" Scott began.

"The medical emergency room is on the hundred and ninth floor, and the fire department is on the eighth."

"Thanks," Scott said, rushing him out and into the next glass walkway.

They moved into the next building, a set of apartments. After climbing to the next few stories, they crossed again into an actual office building, then past a food court with every food and smell he could imagine. Then, a bowling alley crashed and boomed in harmony with the thunder. A spice shop was three floors up, then a holistic healing market with women dressed in richly perfumed drapes. They walked past a metaphysical store: jars of herbs covered the walls, boxes of tarot cards, oracle decks laid on bookshelves, stones glimmered, and incense chased them down into more apartments and across another bridge.

One of the apartment buildings smelled faintly of a meal his mother cooked once; in another, someone kissed piano keys against the wind of the storm; down the hallway, Wolfe listened to the sound of thumping sex, beating rhythmically against the wall beside them as he turned Lett towards the staircase.

"Lower York General Hotel, would you like a room?" an oily man called as they meandered through the thundering halls of a blackened hotel before sinking into the next building.

They sunk deeper and deeper into the fourth street apartment with her smoke-stained walls. Hallway after hallway of apartments stretched on. Loud music hummed through the walls, and smoke crept under a door while someone inside laughed. They went down three more flights, and they were underwater; the cold air sunk in from the windows, walls, and air around them. Yellow lights flickered against the dark, rushing water.

"If you loved me you'd quit fucking around with any goddamn whore you picked off the street!" Wolfe heard a woman wail before the sound of shattered glass twinkling on the hardwood floor echoed through the halls. Lett lurched closer to Wolfe as they passed. Another slamming door made the lights flicker above them.

A man and a woman walked past them holding hands with tired, shallow eyes, two brown bags wrapped tightly in their veined hands. They stumbled into each other, giggling. The man flicked kissy lips at him and Lett when they passed. Wolfe knew those eyes; they were high on PDT.

They slipped down the next flight of stairs.

"Was it up or…?"

"Looking for sumthing hun?" A tall beanpole of a woman with a head shaped like a sunflower leered over them. She and a group of dirty-looking men were talking in the hallway. Greasy shadows were draped across their faces. One of them had red spots up and down his face, another had arms painted black with tattoos, and another shook every few moments, his lips trembling like jowls.

"Yes actually, the—" Wolfe said before Scott cut him off.

"We're fine, actually," Scott spat.

"There ain't no need to act like that, only a question. Lottsa lost people here." The group laughed when she said it. Scott stomped towards them, budging past them as they giggled at each other.

"Don't be like that," she sneered, stepping in front of Wolfe and Lett, stopping them in their tracks. Scott was on the other side of them, detesting loudly.

"Come on, let them through!" he yelled, pushing against one of the most prominent men.

"Alright, cough up your credits. I know you ain't from around here so cough em up."

"We don't have—"

"I said. Cough. Them. Up."

Wolfe felt alive with lightning coursing through his veins.

"And I—"

"Alright. Come here." The woman reached out, her other hand in her coat pocket, and drew Wolfe close by the neck. Lett cried out.

"Marie."

A calm, crisp voice spit over her shoulder. The woman above Wolfe sneered and dropped him.

"Marie!"

The woman turned around quickly. Wolfe saw a door had opened over her shoulder, a split crack where a woman was spliced. She was a short, rounder woman with delicate features and cold, unnerving eyes.

One of the prominent, bald men, with pocked cheeks and red marks across his face and down his arms, was already trudging towards the door. Marie stomped across the smoke-stained carpet and pushed her nose against the crack in the door.

"You step foot in this apartment it will end like last time," the woman through the door hissed. The other woman glared back at her.

"Please, what would it matter to you, Patuanak?" Wolfe could practically hear her growling. "You're ain't gunna be here soon, this idn't your apartment to guard," Marie said

"Until the day my ass steps over this threshold and doesn't come back, it's my apartment to guard. Besides, shouldn't you be off robbing some old woman or harassing a bouncer? At least an old woman might feel bad for beating your ass," Patuanak said.

The men hovered around Marie, muttering and glaring. Another woman down at the end of the hallway flicked her head towards them, beckoning them away and further down into the complex, deeper beneath the sea.

"You'd better watch yourself when you sleep tonight."

"I told you before, I don't swing that way, Marie."

Marie tensed, searching to make a move, but Patuanak inside refused to move, blink, or breathe.

"Go if you're going to, go."

Marie glared between Wolfe, Scott, then Lett before sulking

away down the hallway with bitter glances shot over her back, whispering under her breath.

"Thank you so—" Wolfe began, pulling himself off the carpet and picking black chunks of dog hair out of his scalp and tossing it onto the rug.

"Get where you're going." And the door slammed shut. Wolfe listened to the door click and rattle into silence, followed by muffled footsteps. Wolfe glanced up at the rusty seventy-three hung above the door.

Chapter 27

The Phoenix

"Hello?" Scott asked.

Silence.

"Is this seventy-three, tower forty-two in Lower York?" Scott asked, rolling his eyes in exasperation.

Silence.

"Hello?"

Silence again.

"Please, we came all the way from Mexico City and we…I don't know why we're here. We just heard that you might be able to help us." Wolfe thought about how empty the halls were, how quiet his mind was, how cold he was. Scott rubbed his shoulder, and Wolfe had never felt so alone. "I…we need… Phoenix?"

"I don't do that anymore. No one calls me that," Patuanak said through the door. Wolfe listened to the shifting sound of wood and the roar of water.

"Please, we really need—"

"No."

"Our lives depend on it."

The door creaked open a bit, then more, until she stood right before them. She eyed them up and down, looking both ways in the hallway. Then she pulled the door wider and stood coldly before them. Her arm traced the back of the door. Wolfe eyed the dark sliver behind it, glinting like a wedge of the moon.

She followed his eyes to the door, then back to him.

"Still no."

"What do you even do?" Wolfe begged.

"What?" she snorted.

"I said we don't know why we're here. We were in Mexico City, and this army medic woman told me there was a man who could help people, he sold contacts, he could change our lives. But he's dead, and this location was in his house. So we figured you must be able to help too," Wolfe ranted to her.

"Hmm. Still. Not my business. It's a shame but if they got him, we'll probably be dead in a week. You should get going."

"Please. We have diamonds. Gold." Wolfe pulled the last of Mrs. Bredenbury's jewellery out of his pockets: a diamond ring, a pair of garnet earrings, and an emerald anklet. She surveyed them, looking between Wolfe and the precious gems wrapped in gold and silver in his hands. Then her eyes landed on the jewelled cross hanging around Wolfe's neck.

"What's that?" she asked, nodding her eyes towards the cross. Wolfe crossed his arms in front of himself to obscure the necklace. They watched her. Patuanuk watched them.

She stepped back slowly, and with a blank expression on her face, held the door open for them. Lett looked down at the black fur rug as they entered.

"It's faux," she said.

Her eyes shone blue above him now, glowering over him. She watched them as they came in, letting her eyes sink and settle over Scott as she closed the door.

The blinds were drawn shut, and a few lamps lit the apartment. Patuanak walked around the edge of the room, pulling her finger along the blinds, making sure they were closed. She flicked on lights as she walked, bathing them in light.

Wolfe looked behind the door and saw, glowing in a soft orange lamplight, one of the BESNA officers' signature metal hooks painted pink and silver, bejewelled with stones, resting behind the door, its shiny silver neck winking at him.

"Names?"

"What do you do?"

"You actually don't know. Hmm. I basically create new people. I can make you anyone need to be," she said. "Aren't many of us left, good ones anyway. A lot of them work for

BESNA or they don't have the same connections I do. Names?"

"Wolfe Bredenbury. Lett Bredenbury. Scott Kelvington," Wolfe said.

When he said their names, she looked up and stared at them. She smiled for a moment. "I've seen your ads, you guys aren't nearly as scary in real life," she said, smirking.

—

They sat for nearly an hour as Patuanak formed new lives from ashes. Wolfe had scrounged the kitchen for food, finding some water and a bag of stale, unsalted pistachios. He walked around, touching every curtain, feeling the floor through his socks, and listening to the air whistling through the vents.

The apartment was strange. The paint was a bright cherry red mixed with a macabre Lovecraftian purple, like black, slimy tentacles would pull themselves up through the vents and devour them whole. A few neon signs hung on the wall, books of every shape and size rested beside burning candles, feathers and animal fur draped from every wall with bundles of dried herbs. Wolfe felt like they were intruders in an old vintage film from the seventies, living in a devastated cyberpunk dreamland.

Patuanak was still typing away, completely taken in by the glowing modem, with her pin-straight hair braided down her back. Books, papers, tablets, and cords were stretched across the small kitchen table and the counters, while empty dishes lay around piles of clothing.

"You're lucky Scott, like miracle lucky. Not a camera has picked you up since before you were in Landia. Pretty amazing stuff, buy a lottery ticket or something," she muttered out of the blue before sinking back into her typing.

Wolfe sat down on the couch beside Lett, rubbing hair out of his face. His eyes squinted, his lips trembling.

"What's up?"

"Mommy isn't coming is she?" Lett asked.

What could he say? *I've lied to him twice now.*

"I don't think so."

"What am I supposed to do?"

"I promised your mom I'd keep you safe until she came for you, so that's what I'm gonna do."

"I miss her. Do you think she's hurting?" he asked as tears crusted along the edges of his eyes.

"No. I know she's not hurting. She's thinking of you right now. We'll see her again, I promise." It stung when he said it.

"So. The good thing is that York is a busy place at the best of times. Two brothers from the rust belt moving here wouldn't be the strangest thing by a long shot. No one questions money here," she spoke finally. Scott jumped up and stretched over to her.

"Okay…"

"Okay. So we can get you a car, a job, and a suburban house in Lower York with a mortgage," she said.

"How?" Wolfe asked. Leaning over the chair and seeing mountains of files and documents. Passports and GEDs. A bare law diploma and fake signatures on the mortgage.

"A job?"

"Well, I saw Scott here got his bachelor's degree in social sciences. I'm sure I could get him a job teaching somewhere."

"And me?"

"You'll be a stay at home dad, raising your son, working from home." Wolfe and Scott looked at each other.

"Jesus, this is a lot."

"Yes, it is. But it's important. This isn't just an alibi, it's your life, it has to be bulletproof, and you have to remember everything."

"Okay…so what about the back story?"

"Oh, that's the fun part. I'll get to that in a minute."

"First…this is your law degree and your high school transcripts. Wolfe's commercial cooking lessons and your mortgage, car loan, etcetera."

"How did you get a mortgage?" Wolfe looked over the paper in awe.

"Certain people will do certain things at the threat of other certain things happening to them. It's easy if you have the right cards to play."

"What if we have to prove any of these?"

"Look. I'll be gone tomorrow, and no one will find me. Deal with what you gotta, any way you gotta."

"How do we pay you?"

"You don't."

"What? Why?"

"If I'm careful, I can get anything I need out there in the dataverse. If I ever need something, I'll be back. And doing one over on me; A, doesn't work. And B, is the worst mistake you'll make. Got it?"

"Got it. We owe you for the rest of time."

"There you go."

"You know," she looked over at them, "it wouldn't hurt to wear glasses, grow some facial hair, cut your hair maybe…"

She worked a little longer before turning around, smiling, and looking at them both.

"Well. If you ever wanted to change something in your life, now is the time. So tell me, who would you like to be?"

Chapter 28

Jubilation Day

The golden sun rose across a colossal, unyielding sea of cobalt blue, pouring sunlight over the dewy pavement. Wafts of cool air evaporated into the sky as cars and bicycles rode back and forth down the street.

Wolfe and Lett bobbed through the sea of people moving down the road. Trains tore overhead to the sound of hooting and hollering. Radio stations blared music out open windows, people stirred with the scent of fresh fruit and cooking oil, and brown streamers danced limberly, flitting back and forth in the breeze.

Across the street, in a park filled with oscillating heads, a voice carried through loudspeakers and over screens. "Fascists! Communists! Insurrectionists! Around the world, those weak, cowardly, and dark-spirited people are weeping! One hundred years after Martin Luther King Jr. fought to liberate our brown-eyed people, we have liberated the world. Democracy has won!" As the man spoke, horns honked in the streets, bicycle bells hummed, and people cried out their support.

On the screen, a man was standing on a platinum stand, dressed in dark brown pants and a white and green dress shirt. He grinned into the microphone, a sea of images behind him showed their victories overseas: pictures of violence, war, murdered women and children, and the horrors of the blue-eyed regime in Mexico, Japan, Hawaii, and Bolivia.

"We are the cornerstone of democracy. And we, with the help of our allies worldwide, have brought democracy, truth, justice, and the will of the people back into reality! We have made the world a better place! Today, leaders of OCHS will be brought to The Hauge and tried for their war crimes!"

Wolfe stopped listening. His face was contorted into a smile, but he was an inferno inside. Aflame with fear, a churning, burrowing heat inside himself, pushing emotions down further and sweat to the surface. The endless torrent of thoughts assaulted him with images of what had happened and what was yet to come.

"We have entered a new age. The golden age, the awakening, was spurred by the true civilizations of the past millennia. We are one, we are united, and we are victorious! And because of you, your hard work, your money, through your marriages, and little brown-eyed babies, through us all, working together, we have become stronger than we ever were. Because of you, our life as we know it will prevail!" he cried, pointing fingers into the crowd.

"You were just listening to BESNA Vice Chair Stewart Valparaiso, speaking to you live from Lower York Park. What a speech. Tell me, Ann, what is the crowd like out there?" a news anchor spoke through a tree of speakers.

"Well, let me tell you, the crowd is just radiant out this way. And by no surprise, what a speech! I'm told we're waiting for Mr. Bredenbury, the survivor of the Bredenbury Plantation Massacre, to give a talk just a few moments after Mayor Asquith speaks. Then, we can expect an official announcement on who will be running with Mr. Bredenbury for vice prime minister in the coming months," another news anchor said from beside them.

A large, dumpling-shaped man strolled onto the stage, heavy with weight and sagging with perspiration under the squeezing summer pressure. Large, reddened cheeks wagged as he opened his mouth to speak over the humming of the national anthem through speakers.

Wolfe moved aside to let a family of seven move past and dove into a shop with Lett clenching onto his side. The shop was large and well lit; the windows let in unfurling lashes of white light, and the smell of baking waffle cones and sugar swirled around him in dizzying circles.

Two children ran past him with ice cream bleeding red down their hands. A boy and a girl, one dressed in soft velvet suspenders and a blouse, the other in a two-piece brown suit. They ran outside, and their parents followed, calling out and laughing. Wolfe met their eyes, and the father tipped his hat as he walked.

Wolfe ran a hand over his face, pulling his hair out of his eyes, giving him a chance to feel for a smile. Wolfe stood in the middle of the ice cream parlour and gift shop, frozen with terror. Scott had gone to pick up their car from the other side of town, to run errands, and Wolfe had been instructed to take Lett out for the afternoon and try to avoid the culture shock.

"Culture shock…" Wolfe had scoffed. And yet here he was, standing in the snake pit. Somewhere in York, the villain was standing, preparing to spew lies.

Wolfe looked down. Lett was pointing out a small animal figure made of porcelain. It was wearing a t-shirt and holding a baseball painted in national colours. It swivelled, stirred, and dipped, dancing to a jaunty tune. Wolfe blinked through the spots on his glasses; smears and grease blurred his vision through the thin film. Wolfe's eyes burned from the contact lenses pressed against them.

"—and with his vision of horror, the terrors of the mob, the violence we all lay at night fearing, holding our kids, our houses, our stores close, this man suffered what we all fear. Please heed his cautionary tale, please help me welcome Mr. Bredenbury."

Wolfe felt bile in his mouth, stinging his tongue like venomous barbs. He would have said he felt scared. No, that wasn't it. Decimated. The world had lost. There was no holed-up resistance; there would not be a light at the end of the tunnel. They were waiting for nothing. No one was coming for them. This was a new dawn.

The rest of the gift shop was mugs and bracelets, flags and t-shirts, backpacks and tiny Mos. The prices on small little electronic price tags flashed repeatedly. Fourty-five credits, seventy credits, a hundred and thirty credits, on and on. Wolfe blinked and saw the Worker's District again. They made thirteen credits a day. People had been crammed along the phone booths, pissing their money away, trying to console their crying relatives through the phone if they could locate them.

Wolfe was staring at the tablet strapped to his wrist. He'd called Scott four times this afternoon, and he refused to answer. Wolfe tried a fifth time and watched Scott's face shimmer as it rang, and rang, and rang, and rang.

The bookshelves caught his eye, and he turned to look. On the shelf, novels with unfamiliar authors watched him.

The Science of Colour by S. K. Broderick. Scientific Truths to Stun and Amaze! By Calder Harris. A Thousand and One Brown Eyed Inventions of the Past Thousand Years by Codette Duff. They lined another wall with brown-eyed books that pushed colour, which devalued the collective human growth of history. Next to those stood the several styles and editions of the Order of Truth and Justice. Wolfe felt it in his hand, massaged its spine with the underside of his finger, and tasted the sinister energy leaking through its bound back.

A knife pulled at his stomach, twisting in his guts. He was going to be sick. They slipped past a group of families muttering about veterinary bills and meal plans while waiting in line, molesting the air with their conversation.

"Denzil just got back from the Boreal front, I'm just so proud!" one portly woman cried to another, holding her arms close against her.

"—they tried as hard as possible to avoid work, fought our kindness, threw our honesty and conviction back in our faces. By the time I'd realized a rebellion was brewing and brought it up among my staff, they had abandoned me, working with our workers to burn, loot, and murder everything within reach. They started with the guardhouse—" Wolfe heard Mr. Bredenbury's voice, thick with emotion.

"Do you have a bathroom?" Wolfe asked the teenage worker behind the counter. His face was a red, boiling crater of pimples and zits.

"Um…yeah, just around the back there," he said, pointing a dripping ice cream scoop towards the back of the store.

"Thanks." Wolfe smiled as bile rose in his throat again. Lett might have been behind him. He didn't care. He pushed into the cool bathroom, a welcome relief from the hot, sweaty, pounding headache slithering up his spine.

He slipped into an empty stall and unfurled into the toilet. Retching up batch after batch of stale pistachio nuts. He came undone into the bathroom, trying not to let the next wave of sickness overcome him.

He could finally stop smiling, stop waving and dipping, wiping his shirt with the back of his hand. He could stop *being*.

"Why does this feel like a prison?" he asked himself out loud, barely whispering it to himself in the loneliness of the bathroom. "Maybe if you just put on a strong face and…" Wolfe crumpled over the toilet again, drooling out another mouthful of acid into the already slimy bowl.

This is what you wanted; this is your freedom. Wolfe thought, *why does it feel like this then?* Another voice in his head asked.

Stubble was growing in over his cheeks again. His hair was greasy and heavy, laying across his forehead like damp fur. His face was red, gleaming with sweat. With dripping eyes, he let his nose leak into his shirt. A trail of spit was strung across his lips and stretched across the bottom of his chin. He tried to call Scott again, but the call never rang.

Wolfe was wearing a chestnut brown coat over a white striped shirt cut off at the elbow, jeans, and brown dress shoes they'd bought last night at some department store he couldn't remember. He remembered the cashier staring over them with cautious eyes.

How was he supposed to go outside, look at Lett and tell him to fight for what is right? Tell him he has nothing to fear? *Is it not better to die for something you believe in valiantly rather than die lying to yourself?*

"Don't be silly, the bathroom of an ice cream parlour in Lower York is not the time for a rebellion." He could hear Unity in his mind, see the outline of her face, see her standing there, arms crossed. Her face was fuzzy, slipping in and out of sight.

Wolfe didn't even know what to tell himself anymore. The war was continuing inside him. Someone flushed a toilet beside him, and he heard shoes snapping across the ice white tiles, the sound of water, and then the steps were gone. Wolfe felt his temples bursting, and he tried to call Scott again. It didn't ring.

"Wolfe?" Lett whispered as he fished a hand underneath the door.

"I'll be out in a minute Lett." Wolfe sniffed, rubbing his face dry. He looked at himself in the mirror: his eyes were bloodshot, his ears rang, his nose was clogged, and his throat burnt. He tried to rub vomit off his shirt, listening to the radio drone about the national surplus, industry regulation, and overseas African coups. "And another powerful speech from Mr. Bredenbury, with his official announcement for running for prime minister. Now, the much anticipated reveal of the vice prime minister. This is ninety-three point zero, FM radio."

"You got it, kid. You're good. You're okay," Wolfe told himself. He wiped his face again, forced a smile over his teeth, and walked out into the store again. Every screen showed a live feed of an empty podium. Mr. Bredenbury was just standing there, and Wolfe waited with everyone else to see the vice prime minister's announcement.

Wolfe tried to phone Scott again, and he didn't pick up. Wolfe swallowed hard, feeling it ride the length of his body from his throat to his knees. The air was different today.

The screens waited, and waited, and waited. The air was sucked out of the room, and Wolfe watched the empty podium with everyone else in the country. Wolfe felt something heavy settle in his guts, scratching at his brain. A broken glass, with all its edges minute and endless, had its place. It all could fit if he had the dexterity and patience to glue it back into one. He knew he could piece the truth together, but the expansiveness of it didn't feel like reality. *It can't be.*

He ran his fingers along the books, felt the rim of shelves, and tried to determine the cause of the growing heaviness in his chest. Wolfe looked up to the screen and saw a glimpse of someone he thought he'd met before. The broken glass regained it's form, his heart began to pound, the air grew hotter and heavier. *No. No. No.*

Wolfe tried to ignore the pounding of his heart in his throat and turned away, moving towards the counter with Lett's toy. A voice from the screen began to spiel. Wolfe turned his head slowly to the left, his whole body trembling, a shaking, heaving, mass, weeping with sweat.

"And still, I fought to believe there was hope. I have fought for the last two months to overcome my fears and to realize that any or all of my hopes for blue-eyed people have been extinguished. There can be no unity with immoral, illogical monsters. I know more than any, since my own brother, Wolfe Bredenbury, is one of those monsters." Wolfe turned to face the screen, and Arcola stood at the podium. The glass was rebuilding itself. The curtain behind the podium fluttered.

With every breath, something was croaking inside Wolfe, rising and falling with him in unison. Goosebumps climbed his arms, raising the hair in ridges along his neck. Wolfe stumbled backwards, and a cigar box slipped off the shelf and spilled across the floor, sending silver lighters and bundles of unburnt smoke across the floor. No one noticed. The broken glass regained more shape, less damaged, and more concrete. The curtain fluttered again, and a man dressed in a suit and tie was preparing to step onto the podium.

"That is why I'd like to introduce the one who's been closest to it all, fought the blue-eyed mutation up close, my husband, and your up-and-coming vice prime minister, Mr. Scott Kelvington." Applause erupted across the street as Scott stepped out on a stage somewhere in York. Horns honked in the street, people burst into hoots in the store with Wolfe and Lett, and ads started to spiel from every corner of every store.

"Vote the Bredenbury - Kelvington ticket for a future for your kids." The national anthem erupted from bands across the street, and fighter jets raced strips of gold and brown overhead. Wolfe's tongue was blistered with drought, his eyes were shattered with coastal storms, his hands were stricken, and his entire body quaked. Wolfe wandered out into the street, and leaflets were raining from the sky. Thousands of brown and white pamphlets poured from the sky, glinting in the sun. On its face, both Scott and Mr. Bredenbury watched him, incandescent against the crisp paper.

"Together we will overcome. The brown-eyed people will overcome. Vote for your next vice prime minister," Scott cried from the leaflet, a blinking, BESNA golden eye resting on their brows.

The world sunk into the void. There was nothing but the pounding in Wolfe's ears. Sounds must have come out, but nothing could overcome the roar of blood through his veins. People across the street were unfurling a large full-colour banner that screamed at him. "Vote Bredenbury & Kelvington."

"I have spent the last two months under the forced control of Wolfe Bredenbury and his band of radicals. I spent every night, day, and morning fearing today would be the day they finally decided to kill me. This scar…" he said, showing the gunshot wound he'd acquired fleeing through Landia eons ago. "…was given to me by a thankfully now dead Unity Bredenbury, who tortured me in an attempt to elicit information from me. I know firsthand the horrors they can commit when they are allowed the freedom to do what they like, and since they do not think, behave, or reason like you or me, they are not humans like you or me. If you vote for The Bredenbury - Kelvington ticket, I will ensure the that blue-eyed mutations are absolved from their abuses in the way God sees fit. I will ensure their servitude to the human race serves this great country until the end of time," Scott cried, standing on the stage and letting tears of joy run down his face.

The crowd was screaming with him, and the world knew they were looking at a future prime minister.

"Why, Scott? Why?" Wolfe whispered with the most energy he could force himself to muster, his heart pounding against himself. Wolfe felt his ears rot from where he had heard his words, squiggling deep into his brain until he could listen to nothing but grinding teeth against his nerves.

He scooped up a pile of pamphlets and tossed them into the air, letting them sprinkle down like spring rain. Wolfe was standing in the gift shop again, and a box shattered against the shelf, sending the books on the wall spiralling down. Wolfe shoved a shelf back against the wall, and the bottle of hand sanitizer wobbled back and forth, drunk on its feet before falling, smashing against the ground, soaking leaflets and books.

Wolfe was screaming. He could taste blood. A cabinet filled with toys was weeping out onto the floor. The shelves were bare, and the bodies of books lay twisted like broken butterflies. The sunlight spun through broken glass, sending a glistering, dancing light across the walls. His fingers were scarlet, dripping with his blood . His pants were torn across the knees, his shirt stained with his own ochre handprints. A lighter fell into his hands, flickering silver, red, and orange. Then, without thought, without control of his own hands, he tossed the lighter glowering with flame onto the floor and watched it crumble into ashes.

A demon burst forth from hell, crawling his long arms of flame up the curtains, scampering like mice across the books. The books and their paper wings turned black and curled in on their bodies, simmering into an undulating ball of flame. The demon made of flame lashed out into the store, filling the room with tar-black smoke, eliciting screams.

Wolfe heard screaming but could only marvel at the flames before him, watching as the room turned back into the dirt. He watched Scott's and Mr. Bredenbury's faces bubble on the paper before shrivelling out of sight forever, back into nonexistence. *Is this how it is supposed to end?* Sirens and alarms wailed.

Wolfe backed out onto the street. His shirt was razed, and Lett was tugging on him. A group of people were stuck near the washrooms, and the zit-covered employee was one of them as he tried to stomp out the flames, pushing them further back. Fire licked the windows, shattering glass out into the street, painting black streaks over the ceiling and onto the roof. The fire leapt out of windows and onto stores on either side of them.

Hoards of people scurried around them. Some whimpered; others cried out for their children and partners trapped inside the flame-filled store as the fire started pouring out into the street, catching against the trees. Wolfe led Lett by the shoulders through the throng of people spreading into the street. A man was standing at his car, a tablet in his hand.

"You alright, Mr.?" he asked, dropping his tablet to his side and rushing around to them. When he turned back to grab a towel out of his car, Wolfe fell over him, and his tablet turned from glass into sand again on the pavement. His cries were drowned under the screaming around them. Then the man was asleep, and Wolfe was pilfering his pockets after he'd beaten him. The roof of the building grew into the mouth of a monster. Black smoke plumed through its gaping maw, sending black air out into the sky.

Wolfe tossed the man's tablet, watch, and wallet into the car, still humming on the street corner. A second later, they were sputtering out into the street and around the corner. He ran his fingers through his hair, leaving streaks of ash as he tried to think. He tasted blood in his throat; it burnt to breathe. *We have to get away from the cameras. BESNA will look for us.*

He pulled the car down a back alley behind another string of buildings, heading north out of the city. Then he needed to head west without being seen. He would need money, but Wolfe didn't have an account. But, regardless, Wolfe felt a peace blossom over him as they fled. The air *was* different today. Change was coming.

Wolfe's mind was a bowl of soup, running ideas through his mind. They could make it maybe two thousand kilometres before it needed to be charged, certainly not into the mountains. They needed food; they needed water; they would need money first.

"If you knew how this ended, would you change anything?" Scott's words echoed in his mind. Wolfe emptied his pockets out the window as they drove, leaving a trail of his life in the street. They left the city in silence, the sun flaring, and a fire burning behind them.

Chapter 29

The Last Place on Earth

Wolfe drove northwest through the day and into the night. Undoubtedly, the horror of their actions would be tattled about them as they drove, nasty little seeds spread and sown across every screen in the country, thrown like hand grenades. They were driving along an older highway that no one even knew to drive anymore. Maybe the odd farmer, but then again, maybe.

Farmers didn't exist in this world anymore. The best overtook the biggest and the finest, and now there was Bredenbury and Bredenbury. How anyone could rise against them was unthinkable. Wolfe had to have been blind; it was stupid to imagine it could be done. Everyone who could rise against them was too busy arguing which of Bredenbury's three brands was best for the environment.

Yet Wolfe wondered what 'rising' would look like. It would look like the Bredenbury plantation; it would look like the protests of his youth, then the riots of his youth, the desperate plea for their rights beaten down with water cannons and tear gas. It couldn't be done. Rising up looks like terrorism; terrorism leads to death and prison.

Wolfe realized the world was strange as he drove. They had dug up the trees and flattened the hills. The roots that sucked up the water were long dead, the fields flooded every spring, and heavy tankers with wheels like spider eyes would come to suck up the water and sell it back to the acreages for thousands of credits per gallon. The systems and rigours of nature had been abandoned, and Wolfe felt like a lost soul drifting in a new world.

Who drove anymore? So they missed out on the beauty and wonder of life. Who walked? So they missed the bloom of lilacs, the smell of roses, the falling birch pollen, the leaking, swollen rivers teeming with birds in the spring. Who reads? So they forgot to imagine. Who imagined? So they forgot to think. Who thought? So they forgot to believe.

It was such a shame, a world of the lost, stirring around in perpetuity, beating themselves senseless against the walls built by men like Bredenbury. But they fawn and cry, begging to be seen and have that same power. *Yet the power, and the yearning for it, is why the rest of us have to fight each other.* The world, a place of wonder and imagination, was lost. *Are these not the questions and pondering of an old fool?* Wolfe asked himself. *A man who never notices that he is an outdated relic, an archaic remnant of a past that does not, cannot exist? Maybe.* He reconciled.

Wolfe fought a battle between himself on that long, ponderous drive through the dark night as the charge of the car dwindled. *Do people honestly not think? Do they not feel? Or are they pushed into it, believing they are the saviours of a new age?* The screens blinded them, the tablets numbed them, and distractions leapt through the dataverse into the waiting hands of the hoards who'd rather a comfortable lie than a painful truth.

Snow fell.

Only the gentle humming of the car and the rumble of the road beneath him kept him awake. Lett was sleeping in the back as they drove west. The highway tumbled into gravel when he turned, and when Wolfe turned again, it slipped into dirt. The warning lights were flashing; only fifty kilometres left before the car shut off. A glow in the distance shone up through the night against the hazy blur of late fall skies.

Wolfe opened the door and stepped out, standing in the chilled night. He left Lett sleeping, and he crept up to the house. He jiggled the handle, and knowingly, it stayed shut. Wolfe fought against a wall of memories.

He walked around the edge of the house and reached into the drainpipe, pulling out a small plastic capsule that had the keys in it. Wolfe walked back around to the front of the house, catching visions of himself in the black windows, the concept of a person he no longer was; not as tall, old, or dark, but young, short, and bright instead.

He pulled Lett out of the car and dragged him towards the house. *Thank god I never told Scott about this. No one will ever know; we will be safe here for now.* Maybe he'll find a truck here; his uncle will have some gas.

Wolfe jiggled the handle and lifted it just like he was supposed to do, staring at the black living room, frozen in time. It felt like three decades had passed, but it hadn't been five years. He and his family were standing in the living room, discussing their next course of action.

"It's useless, it's foolish, you're crazy!" his mother had cried to her brother as they stood in the warm glow of the living room. The paint wasn't cracked, the flooring wasn't peeling up, and the furnace was roaring a painful heat.

"They'll make me do my mandatory military service, Elrose. So please, leave, I don't want to have to hurt you or..." he cried. Wolfe sat on the couch, watching the scene play out. Arcola, already in her late teens, was listening intently, and she and Wolfe shared a glance. Later that night, she told him it would be alright; they were always family no matter what. Did she know she was lying?

Wolfe found a pile of wood by the fireplace. The same wood was there the night they left. The same wood that Wolfe had peeled the bark off absently, listening to the adults yell, his childhood fingerprints scratched into the wood. It was the night they fought, the night his parents drug him away by the sleeve and into the car because he had school the next morning. Then BESNA came, and his life changed forever.

His uncle was going to Bermuda, and maybe he had followed through on that promise. Wolfe saw him basking on a beach somewhere, blissfully unaware of what the world was like. His uncle would have tried to get him to leave Scott with his soft words and wise tongue. He would have smiled at Wolfe, and his eyes would have swirled. "What do *you* want?" he would have asked, and the world would have seemed less scary.

Wolfe fought with the fire until the light unfurled across the house. Wolfe lit candles until they glowed. The house was the same: the sink was filled with the dishes from the supper they had eaten, the bed Wolfe slept in was still unmade, and everything was as it had been.

He would have given anything to go back and become the kid he was. Tell them all to fight for every moment, tell them to run and hide forever, bury yourself as far away as you could. He tucked Lett into bed at the back of the house, and instead of sleeping, he walked. He had no intention, so he simply steered himself in circles.

Wolfe sat on the couch, his back to the window. He closed his eyes and saw their faces. His blue-eyed cousins warped with fear, his blue-eyed aunt shaking with anger at her husband, his defiant mother, and quiet grandmother. He tried to remember their faces, the little things, the edges around their nose, the length of their eyelashes, anything that might make them more real in Wolfe's mind. Some were just lumps, black voids with names he couldn't see. He couldn't hear their voices anymore.

What was he supposed to do? He'd have to do something. They needed food for sure. The pantry was empty, the fridge reeked, and the cupboards were only full with water bottles, tea, sugar, and flour. Wolfe could cook, but not without power.

Wolfe burnt the car near the lagoon, and watched it roar and tumble into the water, blinking, blinking, then resting along the rocks at the bottom. He searched the barn and found a rusting red truck, a wall of tools, and a gas tank. The cellar was filled with canned potatoes and salted chicken thighs. A radio was resting on the counter, but the batteries had leaked acid and melted. If Wolfe wanted, they could make it to the Desolation again, out to the mountains, or Wolfe could go find Liberty.

Wolfe felt broken, like an unspooling sweater, a letter someone stopped writing halfway through, like an unwrapped Christmas present, or a half-finished book resting face down on a shelf somewhere. There were so many options, but none felt right;

nothing felt like a choice he wanted to make. Then he felt sleep pulling at his eyes, so he walked along the walls of the house, blowing candles out and plunging them into darkness.

He was standing in the doorway, watching Lett sleep, when he saw himself in the mirror above the bed. He felt a twinge. His cross was hanging on his neck. He pulled it off and flipped it over, marvelling at it in slow motion. It meant so much more now, so much less. It symbolized his oppression, all the lies Scott had fed him over the last four months. Wolfe could see the love in Scott's face but the emptiness in his eyes. It was all a lie. Scott was truly never anything other than that man in a suit and tie.

He pulled the necklace off his neck, holding it between his fingers, and chucked it into the living room. Wolfe pulled off Tisdale's wedding ring he'd worn since Mexico city just a few days earlier and laid it on the shelf. As he crawled into bed beside Lett, he drifted off, a welcome relief from the pounding thoughts inside his head.

—

Wolfe woke up trembling. The moon hung in the starless sky, drawing all the light toward its surface. The snow from the freak storm was gathering along the windowsill. Wolfe sat up, resting his feet on the floor while Lett slept beside him. He was free, but freedom was lonely. If someone went wrong, who did he point his fingers at? Who told him what to do next?

Wolfe looked towards the lantern in the living room ahead of him, not something he'd remembered lighting. His feet were sitting in pools of water; his dreams showed figures and more sleep.

A board creaked somewhere in the house. He peered out the window, and ghostly footprints swung around the house, slowly disappearing under drifting snow. A gentle creaking somewhere in the darkness alerted him again. Through the bedroom into the rest of the house, a light shimmered. He strained his eyes against the static. He pulled himself closer to the door and pushed it open, stepping forward.

He must have done it, though he couldn't remember. *I'm*

dreaming. He'd shattered the man's tablet, destroyed his watch, and burnt the car. *No one can find us.* Still, he wanted to grab Lett and sneak away back through the window and dart into the night. He wouldn't be caught again. The floor shrieked beneath him as he stepped, sending ice through his veins. He saw the silver pocket knife in Lett's hands, so he slipped it into his own, flipping it open as he steadied himself. Wolfe peeked through into the living room.

"Hello, Wolfe."

Scott was standing there, one hand held up with guards on either side of him, plastered in the dozens around the room. The other hand, swinging his wooden cross in his hand.

"You really thought you could escape? Ever? Really, Wolfe?"

There were no thoughts, nothing that would console him, nothing that could help it all make sense. Scott tossed the wooden necklace aside, and Wolfe watched it fall. Scott raised a foot and let it fall, crushing it into a wiggling pile of wires and chips, beeping and flashing with lights like melted wax, like a broken moth hissing on the floor where it lay. A fragment of a chip shimmered out of the pile of wood and wire and started buzzing on the floor.

"Now you have a choice Wolfe. You—" Before Scott could finish his sentence, Wolfe had turned to run. A crushing pressure fell over him. His ears were ringing, and his feet were clattering violently against the floor.

His arms twisted horribly until Wolfe was sure they would shatter. Voices laughed above him, mocking his inability to free himself from their death grip. Darkness was coming, and as he lay there on the floor, he felt himself slipping into oblivion. Wolfe slurred his words, fighting to get to Lett. He was never truly free. He never could have failed.

Chapter 30

The Hospital

Bald, sterile lights flash above him, gaping down on him like wide-eyed streetlamps. Hard and crystalline, white and starched, cold and unyielding they swayed, dancing above him. Wolfe tried to move his head but found himself rigid. He couldn't move, his neck was made of stone, his body encased in cement. He laid there, watching the lights slide.

He tried to slug through his thoughts. Where was he? Where did he come from? *Before? After?* He felt like he was fighting against his own mind, an hourglass, slowly sucking himself deeper and deeper, forceful, instant, unyielding. The prying hands of time tried to end his thoughts forever, pulling him towards sleep.

He tried to think about where lights would be, in this shape, elongated squares stretched across the ceiling, and then he knew. Then he didn't. A bowling alley. Why would he be in a bowling alley? A few noises hissed from behind him. *Voices? Whispering? God?*

As he watched the lights, one would appear at the bottom of his vision, then it would slink out of view above him, replaced by another one without hesitation. There were black lines in the white sky, was it even a sky? Every few steps he could feel himself jolting. Was he laying down or standing up, walking or running, sleeping or awake, dreaming or...

The lights began to dim. They seemed to blink on and off. Wait, or was that his own eyes closing and opening? Wolfe felt like he didn't have eyelids, and whatever thoughts happened had to be true, he was a feather after all.

He awoke again. Something cold pressing into his neck. His eyes were draped with gauze, like something else completely.

Dusky figures drifted aimlessly above him, gliding like angels around him. His neck was no longer cement, but rubber, springing back up every time he peered down at the rest of his body. Now he was certain he was lying down, on a table no less. *Who lays on a table?* He must have been put there, Wolfe thought to himself. Maybe? He was trying to sit up and he felt like he was gliding through the straps on his arms. Why was he tied down? Where was he?

Someone was hovering over him and they seemed to bob up and down like a bottle in a stream. Wolfe felt his head glued down, pulling at his hair. Why did his fingers feel like they were lightning? Electrical. *What is electricity? A fire that moved cars and charged tablets. How?*

He closed his eyes again and woke to the lights above him. Large, round lights, they spun in little circles, flashing colours around him. He felt arms on him, touching him, wiping his forehead, his eyelids with something cool and sticky. It smelt like metal.

It ran down his neck, under his back, he felt like he was piercing something. He tried to tell the figures around him that the big lizard was peeing on him, *it's true, it really was.* Wolfe felt himself crying, why did they smile, why was it funny, why would they let the giant lizard actually pee on him, why would they do that?

Wolfe forgot before he could remember, he felt something move behind him and he was looking at a wall, there was a clock on it, but the hands moved too fast, spinning into a gray blur. Then poked him in the side, like a rough jab. He turned to get mad but no one was there, only the same grayness on the wall encasing him in bleak amber.

"Wh'erddaygo…" he grumbled, and to Wolfe, it made perfect sense.

Without warning, the room around him began to move. Slow enough at first then faster and faster. Then it froze, and his stomach kept spinning, but his head flew detached. The clock on the wall stopped moving, and the letters seemed to vibrate off the white wall. The words in his head seemed to grow louder and more persistent. He felt like he was floating like he was off the table and he was holding the lizard, small and slimy in his hands, reeking of urine.

He lost all concept of space. He was floating in the room, the only to fill the void was Wolfe and the clock. The letters turned into numbers, then back again as colours moved behind his eyes. Were they closed?

Wolfe sat back down, though he never stood. The sounds in his ears grew louder as if he were standing in a tunnel as storms tore the grass above him into sand. The entire room began to shrink, first into the tunnel, then the eye of the storm, into a dot, then the world was drawn into a pinhole.

The world around him was sucked into the dot until he was a black hole, staring down the barrel of a gun. He was the gun, then the black hole, then the gun, then the black hole. He was something but nothing. His words slurred together until it all stopped working.

The world started to come together, then apart in an instant. Then he was struck back into reality, like a thin acid was crawling through his blood, burning the soft, pink flesh behind his eyes. Darkness again, this time with eyes open. His eyes burnt backwards into his skull.

He was sure he screamed, but no words came out. He tumbled over backwards, gone forever, the covenant of his mind a sealed cavern. His mind, a tomb, and the final resting place of Wolfe Bredenbury. He tried to make sense of it all, but the world was lost to him.

He sat up, and then back down. He knew he was on a cruise ship with a swinging porthole. His legs bent backwards, swinging from window to window, pressing against his knees. His parents were there, reeking of boiled turnips, their heads screwed backwards.

His thoughts still pounded in multitudes. Some crying, some laughing, some talking. The world was inside out, and he felt the coolness with his tongue. Bitter. Salty. Acidic. Sour. His eyes smelt like flaming souls and his eyes tasted like porcelain dolls in some mouldy basement. He lay there, undone. There were no more words left to describe himself, he was lost. Undone. Unravelled. UnWolfed.

His ears pounded. A river, a ringing of divinity cried in his ears. Harsh. He cried out and felt his tongue grow fat in his mouth. He saw his vision go in and out, his fingers grew fat and elongated, he gasped but his lungs were stone, unable to pull in a breath. By the time he'd managed to pull himself out from under the ocean, he was aboard the sinking ship.

He flailed, thrashed, beat against the metal bed screaming as hard plastic straps forced him down onto the bed. It wasn't long after this that his world exploded. All around him, the faces began to dip and dive in and around him, their faces swelling and shrinking in size. He tried to move his fingers and they flurried before his eyes. They were yelling and he strained to hear them over his pounding blood.

Somewhere a man laughed. "They don't feel pain like real people." As a piercing hot pain seared through his neck, he heard his father.

"Why Dad? Why are you hurting me?" Wolfe cried out loud to the sound of laughter and sneering. The pressure in his head tried to kill him, the burning behind his eyes fought against his skull.

This didn't feel right, he had to get out of here. *Why is that tapping so loud?* Why was the world going faster than Wolfe could feel?

The objects in the man's hands flashed back and forth violently until the point where Wolfe couldn't tell if he was looking left or right. A white coat, a woman with a tablet, medical equipment. Then the process began anew with the same flashing lights.

Chapter 31

A New Dawn

Gold leeched down the walls, rich plum velvet lined the windows, and curtains adorned with gold tassels hung on the drapes. Busts and wrinkly, leather-bound books stared at Wolfe from alongside the pointy visages of unfamiliar brown-eyed men, staring over the edges of their paintings.

His mind was bandaged in fog; he was lost in some icy hedge maze just outside the corners of reality. Every time he scanned the room, he'd make a wrong turn and find himself lost, starting over from the other side again. His thoughts weren't where they were supposed to be. He tried to find his name, but it floundered on his tongue, dragging itself back down his throat.

He spun his eyes around the room and memories slipped back towards him, falling back through the cracks of his brain. A house, windswept, cold. Black figures, guards, pain. Somewhere deep inside himself, a twinge of anger and sadness rang without understanding. He scanned the room again, and this time a man was sitting on a spindly chair, legs crossed, reading an actual book, flipping the leathery pages with gentle, trembling touches.

The face was strangely familiar, a distant relative, a friend he'd once known. He used all the strength in his body to force himself to his knees, then to wobbling feet. A mirror glimmered when the sun peeked through the curtains to his left. When he tried to find what he knew himself to look like, only a misshapen creature hobbled towards him as he tumbled forward towards the mirror.

Wolfe pulled at his own distorted and uneven face, half-melted and soggy, the left side painted white; a foggy, crystal-coloured eye drifted around in its socket. Then he realized he was blind in his right eye, and upon feeling the rough, pale skin, he realized he felt no touch.

"It's a new procedure, trying to stop the mutation from taking contact lenses. Worked for one, not the other," the man said from the corner of the room, resting Gulliver's Travels face down on the stool beside him.

"Why…" Wolfe's voice faltered, a crunchy, gravely voice he had never heard before. Wolfe fell backwards onto the floor at the side of a bed and just stared with the few senses he could muster.

"You were always so stupid," the man chuckled and held his hand up under Wolfe's chin, studying what they left of his face. Memories came flooding back. Scott. The Bredenburys. Scott pushed him back past the rug, and Wolfe fell, not enough energy to stop himself.

Wolfe just laid there, letting his mind run through it all. He'd fought so hard, lost so much, was so close, and failed. Wolfe felt a twinge in his neck, and he touched the top of his spine. He felt a chip humming away.

"You're so dramatic," Scott snapped, standing up to pace the room in circles, hands in his pockets. He picked up the book and tossed it on the shelf. Wolfe looked up at him through his seeing eye. "Why?" Wolfe gasped through heaving breaths.

"God, do I have to explain everything to you?" he snapped, turning around to look down at him. "Get up. GET UP." Wolfe pushed himself up onto his knees and backwards against the bed frame.

"Why?" Wolfe whispered again, tears threatening to pour over the edge of his working eyelid. "Where is Lett?" Wolfe asked, as calm as he could, holding back the shaking in his voice.

"He's fine.

"What are you planning to do with me?"

"That I'll have to save for Bredenbury."

"Fuck that," Wolfe groaned, shifting against the floor.

Scott turned around, and with a flick on his tablet, Wolfe was thrown over onto his side, trembling with energy. He tried to scream, but his tongue was spasming in his mouth. The pain was unbearable, like his blood was acid, his limbs were made of metal, and he was hooked to electricity.

"Don't disrespect your owner," Scott whispered, shutting off the tablet.

Wolfe roared with rage, banging his head on the carpet as the pain simmered away. He wanted to beat his brains out on the rug; he wanted to bite his fingers off, tear out his hair, and scoop his own eyes out with his fingers. He screamed so loud he could feel his vocal cords stretching, threatening to tear. The dust dislodged itself from the ceiling. His lungs burned and pushed against his ribs. The veins in his wrists bulged, his brain shook inside his skull.

"You truly never cared?" Wolfe asked, eyes staring ahead at the open window. Everything had been exorcised, leaving him with nothing but his sadness. Tears stirred along the edge of his working eye, finally falling like apple seeds along the left side of his face, trickling along his lips.

"No, not really," Scott said, sitting down beside Wolfe, and they stared out the window together, looking up at the brilliant blue sky. A cold winter wind froze Wolfe to his core, numbing his fingers, but he didn't care. "Look. It...it wasn't all like that. There were days I thought I was in it for you, but..."

"Then why lead me along this entire time? Make me think that you cared? Just to hurt me?" Wolfe moved his hand against Scott's, and he snatched it away, pushing himself off the floor.

"I *wanted* to help you! I was going to!" he cried, pushing his hands against his face. "Alright. Shut up and fucking listen to me," he said, pushing a finger against Wolfe's face. Wolfe refused to look away.

"When they took Arcola I was going to kill Bredenbury. I would have. I was going to tear his guts out and choke him with them. Then you were just *there*...and I...I knew he'd kill you, and it all became so much more complicated, and I—" He paced back and forth, running his hands over his face and through his hair. His breathing increased, and his eyes never met Wolfe's.

"How is that—"

"Shut up!"

"*How* is that—"

"I said SHUT UP. I'm trying to tell you that it wasn't my fault. Bredenbury knew about the uprising. He let it happen, he made me go with you or he'd have me, Arcola, and my son killed, I had no choice!" Scott cried, shaking his hands down at Wolfe. "He knew we were going to escape, he knew he'd be able to turn your escape into a political campaign, he knew he could become prime minister because of the escape. And…it was to help him, or die." His lip trembled, and his eyes were rimmed with dew. He ran his tongue over his lips again.

"Then die. I would have never turned myself into a pawn, let myself wander around for months like Bredenbury's bitch. At least you could have died knowing you were useful. How many people suffered because you let us believe we could be free?"

"Don't talk to me about freedom!"

"Then stop acting like you didn't have a choice!" Wolfe felt tears breach the edges of his eye, and tears rolled down his cheek again. Every time he blinked, he saw a new memory shattered. Holding his arm on the steps of the workers' barracks, watching the house burning, peeling beets in the kitchen, holding him in the church basement, watching the burning city, kissing him on the train. The entire time Bredenbury was watching him.

He never escaped.

"But you never loved me?" Wolfe whispered, barely more than a shiver.

"Fuck, Wolfe. You're so gullible. At points, maybe I thought something…but Wolfe I have a son, and a wife and I…" he tapered off, and they sat in silence. A silence that sucked the air out of Wolfe's lungs and pushed in on him, threatening to stop breathing. They sat together, staring at the sky, listening to the sound of the street below.

"Where are we?"

"York. I'm sorry Wolfe."

"You don't need my forgiveness Scott, you have to live with this, not me."

Every moment between them was dissolving. Every kiss, every touch, every trace of fingers over skin meant nothing anymore. So many people died for him. So many people died thinking he was on their side. He was everywhere, like a disease on Wolfe, over him, around him, and in him. There was no memory he could have without seeing Scott's face. Every smile was wrapped in pain; every look was laced with venom. He had taken his future, and with his cruelty, he had taken Wolfe's past.

"Everyone who came in contact with you died. How could you do that to them?"

"I tried to stop you, you can't put that on me, violence isn't the answer."

More tears fell at the impossibility of it. "So I'm supposed to be beaten, raped in a garden by people like you. How can you sleep knowing that that girl you forced to have sex with you at the Midsummer Night's Festival can still feel you inside her, feel your hands on her wrists?"

"That's such fucking bull—"

"I can still feel where you've touched me. All the *soap*, all the *bleach* in the world could *never*, *ever*, make those feelings go away."

"You don't get to talk to me about that."

"Yes I ca—" And before he could finish, Wolfe felt electricity again.

"No. You don't. Not anymore. I didn't fuck you; I fucked Bredenbury's property, with his permission. And if you don't learn your place, it's going to be a dark life for you, Wolfe. You will hold your tongue. It isn't your's anymore. And you will learn to respect your master." Scott towered over him, and, through Wolfe's tears, he could see Scott crying with him. He was in the gravel dust at the plantation again. *He has always been the same. You were a fool.*

They heard steps down the hallway, and by the time Scott had stepped towards the door and wiped his tears, painting his falsity across his lips again, the door had already swung open. Mr. Bredenbury reeked of cologne and had the most enormous smile he'd ever seen, with the brightest, largest teeth. Hot pink gums shone. He wore a brown suit with a dark black coat dusted with snow along its edges.

"How's my election campaign doing?" He leered down over Wolfe, smiling that same stupid grin he had seen so many times before. Wolfe refused to look away from his eyes, staring deep into the almost black craters.

"Still feisty, I see," he said, smiling. "Did you explain it all to him?" he asked, prowling around Wolfe like a wild animal preparing to feast.

"Well, not all of it..." Scott said, gulping.

"Why?"

"I don't—"

"No matter," he said, looking down at Wolfe again. "Wolfe? Oh, don't worry. I'm not going to do anything to you. If you have questions please don't hesitate to ask."

Mr. Bredenbury sat in the oversized plush chair by the window, closing his eyes and letting himself leaf through memories.

"I've wanted to run for Prime Minister for years and when your 'escape' threatened to tear apart my business, I figured it was a gift from God. Rather than quell it, I could use the fear that I built around your insurgency to win the upcoming election." He smiled to himself as he recanted his story. "Govan told me who was involved, and Chester confirmed it. I summoned Scott and he was willing to burn the entire plantation down over something as silly as a missing wife."

He paused, chuckled, then continued. "He came running up into my study in socks, half undressed, and I told him I knew about the uprising and I would have to kill him. Well, the look on his face was priceless. He stuttered and tripped, falling over himself in circles like some pathetic inbred. The idea came to me while he was snivelling at my knees, begging for his life. Then I made him a deal. I let the insurgency continue, shoot a couple of you, and he had to keep tabs on you and make sure you don't do anything too stupid. I gave him the necklace, but by then you'd already gotten a little carried away. No, I didn't expect you to burn down my house and kill my family but…you can get another wife, younger, more fuckable too."

Scott was staring out the window with shame in his eyes.

"Because I realized that if I captured you, the fear, excitement, and mythology around you would have died by the time I ran for prime minister. And that's what led to my plan. Rather than capture you, I needed to build a campaign around your violence. And if I kept Scott on a short chain by holding his wife and kid above him as punishment for letting you burn down my plantation, I could snatch you back whenever I ran for prime minister. And I mean, marvellous work on Scott's part. I think two months with bluies should serve as enough punishment.

"We weren't murderers," Wolfe barked. "We didn't hurt anyone."

"No?" Bredenbury smiled, flicking Scott over to him with a tablet. "My wife and four children, eleven civilians burnt to death in my home, civil damages upwards of seventeen million credits, thirty-four BESNA officers, a young boy named Jansen, and a mechanic of some sort. Not to mention the fighting you spurred on across the country."

"You started it! You killed us off while we were working on the plantation, you raped, and beat, and—"

"I can do whatever I want with what I own, and my property does not have a right to kill people." Mr. Bredenbury spiralled into a rage, throwing the tablet against the wall, shattering it into dust and towering over Wolfe, heaving heavy, fat breaths over him. His smile was gone; the last slivers of light in his eyes were emptied, and only dark holes remained. He had never seen him so mad. Wolfe still refused to look away. They would have to kill him.

"We spun your escape into a nationwide terror. You were on every billboard every day, every night, for months. You could have been in any shed, garbage bin, or basement in the country, and I needed people to see the actions of the escaped, bluie militants. Anyone you contacted had to go, that couple that shot Scott in Landia, the church, those freaks in the Desolation, that kid you killed and his family, 'The Phoenix'..." he mocked, dragging out each statement.

The smile had come back and glittered over Wolfe, slivers of light seeping back into his eyes, a bright sincerity sinking over him. *No, he's lying*. Wolfe thought.

"No, I'm not lying. Everyone you've met is dead," he said, reading the expression on his face.

"Then Brieux and the rest of your 'group' had to go. And I convinced the world that you turned on your own friends. You are so unstable, that you killed the people who trusted you. How could you do that, Wolfe?" He smiled again.

"Then there is that boy you abducted."

"Abducted? You killed his mother!"

"And he is my property. If I let you spend time together before I sell you, it will be out of kindness, and I can take that away from you at any time."

"You're a terrible person," Wolfe cried, looking up at him with tears in his eyes.

"All depends on who you ask."

"Why me though? I have done nothing more than anyone else in this fucking country. Why me?"

"I'm afraid you were in the wrong place at the wrong time, and your close relationship with my Administrative Overseers didn't help with that."

"And why us? We're just people, like you, like Scott, like anyone else. You know that," Wolfe said, crying, letting tears slip down his face and into his mouth.

"Sure. I know people are people, but what does it matter? Have you heard the saying the greatest good, for the greatest number? Because of your sacrifice, and the sacrifice of people that look like you, billions who lived in squalor finally have a shot at economic prosperity. There is no more hate, no more crime, no more poverty, and all for the price to pay of the blue-eyed mutation. Someone has to be at the bottom, it's almost heroic."

"I didn't ask for this," Wolfe grumbled.

Mr. Bredenbury grew irritated, standing up and resting his back against the bookshelves. Tossing up his hands.

"None of us ask for what happens in our lives. We don't choose to be born poor, born weak, born sickly or stupid. When I was born, my family and I lived in the poorest county in West Virginia. All there was were drugs, alcohol, laziness, and welfare. No one had any drive, any vision, any *desire* to better themselves! They were happy to stay stupid and poor, doing nothing with their lives. I did. I have done everything to leave that part of my life in the past. It doesn't matter if it's the fags, the niggers, or the wetbacks, someone is going to be on the bottom, so why should I care if it's you?" he asked, rolling his eyes around in slow circles like Wolfe was the stupidest person alive.

"But why—" Wolfe still tried to grapple with it all, trying to understand who could care so little, who would put money and power over the living, breathing people that roamed the earth.

"God, you people are so naïve. I see it over and over and over again, and you never see it. If you're free, you're forcing a woman across the world to be my slave. If you're free, you're forcing a kid down in Mexico to till my fields for slave wages. If you're free, you're subjecting some eight-year-old Indians into canning factories and laundry rooms. Freedom for you equals servitude for others because you may not be here, but people like me will *always* be here. We will always get our way."

"So I just have to kill you."

"And then ten more people will take my place. Kill me, and more people will follow the scent of my blood to the top. You will never get rid of us. If I don't use you, someone else will. Why are you so important that you think you should be free rather than those you've never met? Do you think it's about eye colour? I would gladly throw my support behind the green-eyed supremacy movement when it rises, if it means I get left alone and I get to make my money. I don't give a fuck who invades who or what riots fill the streets because money is influence, influence is power, and power is control."

"You're a monster."

"People look for monsters. They want to see villains with glowing eyes, and bright green horns because then they can point fingers. As long as I'm at the top, people will be at the bottom. Whether brown, blue, green, or purple, I don't give a fuck, just so long as I'm at the top. That's just life. Every shirt you wear, every tablet you use, every vegetable you eat, there is another person just like me behind it. But it's okay for you to use my tablets and eat the food, but if I make it I'm the villain? Why aren't you a monster too? You're just as guilty as I am."

"But…"

"And then you think it's all about you. It isn't. Brown-eyed people work for me too, and as long as they're too busy fighting over the best toothpaste brand and whether they find whatever celebrity nudes are floating around, they will never notice. They will slave away as much of their time as you do, and still think they're better. The human mind is a bizarre place, Wolfe. You'll see." Mr. Bredenbury had finished his rant. He straightened his jacket, checked his watch, and Scott passed him another tablet to glare over.

"So you'll just kill me then? And Lett? Put us out of our misery?"

"No, of course not. I've convinced the world you're violent, why would I let that imagine slip away so easily? They need to see that I'm not the evil, mean, vicious monster you say, and by letting you spend the rest of your lives working for me I'll prove that. You can go back to my canning factory in the Redemption City Worker's District, and fall into a PDT addiction like the rest of your kind, and everyone will have been right about you."

"You're going to die," Wolfe said, looking up at both men as a group of BESNA officers came towards Wolfe.

"Of course I'm going to die Wolfe. We all are. But I'll die revered and loved, and you'll die after living a long, long, long life, making me my millions. It's not personal Wolfe, but that's just life. No one is going to do anything. I'm going to be two steps ahead of everyone. Hell, I'll be the first to lobby for you to get your rights back when the time comes and we're plunged into civil war. Do you want to know why Wolfe? Because people are stupid, and complacent, and afraid of questioning what should be questioned. I'm not."

Wolfe was pushed to his feet, and they led him away from Scott and Mr. Bredenbury, further into the building.

—

"Mutt! Bluie!" a man yelled at him as Wolfe walked past him, pulling Lett closer to him. Wolfe heard spit hitting the ground. Every time he lifted his head to look around the lobby, the BESNA officers barked at him, so he counted the tiles: gold, brown, sepia, and sandy green. A hundred and seventeen so far. Mr. Bredenbury allowed Wolfe and Lett to spend fifteen minutes together under BESNA surveillance before being led out of their hotel.

Some people jumped back from them, like they were lepers in the street; some walked behind the guards calling insults and reaming them with abuse; others walked like they were nothing, not even bothering to look up from the tablets as they scurried. Screens were even on the buildings in York, and Wolfe watched Arcola and Scott give a speech to a crowd of screaming brown-eyed voters.

Wolfe was the boogeyman, the ghosts, the mythology kids scared themselves with. He was the big bad wolf, the evil that people loved to see beaten. Wolfe felt green horns sprouting from behind his ears as he walked. He was a pawn, a life given away so others could live whole, happy lives. Wolfe was just a bubble among rapids, sent to tumble through this same cycle of birth, fear, hope, depression, and death. They would pass in circles repeatedly until they were eventually all destroyed. They were aimless people, nobodies, and that's what was required of them.

They were shoved into a copper semi-trailer and ridden through the streets in the chill. Wolfe didn't know where they were going, and he didn't want to wonder. Wolfe saw a glimmer of light, slivers of dust cutting back and forth.

He looked down at Lett, sitting beside him, staring out through a slat in the truck. How could Wolfe have known Lett might have been safer, happier if he hadn't been free? He had failed Sandy, and she would watch him for the rest of his life.

When the doors were flung open, the stench of sweat and fear poured out with them. Wolfe clung to Lett's hand as they were pulled out into the light.

The guards talked to each other as the workers passed.

"A Bredenbury shipment?"

"Loaning workers out globally. It's really valiant."

The man stared them up and down, his authentic features hidden behind the darkness. Then he scratched a seven on Wolfe and a four on Lett, pushing them both to the left. They were standing in a brown park, a winding roundabout encased them. All around them, towering office buildings blocked out the rest of Lower York.

Hundreds of thousands of other men and women swirled around the park in circles. Trucks were backed in around the park, and each had a number painted on its side. Lett's eyes lit with fear. They were already hustling people into their transports. A large plastic barrier around the park kept them encased like gerbils.

"Wolfe, I don't want to go. Please don't make me go. I'm scared," Lett cried, holding onto his arm as they walked towards the park's centre. Wolfe looked down, smiling. "It'll be alright," he lied. "When we're free, we will meet up on your birthday in Oasis," Wolfe lied.

Lett sniffled. "Are we going to be okay?" Lett asked, staring at the gaping void of the truck.

"Of course," Wolfe lied again. Lett turned around before they pulled him off Wolfe and wrapped his arms around his middle. Wolfe smelt his hair and pulled his head into his chest. The cars swirled in a monotone blur.

"I miss Unity and Brieux. I wish we never left that town in the desert."

"I know, me too."

As Lett sniffled his way into the back of the truck, Wolfe watched the doors shut and seal. The words Vanscoy Textile Co. fell into view. He watched the truck slide away, knowing he would never see him again.

"You ain't going to see him again," a man crowed. "They are going overseas."

"What if it's all a ploy? I heard Mr. Bredenbury is actually a blue-eyed man with contacts."

"There is a resistance holed up in the Rockies, it's true, my cousin told me."

"I heard they're going to start reissuing marriage licenses again. You even get your own house."

Wolfe imagined meeting a woman in the ghetto and forcing himself to have kids with her. *At the very least, I won't let the truth die with me.* Even if Wolfe had to be sacrificed to get there, there was still hope in the hundred, two hundred, thousand years to come and the millions of changes and new generations they would bring.

There may be a future, four thousand years from now, where someone looks back on Wolfe and heeds his cautionary tale, rife with misery, and stands. A future where someone decides not to let Wolfe's story be in vain and decides to fight before it's too late. *Maybe only thousands would have died instead of millions if we'd spoken up earlier when we were convinced to stay quiet.*

Wolfe milled across the park, numb from cold and pain. In the middle of the park stood a towering copper statue of Prime Minister Windthorst. Wolfe hacked up phlegm, and in defiance, he sprayed it across his giant legs.

Wolfe couldn't help but smile. The smile wasn't one of happiness, not because he held high hopes of what was to come, but because he knew if he was going to survive, he had to try and forget. *I'm fine. I never even left the ghetto.* The nightmares would rear their ugly heads, and he would do anything to block the pain. The alcoholism would come, the PDT would come, the sex would come, and he'd survive for Lett.

The truck was filling up as he crunched along the frosted grass with the eyes of the bronze prime minister up his back; the words Redemption City Workers District were printed across the side of the truck. Tired, weak men hobbled into the back of the semi-trailers, their bones creaking, their taut skin crying out for relief from the cold.

Wolfe laughed, a laugh that started in his toes and came bursting out of his mouth as BESNA officers pushed him into his copper tomb. There was nothing more to do, Wolfe was going back to square one. There were no other paths. They all led him here to this moment. Wolfe forced himself to believe there was hope, *someone will champion change instead of silence, truth instead of lies—*

"Haven't you heard the rumours? There is going to be a rebellion at the Tobin plantation. I think we owe our safety to kind people like Mr. Bredenbury or the Tobins, I don't know why anyone would try and *kill* them, a man said incredulously to the rest of the men in the truck.

Maybe not. Wolfe thought to himself as he sat in the semi-trailer, going home to the fields.